When THEO
Came Home

A Novel by Ron Rhody

Outer Banks Publishing Group
Raleigh/Outer Banks

Cover design by
Gary Val Tenuta
GVT Grafix
GVTgrafix@aol.com

FIRST EDITION
ISBN 13 - 978-0-9829931-0-1
ISBN 10 - 0982993102
eISBN 13 – 978-1-3011781-0-0

November 2013

FOR PATSY
Who is delighted this is finished.

ACKNOWLEDGEMENTS

A town and a newspaper figure prominently in this story.

One is real.

The other is not.

The town, Frankfort, the Capital City of the Grand & Glorious Commonwealth of Kentucky, is real. It's there. A Bluegrass Camelot. I grew up there. You should see it.

The newspaper, the *Journal*, is imagined. I've borrowed the location and part of the name of a real newspaper, a very good one, the *Frankfort State Journal*, the paper I grew up on, for the story, but this one isn't that one.

The characters are made up, too. Like all fictional characters, they're composites of people the author has known or seen or imagined. If they suggest any real person to you, it's unintentional.

This is the last you'll hear from me about Theodore O'Hara Clark. He's come full circle now and deserves to be left alone to do whatever it is he's going to do without me looking over his shoulder.

As Theo walks off into the sunset, my considerable thanks again go to my sister, Ann Rhody Hatterick, her husband, Arthur "Dutch" Hatterick, and my brother, Don Rhody. Their enthusiasm for Theo and his story and their wealth of knowledge of Kentucky government and politics has been invaluable and has informed all three books.

Darden Chambliss, an Associated Press reporter when we met in New York and later the executive in charge of public relations for the Aluminum Association, and Don Wheeler, for many years head of the University of Kentucky's broadcast operations and before that a print and broadcast newsman, have been in from the beginning too. They've tried to keep me lucid, interesting, and honest in the telling. If I've failed, it's not because I wasn't properly coached.

Roe Rogers and Karen Piedmont and Hilda Willoth read all this copy in draft form and helped me shape it into a better story than it would have been without their contributions.

And Linda Hobson, who edited the first two Theo stories, put her fine mind and expert's touch to this one, too.

I am beholden to them all and I thank them.

And you, dear reader, I thank you.

If you've made any, or all, of the journey with Theo, I hope you've found it worth your while.

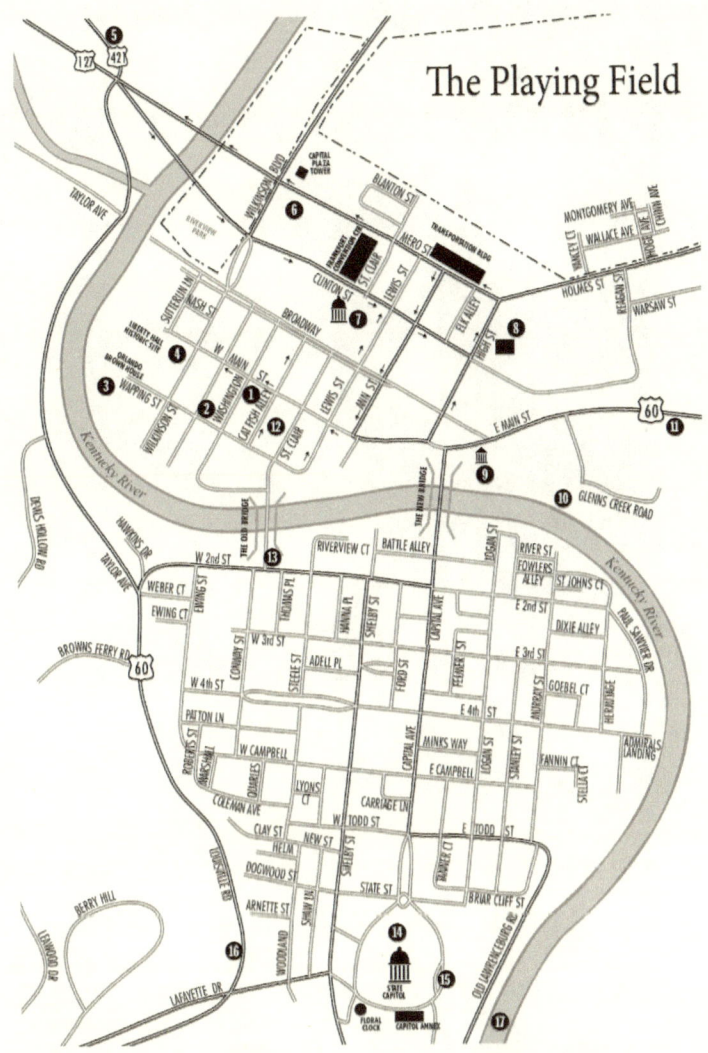

The Playing Field

❶ The Journal
❷ Theo's Apartment
❸ Julie Colby's House
❹ Liberty Hall
❺ To Dulin's
❻ Capitol Plaza
❼ The Old Capitol
❽ State Office Building
❾ The Arsenal
❿ The Cemetery
⓫ To The Forks & Lexington
⓬ The Court House
⓭ Pete's Corner
⓮ The New Capitol
⓯ The Executive Mansion
⓰ Louisville Hill Overlook
⓱ To Big Eddy

CHAPTER ONE

April

Michael was dead and buried.

And Jesse Bristow.

I waited until the furor died down and the new governor was seated, then I left.

Not that anyone suspected me.

There was nothing to link me to Jesse Bristow's killing. But a grey fog of depression wrapped round me. I could find neither peace nor comfort where they had always been. So just before daylight on the second day of the new year, I left.

I didn't slip away. I was too well known to simply disappear. I wound down my column, wrote my swan song, closed my affairs and made my way out of town as inconspicuously as possible.

I had already said my goodbyes to those closest to me. Rhae Dannan kissed me on the forehead and said "remember who you are." Marne understood, but cried. Dulin wished me well. There were no others I needed to tell.

Except Allie.

That was almost ten years ago.

I had no intention of returning.

Yet here I am—in the cemetery overlooking the river—kneeling beside Rhae Dannan's grave and not embarrassed by the tears or the hurt in my heart.

Word of her death didn't reach me until days after it happened. By the time they found me and I'd managed to get back, I'd missed all the ritual of leave taking—the eulogies, the funeral, the going to ground—not even a rose from her casket.

Ah, damn Rhea, I hated not to have been here.

"Rhae Hopkins Dannan," the headstone read, "1913 – 1980. She made us better than we were. And loved us more than we deserved."

I don't know who wrote those words. Paul Isham probably.

She lies beside her husband and her son, all taken by violent deaths. Benjamin, her husband, found dead on the side of a lonely road in the mountains east of Kentucky. Her son Michael shot down in the final stage of his run against Jesse Bristow for the governor's chair.

Now Rhae.

For most of my life, Rhae Dannan had been my champion. She gave me my first real job and watched over my career. But what mattered most was that she held me in that circle of love she drew around Michael. He and I were as close as brothers. She treated me like that.

Dammit, I should have been here to see her safely down.

I stood, brushed the grass from my knees and looked slowly around. The cemetery was deserted. Great oaks and maples rose among the headstones, their branches catching the wind and their leaves forming a canopy through which shafts of sunlight filtered. A few dogwoods added splashes of pink and white to the scene. The only sounds were of the wind in the trees and birdsong.

I pressed my fingers to my lips, touched the kiss to Rhae's headstone and started to leave, but the afternoon coming on was so peaceful that I lingered, walking slowly across the grass and between the markers, reading some of the inscriptions, noting some of the dates, and letting my mind clear of thoughts of things I could have done but didn't—of things that might have been but weren't.

I wandered with no destination in mind, taking care not to step on anyone's grave and trying to picture the person the lines on the gravestone memorialized. *Private Joshua J. Johnson. Army of the Confederacy. Lost at Antietam. Our only son. Lord care for him now.* I could see him. Seventeen, eighteen perhaps, smiling and proud as he stands as still as he can for the photographer, his new uniform crisp and spotless. On another stone, one almost hidden, the grave neglected and overgrown, *Abner Hotchkiss. 1878-1930.* That's all. A name, a date. A bachelor farmer, I thought. No family. Hard working. God fearing. Living alone in an old farmhouse, back a gravel lane near the creek. Poor Abner.

The line that stopped me was on a moderate-size stone of white marble with violets carved along the side. It read: *Wheresoever she was, there was Eden.* My Lord, I wondered, what sort of woman could inspire such a thought? How rare the woman who could. I tried to conjure up a picture. Nothing came. Nothing has. I have hopes something may.

When I came out of the reverie this unexpected encounter produced, I found I was on the cliff above the river with Daniel Boone's grave in front of me.

The view was magnificent. I stood high above the town, able to see all the way upriver to the bend before Big Eddy and downstream to the long curve that embraces the old mansions along Wilkinson Street. The Capitol Building sat proudly among the homes on the upslope of Louisville Hill. I could see almost all of South Frankfort and most of downtown—the two separated by the river but joined by the two bridges. At the foot of the Old Bridge on the downtown side, the Post Office spire and the Catholic Church steeple rose into sky, forming the image made so memorable in Paul Sawyier's watercolor.

I stood for a while, entranced, remembering. A squirrel chattering on a limb behind me broke the spell. My mother's and my father's graves were here as well. I hadn't been to them since I left. I'd made arrangements for their care—flowers on their birthdays, trimming and weeding to keep the site neat, but I hadn't been to them. I'd go later. One grave was enough for one day.

Almost ten years.

A lifetime. A blink of an eye.

To me it seemed both.

A lifetime since I left.

Or yesterday.

From the Louisville Hill overlook as I came in, the sight of town spread out on the valley floor with the river glistening like silver in the sun made me feel I was home and had never left. The white carnation in my hand from the flowers at Rhae's grave made me know it wasn't so.

I had knelt in Michael's blood and waited with Rhae while he died. I had held Allie while she cried like her heart would break.

I won't stay. I'll stay a day or so. I'll stay long enough to see Dulin and maybe one or two others. Not Allie. I won't see Allie.

Paul Isham was waiting for me at the country club. Though he was into his seventies, he was ramrod straight and carried himself with that air of natural dignity that automatically commands respect. He was standing outside the clubhouse on the cart path above the eighteenth green, watching a foursome come up. His hair had turned silver, and he was dressed in a well-cut, navy-blue suit. He was tall and trim, and as he stood there, I could picture him in an earlier time in a string tie and a ruffled shirt, wearing a swallow-tail coat, planter's hat in hand, standing in front of a columned mansion, holding the bridle of a young colt and looking out over rolling Bluegrass pastures. It would have been a fair enough picture. The Ishams were Bluegrass aristocracy. Most of their money vanished in the aftermath of the Civil War, but the family did well enough, and the name was honored in all the circles of Bluegrass society.

Paul saw me as I came up and started over with his hand out and a welcoming smile but then remembered why I was there, and the smile dissolved into that somber face we put on in the presence of death and misfortune.

"There is a table waiting for us inside," he said.

He had the staff set it up in the far corner of the big dining room. Most of the members took lunch on weekdays in the bar next to the pro shop downstairs, and since it was well past the usual lunch hour, we had the room to ourselves.

Paul had been the one who got word of Rhae Dannan's death to me. He had been Managing Editor of the *Journal* during the time of Michaels's run for governor. Now he was Managing Editor Emeritus, having given up day-to-day responsibility for the paper but retaining responsibility for the editorial page and serving as Rhae's right hand on all matters editorial.

Neither of us was interested in small talk and after exchanging a few meaningless pleasantries, I asked, "How did you find me?"

"Your agent," Paul said. "Thank God you leave word with someone. She knew you were in Afghanistan. I had to call in my chits with Senator Ford, but his people managed to find where you were and get you out."

I nodded in appreciation. Vintage Paul Isham—analytical, thorough, determined.

"We were about as far in-country as you can get," I said. "No roads. Only encrypted, short-wave contact. I had no idea what was going on. Neither did the CIA crew chief. 'Message from HQ,' he said. 'They want you out of here. Helo's on its way.' It was black night and a storm blowing. The pick-up spot a ledge on the mountain side. Too small to sit the helicopter down. They hovered and took me out by harness."

A waitress appeared over Paul's shoulder.

"Mr. Isham, what can I get you?"

Paul looked up, saw the waitress.

"Irene? Yes, Irene. A drink, Theo?"

I shook my head. What I wanted was to know how Rhae Dannan died. "Just coffee, please. Black."

Paul said, "Ancient Age on the rocks, Irene. We'll order later."

Smiling, pleased at being recognized, Irene beamed and walked away.

Paul picked up his fork and moved it slightly to his right. He lifted his knife then put it back down. He looked over his shoulder out through the big picture window to the day outside. He turned back to me.

"It was almost dark," he said. "They were making the turn off the Lexington road onto the Versailles road. You know the spot?"

I did. It was the road most of the Frankfort folk took to get up to the University for the ball games.

"She was coming back from Keeneland. The spring meet. The Saturday card. There was a filly she was interested in. Her foreman was driving. She was up front with him. Jake Wainright—he owns the new auto parts plant that came in last year—was in the back seat.

"A pick-up truck trying to beat an old lady in a Buick to the intersection accelerated out to pass, lost control, jumped into the oncoming lane and hit them head-on. At full speed. Rhae was killed instantly. A broken neck. The foreman is still in critical condition. Wainwright's okay. Some broken ribs."

"The driver of the pick-up?"

"Dead," Paul said. "Died on the way to the hospital. A kid. Sixteen years old. The girl with him has two broken legs, a ruptured spleen, and a severe concussion. Her face went through the windshield. They're hopeful plastic surgery can give her back a decent look."

"Was he drunk?"

Paul began to shake his head from side to side, a look of disgust on his face.

"Just showing off," Paul said. "Just by-damn showing off! To lose her that way, that senseless way. . . ." He closed his eyes and dropped his head, and I could feel the anger radiating from him.

When he opened them again, he managed a weak smile. "Well, it was a beautiful funeral. The church was full of flowers. The sun was shining. People from everywhere were there. Allison Sinclair was there. She asked about you. And Dulin. He asked if I'd heard from you. A lot of people asked about you."

Dulin, I thought. Bless his heart. He taught me. He shaped me, him and Will Owens. Of course Allie would have been there—for Rhae, for Michael.

"Well," Paul said again, "you're here now."

"Thanks for going to all the trouble to find me and getting me back here."

He waved the thanks away. Then, "Do you ever think about coming back?"

I frowned. In the context of what we were talking about it seemed an odd question. Then I realized it was an entirely reasonable question. My hometown. My family is buried here. I have family and friends here.

"No. I don't think about coming back, except maybe to be buried. Why?"

"Rhae's estate," he said. "I am the executor."

I wasn't surprised. Paul Isham had been Benjamin Dannan's best friend, and after Benjamin's death, had become Rhae Dannan's closest advisor.

"It's a big estate," he continued.

Again, I wasn't surprised. Rhae's family fortune had been building since her great-great grandfather, Captain Thomas Hopkins, Army of the Confederacy, came limping home in a tattered uniform and leading a lame stallion. The countryside was in shambles then. No one had money, and land was going for a song. Somehow, Captain Hopkins had Yankee dollars, and he began buying up bottom land along Elkhorn Creek, adjoining his father's small farm at Peaks Mill. By the time the carpetbaggers slinked north, he owned more good agricultural land than anyone in the county and was breeding thoroughbreds and thinking of running for the Senate.

There was talk that the money to start it all came from a Union payroll that Captain Hopkins waylaid on his way home from Appomattox Courthouse. How a lone man could ambush an army pay-wagon and make off with a small fortune was never explained— or even questioned. He was, after all, a Kentuckian, a Confederate Officer, and a Hopkins.

Over the years, subsequent generations of Hopkins had added to the Captain's start, and today there were few family fortunes anywhere in the Commonwealth that were larger.

I nodded, smiling, remembering how Rhae had told Michael and me the Captain's story one summer night on the porch at the farm as we watched fireflies in the meadow and how much pleasure she took in it.

"The saber," I said, "Captain Hopkins' saber? She had it hanging over the fireplace in the library. It's still there?"

Paul ignored that. "You understand? It's a large estate— the farming operation, the paper, the stables, and an investment portfolio of considerable worth."

I wasn't arguing. I believed him. But he wasn't getting the sort of response I guess he wanted. The size of Rhae's estate was a matter of indifference to me. Now that he had raised the subject, I was interested in who the *Journal* would go to, but for the rest of it, I wasn't even curious.

Over his shoulder I could see Irene approaching with her order pad in hand. Paul sensed her and waved her away without looking. He sat his drink down, moved the little flower centerpiece to have an unobstructed view across the table to me, leaned forward and said in a voice so quiet we could have been in church, "She left it all to you."

CHAPTER TWO

Paul Isham was as near an acolyte as lay society permits. His paragon was Benjamin Dannan. Paul became a convert while completing his graduate degree at Columbia University's School of Journalism. Columbia accepted only the best, and Paul Isham was foremost in his class. He fell under the Dannan spell when Benjamin was on campus, speaking on his experiences covering the mine wars in the mountains of east Kentucky, one of the bloodiest times in the state's history. The miners, after a lifetime of maltreatment and exploitation, were trying to form a union to protect themselves against the greed of the mining companies. The owners were dead set against it. Carnage and mayhem followed. Benjamin Dannan was in the middle of all of it. The companies had the money and the muscle and virtual control of the local politicians and police. They figured no one of consequence would notice a brawl in a remote corner of the Appalachian Mountains.

Benjamin Dannan's coverage proved them wrong. His reporting and writing drew national attention to the fight and played the major role in the miners finally winning.

Paul was being courted by big Eastern newspapers when he heard Benjamin. After that, all he wanted was to return home to Kentucky and play on the Dannan team. He was not only Benjamin's acolyte, in time he became Benjamin's best friend. But even before that, he fell in love with Rhae Dannan.

Rhae had a charm and grace and a natural warmth that drew people to her. Yet there was a core of steel in her that made me think of a goddess of war in mythology. She was a superb horsewoman and an unrelenting competitor. She took no enemies and lost no ground. The unfortunate few who thought they would have the advantage of her when she took over after Benjamin's death, learned rapidly and to their regret how wrong that assumption was.

I don't know what Rhae looked like when she was young. When I knew her, she was a beautiful woman, tall, with hair as black as a raven's wing and eyes the color of amethysts. She had a way of smiling that made you want to please her. I can imagine the effect on the young Paul Isham, working at the feet of his hero and basking in the radiance of Dannan's bride.

As a new hire and yet to be proven, and later, having earned the trust of Benjamin, he couldn't admit, even to himself, how he felt about Rhae. All that was left for him was to try to be Rhae's best friend, too.

Paul and I were never close.

Don't misunderstand me. I respected him—as a professional and as an individual. He was a first-rate journalist. No one had a better sense of where the real story lay or could turn out better copy under pressure. But there was no warmth between us, no chemistry. You work with someone on matters that are important or exciting, and a certain camaraderie develops—even a degree of affection. This happened with Dulin Monroe and Will Owens. Not with Paul. I'm not sure why. We didn't dislike each other; we just were never close.

What Paul was telling me came as a real shock. Me? Why? Almost as disturbing was my strong feeling that he didn't approve. His frown and his tone of voice said so. I couldn't fault him for that. Neither he nor Rhae had seen me in almost ten years. I had no business experience. I had no apparent anchor? A good idea?

I should have let it go. I had come non-stop from a remote pass in the mountains of Afghanistan, by helicopter to Karachi by Emirates

Air, to Berlin, by Lufthansa to Dulles in Washington where the company jet met me and brought me to Louisville and by Hertz from there to the cemetery.

I'd had practically no sleep and far too much caffeine. We sat there in silence, Paul studying me while I tried to digest this news. Rather than ask the important questions, I reacted instead to his attitude. "You don't like this, do you?"

Paul sat his drink down, leaned back again, folded his hands together, stared at me, then "Rhae didn't ask my advice. Usually she did. Not this time."

"What would you have told her?"

Eyes steely, chin jutting, "I would have told her she shouldn't confuse you with Michael."

CHAPTER THREE

Rhae had no living kin. Michael was her only child, and she, herself, was an only child. If there were Hopkins around, she was close to none of them.

Michael and I had practically grown up together and had been best friends since we met in the second grade. I had helped him through the terribly difficult period after his father's death when neither of us knew what death was or believed it could take someone we loved. We became even closer after that, and Rhae came to count on me to not let Michael sink into despair or be eaten by his anger.

We were nine that summer, and I spent most of it on the farm with Michael. We helped in the fields and with the livestock. We fished the creek from the main house all the way down to Strohmeier's Camp where it joined the Kentucky River. We spent lazy evenings on the big front porch watching fireflies and listening to Michael's grandfather's stories.

People often mistook us for brothers. We didn't really look alike. It's more that we were similar. We grew into young men of adequate size; not big, but big enough. We both had blue eyes and black hair and the fair skin of our Celtic genes. We had friendly natures and smiled easily and were comfortable in most people's company and definitely in each other's.

Michael had that kind of disarming charm you find among certain boys. I was polite and watched my manners. We did almost everything together and were good at everything we did. Rhae said we were handsome boys and called us kings of all we surveyed.

We competed, of course. What boys don't? It wasn't a jealous competition. We weren't particularly interested in proving which one of us was better, only that we were better at whatever we were doing than anyone else. We didn't particularly care which one of us won, only that one of us did. We had the kind of confidence in ourselves that made us expect to win—every time. That didn't always happen, but it happened enough that we never lost the conviction—even in our competition over Allie. Maybe I'm understating that, but our contending for her wasn't something that eroded our friendship.

We were together until the summer before our sophomore year at the University. The Korean War started that summer, the summer of 1950, and the Marine Corps reserve unit I'd joined to make a little extra money to help pay my way through college got activated. Michael didn't need the money, so he hadn't joined. When I got back from the war, Michael was at Stanford working on his masters. Allie had married and divorced and was the mother of a baby girl.

I re-enrolled at the University to finish up my journalism degree. Rhae gave me a job at the *Journal* so I could pay for it. Michael and I saw each other when he came home on holiday, and we always had New Year's Eve dinner at the farm with Rhae—just the three of us.

Michael and I stayed in touch while we worked at our careers. When he resigned as head of McKinnon Industries in California and came home to run for governor, Rhae and he and I became a team again.

Rhae never confused us. "You are of a piece," she told us, "the same, but different."

No. She never confused us.

CHAPTER FOUR

I left Paul Isham at the club, checked in at a motel down the road, grabbed a couple of hours sleep, then struggled awake. I shaved, found a clean shirt and a pair of not-too-badly wrinkled slacks, hung my blazer in the bathroom to let the steam take some of the creases out while I showered, splashed on some after shave and left to go see Dulin Monroe.

The news that I'd somehow become heir apparent of the Dannan estate stunned me so thoroughly that I didn't grasp the consequences. Dulin would know.

There was still light in the sky as I drove down East Main hill and through town to cross the river on the new bridge where the Craw used to be. A massive new complex of state office buildings now rose on the riverbank out of what had been the roughest, toughest, most dangerous and talked about section of town—the fruit of urban renewal.

On the far side, a wide two-lane highway curved up through limestone cliffs to carry traffic to Devil's Hollow Pike and from there west and north to Ohio.

I found the turnoff to Dulin's place near the top and pulled up in front of a large fieldstone house set on a bluff amid cedars.

Dulin had the door open before I could knock.

"Well I'll be damned. The real Theodore O'Hara Clark." He was smiling broadly and almost—almost—hugged me. But he caught himself in time, shot out his hand and, beaming, pulled me inside.

"Let me look at you." An exaggerated head to toe scan of me standing there. "Not much the worse for wear. No grey yet, no gut yet. A little more mature."

He laughed out loud. "Theodore O'Hara Clark, by God, present and accounted for. By damn, boy, it's good to see you. If your by-line hadn't started turning up, we'd have given you up for lost."

And in the midst of that boisterous welcome, I felt embarrassed and ashamed.

In all the time I'd been gone, I'd made contact with no one at home. Not Rhae, not Dulin, not Allie. I hadn't written, hadn't called—anyone—in almost ten years. I hadn't considered that there might be some who were concerned about me, hadn't thought there might be some who were anxious or troubled that no word had come from me, that the only knowledge they had of me was a chance by-line in a national magazine.

That first year, I could make excuses for that. I was hurt, and I was hibernating and licking my wounds. And the second year, I was just beginning to heal and come out of it. But after that, after I started finding my way again, after I began writing again, after the assignments started coming, and I began to regain a measure of success and feeling good again, after that, the only excuse I could conjure up for my conduct was that I was a coward. I didn't want to risk being reminded of the times that bore me down.

"Ah, Dulin," I said, "I'm sorry for that. I should have been in touch."

His hand was still on my shoulder, but the smile went away.

"Yes, you should have. Rhae worried. Hell, even I worried."

He frowned, then smiled again. "That's yesterday. Come in and sit down and tell me what you've been up to."

He led me through the living room and out on to the deck. Twilight still held on the horizon, but shadows were beginning to ease into the creases of the hills.

"Like it?" he asked.

The view was astonishing. I could see almost all of the valley from where we stood. I turned to him, smiling and nodding.

"I found it after I retired. I was quail hunting up here and ran across this little rundown farm." He was standing at the railing at the edge of the deck, slowly scanning the scene before him. He turned to me with a face full of pride.

"I tore down the old house and the barn and built on the crest of this ridge, so I could see it all."

This was a view of the town I'd never had. I couldn't imagine how the previous owner had thought he could make a go of farming up here. We were in scrub-cedar and worn-out soil country where there was barely enough dirt to cover the limestone ridges. Farmers are eternal optimists or unacknowledged masochists, or maybe just hopeless optimists. There was no way a man could raise a crop of anything but goats off this land.

"Absolutely awesome," I repeated.

"Enjoy it. I'll fix us a drink," Dulin said.

The night was pleasantly chill, just enough cold in the breeze to make you want to keep your jacket on, but not enough to be uncomfortable, so we sat outside sipping bottled-in-bond Ancient Age and watching car lights blink across the river as the first of the night's stars began to poke through.

Dulin caught me up on the years I'd missed. His wife, Edna, had died. She wrote for the *Kentucky Coal Journal*—an uncommon interest for a woman, coal mining—it seemed to me, but she was good at it and respected. She also wrote children's poetry, although they had no children themselves. She was a small, intense woman with a penetrating sense of humor. I was sad she'd died.

That was five years ago, the year he retired. Dulin said he had adjusted. He bought the place two years after her death. The planning and the building and the moving helped take his mind off it.

He was enjoying retirement. He taught a class every other semester at the university. He traveled, mostly for bird hunting— quail and dove down in west Kentucky where he grew up, and regular trips to the quail plantations in Georgia, and sometimes out to Nebraska for the pheasant. No writing except for an occasional guest editorial for the *Journal*. He was reading all the stuff he had always wanted to read but never had time for, even *Ulysses* and *War And Peace*. He was sorry he'd wasted the time on *Ulysses* because he thought it dense and boring, but he'd read all of Ray Bradbury with delight and Stephen Vincent Benet with admiration and was now in the middle of *The Seven Storey Mountain.*

He wasn't a farmer, wanted no part of it. The work was too hard. The few acres he had, he'd leased out. A little additional income most years.

He and Rhae Dannan kept in touch, lunched regularly. And he kept an eye on the *Journal* and on the "new" managing editor Lew Arbogast, two years into the job, brought in when Paul Isham moved to Editor Emeritus. A good man. University of Missouri J-School graduate. Lured away from the *Dallas Times.*

He paused, tilted his glass back to finish off his bourbon, reached for my glass and said, " I think we need a bit more."

When he returned, he handed me mine and said, "Now it's your turn."

It was full dark and still and quiet. There was just enough light from inside that we could make out each other, but indistinctly. I sat in a big, old wicker arm chair. A long, low pine coffee table was in front of me. Beyond that was the deck railing, and a few yards beyond that, the cliff.

Dulin had pulled his rocker to the far end of the table, put his feet up and settled back comfortably, waiting.

I sat my drink down, stood up and walked to the railing. Way up the valley I could see the Capitol dome bathed in spotlights. From this distance, it looked like a small beacon set in deserted country to guide the faithful safely home. In front of me, the town's lights sparkled on both sides of the river like clusters of jewels. Down the valley, a barge was making its way upstream with its running lights glowing green and red.

I turned from the railing to face him. He was waiting patiently for me to get the explanation out. He already knew why I left, or knew as much of it as I could explain at the time. What he wanted now was an accounting of where I'd been and at least a hint at why I'd cut myself off from everyone for all those years.

I owed him as much. Dulin saw more in me than I ever saw in myself. His reputation and his word got me hired by the *Herald-Tribune.* His coaching after I came back from New York and was trying to make my way through the cut-throat competition of political reporting in the Capitol, gave me the edge I needed. His friendship and support was a rock I knew I could hang on to.

I owed him.

So I began, not sure how much I'd tell him.

"That night I left, I said goodbye to Rhae out at the farm. It was just beginning to snow. We stood on the back porch watching. I knocked on your door about eleven-thirty. I knew you'd still be up. We had coffee and brandy. I told you what was on my mind, or most of it. You listened. Didn't ask any questions. Only said, 'come home when you're ready.'

"I had left twice before. But I came back each time. The Marine Corps took me away the first time for the war in Korea. I was a kid. I told you about that. A little later, you opened the door for me to Manhattan."

Dulin smiled, remembering.

I remembered, too. The editors liked the way I went after stories and the way I hung words together. They said I had real potential.

But neither my growing reputation nor the glamour of the city overcame the loneliness I felt in the canyons of its streets or the remorse I carried over Rose Baltar.

That was my biggest story. I exposed an Asian gang that was luring young girls out of the back-country provinces of the Philippines with promises of exciting lives in America. They would be domestic help for wealthy Asian couples, live in luxurious apartments, make more money than they ever dreamed possible. Instead, the girls, some no older than twelve, none older than eighteen, once ensconced, barely speaking the language, alone and frightened, became virtual slaves. They worked twelve-hour days, seven-day weeks, were paid almost nothing, were seldom allowed to leave the places they worked, and in many cases were forced into sex—usually by the husband but often for any of the males living in or visiting the house.

Only one girl, a girl I made friends with as I began probing into the story, had the courage to go on record. Her name was Rose. I used her as my subject. When the Manhattan district attorney indicted the ring's bosses, I convinced her she should testify. I promised her the police would protect her. She trusted me. On the morning after she gave her testimony, her savagely beaten body was found in the street in front of the house where she worked. No other girls would testify. Rose's, though, was enough

It broke up the ring.

Rose died.

She was seventeen—sweet, trusting, had never been beyond her village. Manhattan, what little she saw of it, was a magic place to her. The high-rise condo where she lived and worked overlooked Central Park. She could see the trees and the joggers and sometimes the carriages with their happy tourists rolling through. She walked in the park only once. A Sunday, during one of her few afternoons off. Her life was a hell she could never have imagined. Her courage in standing up against the gang is something I can't explain but will always admire.

I lapsed into silence for a moment, considering. My series of stories, the stories Rose made possible, saved some, a few, maybe a lot of other young Filipino girls from similar ordeals.

She died. I got front-page bylines and a Pulitzer nomination.

Dulin understood what I was thinking. "You can't fault yourself for the police failure to provide her protection."

Ah, but I could. I did. She trusted me. I failed her.

"Maybe," I said. "Anyway, I didn't want to play that game anymore. I came home. And I had no intention of ever leaving again."

It was quiet on the porch. We were too far back in the hills to get any road noise. The dark was complete. There were no houses anywhere in sight. There was only the faint light spilling out from the kitchen and, far away across the valley, the lights of the town.

""Strange how things work out, isn't it?"

I could sense Dulin shifting in his chair, hear the tinkle of ice as he raised his glass.

"So we shook hands and I climbed in my car and headed out. I went up on Louisville Hill for one last look at the town. After that, since I was headed west, I just kept going.

"I took my time. Out across the Mississippi, up through the Badlands. I stopped at the Little Big Horn to walk the Custer battlefield then went on up through the Rockies to Yellowstone. At Ketchum, I stopped to pay my respects at Hemmingway's grave and make a couple of casts into the Big Wood where he fished while he lived there.

"The road ran out at Arcata on the California coast not far from the Oregon border in the heart of the old-growth redwood country. They're magnificent trees. The oldest trees in the world. Some over a thousand years old. We don't have anything like them. Taller than you can imagine, hundreds of feet tall, yet graceful and with a dignity that makes you feel you should whisper when you're in among them.

"Arcata was a provisioning center for the gold mining camps in the Klamath and Trinity Mountains in Gold Rush days. Now it's a lumbering town. There's a small college there. Brett Harte lived and wrote there once, and much later, Raymond Carver. Some of the best steelhead fishing in the world is nearby on the Mad and the Klamath and the Eel.

"The feel of the place suited me. Grey. Somber. Gauzy wisps of mist in the treetops. A little sun now and then but not enough to spoil the mood.

"I found a small cabin in a stand of trees out a gravel road north of town. Spartan. No neighbors.

"On days when there was sun, I sat on the porch and watched the play of the light on the crest of the waves. And on days when there wasn't sun, I sat on the porch and watched the wind etch designs in the fog. And when it rained, I built a fire and stayed inside and read. I slipped into a trance-like state, waiting for the black dog to go away. But he wouldn't leave. How long that might have gone on I don't know. Maybe until I shriveled up and blew away.

"Then the storm came, the first big Pacific storm I'd experienced.

"Rain hammered at the walls, blew through the window jams and under the door. Wind like none I'd ever felt. It took the cabin in its fist and shook it like a toy. Every crack spewed water. I pulled the covers over my head and waited.

"When the wind died to a constant hiss, I poked my head out to see if the walls still stood. What was left of the cabin was dark. The door was gone; a part of the roof open to the sky. Through the hole where the window had been, I could see a red dawn breaking and behind it, a black cloud bank boiling in from the sea.

"'Oh hell,' I said.

"I'm not sure who I was talking to. God maybe. The demon. Or whoever or whatever was responsible for all that foolishness. I was cold. I was wet. I was mad, and I was sad, and I knew things weren't ever going to be like they were ever again.

"In my ear, I could heard Rhae Dannan's voice. 'Deal with it!' When we ran up against something we didn't want to face, that's what she'd tell Michael and me, 'Deal with it!'

"After the storm, wet and cold and wind beat, I slowly began to accept that I had been babying myself. I was running and ducking and hiding from things that, dammit, I just ought to face up to and deal with. There is this little click in my brain. When I can get it turned, my discipline is rock solid. I managed to get it turned that morning. No more running and ducking and hiding. Time to come out to the real world again.

"When I did, I had no desire to do anything in particular, just smell those roses people kept telling me I should take time to do. I had money enough. The *Journal* had paid me well, and the fees from the pieces I'd done for *The Atlantic* and *The New Yorker* during Michael's run for governor and then at his death, bolstered all that.

"That was a sweet interval—relaxed and self-indulgent and untroubled. I fished when I felt like it and walked the redwoods when I didn't. I made myself welcome at the old saloon on the road to Samoa when I felt like company and enjoyed my privacy when I didn't.

"But a year of it was enough. The black dog was off sniffing elsewhere, and I was almost suffocated by the smell of roses. I got bored. Then I started getting curious again. The detective sergeant from Cincinnati, working as a deck-hand on a fishing boat out of Eureka, was there a story there? The growing aggravation among the lumberjacks about California hippies making trouble for the logging operations in the old-growth redwood forest, where was that going?

"I made contact with an agent I'd worked with. Assignments started coming. With the assignments came the need to be more mobile, so I closed the shutters on the little cabin at Arcata and moved down the coast to San Francisco. From there I could get any place in the world fast and without fighting the hassles of Manhattan or Chicago.

"One story led to another. I wrote about politics and wars and people. The editors I wrote for liked it. They kept giving me assignments.

"I have a twenty-second floor apartment in a new high rise on Russian Hill now. I can watch the evening fog slip in through the Golden Gate from there. And be in walking distance of the best restaurants in the world, and the best music, and the prettiest women. Well, maybe not in walking distance of all the pretty women. Sometimes I have to take a cab. And I've made good friends with some of the free spirits and the outlandish thinkers who give the city its special aura. There's no place like it.

"A little over a year ago, *The Atlantic* asked me to become an Editor-At-Large. They let me pick my subjects, cover what I want within reason. That's when you started seeing my byline. It's been great, Dulin, really great. And I've been an unthinking ass for not being in touch, and I apologize."

Dulin shifted in his chair, then stood up.

"Yes, you have been," he said quietly. "Yes, you have."

I couldn't see his eyes in the darkness, but I knew they were on me. He bent down for the glass he'd set on the table. Straightening up he said, "OK, then." He reached for my glass and started inside, "We'll start a new story with Ancient Age."

When he came back, he took his seat in the rocker and leaned toward me.

In the quiet, I could almost hear him turning the situation over in his mind. Then he took a sip from his drink and said, "You went away and had it all figured out. Now Rhae has complicated your life."

"You know about her will," I said.

"She discussed it with me before she made the decision."

"Paul Isham thinks it's not a good idea."

"He could be right."

Ice tinkled in the silver julep cup as raised his drink to his lips.

"You're changing his life, Rhae, I told her. She smiled that smile of hers and said, 'It's time he came home.'

"Maybe you're expecting him to be something he doesn't want to be. Something he doesn't know how to be. All that money, Rhea. All that responsibility.

"When Michael and Theo were boys,' she said, 'I used to set them tasks around the farm just to see what they would do. They were eager, fearless, smart as hell and absolutely sure of their ability to get done anything I wanted done. If they didn't know how to do a thing, they found out how. If they didn't have the tools or the strength to do a thing, they charmed the people with the tools and the strength into doing it for them. Tom Sawyer was an amateur compared to them. They never failed me. When they became young men, they were masters of all they surveyed. Neither one of them ever disappointed me. Theo won't disappoint me now.'

I couldn't decide if the look on Dulin's face as he told me this was one of concern or curiosity. Ah damn, Rhae, I thought. That ain't fair.

"What does she want me to do?"

Dulin sat his drink down and began to stand up. "You're meeting with her attorney Monday. You'll get all the details then. She left a letter for you, a private letter. That will tell you more than the language of the will."

He walked to the door opening onto the deck. "Come on outside. I want you to see something."

We'd left the lights off. Inside was warm and pleasant. Outside was dark and chill. I shrugged and followed him.

The moon was in its last quarter, waning and not rising until just before dawn. For now, the sky was clear and the stars brilliant.

I moved to stand next to Dulin at the railing.

"This is part of what comes with the package," he said, sweeping his arm in a lazy arc.

In the distance, the Capitol Dome glowed in alabaster light. Floodlights illuminated the Arsenal's towers, standing guard on the cliff above the river. Beneath me, the town spread out on both sides of the river in sparkling grids, streetlights twinkling through newly leafed trees. Downstream, lanterns glowed faintly on the few boats anchored in the water beneath the dam where fishermen were after the monster catfish that lived there.

When I turned back, Dulin wasn't looking at the view; he was studying me. "You're going to be a rich man."

I flicked a half-hearted smile.

"Setting the money aside, any interest in coming back?"

"None," I answered, without hesitation.

"Putting the money back in the equation; that change your interest in coming back?"

"No," I said.

"Hmnph," was all he said. He turned to look back out over the valley. Nothing had changed there. The Capitol Dome was still lit. The guys were still fishing below the dam.

"I didn't think the money would make a difference," he said. "Well," he said, turning back to the open door, "I'm out of Ancient Age. Another?"

We talked until almost dawn.

CHAPTER FIVE

Rhae Dannan's will would be filed with the Franklin County Probate Court on Monday. Its contents would become public, and at that point, anyone who cared would know that the Dannan Estate was in the hands of "Theodore O'Hara Clark, a Frankfort native, presently a resident of San Francisco. He may be remembered as a writer, reporter, and political columnist for the *Journal*, now Editor-At-Large for *The Atlantic Magazine*."

That's probably about all that would be said in the newspaper report. What else might be said privately would depend on how well people knew me or whether they'd been the butt or the beneficiary of one of my stories.

For the time being, I was incognito. Only Dulin and Paul Isham knew I was in town. I had the weekend to myself.

After leaving Dulin's, I checked out of the depressing little room in the motel with the dim lighting and the worn carpets and moved to a newer one out on the Louisville Road.

Then I went shopping. I didn't know how long I'd be there, and the only clothes I had with me were field gear for the mountains: a sports jacket, a couple of dress shirts, and a pair of slacks.

But Fayette-Crutcher wasn't there. A lot of things that used to be downtown weren't there. The Police Station had moved. The Capitol Theatre was shuttered. Even Mucci's and Kings Bar were gone. And Main Street had been turned into a one-way street—the wrong way.

Downtown looked like it had closed down. There were no people on the streets. Almost no traffic. On a fine spring Saturday morning in the heart of town! I thought of Rip Van Winkle.

Crutcher's had been the busiest men's store around. It was one of those classic shops found in every city of any size in the Bluegrass, big windows full of tasteful display, always people in and out. If you've traveled to Southern college towns or done country club evenings or big game days, you recognize the look—fashionably proper, classy but understated—different from the Ivy League, not so self-conscious—comfortable and easy but never careless or offhand.

I gambled that Graves-Cox would still be there, the company store for the well-dressed man in Lexington, prospering in the shadow of the University—a half-hour drive if I pushed it, and no Troopers were patrolling the Versailles road that morning. They weren't, and I was.

By noon I was outfitted and had a promise from the manager that he would rush the tailoring of the new slacks and jacket to have them ready first thing Monday morning.

I went back to the motel and slept through the afternoon—a deep, dreamless sleep. When I woke, I showered, shaved, and changed into a fresh shirt and a neatly creased new pair of khakis. I had no plans for the night. No one to see. No place to go. So I stirred myself to make the call I should have made the day before. Kit Bedrosian hadn't heard from me since I'd left.

Six o'clock Eastern time; three in the afternoon in San Francisco. A Saturday. Low odds she'd be in her office.

But she was.

"So you've finally decided to check in. Where the hell have been?" was her greeting.

"Kit—"

"Don't Kit me. The last I heard they were trying to find you somewhere in the mountains of Afghanistan with a war going on. Where are you?"

"I couldn't call before. I'm calling now. Be nice."

"Sometimes you really tee me off, you know that? Are you okay, really okay? Don't give me your macho impersonation," she said.

I sometimes thought I could love Kit Bedrosian. She had the looks. She brooked no bull. She was tough and tender and almost as smart as me. And she was the best agent I'd worked with.

"I'm fine. The Afghan piece is going to be strong, maybe strong enough for a cover. Let them know in New York. But it will have to wait. Strange things are going on here that I have to take care of. Shouldn't take long, and there's no need to rush the story. It's only going to get bigger."

She listened patiently as I brought her current with what had happened since we talked last and with what I had to do now. She didn't interrupt. She listened. That was one of Kit's great talents..

When I finished she said softly, "I'm sorry about Mrs. Dannan. She must have been very special." She paused a moment, "I'll take care of New York. You take care of what you need to take care of and get yourself back here," then softening, "Be careful, Theo."

CHAPTER SIX

The reading of Rhae Dannan's will turned out to be a public event rather than the private affair I'd thought it would be. I had pictured myself and Paul Isham sitting in the fifth floor office of Cantrill & Livingstone in the McClure Building on the corner of Main and St. Clair in downtown Frankfort while the Court House clock struck twelve and attorney Oscar Cantrill read from the document in front of him. He'd be a courtly gentleman, bow-tied, soft voiced, very formal, but friendly. The whole affair would take perhaps half an hour. I'd have no questions. We'd stand and politely shake hands and take our quiet leave while Attorney Cantrill proceeded with whatever else he had to proceed with to make it all legal.

Instead we walked into an anteroom full of reporters. The disposition of the Dannan estate was news in the Blue Grass. They all knew Paul Isham. More than a few knew me and looked up in surprise when they recognized me. The *Journal,* of course, was there. And the Lexington and Louisville papers, a man from the Associated Press, a woman who looked familiar, from WHAS I thought, and a young woman who Paul whispered to me was from the *Kentucky Post* in Cincinnati.

The reading of the will was private, but Cantrill & Livingstone, not averse to a bit of public attention, had announced the time of the meeting and let it be known that copies of the will would be available to the press immediately after it was filed in probate court. It wasn't the usual practice, but it had been approved by the Executor of the Estate, who recognized the high degree of local interest in the matter and wanted to save members of the press the time and trouble of trying to get copies made under tight deadlines.

So they were there. Waiting.

I smiled and nodded to those I knew as we made our way through the throng and into the inner office.

Damn. Was this going to be a bigger deal than it needed to be? Was Paul intentionally generating attention to the change?

Cantrill was not what I expected. He wasn't ancient or formal. He was a tall, amiable, sport-jacketed man about my age, with a quizzical smile and a soothing voice. He was a liberal arts graduate of the University of Kentucky and product of the University of Virginia's School of Law. I should have known Rhae would go for talent, not tradition.

"It is a straightforward enough document," Cantrill said as he ushered Paul and me to seats. "Mr. Isham already knows its contents. I will go over the provisions for you, answer any questions you have and then have the document filed with the probate court to begin the formal legal process. There should be no problems."

He paused then and reached into his desk drawer. "Before I begin, Mrs. Dannan left a personal letter which she wanted me to give you before you hear the terms of the will." He reached across the desk and handed me the envelope. It was addressed, in Rhae's elegant hand, simply *Theo.*

"We will give you some privacy."

They left. I was in the room alone. It was peaceful— the soft light of afternoon filtering in from the street-side windows, book-lined walls, the smell of leather and ink—quiet, comforting. I hesitated to open the envelope, not wanting to go further.

Perhaps this is just a dream, I hoped. I'll wake in a moment and be freezing in a sleeping bag in the cave in the mountains. One of the team will already have started the coffee. The lookout will be shivering in a blanket at the edge of the ridge.

The envelope in my hand was real.

I opened it and began to read:

Dearest Theo,

That you are reading this means, well, it means what it means.

Paul will say that I am confusing you with Michael.

Dulin will say that you have your life in hand and I shouldn't tamper with it.

I have never confused you with Michael. I have always known who you are and loved you for your own unique self. As for Dulin, he may be right, but even so, all that I have, I entrust to you. The farm, the Journal, the printing company, the stables—I entrust them to you.

These are my family's legacy ... my legacy. I want that legacy to survive. Whole and independent. I don't want it broken up and parceled out to men whose only consideration is profit and or be under the control of those who have no real concern for our people or this place. Especially the Journal. It was Captain Hopkins' pride. It has been mine.

A bond forms between a newspaper like ours and its town. The newspaper becomes the people's voice and the town's conscience. It keeps watch. It challenges power and punctures influence. It exposes villains and honors heroes. It informs and educates and entertains. It outrages some and inspires others, but it never loses sight of its responsibility to search out the truth and tell it ... so that the people know ... so that they can't be mislead or manipulated or taken advantage of by the charlatans and the messiahs because they've been told the truth.

I want you to shepherd that legacy.

Will it change your life? Probably. Will you want the responsibility? Probably not. But I'm counting on you, Theo. This is important.

Come home. You belong here.

Rhae

Home.

Belong.

Where was Rhae when she wrote this? Was it night? Was she sad? Had she some premonition?

I pictured her at her desk in the library at the farm. Just before bedtime, the sound of the creek whispering in through an open window, pausing, looking up, brushing her hair back from her eyes, then bending down again to make these words on this paper.

Ah, Rhae, what are you doing to me?

CHAPTER SEVEN

The story of the disposition of the Rhae Dannan estate made the evening newscasts. It didn't lead, but it played high. That meant the play in the morning's papers would be prominent and more exhaustive. The broadcast reporters have only a minute or so to get their story told. My print colleagues have no such time constraint and the space to tell what they want to tell—or know. That didn't make me happy. I didn't want the Dannan-Bristow matter resurrected.

When Michael Dannan resigned his job as chief executive of a large multinational corporation headquartered in California to come home to run as a dark-horse candidate against Jesse Bristow for governor, he captured the state's imagination.

Michael was young and handsome and so charismatic that people flocked to him. He was Sir Galahad come to free the Commonwealth from the grips of the evil barons.

The Democratic machine owned the state. It had been putting its candidates in the Governor's Mansion like clockwork for the past forty years, and Jesse Bristow was the Party's latest pick. That someone with no political experience and no organization would have the effrontery to take on Bristow and the Machine galvanized everyone.

As time ticked down to Election Day, all the polls had Michael well ahead. In the final run-up to the voting, his managers scheduled a rally in Harlan—Harlan, the heart of the coal country in the eastern Mountains that was Jesse Bristow base—Harlan with its history of blood and violence—to show how strong Michael's support was throughout the entire Commonwealth—even in Bristow country. I argued against it.

Michael was shot dead there.

I was with him.

His blood splashed me.

Michael was making his way through a crowd of cheering, shouting supporters to the speaker's platform. I was right behind him. A young man stepped out of the crowd. Michael recognized him, turned to offer his hand. With it came the sound of a shot. Michael rocked back, staggered, dropped.

Before anyone could react, the young man raised the pistol in his hand to his mouth and blew his own head away. A forty-five. A cannon.

There was talk that Jesse Bristow contrived the killing. The young man worked for Bristow, and like Bristow, was a Melungeon.

Nothing ever came of it.

I knew it to be true.

A few weeks later, Jesse Bristow himself was killed— by a little twenty-two slug delivered squarely to the center of his forehead while he worked late one night in his office not far down the avenue from the Capitol.

Despite a massive effort, Jesse Bristow's killer was never found. No suspects were even identified.

I clicked the TV off. The phone rang as the screen faded to black.

"Welcome home!"

I recognized the voice at once. "Julie!"

"It's too early for you to have eaten. Come on down here. I want to hear all about everything."

"Julie—"

"I haven't started dinner. It's just me and Jim. We'll have the bourbon chilling."

"How did you find me?"

"I called Paul Isham. Quit wasting time."

Julie Harrod—Julie Colby now. I'd known her longer than I'd known Michael. She and I started first grade together. She was as close a friend as I ever had, as close as Michael, closer than Michael in many ways.

At one point, that second year of high school I think, we both thought we might be drifting toward something more than being friends. We liked the same things, laughed at the same things, got mad at the same things, were at ease and satisfied in each other's company. But going further made us both uneasy. It was better that we were friends. No, we were more than friends. Julie knew me better than anyone. I talked with her about things I would never have discussed with anyone else, trusted her totally, knew that she cared for me unselfishly.

She and Jim Colby started dating later. Jim was a year ahead of us in school, president of the Senior Class and star of the Debate Club. He was headed for Vanderbilt on a basketball scholarship. Julie graduated from UK with a degree in English Literature and Jim from Vandy in Economics. They got married as soon as Jim got his law degree from Georgetown. When I left, he was on his way to a partnership in the most successful law firm in town. Julie was concentrating on raising their kids, two boys and a girl. The boys must be in college now; the girl in high school.

Julie had the bourbon chilling in the fridge when I got there. It was the house she grew up in—a rambling two-story white Colonial with green shutters at the foot of Wapping Street on the river. A screened-in porch ran across the back of the house and looked out on a carpet of grass that ran down to the river. On lazy afternoons in the summers, we'd sit on that porch reading and talking and sipping lemonade, waiting for the occasional breeze and watching bumblebees in the honeysuckle vines by the steps.

Julie, unchanged in ten years, radiating energy, grabbed me and kissed me and took me by the hand and led me out to the porch where Jim was. She poured enough bourbon to cover the two ice cubes in the julep cup she handed me; fixed me with a hard stare and said, "You didn't call when you left. You didn't call when you got back. Explain yourself."

"Oh, hell," Jim said, laughing, "You're not mad. Leave him alone."

She laughed then, too. "No, I'm not mad. I'm just glad to see you. You can tell me what you want to tell me when you're ready." She kissed me again and pointed to the swing—an old style porch swing with big cushions and squeaky chains. "It's been waiting."

I settled in as if I'd never left.

We ate and talked and told stories and laughed, remembering. Jim was a little heavier, Julie still as trim and sparkling as she had always been. They caught me up with people I asked about. I didn't ask about Allie.

They caught me up with what had been happening to the town.

I did bring that up.

I still couldn't comprehend that downtown was practically empty on a Saturday morning. As I remembered, its streets were teeming on Saturdays. Downtown was the place where everyone in the county shopped, especially on Saturdays when the state workers had the day off, and the farm families came in to get their weekly shopping done. The block of St. Clair leading down to the Old Capitol where the J.C. Penny and the Five-and-Dime and the A&P store and Yancey's Wheel Cafeteria stood used to be so full of people you could hardly make your way down the street.

Was it a matter of a bad local economy? Over the years the town had always been insulated from the ups and downs of economic swings. Its two biggest employers were the distilleries and the

Commonwealth of Kentucky. Had people stopped drinking? Was state government closing down?

"No to the former, thank goodness" Jim said, raising his cup and smiling. "The latter is in question."

"I don't follow," I said.

"We have a new governor. He's a high profile businessman. Young. Flamboyant. Big ego. He wants to run the State like a business is run. He thinks there are too many people on the state payroll and intends to fix that the way they do in business—fire a lot of people. He's surrounding himself with his business cronies and has put them in charge of the big departments—highways, personnel, finance, natural resources, and so on, and is letting them make the cuts. They're eliminating about five thousand jobs—more than a third of them here in the county—almost two thousand local jobs! The impact on local business is huge. Stores and shops that have been doing well for years are closing or moving out to the malls around the new housing developments east and west of town. It's killing the down-town businesses. He's also making a run at the Merit system."

I remembered what that was—the Commonwealth's civil service, the core of government. Merit System employees got their jobs through competitive testing. They're not political appointees and can't be hired or fired for political reasons. Theoretically, it gives the state a cadre of qualified, experienced, non-political employees doing the work of the people without regard to whether some politician wants it done or is going to profit from it. They're the professionals who keep the government running while the political hires come and go with each administration.

"The new Governor wants to change that. He wants to hire and fire just as they do in business—anyone at any time for any reason—forget the Merit System rules."

"Can he do that?"

Jim turned to Julie.

She frowned, looked at us both. "Tell him later," she said. "Talk about something else. Talk about what Theo's going to do. I'll make the coffee."

We ate outside by candlelight. Dark came on pleasantly; the sky across the river fading delicately from salmon pink to back-lighted blue; a soft breeze carried the scent of honeysuckle; crested flycatchers darted over the water. Jim cleared the table and left me alone on the porch.

Talk about what Theo's going to do? I had no idea. Tomorrow. I'd think about it tomorrow.

Julie came out with the coffee; set my cup before me. "A little sugar, a little warm milk, and a lot of bourbon."

"Perfect," I said.

The night, the setting, the comfort, the company—damn, I thought. Golden. Let no black thoughts come creeping in; let no malevolent spirits hover near.

Julie's soft voice intruded.

"You left without telling me."

In the candlelight I couldn't make out her eyes.

"Why did you go?"

I reached for her hand. "I explained in the column I wrote when I left."

Julie shook her head. "You just made up a story people would believe. You could always get away with that. Except with me. I know you, Theo Clark. You were running from something. Did you run far enough? Is it behind you now?"

The candle flickered. I heard a whippoorwill down by the river. Julie waited. She knew me.

CHAPTER EIGHT

Had I run far enough? Was it behind me?

I had killed before.

I had killed in anger and in retaliation and in self- defense. I had killed out of fear and disgust and righteousness.

The Marine Corps taught me how.

But never in cold blood. Except for Jesse Bristow. The strange thing is, I half-way liked the man.

Jesse was almost God-like in the coal country.

He'd gone into the mines when he was fourteen after his father was killed in a cave-in. When the mine wars began, he was still in his teens. When they ended, he was the hero of the region.

The event that made his reputation and announced his character occurred early in the conflict. The mine owners had brought in squads of strikebreakers from the back alleys of Newport and Cincinnati. Thugs and lowlifes mostly, they were to provide muscle for the local police. Answerable to no one but the sheriff and free to run as rampant as they pleased, they bullied and ax whipped and burned families out all over the region. If anyone objected, shotguns and pistols came out.

"No union, you sonsabitches. End the strike! Get back to work!"

One night they delivered that message to Jesse Bristow's cousin who was leading the strikers at the Hawk Canyon mine. They kicked in the door of his little cabin on Dry Ridge, pushed his wife and baby back inside, dragged him out and set a torch to the place. Then they worked him over with their ax handles, fixed a rope around his neck and hung him from a white oak tree. He swung there strangling while his wife and baby died in the smoke and the fire.

The flames on the ridge could be seen from the town where Jesse lived with his young sister and his aunt. By the time he got up there, the cabin was only embers. Women from nearby were gathered around the bodies of the woman and child; some crying; most of them staring into the ashes grim faced and silent. The men were milling about, shocked at the savagery of the act.

Remember, Jesse was only in his teens, eighteen, I think, at the time. When he was seen and recognized, the crowd began to gather around him. They knew him. They knew he was blood kin. Jesse was calm, icy calm it seemed. He didn't say anything. He walked to the tree, took the hanging body of his cousin in his arms and lifted him up, motioning for someone to come and cut the rope.

Jesse walked to a clearing where the women had taken the bodies of the woman and the child and laid his cousin down beside them. There was grass there. The glow from the embers of the burning cabin gave a little light. Jesse stood in the shadows, silent for a moment, then stepped forward. He told everyone to go home. In the light of the dying fire, with the women crying in the background, he stood ram-rod straight and with such a fury on him that everyone felt it. Men much his senior, men the community was used to looking to for leadership, were all around him, yet Jesse took command, and no one questioned it. He told them to go home, that this would be taken care of, that what needed to be seen to would be seen to.

Later that night, Jesse, with Satis Arnow, who later would play an important role in Jesse's run for governor, and two other hand-picked friends, stole up on the cabin of the men who had done the killing. No one had any doubt about who they were. The six of them had been terrorizing the countryside for almost five weeks with the Sheriff's blessing.

It was well after midnight by then, cold and clear. No moon; stars everywhere.

The deputies were inside— rehashing the night's work, drinking and laughing. Jesse kicked the cabin door in and stepped through. The others followed. Jesse said nothing, just blew a hole in the table they sat around, pumped another round into the 30-30 carbine he had in his hands and started toward them. They were startled, then frozen, then frightened.

Jesse made them stand with their hands up. As they did, the shock began to wear off.

"What do you think you're doing, hotshot?" one of the men said, the chief deputy, the leader. "You gonna turn us in? Who to? We're sworn deputies doing our job. You think the Sheriff is gonna do anything? Hell, we work for him. We'll probably get a bonus. Now get your ass out of here," the man said, working up a laugh and starting to bring his hands down.

Jesse hit him across the mouth with the butt of the carbine.

There was no more laughter.

A big cast iron wood-stove stood at one end of the room. "Tie this one to the stove," he said, pointing to a weasely looking man with a drooping eye. Tapping the tip of his carbine against the badge of a the next man, a hulking mass with a gut so big it was hard to imagine how he carried it, "This one to the ice-box." The other four were marched outside.

Jesse began to slosh the cabin with kerosene. The men watched him in disbelief.

When he was finished, he threw a lighted match through the door and backed out.

Outside, he walked the rest of them down the path toward the well. There was a patch of grass there. He made three of them kneel and shot them one by one—in the forehead. He wanted them to see it coming.

The fourth man, the man who had mouthed off, the chief deputy, Jesse hung him from an old elm tree just down the path. He would have found a white oak if there'd been time. Jesse looped the rope and tied the knot himself—a simple knot, not a neck-breaking knot as hangman knots are tied—threw the loose end over a high limb, grabbed it and pulled the horrified deputy up off his feet and held him there—strangling and kicking—until he died. You know how strong a man has to be to haul a struggling adult male off the ground at the end of a rope and hold him suspended in the air until he chokes to death? How furious a man has to be? Flame from the burning cabin threw light on it all.

What needed to be seen to was seen to.

That story made its way by word of mouth throughout the mountains. By the time the mine wars ended, it had taken on the aura of a legend and Jesse Bristow the mantle of protector, avenger, and leader.

I didn't see this myself. It was told to me by Satis Arnow, who was there. But I believed every word of it from what I came to know of Jesse Bristow during the campaign.

Satis was a local banker and good friend of Jesse Bristow until that night. Jesse scared him that night. Satis said that no man made a more loyal friend than Jesse Bristow, that no man he knew could be so tender-hearted or thoughtful as Jesse Bristow, but after that night, Jesse was taken by a Messiah complex. Jesse knew what was right and wrong. Jesse knew what needed to be done. Buck him at your peril.

Satis came over to our side during the campaign. He was with us the day Michael was killed.

Jesse had made himself into one of the most powerful men in the state. He started with small truck mines that Satis helped him finance. He got big enough to worry the corporate mine owners. They bought him out and asked him to take over their dealings with the state and federal regulators and with the union he helped create.

Later the natural gas and oil drilling companies asked the same, and then the electric utilities. Soon, Jesse had more real power than all his clients combined. He was an elder in his church, a benefactor to worthy causes, a hero of the Mine Wars and a legend in the mountains of Kentucky.

And he was liked by all but his enemies.

He was a big man, muscular but slim, likeable, had a way about him that made you feel that no harm would come your way when you were in his company. And his hands. Almost delicate. He played the guitar. When he was young, he and his sister won a folk singing award; she singing; he accompanying.

I didn't regret that I shot him. Yet as the days rolled by and put me further from the event, I began to feel a guilt I shouldn't have felt. I did what I had to do. There would have been no justice had I not done it. I was right to do it. And yet ... Did I run far enough? I thought I had. I almost had. Then I had to come back to where the phantoms were.

CHAPTER NINE

Ah, the phantoms.

They come in the shank of the night when nothing's stirring, when it's so quiet you can hear the dark. They ease in under the edge of sleep and pry the psyche open just enough to let the worries and the sorries and the guilties slide in. And then you lie there, not awake but not asleep, with the pictures playing in your mind, feeling the ache all over again.

Rose, holding tight to my hand and looking into my eyes and trusting me when I told her the police would protect her.

Will, smiling to himself in the mirror behind the bar at King's, raising his glass in toast to me, both of us knowing he's killing himself with each drink he takes.

Emma, wandering at night up to the fence-line of her farm, terrified to cross over because of the Gypsy curse.

Lucas Gwynne, putting the forty-five in his mouth and blowing the back of his head away.

Josh overdosing to escape the pain.

Chad, bleeding to death on that damn hill in Korea.

Michael dying in Rhae's arms.

And Jesse Bristow.

The surprise on his face as I raised the twenty-two.

They still came. Not too often now. At the beginning, in those first months after Michael's death and my settlement with Jesse, they came every night—just Michael and Jesse.

Then, if it was Jesse alone, sometimes the pistol misfired. Sometimes I missed. Sometimes he laughed and swatted the slug away like a housefly and came after me with a hunting knife, and I'd run, panting and terrified. Mostly though, he took the bullet square in the center of his forehead, looking perplexed and confused, making no sound, a thin red stream oozing down between his eyebrows, and I'd stand there feeling righteous and justified and trying to ignore a little voice in my head, asking "who gave you the right?"

With Michael it was always the same. I'm walking beside him. He's smiling, animated, happy, and then a gun goes off, and his blood is in my eyes, and I'm trying to lift him from the ground, and then we're in the hospital, and Rhae is sitting by his bedside holding his hand and telling me through her tears that he's gone.

Yes, the phantoms still came. But I've tired them. Time and distance diminish them. Even phantoms get fatigued.

Now that I'm back, will they regain their strength? Have I brought them home?

CHAPTER TEN

The news stories played about as I thought they might—big in the *Journal* and the *Lexington Herald*, prominent but not splashy in all the others. The piece made Page One in both the *Journal* and the *Herald.* It was a strong, local story for both.

All made mention of the Dannan-Bristow race for the governor's chair and that I had been a principal advisor, and life-long friend, to Michael Dannan. The wire service story that went state-wide noted that Jesse Bristow's killer had never been found.

I laid down my copy of the *Herald* as the waitress refilled my coffee. The restaurant, a truck-stop at the top of Louisville Hill not far from my motel, was busy and noisy, and the scrambled eggs were good, and the home-made biscuits, served hot and with a crock of honey on the side, were superior.

The seats at the counter were filled with truckers, the air full of cigarette smoke and the smell of bacon and onions frying on the grill. What little I could make out of the talk had to do with the Kentucky Derby upcoming that weekend.

I finished my coffee, paid, and walked outside. The sky was cloudless and of that soft blue hue you see only in the Bluegrass in the Spring. A light breeze was lifting the colored pennants by the gas pumps, the air a little cool but with the promise of warmth by midday. No chance of rain. No chance of overcast. A perfect late April morning. Carpe diem.

Oscar Cantrell, Rhae's attorney, was first on my list.

Though it was not quite eight-thirty, he was in his office as I had asked him to be when I'd called the night before.

The rest of the building was just coming to life. I had the elevator to myself, and when I arrived, the secretary had already started the coffee. Cantrell and I made small talk while it brewed, then with hot cups in hand, retired to his inner office.

"You got me up before breakfast," he said, smiling as he sat down behind his desk. I took the chair beside it, joined in the smile.

"Sorry," I said.

He waved it away, still smiling. "Never mind. An early start is good for me. Now what can I do for you? Something in Mrs. Dannan's will? Some provision you're unclear on?"

Cantrell leaned back in his chair, relaxed, a curious, but helpful look on his face.

"Rhae's will seems to have taken everyone by surprise," I began. "Do you have any idea of what was in her mind when she did this? Did she have some premonition? Was there an event that triggered it? Her health, some other concern?"

Cantrell hesitated for a just a moment. "Mrs. Dannan wrote the new will about three months ago. She wrote it herself ... by herself. She had the provisions exactly as she wanted them and no changes were to be made. She brought the document to me to be put into legalese. So far as I know, she was in perfect health. There is no event that I know of that would have prompted the new will."

Cantrell paused, "Except—well, she had a meeting in early January with a representative of a business consortium headquartered in Cincinnati. The group is in the process of acquiring newspapers and radio stations in Kentucky. They wanted to acquire *The Journal*. She had me go over their proposal. It was very generous. Mrs. Dannan turned them down. She seemed a bit disturbed about it. Shortly afterwards, she came to me with this new will."

"What was in her old will?"

"I can't tell you that, Mr. Clark. Only Mrs. Dannan could authorize me to reveal that information. Anything else?" Cantrell asked.

There was. I needed to understand how this process would unfold.

"The provisions of the will don't take effect until the probate process is complete, as I understand it," I said. "How long is that likely to take?"

"Mrs. Dannan's affairs are in good order. Six months at most."

"Six months! Can't it move faster?"

"Probate is a precise and complicated process. There are no shortcuts. For an estate this size, six months will be remarkably fast."

I did the calculation. "October! It will be October before all this is settled. My god. What happens in the interim? Who's in charge?"

Cantrell frowned. "Until probate is complete and the estate's assets distributed, that is, until all the bills and taxes are paid and outstanding debts settled and litigation, if there is any, completed, the Executor, Mr. Isham, has control of the estate's finances. The businesses—the farm, the stables, the newspaper—they keep operating as usual under their present management. Formal control won't pass to you until probate is done. You could take an active role in the management now if you choose. Mrs. Dannan made it clear she wanted you in charge."

"So Paul has control of the money," I said. "What else? Could he, for instance, sell the *Journal* to the consortium you mentioned if he decided it was in the best interests of the estate?"

Cantrell was surprised by the question. "Good lord, no. Not without your approval. The Executor can sell assets of the estate only to raise money to settle claims and debts. There are no debts outstanding against Mrs. Dannan's estate large enough to justify the sale of an asset as valuable as the *Journal*. As the heir at law, you'd have to give your blessing."

Remembering Dulin smiling and saying that Paul would be tempted by the prospect, that was what I really wanted to know.

"Is there a problem," Cantrill asked.

"No. No problem." I hoped my smile reassured him. "Just curious."

"I don't know what your relationship with Mr. Isham is, but let me assure you, Mr. Isham will carry out Mrs. Dannan's wishes to the letter with as much speed as possible."

"Oh, I have no doubt of that."

We talked a few minutes more. Cantrell asked about my plans. I told him I'd made none yet. Was I going to take advantage of Rhae's box on Saturday? The coming Saturday was Derby Day, the Run for the Roses, the world's greatest horse race, just down the road at Churchill Downs. It had been run the first Saturday in May every year since 1875. Rhae loved the Derby. She had hopes her Elkhorn Stables would one day saddle a winner there.

"Put your money on Plugged Nickel. He's a shoo-in," he said.

Paul Isham and I needed to come to an understanding of what our roles would be while we waited for the probate process to be completed.

It's true I'm no businessman. Neither is Paul. We work with words and ideas, not with numbers. Rhae was the helmsman. As the CEO of Elkhorn Enterprises and Publisher of the *Journal*, she directed the businesses and made the business decisions. I had no intention of trying to inject myself into the management of any of the businesses. Still, during this six-to-eight month period, someone would have to fill the role Rhae no longer could.

Paul had more experience than I did. But I wasn't completely untutored. I'd done stories on men who started with little more than an idea and built it into a world-class company. And others who had taken what seemed to be money machines that could never fail and run them into bankruptcy. The in-depth research and interviews necessary for this type of piece is a graduate course in the topic. I learned what the winners and the losers did, and how they did it. The result was that I came away with at least a beginner's understanding of how the game is played. With a little help, I felt I could play it well enough if I had to.

That's the position I took with Paul.

We hammered it out over lunch later that day. He wasn't convinced. "You're coming into this absolutely cold. You've been away from all this for almost ten years. I doubt you ever knew, or cared, anything about the business side of a newspaper. You know nothing about the farming operation, or the stables, or the printing company. Be realistic, Theo. You're out of your depth here."

Paul felt, or hoped, I'd be overwhelmed by the charge Rhae Dannan had given me and willing to defer to his seniority and experience.

I listened politely, didn't argue, no point in arguing when you have the conn, and just said, "Humor me."

My reality check was Dulin.

When I got back from Korea and was finishing up at the University, and Rhae Dannan gave me a job at the *Journal* to help pay my way through the rest of school, Dulin Monroe was the Editor. He was in his early fifties then, brought in from the *Baltimore Sun* to run the paper after Paul Isham moved up to Managing Editor following Benjamin Dannan's death.

Dulin was a sizeable man, broad and sturdy with white hair that curled over his collar and friendly smile—if he felt friendly. If he didn't, you didn't want to be in his path. He was respected and admired by his peers, which was high praise because the Capitol City press corps in those days was a fraternity of the best in the business. They brooked no pantywaists and tolerated no pretenders. Dulin was an unrelenting foe of arrogance and power. For me, a fledgling in awe of the real pros, he could have been a nightmare. He turned out to be a treasure—a mentor of great patience and a valued friend—Dulin and Will Owens.

Will Owens, Bane of the Bad Guys, Champion Of The Little Man, Poet And Scholar and Bravest Of The Brave—Will Owens, the

Journal's star when I was breaking in—they took me by the hand and led me into the world I wanted.

Will drank himself to a young death. He knew he was doing it, but he kept on anyway, not because he couldn't stop but because he wouldn't.

Dulin's coaching and cajoling and prodding and stroking, his confidence in me and his unqualified support during my coverage of the Ashes Murder Case got me to New York, to the *Herald-Tribune*, to the start on the career I fantasized about.

Dulin never danced around the truth with me. If I was doing dumb things, he told me. If I was making bad decisions, he told me.

I saw Dulin that afternoon after leaving Paul's office. He was outside fussing with the dogwoods behind his house. He looked up as I drove in, putting a hand over his eyes to shade them from the sun, so he could see better. When he recognized me, he waved to a little parking space by the barn and started down.

"No blooms yet," he said as he walked up. "The buds look okay but nothing's popped yet. They were beautiful last year. Pink and white. Lovely against the greenery all around."

I climbed out of the car and took his hand. He didn't seem surprised or curious or anything other than pleased to see me.

"Come on up to the porch. The sun's over the yard-arm somewhere. I'll buy you a drink."

He lead me out to the porch on the cliff overlook and told me to enjoy the scenery while he washed up and made the drinks.

When we were settled he said, "It seems to me I read something about you in the papers this morning. Heir to the Hopkins fortune? Croesus in the Bluegrass? How did the *Herald* put it, 'When the estate is settled, Clark will have command of one of the largest personal fortunes in the Commonwealth.' That's you, right?" he said with a big teasing smile on his face.

"Come on, Dulin, this ain't funny."

"I know. Just couldn't resist the opening."

He took a long sip of his drink and sat looking quizzically at me.

"I had a talk with Paul this morning," I said.

"Yes?"

"We got clear on our roles."

"You did?"

"He's in control of the money until the will clears probate. I'm in charge of the businesses"

"Paul went for that?" Dulin asked with surprise.

"He had no choice. That's the way I want it, and according to the attorney, I have the conn."

"You told him that?"

"Yes."

Dulin laughed and clapped his hands. "Damn, Theo, you came out of the gate swinging." He seemed delighted.

"Paul said I'm in over my head."

He stopped smiling then.

"Maybe," he said, and paused and considered then shook his head. "No, I don't think so. The men running the businesses know what they're doing. Rhae didn't hold their hands, and you don't need to either. You'll need to get in and understand what the businesses are all about, but otherwise, let the managers manage. In time you're going to have to start acting like an executive—setting goals and seeing to it that they're met. For now, though, all you need to do is make the decisions they bring to you. You're smart enough to handle that."

"The Journal?"

"Ah," said Dulin, the *Journal.* "It was Rhae's pride and joy, you know. That's where she put most of her time and attention. Lew Arobogast is the Managing Editor now. I told you about him. University of Missouri Journalism School graduate, city editor at the *Dallas Times,* hired away to come to the *Journal* a little over two years ago when Paul semi-retired and became Editor Emeritus. Lew's a good man. He's got the right instincts. He has the know-how.

But he's still learning his way around this playground. Handling the challenges the *Journal* has right now would be a test for even a veteran who knew where the bodies were buried. The city's going through major trauma, and no one knows how that's going to turn out. In addition to the local Armageddon the new administration is unleashing, Lew's got to cover both the State Capitol and the political shenanigans that go on in that majestic building and in the Legislature, and you know the kind of competition the larger news organizations like the *Courier* in Louisville and the AP and UPI can mount. Local politics are no less contentious than when you were here, and he's got to tread between the county's power blocs and special interests and make sure the Rotary Club and the Bridgeport Women's Guild and the high school sports teams get their due. You know the drill."

I almost thought he sighed. But this was Dulin Monroe. Couldn't happen.

"Lew needs hand holding," he continued. "Rhae was a master at it. Paul gets involved some. Not always successfully. Lew and I talk from time to time. He calls if he has something he thinks I can help with."

He'd given me all this conversation leaning forward with his arms on his knees and making sure we had eye contact. He paused then, rattled his julep cup and tipped it up to take a last sip.

When he looked to me again he said, "You ought to go introduce yourself. Go to him. Don't make him come to you. Make him understand you're not a threat, that you want him to be successful. You could be a great team. You're not that far apart in age. My bet is you're pretty close together in the way you think."

Dulin stood up and reached for my glass. "I'm empty. You want to take a time-out while I fill these?

Twilight was beginning to creep up on us. The sun had already slipped below the ridgeline behind the house, and street lights were beginning to twinkle on across the river.

He returned with a julep cup in each hand, "Ancient Age. The second one is better."

He sat back down and continued as if there had been no interruption.

"So you're going to get on to Lew." It wasn't a question. "Where was I? Oh, yes, the *Journal*. This new governor and his administration are making big problems for a lot of people, the *Journal* included. Your printing company holds the State printing contract. It accounts for perhaps ten to fifteen percent of that company's revenue. The Governor's office has put out the word we may lose it. No direct action yet, just that it's being considered. As in all things political, there's a quid pro quo of some type involved. We don't know what it is. We don't know what the politicians want. The printing contract is based on a competitive bid. Lowest qualified bidder gets the contract. We've been that for the past two cycles. The rules could change. They make them. The can change them. Or the crony the Governor's office wants to get the bid may be told what our bid is and simply underbid us. It's happened.

"So there's that. And there is this consortium lurking out there. They have some tie-in to the Governor's office— to the chief of staff I think. I don't like anything about this."

"You said Paul seemed interested."

"He's being naïve," Dulin said. "Paul sees the *Journal* as the flagship newspaper in a chain stretching across the Commonwealth with plenty of money behind it and no worries about competition—a powerhouse. He's ignoring that control would lie with the management of the consortium, not with the editors of the *Journal*. Rhae would never go for that."

"Paul could?"

"He thinks he'd be strong enough to hold on to control." Dulin laughed then. "Other than that, Mrs. Lincoln, how did you like the play?"

There was a full moon that night. Dulin had no plans, and I had no appointments, so he put a couple of steaks on the grill on the far end of the porch, baked a couple of potatoes, made a big salad, and tore off some bread from a fresh loaf of French he'd gotten downtown that morning. He found a bottle of Caymus cabernet to compliment the feast, and we ate and drank and talked until well after midnight.

We decided that I would begin making my visits to the businesses on Friday, starting at the farm. I'd finish them on Wednesday of the following week with Lew Arobogast. We'd meet here at Dulin's place. Dulin would set it up. It would be a relaxed and informal get-to-know time. A few drinks. Grill some steaks. Talk and learn.

Then I'd head to California. I'd make peace with Kit Bedrosian, get current on my correspondence and assemble enough clothes to give me a decent wardrobe for an extended stay in the Garden Spot of the World and the Seat of Culture and Learning. Then I'd collect my trusty Royal portable and swing back through New York for a meeting with my *Atlantic* editors on the Afghan story before dropping back down to the Bluegrass to begin whatever it was I was going to do about Rhea Dannan's summons.

CHAPTER ELEVEN

The bugles wake me.

I catch a glimpse of white shrouded figures flowing ghost-like through falling snow. Pink flashes flare as small arms stutter in the night. Mortar rounds chew black holes in the frozen ground. Chosin. That awful winter of 1950. The bloody retreat from Chosin Reservoir.

I twist in bed as the scenes play in my mind. I'm eighteen, a Marine with an M-1 in my hands, freezing on a mountainside just south of the Yalu River in North Korea. We're surrounded and outnumbered. I'm lying on top of a ridge laying down covering fire as our deuce-and-a-halfs negotiate the icy trail below me. Irv Jansen is off to my right, his legs blown away, moaning between screams.

Sergeant Kowalski taps me on the shoulder, 'Stay focused. Keep 'em off the top.' All I want to do is find a big hole and crawl in it and pull the sky in over me. But I keep firing.

Machine gun rounds start kicking snow in my face. I roll left and then lurch up to move my position. There's a body in the way. I crawl over it and look down to see whether it's one of us or a Red Chinese but it's too torn apart to tell.

When I look back up I'm on the stairs outside the office where Jesse Bristow is working. Everything is eerily quiet. I'm still in my parka but the night is warm and I'm uncomfortable in it. The smell of cordite is in the air.

I wake up fully then.

I hadn't outrun them.

Michael still came, but not often. Allie too—sometimes hand-in-hand with Michael, sometimes holding her arms out to me. The others, Will and Chad and Josh and Rose, I must have tired them out. Or they got tired of the game. If they came, they came only half-heartedly. Even Jesse had begun to fade.

But tonight Jesse slipped in again. Are the memories these streets hold giving them strength? Will they all return to haunt my nights?

The rumble of traffic on the highway outside was muted. A pulsating yellow light glanced against the shades I'd pulled firmly down to keep the darkness in.

I lay awake remembering, not wanting to go back to sleep, not wanting to open the door to my phantoms. Get up and get out of this place, I told myself. But where was there to go at four in the morning?

The only all-night place I recalled was on the corner of an alley about a block from the Old Bridge in South Frankfort. A White Tower. A hamburger joint. I'd stop there sometimes after the paper was put to bed. At that hour of the morning, they had sweet-rolls still warm from the bakery and strong coffee. Worth a try.

The drive down Louisville Hill to look for it took me past Second Street School. Michal and I spent our grade school years there, and Julie, too. Flashes of us on roller-skates whipping around the flag-pole jumped in my mind.

And on up to the intersection at Bridge Street where Pete's used to be. That was our mecca. We'd gather there after dates, after games, standing around the lamp post on the corner, sometimes singing harmony, sometimes walking across the street to sit on the low wall that bordered the softball field to talk about the grand things we were going to do when we finished school.

Pete's wasn't there anymore.

I couldn't tell what stood in its place. It was too dark to read the sign in the window as I passed. But there were no boys singing on the corner.

Just ahead on the right, I saw it. On the corner of the alley where it should have been, all lighted up, a sanctuary against the dark and the dread.

The street was empty; the only movement the flash of the stoplights at the intersections and the only sounds the thud of my car door closing. The air was cold and moist from a slight mist off the river. The morning felt so lonely I could have been the only survivor in a deserted city after the population had fled or the Rapture had come and only us poor sinners remained to wander the night.

I shivered and pushed through the doors.

It was only my mood I suppose, but as soon as I stepped into the light and the warmth of the "tower," I felt I'd made it through a gauntlet and was safe. The phantoms wouldn't come here.

There was only one guy sitting at the counter. He kept his face in his coffee and never glanced up, so I don't know what he looked like.

The boy behind the counter was in White Tower white-white pants, white tee-shirt, white apron, white garrison cap slanted cockily on his head. He was about eighteen or nineteen, plain-faced, friendly and eager for some companionship to break the monotony of the night.

I ordered. No warm sweet rolls it turned out, but an apple Danish and coffee as strong as I wanted.

We talked, the boy and me, about the things you talk about with strangers at dawn just to have the company. He was working the midnight shift to help pay his way through Kentucky State, the college up on the hill, where he intended to earn a degree in biology and get a job with the State as a wildlife biologist when he graduated. He didn't think Plugged Nickel was worth a dime. He favored Genuine Risk, a filly, to win the Derby. Fillies were usually no match for stallions, but he was going to put five dollars on her to win, anyway.

As we talked, daylight came. I looked out through the blinking neon sign in the window to see the night giving way and fog flowing up from the river. It would burn off soon, I guessed, and be another sparkling April day.

I paid and left. Feeling good.

CHAPTER TWELVE

May

I'd been too long away, un-chaperoned and undisciplined. I needed looking after. The matter wasn't open for debate. So sayeth Julie Colby.

We had to find a different place for me to live while I was waiting the completion of the probate process. The motel I was in was too common and dreary. And I needed to begin to reconnect with people in town, get a social life going, keep myself from getting bored.

"You get snarky when you get bored, Theodore, you know you do, and it isn't becoming." I wasn't exactly sure what snarky meant, but I wasn't about to argue.

My re-entry would be at her Derby party Saturday. Julie had her father's box at Churchill Downs and close-in parking and loved the dressing up and the big hats, but she and Jim seldom went. She preferred the Kentucky Oaks, the big race the day before the Derby. It spotlighted the best fillies in the country and had most of the glamour of the Derby without the riff-raff. The Oaks didn't attract the beer-swillers who packed the infield on Derby Day. She thought it altogether more classy.

We'd go to the Oaks. The Derby we'd do at the camp. Her juleps were stronger than those served at the track, and she could see the race better on television.

I had the first of my meetings with Rhae's business managers on Friday. Present were the executive vice-president of Elkhorn Farms Ltd., the general manager of Elkhorn Stables, and the manger of Elkhorn Commercial Printing. Rhae had remodeled the old stone carriage house at the entrance to the farm property into offices for the farm manager and his staff. We gathered there. The windows were open to the morning air. The sweet scent of new mown grass and the soft lowing of cattle in the pasture filtered in. If the managers were nervous about the meeting, the setting couldn't have been more soothing.

I came humble and green. I wanted them to understand that I knew I needed to learn. More important, I wanted to reassure them that I wasn't going to rock any boats, that they should keep operating as usual, and nobody's job was at risk.

It went well. I knew some of these men when I worked summers on the farm with Michael. Some were only a few years older than me at the time. We got along fine then. We'd get along fine now.

I made sure I met with everyone at the same time. What I had to say I wanted them to hear directly from me and not filtered through anyone else and not relying on anyone else to deliver my message the way I wanted it delivered. Too much gets lost in translation.

I planned the same approach for the other meetings, particularly for the meeting with the *Journal* staff. That crew—the reporters, the printers and back-shop guys, the secretaries, the people on the business side—they should still be pretty much the same people who were here when I left. I'd know them and they'd know me. I'd play on that. I'd have Dulin fill me in on who was still at the *Journal* I should know; remind me of things I should remember about them.

And I'd count on Julie to do the same at her party—help me put names with faces, recall little adventures and accomplishments that I should recall but might not.

Julie Colby's Derby Day parties were singular events, usually twenty to thirty friends—never business contacts or society doyens or nice-to-knows.

It was a "for-us" party made up mostly of the little group who had gone to school and grown up together. She staged it at her family's camp near Big Eddy. "Camp" didn't do justice to the venue. Her grandfather, the late Colonel J. J. B. Espy of the tobacco Espys, built it. The layout covered about twenty acres of bottomland and tree-covered ridge on the west bank of the Kentucky River about five miles south of town. The main building was a large, two-story log and fieldstone structure. It sat on a wide, flat, grassy plane that sloped gently down to a sandy beach where a wooden dock extended out into the river with a swimming float anchored about ten yards beyond.

There were seven sleeping rooms on the upper floor of the main building. The ground level was basically one giant, open room with a stone fireplace and big windows in all four walls and a kitchen in the rear. A sitting porch ran across the front of the building. The porch had been built in a way that most of the night sky was visible from it.

Sitting there on summer nights, listening to music and watching a full moon on its course, was a memory I treasured.

For this May afternoon, the sky was empty of everything but blue, and the day was flawless. Bars had been set up on the porch and down at the dock. Round party tables shaded by bright white cafe umbrellas dotted the lawn. The betting window was inside by the fireplace with large televisions on the walls on either side.

The race card began at noon. The Derby itself would be the next to the last race of the day. At post times, everyone would move inside. Some were ducking in and out making bets already. Most, though, were outside in the salubrious afternoon, talking and sipping juleps

The women in their spring colors and their flamboyant hats, the men in blazers of light pink and green and yellow, the white sheathed tables and the sprouting umbrellas—all this against the green of the grass and the sheen of the river, made a picture so arresting it could have been on a movie set or a painting being posed by Seurat.

Nowhere on God's green earth are the women lovelier than the women of the Bluegrass on Derby day. And nowhere are the men more willing to don peacock colors.

Julie had me by the arm.

I knew most of the people, but after ten years away, I wasn't always sure I had the right name with the right face or that I was remembering little things I should remember. Julie whispered the needed information to me if she sensed me floundering.

Jim Colby waved to us from the porch. He was talking with a young woman who smiled and extended her hand as we walked up. "Don't be embarrassed that you don't remember me."

I took her hand, a little flustered, trying to bring a name to mind but not managing it. Hers would be a hard face to forget.

Julie rescued me.

"This is Tracy Jordan, Theo," she said. "She went to the Catholic girl's school in St. Louis. She was here only in the summers, and she spent most of that time out on her uncle's farm. It borders some of Rhae's property."

Still holding my hand, Tracy Jordon said, "We met at the Country Club. I was with one of the Catholic boys from Good Shepard, one of the Coleman boys. He introduced us. You were with Michael and Mrs. Dannan. We met again later that summer on my uncle's farm. You were helping with the haying. I brought water out to the crew."

"I don't believe you," I said. "I'd never forget someone so pretty."

Tracy Jordan was striking—brown eyes and the high cheek bones of a model or a Cherokee princess. Her hair was golden-red, almost the color of burnished copper. It was cut short and styled in a way that made her seem a serious career woman but on a closer look, made you think that might be merely a disguise. She wore a blue blazer over a pink blouse. The skirt was white and pleated and fashionably short. The legs it revealed were worth attention.

Julie laughed. "Stop it, Theo." To Tracy she said, "His manners are usually better." Then she turned to her husband. "You haven't been talking business?"

"A little. The hearing is only a month away. We were just comparing notes."

"Well stop. Today is for fun and games. Get back to your war Monday."

Jim saw the confusion on my face. "I'll bring you up to speed later." He smiled to Tracy Jordan. " OK, let's go see if her juleps are as good as she says they are."

Julie laughed and winked, "I may have to ration you."

Which wouldn't be a bad idea. Julie's juleps are smooth and lethal and can become addictive. I know that for a fact.

They're made from a recipe handed down through generations on the Espy side. In chilled silver julep cups, place four or five mint leaves and muddle with one teaspoon of powdered sugar and one teaspoon of water, then fill the cup with finely crushed ice. Pour in one jigger of bottle-in-bond bourbon and stir until the ice has dropped an inch or two, and frost is forming on the cup. Then fill the rest of the cup with bourbon, stir mildly once or twice, add a sprig of mint dusted with powdered sugar and behold—a certified, can't-be-beat, two's-the-limit, Julie-style Kentucky mint julep.

The afternoon rolled along as those sorts of afternoons do. We reminisced and told stories and laughed. I got caught up on children and marriages and illnesses and golf and was let in on whispered speculation about who might be slipping around with whom.

No one was happy with UK finishing fourth in the national basketball rankings and even less happy with the new governor and the havoc his actions were inflicting on the town. But after the second julep, everyone was mellow, and the world was bright.

When Derby time came, to the surprise of almost everyone, Genuine Risk, the filly, came home first, nosing out Rimbo by a length. In all one hundred five years of the Derby, Genuine Risk was only the second filly to win.

Tracy had her money on Genuine Risk and had tried to convince me to make my play there too. I thought my guys at the truck-stop knew more and put my five-dollars on Plugged Nickel. He ran seventh. There's a moral to that story.

No one was interested in the last race, so the televisions were turned off and someone started the music playing. Speakers on the porch carried the sounds outside. It was still light, but would be dark soon. A few couples began to say their thank-yous and start for their cars. Some had come from as far away as Lexington and some had baby-sitters to get home.

Julie would be lighting candles soon and would find out who wanted to stay for dinner, and Jim would fire up the big grill on the porch and bring out the steaks. I was in no hurry to leave. I had no place to go except back to that dreary little motel room.

The late afternoon breeze was pleasantly cool. The sky was cloudless. There would be an almost full moon later. Julie decided we'd eat outside. She made her survey of stayers and put me and Bobby Layne to setting up tables down near the beach, so we could sit together.

We'd be eight in all. I placed Tracy's chair next to mine.

CHAPTER THIRTEEN

The hearing that Jim Colby referred to turned out to be the reason Tracy was with us.

We'd finished dinner. Everyone had left but us. We were still at the table, sitting silent for a moment, taking in the moonlight.

Jim sat across from me, leaning back in his chair and looking up at the sky. I saw him give a faint shake to his head and heard him say very quietly, almost as if talking to himself, "It's outrageous."

Julie glanced over quickly. "Now don't let yourself get excited. It's a fine night. Enjoy it."

Jim turned and smiled at her, raised his glass to his lips, took a sip. "Right. Nice night. Don't get worked up."

I looked at Julie, questioning.

"Oh explain, Jim," she said with a little sigh. "Theo won't sleep."

He nodded, sat his glass down, and turned to me.

"Do you remember Artie Skinner? A tall, thin kid with a goofy grin. He wanted to play basketball but couldn't dribble, stuttered sometimes. He was serious about everything and willing to help with everything. Got kidded some. Not the smartest guy in the class, but he got by. He graduated with us."

"What about him?"

"He was fired from his job with the State. I'm representing him. We're appealing the firing."

"And that's what outrages you?"

"You're damn right it does. Artie was Merit System. Merit system employees can be fired only for cause: stealing, drunkenness, missing work, that kind of thing. Artie's as honest as the day is long. He doesn't drink. He's never missed a day of work."

Jim stood up.

"The only 'cause' for firing him is that Artie keeps insisting they play by the rules. They keep trying to cut corners, and Artie keeps telling them they can't. They're charging he's incompetent to do the job. And saying he's taking kickbacks. Damn lies!"

From across the table Tracy Jordon added, "Ridiculous. Absolutely ridiculous."

"You're involved in this," I said, surprised.

She nodded. "Artie is kin ... the son of my uncle's sister. They live on my uncle's farm, the one next to Mrs. Dannan's. I was there almost every summer. I practically grew up around Artie." She smiled, "He's like an older brother to me. He's the sweetest, kindest, most responsible person you can imagine."

Jim had moved around the table and was standing behind Julie, his hand on her shoulder

"Artie's job is Assistant Director of Rights-Of-Way. He keeps the records for right-of-way maintenance, schedules mowings, reviews contractor bids. The case they've trumped up charges that he makes constant mistakes that cost the state money and time and that he takes kick-backs from mowing contractors. They're going to say that the reason he makes the mistakes is that he's not smart enough to handle the job."

Tracy slapped her hand down on the table. The candles fluttered. "That's ridiculous. That's just ridiculous. They have no proof. Some fudged up memos, a few mostly illegible handwritten 'reports' from field workers, a letter from a contractor no longer in business, no longer in the state even, that's almost certainly bogus."

Jim broke back in. "Tracy is an attorney—a litigator, a damn good one, with Fosburg & Jamison in St. Louis. She volunteered her help."

"It's you two against the Commonwealth?"

Jim nodded grimly. "I'd feel more confident if this was a jury trial. It's not. It's tried before a Hearing Officer from the State Personnel Board. The hearing is run like a regular trial except there's no jury. Both sides present arguments, evidence, witnesses. The Hearing Officer is the judge and the jury."

"And the hearing is public," Tracy said. "Anyone who wants to watch it, can. That's important to Artie. He's so sensitive to what people think about him."

"The facts are on our side," Jim said. "There is absolutely no justification for firing Artie."

Tracy said, "Artie's going to have to sit there in public and hear all that abuse. It's going to be awful for him."

"Is he?" I said.

"Is he what?"

"Not smart enough to handle the job?"

Jim and Tracy looked at each other and then back to me.

"Of course he's smart enough," Tracy said emphatically.

More mildly, Jim said, "Depends on who's doing the defining. He's slow on some things. And he's shy. But he is not retarded. Can they make it look as if he is? Or at least plant the suspicion? Maybe."

"If they do it will kill him," Tracy said.

There were just the four of us. Everyone else had left. We were alone at the table on the riverbank with the full moon high in the sky and the river shining silver. A whippoorwill called now and then but otherwise there was silence all around.

Into it Julie said, "This case is a cause célèbre. Everyone knows that the new Governor would like to be rid of the Merit System. Artie Skinner could be the poster boy. If they can establish that Artie can't handle the work because he's not mentally competent to do it, they can say the system gives jobs to people not capable of holding them and that once they're on board it's almost impossible to fire them. They can say the system protects the incompetents. It should be done away with and something more effective, like the practices businesses use, should be put in its place."

"And Jim's not making any friends in the Governor's clique," Tracy said.

The import of what I was hearing struck me then. "Am I missing something here," I said to Jim. "If you win, you'll be high on the Governor's enemies list. If you lose, you'll still be high on that list. There can't be a big fee involved. Your firm must get a fair amount of business from the State. What's here that I don't understand?"

Jim was silent for a long moment, looked to Tracy and then to Julie then back to me. He didn't say anything. He just shrugged. Julie gave a little laugh then. "Oh you know Jim. He thinks he's Robin Hood."

Finally Jim laughed. 'Yeah, but what the hell. I can always make my way as a male model."

None of us wanted to deal with the pictures that brought to mind, so on that note we drank a final toast, collected the empty wine bottles, made sure the candles and the fire were out, and called it a night.

CHAPTER FOURTEEN

Tracy.

Tracy Jordon.

So she's an attorney?

A litigator, a trial lawyer. A damn good one.

So what I know about her is that her uncle has a farm that borders Rhae's property. She spent some summers there. We met briefly during one of those summers. She's Catholic. She knows, or knew, the Coleman boys. I know, or knew, them too. Bill, Jim, Eddy. Popular. Handsome. Fine athletes. Went to Good Shepherd, the local Catholic high school. Too bad. If we'd had them, we might have won the state football title my senior year.

She went to high school in St. Louis—to a Catholic girl's school. May have gone to university and to law school there, too. Washington University School of Law has a reputation.

Don't know the family name. Jordan? Don't recall any Jordans. Julie can fill me in on that.

Age? She must be years younger than me. If I had met anyone as pretty as Tracy when I was a teenager, I would have carried that picture around in my mind for a long time. So she must have been too young to notice. Not yet blooming.

Why am I interested?

Kit Bedrosian turns heads when she walks into any room. Maeve Preston skips through the Manhattan media scene like it's her backyard. Clio Marwick's pedigree opens doors at the best clubs in London. No one has a keener mind or a quicker wit than sweet Charlene.

I'll have to think about this.

Allie? I won't think about Allie.

CHAPTER FIFTEEN

Lew Arbogast was already at Dulin's when I got there, and I got there fifteen minutes early.

That impressed me. Punctuality is next to Godliness. Team meetings at the Green Bay Packers when Lombardi was coach started on "Lombardi Time." If a player was late to a meeting, it cost him one hundred dollars for each minute. Coach assumed that if he could get to a meeting on time, his players could too. It didn't take the team long to figure out they better be there early, and that gave rise to "Lombardi Time." The saying was that if you're fifteen minutes early to a Lombardi meeting, you're fifteen minutes late. Lombardi ran the most efficient meetings in the National Football League. Lombardi thought people who were late were undisciplined and not to be relied on. I try to operate on Lombardi time. Barring acts of God or nature, I'm never late.

So I had a good feeling about Lew Arbogast before we even shook hands

It was raining, a driving rain that almost overwhelmed my wipers as I made the turn off the blacktop onto the gravel lane leading to Dulin's. I managed to make the run from the parking area to the porch without getting entirely drenched, but if I'd had any idea, conscious or otherwise, of cutting an imposing figure on introduction, that was gone. My hair was wet, my jacket wet, my pant legs wet. I looked like what I was, something just dragged in out of the rain. Dulin had seen my car lights as I turned in and met me on the porch with a big white towel in one hand and a glass of bourbon in the other. "Damn, Dulin, you could have met me with an umbrella," I said, reaching for the towel.

He huffed and shoved the drink toward me. "Take a sip and come on in and meet Lew," he said, leading through the door into his main room.

The clouds of the fast moving thunderstorm had drawn a shade over what should have been a fine spring sunset, but the light from the fireplace made the room seem cheerful. Lew Arbogast was standing beside it.

"Lew Arbogast," he said, with his hand extended and a smile on his face. Nodding to the rain outside, he said, "I beat it by about ten minutes."

"Get up by the fire and dry-out," Dulin told me. "I'll start dinner. You two get to know each other while I create a gourmet feast. You know where the bar is."

I liked Lew Arbogast from the start. It was clear that he was confident in himself and not at all interested in trying to find out what I wanted to hear and making sure he told it to me.

All I really wanted to do was reassure Lew Arobogast, and through him the whole editorial crew at the *Journal,* that they had no need to be apprehensive. They were hand-picked and trained by two of the best people in the business in Dulin Monroe and Paul Isham. I had no inclination to make changes or rock boats. I told Lew they should keep on doing what they were doing in the way they were doing it. I had some business that needed attending to and would be away for several weeks, but when I returned, I wanted to meet them all.

"Thanks for that," Lew said when I'd finished my little speech. "People are nervous. No one on staff has known any other boss but Rhae Dannan. You can understand they're wondering what to expect. And they've all heard the rumor about the Consortium."

Dulin nodded. "Most of the town has heard it."

To me Lew said," Is there anything you can say about that?"

Dulin held his hand up to me. "Don't go jumping into this with both feet." Looking pointedly at Lew, he said, "Anything you say to us is confidential, but even so, you ought not to be commenting on this. You want the speculation to die. It's unsettling not just to the staff, but to advertisers, too."

I understood Dulin's point. I understood the staff's unease.

"I haven't heard the rumors, Lew. I understand that Rhae turned down whatever this consortium had in mind. I don't imagine I'm about to second guess Rhae Dannan."

I paused to let that sink in, then said to both of them, "Is that good enough for you?"

It was good enough for Dulin. How good it was for Lew I'm not sure, but he accepted it, and we moved on.

Lew gave me a fast run-down on everyone on staff and an update on the major stories they were dealing with or anticipating.

I knew many of the players. There hadn't been much turnover at the *Journal* since I left. Lew Arbogast, himself, was the most notable.

The story that was getting the most attention centered on the big cut in state jobs the new Governor had ordered—twenty percent across the board. Downtown businesses were feeling the consequences. People who were losing their jobs weren't spending. Everyone else was wondering if they were next and weren't spending on anything but necessities. Shops were closing or moving. Restaurants were turning up empty. It was not a good time for the Capitol of the Commonwealth.

I asked about the Skinner hearing. Lew was aware of it but had done nothing on it so far. He planned a piece for the Sunday before the hearing, a page-one piece which would discuss the administration's drastic reductions in the state payroll and the Governor's apparent intent to dismantle the Merit System. The Artie Skinner case was the opening salvo.

"What are the odds," I said.

"On the Skinner case? The State will prevail. On the Merit System? Over ninety percent of the state's employees are covered by it. If the Governor wants to get control of hiring and firing, he has to get rid of it. I don't think he has the votes in the legislature to pull it off, but he is a very impressive guy."

Dulin broke in, "He'll label all the Merit System people bureaucrats and play on the public's ingrained dislike of red tape. They'll liken them to professors who get tenure and can't be fired. They'll spotlight people like Artie to make their case that the system is saddling taxpayers with incompetents. They'll throw around a lot of money and use public opinion poll results to beat up on the Legislature.. I wouldn't bet he couldn't pull it off, but it's a long shot."

"Will the paper take an editorial position on this?"

Lew paused, "That will be up to you."

Dulin came back, "Where the *Journal* stands will be important. Your position will influence other papers. To put this in its crassest terms, the question is whether it's better to have the machinery of government in the hands of "bureaucrats" who got their jobs through competitive testing and have no political obligations or have the state run by political appointees put in place to do the will of their bosses. You, Theo, specifically, will be under pressure from both sides. The administration has the muscle—the state printing contract in particular. Remember the rules about fights. Don't pick unnecessary fights. Don't pick any fight you don't think you can win. If you're in one, throw away the rule book and fight like hell."

CHAPTER SIXTEEN

The Delta non-stop from Cincinnati to San Francisco got in just before cocktail time. Thin tendrils of fog were beginning to slip through the Golden Gate, and car lights made a necklace of sparkles across the Bay Bridge as the evening inched along.

Kit Bedrosian was waiting for me at the Delta gate. She wore a black leather flight jacket and trim British tan slacks that hugged her hips and her legs. A man's-style white button-down shirt and a gray Fedora completed the outfit. The sight of it caused a young businessman rushing by to break stride and turn to look back. Two others waiting across at the gate stared appreciatively.

"This your Indiana Jones look?" I asked, grinning as I came up to her. She ignored the jab, took me by the arm and started hustling me through the crowd.

"See that fluffy looking stuff out there? It's called fog? It's cold. Luggage?"

"Just carry-on."

"Perfect," she said. "There's a car waiting at the curb."

"No hello? No how are you? No welcoming kiss?"

"Get in," she said, shoving me into the back of the town car. She climbed in next to me, closed the door, grabbed me by the ears and kissed me so hard I lost my breath. "Now shut up. We have a ton of work to catch up on, and it's going to take forever to get to town in this traffic and fog. We're starting now. No diversions."

I'd been away almost a month—the time in Afghanistan and then the time in Kentucky. Work and projects had piled up.

Kit had her briefcase on her lap and a clutch of folders in her hand. "The Wind River story for *Esquire*—are you going to do it? Opening another, "That friend of yours at the J-School at Cal wants you to come talk with his graduate students at their seminar next month." Waving an envelope at me, "If you don't pay your electric bill, PG&E is going to turn out your lights." One by one she began shoving papers at me, "Your telephone. Your Visa credit card!" Frowning at me, "How did I get stuck keeping you out of trouble with your creditors, anyway?"

"Because you're a kind, sweet woman who knows I'm only a poor country-boy trying to do the best he can in a world he never made."

"Ha!"

She snapped her briefcase closed and turned to face me directly.

"The *Atlantic*. Your Afghan piece. They want to see you in New York next week to talk about it." Her tone changed then, the scolding melding into concern.

"Was it bad? Were you where guns were going off?"

Soviet paratroopers landed in Kabul city on Christmas Day. Forty-eight hours later, ground forces numbering eighty-thousand accompanied by fifteen thousand tanks rolled across the Afghan border.

They came to rescue a pro-Soviet Afghan government locked in a savage civil war with Afghan nationals violently opposed to the regime's attempts to overthrow the Muslim culture that was the guiding influence over most of the country.

Afghanistan was too important a geographic location in Cold War politics to be ceded to Russian control. Our side wanted the nationals to win. We were beginning to take steps to help make that happen.

I went there in March with a covert CIA team who were being sent to set up liaison with the guerillas, the Mujahedeen, and work on ways to supply them with arms and materials.

My purpose there was to gather information for a possible year-end cover story in *The Atlantic*, one that would define the shape of the conflict and suggest its likely outcome, one that might influence the way policy makers approached the war.

Afghanistan is an unforgiving country. It will kill you if it can. The land is steep and stark. The weather can be murderous. Historians call it "The Graveyard of Empires." No one had managed to conquer it. Not Alexander the Great, not Genghis Khan, not the British in their days of Empire. Afghanistan defeated them all.

Was it bad there?

I'd been at Chosin in Korea in the arctic winter of the first year of that awful war.

That was bad.

I was at the fall of Saigon.

That was bad.

In those first few months after Christmas, the Russians concentrated on the Afghan cities. We were out in the country where the Mujahedeen lived, in the cold and brutal mountains. There were times that got my heart racing, but in the context of bad I had in mind, it wasn't. I had no doubt it would get that way rapidly.

"No. Not bad."

"Will you go back?"

"Yes."

We rode on in silence, thinking our separate thoughts, traffic barely inching along.

We didn't go on to dinner that night. We went to Kit's place. Fog flowed past the windows. We pulled a blanket up to keep warm.

Saturday morning on San Francisco Bay. Sunlight sparkling on calm water. Sky so clear that when you looked up, it looked like you were looking into forever. The air just cool enough for a light sweater but not so cool as to make you want to be inside. From our outside table at the restaurant in Sausalito, we could see all the way down the Bay. Flights of white sails flocked under the bridge and around the tankers lying at anchor in the roads.

"Do you think this is a good idea?"

Kit was buttering a slice of toast.

"What?" she said frowning.

"Fraternizing with the hired help. They say it's bad practice to fraternize with the hired help."

She had on deck shoes, so the kick against my shin wasn't crippling.

"Don't get smart with me, Lothario, I've got the keys to your car."

We both laughed, delighted to be in each other's company on a morning so grand.

I had to be in New York Thursday, so that would give me the early part of the week to get organized for the time I'd be away waiting for Rhae's estate to settle—pack enough clothes to last me, arrange for the mail and someone to look in on my apartment—the niggling details that had to be taken care of to keep my life afloat while I was playing games in the Bluegrass. What I didn't attend to Kit would, but I wanted to impose no more than was absolutely necessary. I'd begin on that Monday. Today and tomorrow were for just Kit and me.

There was a bonus.

The phantoms hadn't followed.

When I boarded my flight for JFK that Wednesday morning, my nights had been serene. Kit kept them away.

The editors in New York agreed with my assessment of the Afghan story. Russian victories in the first few months of the war were to be expected. The early fighting was around Kabul were Russian armor would easily overwhelm the rebels, but once the fighting moved into the countryside, as it must, that advantage would be lost. Russian tanks would be of little use in the mountains and their troops no match for the weather, the terrain, and the assaults of the Mujahedeen. It would be a long war. I'd go back in October and write for the January issue. No one else was working the story. We were ahead of it and would stay ahead of it.

With the timing decided, the meeting wound down, and I had the evening to myself in Manhattan.

When I first came to town, a rookie fresh from the hills of Kentucky, the city mesmerized me. It was the jeweled island where magic was made and dreams came true, where the favored lived and talent ruled—The Capital of the World. It was New York.

I was spellbound by it and came to know it well.

But after a time I recoiled from it. After Rose's death, after I'd convinced her to testify against the gang, after she'd died from the beating she'd taken, after I'd been feted and honored for my reporting, after that, after the depth of the city's indifference became apparent, after the emptiness of its heart chilled me, I loved it no more, and I left.

Young love dies hard, though, and as I matured and my assignments brought me frequently back to New York, I began to forgive and as I forgave, I fell under its spell again.

At the start, as my romance with the city was beginning, I was adopted by a trio who felt it an act of charity to take pity on a poor country boy adrift in the big city. I think my naiveté amused them. They didn't address their elders as sir or ma'am or walk on the curb side of women as all of my kind were taught to do and did instinctively. We became fast friends.

One of the trio was a Tennessean. He was the boulevardier of the group, the man about town, known to all the maître d's at the in restaurants and able to get tickets to the hit plays. He worked in public relations in the second largest agency in town and had an expense account that could accommodate such luxuries.

Another was a reporter like me and no older than me, but an old hand. He came from the Irish of Brooklyn and had that edge the Irish often have, something in the blood that resents privilege and power. He started work at sixteen as copy boy at the old *World Telegram* and worked his way up to the city hall beat.

The third, Benjamin Bolanger IV, of the Massachusetts Bolangers, was an Ivy League blue blood and rising star in an old-line investment banking firm.

How the three of them came together, I never knew. Jay O'Donnell, the boulevardier, and Brian Eagen, the reporter, must have met in the course of their work. Benjay, the broker, the Ivy League lord, how he came across the two of them, or they him, I had no idea. But it was a serendipitous happening.

Jay had arranged for us all to have dinner at Callucci's, a small Italian restaurant on East Forty-Sixth off Third Avenue. We'd been going there almost from the beginning. Gino Callucci, the owner, knew Jay and would always find us a table, even on the busiest nights. But never the round table.

Tucked into a corner behind the little bar at the front of the room, it was the only round table in the room. Some nights it was empty even when the rest of the restaurant was full. Sometimes there was only one person seated there, always the same man—a beefy, full-faced man with heavy black eyebrows that hid his gaze. He dressed in black suits, wore starched white shirts with stiff white collars, and crimson ties, always crimson. Sometimes there were two or three others with him, nattily dressed. They talked quietly, drank moderately, ate appreciatively. The way the table was situated, back in the far corner of the room, it couldn't be approached from any angle without being seen. Gino Carlucci treated whoever was seated at that table with great respect. We thought they were Mafia.

One night, Brian, the Irisher, the wildest of us, the most fearless, smarter than the three of us together, with more gin in him than he should have had, which was not an uncommon thing, and no judgment at all, which was even less uncommon, with the big table sitting empty and the evening wearing on, out of curiosity he couldn't contain and showing off, as he often did to his delight and our chagrin, got up from our table and went up to Gino.

"Is he?"

Gino stared at him.

Brian nodded toward the big round table.

"The big man at the big table," Brian said with a knowing smile, "is he Mafia?"

Mr. Callucci frowned at Brian, then slowly turned to look at each of us. When he finished his inspection, he leaned conspiratorially into Brian and whispered loudly enough for us all to hear, "Don't pry at doors you don't know what's behind." He patted Brian on the cheek, nodded sternly to us, and turned back to his station.

I was the first to arrive.

I ordered an Ancient Age on ice—two ice-cubes, cover the ice with bourbon, please—sat back on a stool at the bar and waited.

From the small foyer where the hatcheck girl sat, the bar was two steps down and to the left. It was curtained off from the rest of the room, so that diners had privacy from curious eyes.

When we first came to Carlucci's, I thought I'd been dropped into a scene from La Dolce Vita. The room was a long rectangle. Sleek women, bejeweled and in low-cut dresses, and men in expensive looking suits sat at tables covered in crisp white linen. A single red rose in a crystal vase stood on each table with an unshaded candle fluttering beside it. The walls were covered in flocked red velvet, and the tinkle of silverware and the purr of conversation filled the air. I wasn't sure what sybaritic meant, but this had to be close to it.

Gino Carlucci was famous for his stracciatella. That night we started with that and let Gino decide the rest, switching from Barolo to Pinot Grigio as the courses arrived. This came to be our regular routine at Carlucci's.

When we were sated and ready to leave that first time, after adding up my share of the tab, I didn't have enough money left for cab fare. It was a little after midnight. I had a pleasant buzz on. Outside there was a soft mist in the air, and the streets flowered with well-oiled people on the move to warm beds or late night bars. It was too fine a night for a cab, even if I'd had the money. I walked— delightedly content.

I might take a cab tonight, I thought. I've got the money. Then I laughed at my own swagger. Don't get flip, Buster. You rich guys can be a pain.

And that's what they ragged me about most of the night.

The O'Donnell started it. "Theodore O'Hara Clark," he called out in a sing-song chant as he came rushing through the outside door, "Midas, Croesus, moneyed-man and nabob! Fat-cat, plutocrat, man 'o means and heart throb! How the hell are you?"

He threw a bear-hug around me and lifted me off my seat, laughing and smiling. Brian and Benjay were right behind him, laughing as well and pounding on me.

"Whoa, guys, Whoa," I said, untangling myself, "Gino'll kick us out of here with all this racket." Then, straightening my jacket and trying to regain a semblance of dignity while they ringed me beaming, "But damn it's good to see you."

Almost two years had passed since we'd all been together. We poked and jabbed and acted like fraternity boys loose on the town; the pretense and constraints of our august positions and reputations for a moment jettisoned. It got better after the surprise.

When Gino ushered us into the dining room, the big round table, the "Mafia Table" was empty.

He led us toward it on our way to our usual table at the back, but as we passed it, he stopped, looked pointedly at Brian, took my arm, led me to the table, pulled out the chair where the big man in the black suit always sat, and ceremoniously seated me.

Everyone's surprise was complete. We looked uneasily at each other. Gino watched us, smiled, spread his arms, bowed, and with great formality said, "Gentlemen, your table."

Whether the big man died, whether his family had been taken over or eliminated, whether he was really Mafia, we never knew. Gino never explained, and we never asked.

After the first bottle of Barolo, after the stracciatella, after the salads and the entrees, the talk turned from joking at each other to me. They'd seen Rhae Dannan's obituary in the *Times* and the reference to the wealth of her estate being willed to "Theodore O'Hara Clark, an editor at *The Atlantic* magazine. That's how they knew.

They ribbed me about it—warned me about the women who would be coming out of the woodwork to attend to my every want, the long-lost relatives mysteriously appearing from strange places like Kansas or New Mexico, hoping to get in on the action, the Tax Man salivating, the deal makers lining up.

"Theo, poor boy," said Benjay "being rich may be more than you can take. Better you should turn it all over to me to look after for you."

That sparked a short, high-spirited argument over whether the burden could be better borne by Jay or Brian. Afterwards, we sat catching our breath, our eyes teary from laughing.

In that moment of quiet, Brian rose slowly to his feet. "All this talk of money makes me sad." He was serious now, not joking. The others fell silent. "Money changes things. Money changes people." He fixed me with his melancholy Irish stare and raised his glass to me. "Well this is all damn fine, fellows, but I want to drink one last toast to the old Theo Clark. He was a damn fine fellow, and I will miss him."

There was a moment when no one stirred, then Jay rose, glass in hand, then Benjay. They stood in a semi-circle around me, glasses raised.

"To the old Theo Clark!"

CHAPTER **SEVENTEEN**

The old Theo Clark.

I ran that scene over and over in my mind as my flight bumped through thunder-heads from LaGuardia down to Lexington—the three of them standing there, the laughter of the moment ago gone, a look part sad, part questioning on their faces, me racking my mind to try to find a funny line to bring the warm mood back.

The old Theo Clark.

Who did they think he was?

Who did I think he was?

That Theo—that Theodore O'Hara Clark.

That Theo was born to a happy Irishman with a tenor voice so pure even the bird's listened, and who could handle a fly rod so gracefully his casts traced perfect loops on the canvass of the sky. He was a foreman at the distillery. Dead at forty-seven. A heart attack. Theo was just south of the Chinese border that day on the frozen road back from Chosen in the first winter of the Korean War.

His mother was a country girl, the sweetest woman who ever lived. She died when he was twelve. He's still hurting.

That Theo grew up in a house next to the river near the foot of the railroad bridge. He raced up and down the riverbank and all over the Old Capitol grounds and played kick-the-can on the corner in front of Liberty Hall on summer nights. He had a paper route and glided along the city's streets on his bike in the early mornings with the sun just rising and lights coming on in the houses along his route. He knew almost every street in town, felt at home in all of them, felt the town liked him. He liked the feeling.

That Theo had a girl he thought he loved and who he thought loved him, but his pride got in the way.

He went to war as a boy and learned to kill. He survived, finished college, became a newspaperman. He went eagerly off to New York to find his fortune but got so badly disillusioned there that he came back home.

That Theo's best friend bled to death in his arms. A few weeks later that Theo killed the man responsible.

He was broken for a while and went away to lick his wounds and when he had done that, he was doing well, that old Theo Clark.

Then Rhae Dannan died and made him her heir.

CHAPTER EIGHTEEN

The letter was there when I got back.

The envelope was addressed by hand to Mr. Theodore O'Hara Clark c/o *The Journal,* Frankfort, 40601. My name was underlined in red. The handwriting was crisp Spenserian script, the graceful curves that the best schools, or the most disciplined teachers, insisted on.

I turned the envelope in my hands. The postmark was Williamsburg, Ky. I remembered Williamsburg. I'd been through it several times during Michael Dannan's run for governor—a small town in the mountains not far from Cumberland Gap. Cumberland College was there. The return address was a post-office box.

Intrigued, I started to open it, but just then a young face appeared around the doorframe and, smiling, asked, "Coffee, Mr. Clark?"

While I was gone, Paul Isham had taken a small office for me. He had intended to put me in Rhae Dannan's office at the *Journal,* but I didn't want that— not yet, not now. I wasn't ready for the Publisher's office. There was nothing else suitable in the building, so he'd taken an office for me in the McClure Building on the floor above lawyer Cantrell's office. From my window I could see down to the Old Capitol Grounds and watch whatever foot traffic there was on what used to be one of the busiest streets in town. There was very little now. People were hunkered down. The State reaper was still out with his job-cutting scythe.

I put the letter aside to open later and smiled back as my new secretary stepped through the door."

"Two sugars, a little milk, the rest hot and black—have I got it right?"

"Prefect," I said, sitting back and savoring. A private office, an "assistant"—these were new experiences for me. I'd spent my time in crowded newsrooms or knocking out copy on my portable anywhere I could find a level surface and a place to sit. A room all to myself, a desk, bookshelves, paintings on the wall, soft lighting and blissful quiet, someone to bring me coffee and answer my phone— lordy, lordy how do mere mortals manage.

"There is a long list of calls, Mr. Clark," Mildred said as she brought in the coffee. "Do you want to start on them?"

"I didn't know I had a phone number," I said.

"People called the *Journal* after the story about you ran in the newspaper. We told them we'd give you the message. There were a lot. You do have a phone now. This office. The number is—"

"Never mind. You were at the *Journal*?"

I'd met Mildred only a short time ago. She was waiting in the office when I arrived. Paul had told me about it and gave me the address when I got back from New York yesterday.

"Yes, sir," she said. "I worked for Mr. Flynn in advertising. I got the job right after I finished at Eastern State."

"And you signed on as a secretary?"

"As an assistant. We don't have secretaries at the *Journal*."

"But—"

"My degree is in marketing. Working for Mr. Flynn in advertising is a good place to start," she said smiling.

"And they shoved me off on you?"

"Mr. Isham and Mr. Flynn thought it would be good experience for me. And that I can help you. I'm thorough. I don't make mistakes. I can take care of your schedule and phone calls and run your errands and get information you want. I don't take dictation but I'm a good typist and I can handle your correspondence if you give me rough drafts first. They said you would. They said you'd write your stuff first anyway. That you weren't a dictator." When she realized what she'd said she blushed and started to stammer. "I didn't mean...."

I laughed.

"Damn, I hope I'm not."

She relaxed a bit then.

"Where are you from?"

"Here."

"Where here?"

"Bellepoint. On the other side of the river. That's where I grew up. I went to Frankfort High.

"Me too."

"Bellepoint?" she said in surprise.

"No, no," I laughed again. "Frankfort High. Not to worry, Mildred Polsgove, we'll get along fine."

She was a tall, pleasant girl. Plain in a pretty way. She seemed confident and competent.

"The calls," she asked.

"Let me see the list."

I spent the rest of the morning going through mail. Most was from people I didn't know—appeals for money, business pitches, invitations to lunch or dinner or golf or a spin on the river, people who wanted to help me invest my money, sell me insurance, fire the editor, contribute to their favorite charity— unbelievable the horde that money attracts. Dulin was wrong, though. There were no offers of matrimony.

The calls were mostly from friends or people I'd known and worked with in my years here. I'd get back to all of them. The letters—I wasn't sure what I'd do about them. Answer them, I suppose, a matter of courtesy. But no hurry. Except for the letter with the red underline. There was something about it I found troubling. I'd have to attend to that.

CHAPTER NINETEEN

Julie Colby pried me away from the mail just before lunch.

"I've found the perfect place for you. You need to see it this afternoon and sign the lease before someone steals it away from you."

She paused and smiled proudly, "Actually, I've already signed the lease. Someone might have stolen it if I hadn't and anyway, you'll love it. So, no argument." She shoved my blazer at me, said brightly to Mildred, "He won't be back this afternoon," took my arm and walked me out the office door.

"Damn, Julie," I manage to get in as we hustled to the elevator, "I just got back."

"Yes, and you should have called me. But you're forgiven. We're having lunch at the club with Tracy; you remember her, then we're seeing your new apartment and after that, you and I are going shopping. The place isn't furnished. You'll need something to sleep on and eat on and a place to entertain all your friends and admirers. Isn't this going to be fun?"

When the hurricane of Julie Colby was blowing full force, the best you could hope for was to be able to hold on.

She was about a half step ahead of me. I grabbed her hand, turned her around, kissed her on the forehead. "You're not my mother. Let me catch my breath."

She stopped then and brushed my check softly with her fingers. " I know, Theo, dear, I know." Then taking my hand and turning back down the hall, said, "Tracy's waiting, and you'll come along quickly if you know what's good for you."

A table on the porch overlooking the eighteenth fairway, two pretty women, sunshine filtering through the trees, and a light breeze ruffling the daffodils in the planters along the walkway—yes, good for me.

Julie took over the conversation immediately with her descriptions of the "jewel of an apartment" she'd found for me and her ideas on how it should be furnished. Tracy Jordan, brown eyes sparkling, buoyantly fetching, fell in with Julie's mood immediately. The two of them seemed to forget I was at the table in their enthusiasm about outfitting the place and getting me settled.

"Sheets and towels" Julie said, frowning. "Big fluffy towels. White. Maybe light grey hand-towels."

"And silk sheets," Tracy said, "light blue. "Blue's your color," she said with a wink and a laugh.

I held up my hands. "Whoa, ladies. Silk sheets? Pastel hand-towels? Leave me a little machismo."

They played with that conversation while we ate, more teasing than serious. We agreed, Julie and I, with Tracy concurring, that the best course of action would be for me to step out of this completely and leave the furnishing of the place to Julie, who was eager for the challenge, and with the understanding she could spend what she wanted, and I wouldn't cry.

"Done. With two exceptions. I pick the bed, and I pick the desk. And no weird pictures and no silk sheets."

"Spoilsport. Done and done. Kiss him for me, Tracy," Julie said, laughing.

Unsurprised and unembarrassed, Tracy Jordan leaned over and kissed me lightly on the cheek with anyone who cared to be watching us free to see. "Think people will talk," she said, smiling wickedly at me.

Julie glanced up approvingly. "I certainly hope so."

Julie was right about the apartment. A jewel it was. On the corner of Wapping and Washington in the most graceful part of town—Liberty Hall a long block away, the *Journal* about the same, quiet sidewalks overhung with great oaks and maples, the river just down the street and churches all around, so I'd have the song of bells on Sunday mornings.

I knew the place.

When I was a young boy just learning to read, it had been the city library—a trim two-story colonial filled with books and the good smell of binding glue and paper. My dad started me on the Greek myths there, and I got so enthralled that I tried to work my way through everything. I spent almost as much time with Mowgli and Kim and Johnny Tremain and Hawkeye as I did on the riverbank playing war.

The city outgrew the little library, and it had become the Woman's Club headquarters. The upstairs was rented out to help cover costs. That's what Julie had found for me. Walking in was like stepping back into a place where all the memories are good, and you feel safe and cared for.

CHAPTER TWENTY

The envelope.

I remembered another envelope from the mountains, addressed not to me but to Michael, and Michael handing it to me and asking me what I made of it. That envelope started us down the road to his death.

I'd put off opening this one, letting the day pass and most of the night. I got in bed in my little room at the motel at the top of the hill, depressed that my new apartment wouldn't be ready for me for another week, not sure I could get to sleep, but the night was far enough gone I had to try.

I wanted to sleep. I didn't want to think about the letter. Good news doesn't come underlined in red. Think about it tomorrow, I told myself. Tomorrow will be soon enough.

Only the little guy in my head who keeps pushing me to do things I don't want to do, the one that keeps sending me out against monsters at the gate, wouldn't let me. Get up, dammit. Don't listen to Scarlet. Listen to Rhae. Deal with it, dammit!

Pulsing red light from the neon sign outside seeped through the shades, road noise from the trucks rolling by filled the room with a hum. Who the hell could sleep anyway?

The shank of the morning again. Dark. Cold. I showered and dressed and headed for the White Tower. Lots of light there and hot coffee.

The same kid was behind the counter, and the place was just as empty as before. A lone guy at the counter. The same guy? I couldn't tell.

The kid recognized me. "You bet on the filly like I told you?"

"Wasn't smart enough. Should have listened."

That pleased him. "Lot of people would be better off if they paid attention to me." He made a swipe at the counter with a towel and fixed me with a smile, a nice, bright smile for a still-not-daylight morning.

"Sweet rolls? Coffee?"

"You have them this morning?"

"The bakery truck was just here. They're still warm."

I took a seat at one of the small tables by the window, looked out on the empty street, and much encouraged by the dextrose and the caffeine, pulled the envelope out of my jacket pocket and opened it.

"*Mr. Clark*" it began. No nod to convention. No "Dear." Right to the point.

"*Mr. Clark,*

I have a manuscript you should see.

My name is Niccan Dye. I am, or was, Professor Marne Young's graduate assistant. Professor Young was Director of Appalachian Studies here at Cumberland College. She passed a month ago. A tragic loss for us all. I am in charge of cataloguing and filing her papers—her personal (personal was underlined in red) as well as her academic papers.

In the process of doing this, I have come across a manuscript written by you. Its title is "The True Story of the Dannans and Jesse Bristow."

I think we should discuss this.

I think you will want to discuss this.

In person."

Mr. Niccan Dye closed with a repeat of the post office box through which he could be reached by mail—he had no phone—to arrange a meeting. Nothing more. No elaboration.

Marne dead?

The shock of it jolted me.

Marne was my guide and interpreter and tender companion during our search for the truth about Benjamin Dannan. Through the long nights following Michael's death, she held me and soothed me and told me I had done right.

And she died, and I didn't know!

The manuscript in the possession of Niccan Dye was only a threat. Marne's loss was a wound.

CHAPTER **TWENTY ONE**

The letter to Michael Dannan from the mountains, the one that started us on the road to his death—Marne Young had written it.

She wasn't a director then. She was a young graduate student working on a doctorate in cultural anthropology at the University of Georgia while helping as an aide at a hospice in a little place in the Cumberland Mountains called Lost River.

Damn, I don't want to live all that again.

What happened? Marne was too vital, too strong to just die. Her body wouldn't betray her like that. Her mind wouldn't let it.

Daylight came while I was sitting there, fog drifting up from the river, the stoplight at the corner obscured in mist. A lone car passed. Nothing else moved. Looked cold out there, and lonely. Inside there was just me and the White Tower kid. The coffee urn was full; the grill was hot; the counter was sparkling and the few tables wiped off and ready. But it was too early for his morning regulars. The kid fidgeted and rearranged the menus on the counter, fighting boredom and eager for action.

Me too, I thought. No point in wasting more time. I signaled for the check, took the last gulp of coffee, folded the letter back into its envelope and stood up to leave.

"You gonna leave me here all alone," he said as he handed me my change. I waved it back to him.

"You'll be frying eggs and flipping burgers before you know it. Have a great day."

"That's my line," he said as the door closed behind me.

Nowhere to go but the office.

I turned up my collar against the cold and decided to walk it. Would be good to start the day that way—on foot. My car would be okay in the little lot in the alley. The walk would clear my mind.

I angled across to Pete's Corner and then turned onto Bridge Street to cross the river. Sounds were muted by the fog, and the outlines of the buildings blurred. I was a specter moving in a dreamscape.

I saw no one. Heard no one.

From the center of the bridge, fog hid the river and was fingering into downtown and edging up against the homes on the streets that flanked the water. By mid-morning it would be gone. The sun would come up over East Main Hill. The fog would melt. A sparkling May day would slide into place, and all would be right with the world.

Are you listening, Theo? That's the way it happens here—in the garden spot of the world—in the seat of culture and learning—in little-Frankfort-nestled-among-the-hills. I grew up here. I know it to be so.

That's what I told myself walking down the empty street to the corner of Main where sat the McClure Building and my new, and I hoped, warm office.

CHAPTER TWENTY TWO

My prediction didn't disappoint. By ten the day was gorgeous—bright sun, clear sky, salubrious temp. See, Theo old buddy, what'd I tell you? Listen to me, and you'll go places. Garden spot of the world, hands down.

Mildred was in the office when I got there. Six-thirty, seven o'clock? We had to be the only two humans in the place. All the offices were dark except mine. What's she doing in so early? The coffee was on. I got its rich aroma when I opened the door.

Mildred looked up, surprised.

"Are you trying to get on steady," I said.

I meant it as a joke, but she wasn't sure. She looked flustered and started to stand.

"I'm joking," I said quickly, motioning her to sit. "Why are you here? It's just barely daylight."

"I wasn't sure what time you like to start. I wanted to be here before you. I wanted to have your coffee ready and the morning's papers on your desk." She pointed to copies of the *Journal*, the Lexington *Herald* and the Louisville *Courier-Journal* waiting to be taken into my office.

"How'd you get these so early?"

"I picked up the *Journal* on my way by. There's a newsstand at the Greyhound stop on Broadway. The out-of-town papers make their first drops there."

I shook my head in appreciation, smiling, "You're a jewel, Mildred, a certifiable jewel."

Good old Mildred, wide awake and cheery, she cracked the shell of gloom I'd let form around me. By the time I'd had my second cup of coffee—a little milk, two spoons of sugar, just right, thank you—and finished the papers, I was ready to begin focusing on the problem Mr. Niccan Dye had thrown me.

The priority was Marne.

The best source of immediate information would be her local newspaper. Her obituary. With Marne's position at the college, she would have been prominent enough to be worth more than a passing mention. I didn't have the date of her death, and it was unlikely that the local paper would have the staff or the time to send someone searching through the files to find the information for me. I'd have to do it myself. But I was reluctant to draw attention as I undoubtedly would if I showed up asking to see the files on the death of Professor Marne Young.

Mildred.

I'd send Mildred.

She could pose as a family friend or a former student if anyone got curious. She might even be able to get a lead on the mysterious Mr. Dye.

On the roadmap, Williamsburg looked to be about a three-hour drive. If she left now, she could be there by mid-afternoon and back here by eight at the latest. I'd take her to a late dinner. I showed her the letter, told her what I wanted her to do.

"Are you okay with this?"

"Yes, oh, yes" she said, ready and eager.

"Get copies—the obit, the story if there is one, whatever might have played. I doubt there'll be time to check on Mr. Dye, but try. And drive safe. You're a good driver? I don't want you on my conscience."

"Of course," she said. "What about your phone?"

"If I'm here, I'll pick it up. If I'm not, they can call back. Go."

The afternoon passed slowly.

The phone rang, but I ignored it. The pile of letters stared at me, but I didn't make eye contact. I took a long, slow walk through downtown. Except for a smattering of people at sidewalk tables in front of a few small restaurants, the streets were deserted. One or two cars passed. I felt like a character in a Ray Bradbury story who found himself dropped into a picturesque little town that some threat of impending doom had emptied.

Later, I got my car and drove out to the Forks of Elkhorn and parked in the lot at the Buck Run Baptist church by the banks of the creek and watched the water flow over the damn at the Fish Hatchery upstream.

Elkhorn ran full and emerald and flashed sparks of sunlight as it slid past. I moved up to the bridge to watch the North Fork coming in from Georgetown to join the South Fork and form the main creek. It would run past Rhae Dannan's place at Peaks Mill to join the Kentucky at Strohmeier's Camp, then north to meet the Ohio at Carrolton, then turn west toward Louisville, weave down past Paducah, go all the way to Wickliffe on the western border of the state, then make a left turn, flow into the Mississippi, and drop south to the Gulf, there to be taken up by sunlight, turned into clouds, and brought back home to the Bluegrass as rain.

Is that reassuring?

I decided not to think about it. I decided to think about the tune the creek hummed as it ran under the bridge, the pictures the clouds made in the sky, of Allie golden in the sun on a blanket in the grass by the side of the creek.

Eight o'clock came, and Mildred wasn't back. By eight-thirty I was ready to call the State Police. I had the phone in my hand and was dialing when she walked in.

She was beaming.

"You promised me dinner," she almost shouted in her excitement as she burst in, a carefully folded newspaper in her hand and an envelope under her arm.

"You got it," I said.

"Got it. And more."

I rose, relieved and smiling.

We spread the papers on my desk—the daily, the *Corbin Times*, and the town weekly, the *Whitley Republican*. The story was page one in both.

I looked up to Mildred in disbelief.

"A rattlesnake! She died from a rattlesnake bite!"

Mildred was standing at the corner of my desk; her hands clasped in front of her, watching me.

The stories were clear enough, yet I recoiled from the facts.

"Corbin, March 2—Marne Young, Director of Appalachian Studies at Cumberland College and one of the nation's leading scholars in Appalachian cultures, died Monday from a rattlesnake bite suffered during a religious service at a mountain church in Harlan County. She was thirty-eight."

That's the way the lede ran in the Corbin paper. The *Whitley Republican* had it about the same.

Mildred rushed to try to explain.

"She was doing research. On snake-handling religious cults in the mountains. The girl at the desk at the *Republican* told me. She was one of Miss Young's students. When I told her what I was looking for, she couldn't stop talking."

"Tell me," I said.

Mildred and the girl hit it off immediately. The girl, still in school and working part time at the *Republican*, told Mildred the college was devastated. Everyone loved Professor Young. Everyone took her class in the Peoples of Appalachia. Many went on to her courses in Melungeon Studies, some who had Melungeon blood but didn't want to admit it; some who were proud of it and said so, like Niccan Dye, her graduate assistant. She knew Niccan. He was working on his masters, planned to go on and get a doctorate at the University of Georgia where Miss Young got hers. He was something of an agitator. Melungeon Pride, the campus organization for students with Melungeon blood, was his creation.

Niccan Dye was with Professor Young when she died, the girl told Mildred.

CHAPTER TWENTY THREE

We had dinner at the club. Mildred had not been before. Though I wasn't a member, everyone expected me to become one, and Paul Isham had arranged for my use of the facilities until that happy day came.

Mildred was concerned that she might not be dressed properly. I told she looked fine for a late dinner on a weekday night, so she fixed her hair, put on fresh makeup, and we made our entrance.

The dining room was almost empty. The Capitol City elite dine earlier than nine-thirty. In fact the kitchen was already closing, "but we're happy to serve you, Mr. Clark, no problem," the maître 'd reassured me. "We're looking forward to seeing a lot of you here."

He escorted us to a table in the far corner of the room that looked out to a stand of poplars that were up-lighted and swaying gently in the night breeze.

"You'll have a cocktail?" I asked her.

"Definitely," she said.

She ordered a Beefeater martini, which surprised me, up, no olive.

"What?" she said as I glanced up at her.

"I had you confused with someone else."

"Who?"

" A proper Southern Baptist lady who never lets liquor pass her lips."

She smiled at that.

I had the newspaper and the envelope with me. I laid them in the seat of the chair across, and we sat silent as our drinks came. Mildred was sensitive to my mood. She was pleased with herself, excited at having delivered what I wanted, almost bursting to know what this was all about but not poking, waiting to take her lead from me.

When our drinks came, I raised mine to her and said, "Thank you. Well done."

She looked pleased, a glint of pride in her eyes. "I told you. I can help you. I can do research for you. I can go places, find out things. I'm not bashful. People like me."

I had to smile at that.

Shyly now, not sure whether I would take it as prying, "She was a friend of yours?"

A friend of mine?

I looked out the window to the light on the trees. The wind was picking up a bit.

Marne Young was about Mildred's age when we met. She was a slim, pretty brunette, so serious and caring that Michael and I both were taken.

The letter she wrote lured us to Lost River. It was for Hannah Collins.

Hannah Collins was dying. Marne Young was there, doing research on Melungeon history and helping care for her. Hanna Collins said she couldn't die in peace until she'd settled something with Michael.

We were just beginning Michael's run for governor then. Hanna Collins died before we could get there, but she left for Michael an antique silver box that held one old photograph and three faded newspaper clippings.

The photograph was of Michael's father, Benjamin Dannan, and at his side a young woman of striking beauty. They were smiling fondly at each other. The clippings were stories about the sister of Jesse

Bristow. Nothing more was there. No request. No explanation. Nothing more.

Hanna Collins was a Melungeon. Full-blooded. Jesse Bristow was half. His father was an Irishman who chanced into the mountains looking for his fortune. He didn't find it, but he found Jesse's mother. She was Hanna's younger sister. The Irishman and the Melungeon beauty fell in love, and he went into the mines to make their living.

A cave-in killed him. Young.

Jesse's mother died shortly afterwards from what was called a fever, but medicine in the mountains was so bad that no one really knew. Hanna Collins took the children, young Jesse and his baby sister, and raised them.

Somewhere, somehow, there was a connection to Michael.

Marne Young was our guide as we tried to find it.

Through it all, Marne and I became more than friends.

When I left, I asked her to look after my stuff. She had the key to my apartment where it all was—my books, my files, the drafts of stories I'd finished but hadn't pushed to print yet. Marne would take care of them. Marne would find a place for them.

I turned from the window back to Mildred, trying to mask the regret in my eyes.

"Yes. She was a friend. But I went away and we lost touch."

A line from the lyric of Danny Boy kept running through my mind:
"And you will come and find the place where I am lying,
 and kneel,
and say an Ave there for me."
I would.

CHAPTER TWENTY FOUR

June

I didn't respond to Niccan Dye's letter.

I was curious to see what he'd do.

A week passed. Then another.

I moved into my new apartment above the Women's Club, started getting familiar with the people and the operations at the stables and the printing plant, returned phone calls, answered letters.

May segued smoothly into June. The days got longer. The nights got softer. Sleek yearlings played in bluegrass pastures along the road to Lexington; corn grew succulent in the bottomlands by the river. My nights again opened to phantoms.

On the fifteenth day following the receipt of Mr. Dye's red underlined letter, his follow-up came.

Mildred walked it into me in the late afternoon. I'd just gotten off the phone with Jim Colby. There was a development in the Artie Skinner Merit System case. Jim wanted me to come to dinner at his place, tonight if I could make it.

Mildred handed the envelope to me with an anxious look. I hefted it, turned it, inspected the front. The hand was the same elegant Spenserian. There was no red underline, but there was a return address.

"Mr. Dye comes announced this time, I see."

She nodded. "By registered mail. I had to sign for it."

Mildred didn't look happy about this.

"What if I don't open it?

She gasped.

"I'm joking

"Will you tell me what it says?"

"Only if it's something really bad."

A frown creased her forehead, then she smiled. "Stop teasing, Mr. Clark."

Niccan Dye's letter was nothing to make light of. If the manuscript was the one I thought it was, it would be more than a problem; it could be a disaster. But I'd learned not to rush foolishly into battle without surveying the ground and understanding the enemy.

Chosin taught me.

We were hell-and-gone up in the mountains just south of the Yalu River—eighty miles out in front of our lines at the tail end of the planet, surrounded and outnumbered with hordes of Red Chinese coming at us in weather so cold our weapons froze.

The world thought we'd be massacred.

Thirteen days and nights it took us, thirteen hellish days and nights of snow and blood and moans of the dying and the wounded.

But we fought our way out, the god-blessed First Marine Division; we fought our way out. And we brought our dead and our wounded with us.

We should not have been there. General MacArthur and his sycophants rushed us in without knowledge of the terrain, without assessing the strength of the enemy. Rushed us in for ego and glory. Damn their eyes.

No rushing. Not for me.

"We'll get to it tomorrow, Mildred. Jim Colby asked me to dinner, and I'm not gonna let Mr. Niccan Dye spoil my evening. Tomorrow's soon enough."

CHAPTER TWENTY FIVE

Jim Colby walked me out back almost as soon as I arrived. Tracy Jordan was already there, looking serious and concerned.

"Remember when we played Danville our senior year?" Jim said as he put a bourbon in my hand.

"They had this big fullback. Weighed maybe two-ten. The sweat through his jersey when you hit him smelled like beer. Remember? Our biggest guy was Josie. One-hundred ninety-five. You were what, one-seventy? Michael about the same.

"They were heavily favored. They were killing us. You scored once. Popped through my hole, ran over the linebacker and out ran everybody to the goal line. Michael hit Bruce with a short pass in the end zone for our second score, but we missed the extra point, and we were down thirteen to twenty-one and it stayed that way until the last few minutes of the game. They fumbled on their five. Gordy recovered it. Bruce made that unbelievable one-handed catch in the end zone. We're down by one. An extra point ties it. A two-pointer wins it. Coach decides to go for the win. Their defensive line was tough as hell. He decides to try a play action pass into the flat.

"We line up in spread formation with Michael back. The ball's snapped. Michael gets it, but rather than setting up to pass, he takes a step back. Then to everyone's amazement, he drop-kicks it. A drop-kick! They went out with Red Grange. But damn he did it, and he made it. We won. Remember. We won! On a drop-kick! One of the first guys on the field to help hoist Michael onto our shoulders was Artie. Remember?"

I remembered. That game won the conference championship for us. No one expected us to win, not even us, but Michael kept saying we can do this.

So we played like we could. And we did.

And Michael. Damn. Michael.

None of us expected that drop-kick. I'd seen him kick it sometimes after practice just fooling around. I think coach almost had a heart attack right there.

What are the odds? The kicker has to catch the snap, drop the ball with the nose down while he's striding forward and make contact with it a fraction of a second after the ball hits the ground. He's kicking at a moving target and arching it up and over rushing linemen and sailing it through a set of goalposts twenty yards away.

Impossible. So impossible it's worth three points, one more than we need.

We win by two.

Tracy rose off the swing and came to stand beside Jim.

"Artie's hearing is next week. We've drawn a Hearing Officer who owes some favors," she said.

I was still on that playing field in Danville—field lights clicking off; the orange and blue of the Panthers and the blue and the white of the Danville Admirals mixing and swirling as fans file out, ours cheering and laughing, theirs subdued—helmet off, standing by myself, beginning to notice the aches where I'd been hit, feeling the chill of the November night, looking at the scoreboard and realizing we did it, we by-damn really did it! Winning when no one expects it— winning when you're so beat up and tired you can hardly stand—the exhilaration, the pride, the feel of it, the sheer sweet feel of it. Ah, damn. After all these years, I still remember.

"Do you understand, they've stacked the deck against us," Tracy said, bringing me reluctantly back.

"Get him changed." I said.

"Won't happen," Jim countered.

"But we have a strong case," Tracy continued, "and if we lose, we can appeal. The thing that worries me most is that if the Highway Department's attorney puts up witnesses who say Artie is a little strange, a little slow, not very bright, not smart enough to handle the job, if they say those sorts of things in open court for everyone to hear, if they give the impression they think Artie is retarded, whether they say it outright or not, it will kill him. He won't be able to hold his head up. He'll be humiliated."

"Making that assertion is against the law," Jim broke back in, "Federal regulations won't let any discussion of a possible handicap be introduced. The state can't discriminate against the handicapped."

"Makes no difference," Tracy said. "They can infer it, and we can't do anything about it."

"They can't win on that basis. They have to show incompetence. They have to prove inability to do the job. And the record favors our side."

"But you're not confident that facts will win the day for you," I said.

"No. I need a drop-kicker."

He raised his glass, took a sip, and looked at me over the rim.

"That's you."

"You're joking," I said.

Tracy stepped toward me; put her hand on my arm.

"We need to make sure that the Highway Department and the Governor's office understand that a lot of attention is being paid to this case. They need to know it's going to be in the spotlight, that they can't shove poor Artie over the cliff, and no will notice."

Tracy had those brown eyes of hers boring into mine. Jim was standing there staring at me expectantly.

I felt like I was an onlooker being dragged into a big fight that I just happened to be passing by.

"The *Journal* is the spotlight," Tracy said.

"You're going to cover it, right? You're going to give it big play," Jim said.

And there it was. The shove.

"Whoa, Jim," I said. "I'm not making the calls at the *Journal*. Lew Arbogast's the editor. I think he's planning a Sunday piece. He'll know the significance of the story. He'll give it the play it deserves."

"And you?"

"I'm just a bystander."

'No," Tracy Jordan said, pulling me around to face her. "You can't be. You have to be involved. Just talk with Artie once, and you'll know you can't let this happen. I'm going to set it up. We'll go to lunch. Tomorrow. You can make tomorrow. A special favor."

I took a minute, then surrendered.

Julie walked out on the porch at just that moment. She took in the three us standing there and felt the tension in the air. She considered for moment, shook her head and said, "Are they ganging up on you, Theo?"

She walked over and kissed me on the check. "Well, it's in a good cause, but it's going to stop. I've been slaving over a bridge table all afternoon, and I'm ready for a relaxed cocktail and dinner out some place that's nice, maybe Lexington. Jim, my dear, please get down off your white charger and make me a big Manhattan. Tracy, darling, please fill your and Theo's drinks and let's all sit here on the porch and make polite small talk while the sun goes down. Then we'll go see what we can find that's fun up the road."

CHAPTER TWENTY SIX

Artie Skinner.

He takes a competitive test that says he's qualified to do a specific State job. He's hired. He does that job well for over twenty years.

Then someone decides to use him as a tool to start whittling away at a system that limits the politicians' ability to load the State payroll with cronies. In the process, they will strip him of his dignity and rob him of his identity.

I hadn't seen Artie or thought about him since high school. Didn't even remember him very well.

So he came, walking up the path to the Upper Pond at the Game Farm. Tracy chose the meeting place. Artie would be more comfortable, more relaxed at the Game Farm. We'd have a nice, sociable picnic, she said.

No argument from me. The State Fish and Wildlife Department had transformed a little farm on out in the county on the way to Louisville into a park-like, wildlife education and recreation center. There were grass-banked ponds stocked with bass and bluegill, a wildlife museum, hiking trails, and an enclosed area where some of the game animals and birds that made the state an outdoorsman's magnet could be seen in a natural setting. Picnic tables were scattered around the ponds and under the big oaks and elms that graced the place. I got there first and staked out a spot that was shady and fairly private but with a good view of the ponds.

As they walked toward me, Tracy had her left arm hooked through Artie's and was carrying a big wicker hamper and was laughing and talking. Artie walked beside her, nodding and smiling back.

What I recalled of Artie, and that only vaguely, was a tall, skinny kid with a burr cut. He hung around all the practices and helped wherever he could. He could sing. He had a full rich baritone voice and sang solos in the school concert choir. A nice guy. Good natured. Easy going.

I waved, stepping out of the shade, so Tracy could find me, and waited there in the sunlight looking friendly. I didn't take a chance on there being any awkwardness. I walked out to meet them and started talking before anyone else had a chance.

"Artie, damn, it's good to see you. It's been too long."

Tracy sat the hamper down on the table and kissed me lightly on the cheek. "Nice spot," she said, looking around. "I've got ham and cheese and roast beef sandwiches, potato salad and deviled eggs, sweet pickles, chips, soft drinks, and Rebecca Ruth bourbon candy for desert. Suit you?"

"You read my mind."

Artie nodded in agreement.

"You two want to get reacquainted while I lay this spread out?" She began opening up the hamper and motioned us away from the table.

Artie wasn't sure what to do. Nor was I. He was shy, and I was trying not to show the feeling of embarrassment I had. I'm not sure why I was embarrassed. Because I had forgotten about him? Because of the situation he was in? Maybe because he might be expecting something I couldn't deliver.

But whatever awkwardness or nervousness was in the air Artie dispelled when he looked up and said, "I was sorry when you went away. I'm glad you're back."

It was such a simple, sincere thing to say that it completely disarmed me.

I relaxed. Artie forgot to be self-conscious. We talked easily about the things we remembered from high school—funny things, good-to-remember things. I was surprised at how much I remembered that I didn't think I did until Artie touched the key. And surprised at how much he remembered of Michael and me.

"You and Michael looked out for me," he said. "You wouldn't let people make fun of me. That day in the gym when we were sophomores? Vick Ansel and that gang? They were going to pants me. Make me walk home in my underwear. I was by myself. Sweeping up after practice. Helping Coach out. Vick poked his head in and saw me. "Well lookie here," Vick hollered. "Coach's little helper all alone. Sing a song for us, dreek.' Then he changed his mind. 'No. Let's pants him. Send his little retard self home with his bare ass hanging out. Get him.

"Before I could run, they had me and my pants half way off and Vick laughing like crazy and sing-songing, 'Sputter, sputter, peanut butter. Pinch his cock and make him stutter.'

"You and Michael came out of the locker room about then. Your hair was still wet from the shower. You all didn't say a thing. You just looked at each other. Michael had his small duffle in his hand. He sat it down. There were four of them. They had me stretched out on a bleacher bench. One guy was holding down my head, two others had my arms pinned and the fourth guy was tugging my pants off. You came across the floor shoulder to shoulder, not rushing. When they saw you, one of the guys holding my arms let go and started to run but Michael grabbed him and smashed him in the face. You backhanded the guy on my other arm, then hit the guy pulling my pants down square in the mouth and sent blood flying everywhere.

"Come on down, Vick" you called, 'join the fun.'

" But Vick started for the door. The others crowded behind him.

"You yelled after them, 'Don't touch this kid again. If you see him coming, get out of his way.' Michael helped me up and made sure I was okay. He had his car. He was going to give me a ride home, but I wasn't finished with the gym, so I stayed."

Vick Ansel. Him I had forgotten completely. He came back to me now. He was big. He was fat. He was a bully. A lard-ass bully who never came out for any of the teams.

"Did Vick ever bother you again?"

Arnie shook his head. "No one else did either. The message got around. Don't mess with Artie Skinner. He's a friend of Michael and Theo's," he said beaming at me.

Unnoticed, Tracy had walked up behind us.

"A friend of Theo's," she said softly behind me. "That must have been a good feeling." She moved past me to Artie, took his arm and stepped toward me. There was just the hint of a tear in her eye. "A thing like that could make people think you have a caring nature, Theo Clark." She smiled, slipped her other arm through mine and walked with us arm-in-arm to the table in the shade.

Artie Skinner loved his job. He took pride in it. Took pride in doing it well. And it gave him pride. He was a somebody. Not a big somebody, but big enough to suit his ego. He was an Assistant Director, in his mind an executive, a manager doing an important job for the Commonwealth. A man of stature.

He had never missed a day's work, had never been late, never left early. He'd been recognized for his contributions with two Employee-of-the-Month certificates. He'd been awarded the Meritorious Service Medallion on the occasion of the twentieth anniversary of his time in the job.

Artie Skinner was a solid citizen and a loyal and trustworthy employee. Most people liked him. His new boss at the Highway Department didn't. That man came in when the new governor came in. He was from somewhere in west Kentucky. He didn't like it that Artie, when he was excited, sometimes stuttered. He didn't like it that Artie wasn't as fast as some of the others at understanding the new practices he wanted to put in place. He didn't like it that Artie sometimes told him, never disrespectfully, always trying to be helpful, that the regulations didn't permit them to do some of the things he wanted them to do.

Most people liked Artie, though. The few who didn't, he tried to be nice to anyway.

These are the things Artie wanted me to know that came out as we talked over lunch.

"You know what these new people are trying to do to me," he said. He said it in a way that made me feel his embarrassment and distress—and his anger.

"It isn't true, Theo. It isn't fair."

He didn't ask me to do anything. He only wanted me to know what was going on, so that I wouldn't think less of him if I heard some things that might be said.

They left me sitting in the shade under the big oak. A school bus had just unloaded a passel of kids at the Wildlife area who were running and whooping. A lone fisherman on the far bank of the Upper Pond was sitting back down while his bobber settled after a long cast out to the center. Tracy had her arm hooked through Artie's, and he carried the hamper in his other hand. They were walking slowly. Not talking. Just being together. A gentle soul, Artie Skinner. Too few of them.

I called Jay Arbogast at the *Journal* as soon as I got back. He planned a large piece on the Artie Skinner hearing, but had decided to run it on the morning of the hearing, this coming Wednesday, four days away. The story had originally been scheduled for this Sunday, but more time was needed to develop the piece in the depth he thought it deserved. Interviews with Jim Colby and with the attorney representing the Highway Department were still needed, and he hoped to get Colby to let his reporter talk with Artie.

I relayed the information to Jim Colby by phone, then had him transfer me to Tracy. "Artie will never do an interview, Theo, he's too shy," she told me. "We wouldn't let him anyway. Too much could go wrong. We're going to start preparing him tomorrow. We'll explain what he should expect to hear from witnesses for the State and go over the questions he's most likely to get from the State and from us when he's on the stand. We'll work on his answers, but the chances that he'll remember what he's supposed to say when he's nervous and under pressure aren't good. If he starts stuttering, if he gets frightened or angry, we're lost. We're going to have to prepare him to be accused of not being up to the demands of the job, of being slow. That will devastate him. You saw how proud he is. He'll just dissolve."

"Do you have to put him on the stand?"

"We can try to make the case on the evidence. But the Hearing Officer has the right to question Artie. He will. There's no doubt of that. If this wasn't so important to Artie's sense of himself, I'd drop the case right now."

"Why did you let him take it on in the first place if you felt it was too big a risk to his ego?"

"Artie was mad. We were mad. The facts were on our side. We weren't going to let them get away with it. We didn't know they were after something bigger than Artie."

"Pull him out then."

"I don't think Artie will let us."

That was Friday, a fine sunshiny June day.

Jim Colby and Tracy Jordan had their briefing session with Artie Skinner the next day, a Saturday. The moon was in its last quarter. Mujahedeen guerillas were pounding the Russians in the Panjshir Valley. Julie Colby pronounced herself pleased with the shade of pale blue in which my bedroom had been redone.

Sunday was hot. Elkhorn was running clear. I spent the morning working nymphs down the riffles of the Main Creek near Peaks Mill. Tracy went to church with Artie and his mother at Buck Run.

The next day, Monday, two days before his hearing, at approximately four-forty-two in the afternoon, Artie Skinner jumped from the top of the State Office Building in downtown Frankfort onto the esplanade fronting Ann Street.

The State offices were just closing for the day.

No pedestrian was hit.

Artie Skinner died immediately.

He wore a blue suit with a white pocket-handkerchief, a white shirt, and a blue-and-red striped rep tie for the occasion. Artie had in his pockets the Meritorious Service Medallion he'd received in recognition of his service to the Commonwealth, the medal he'd won for male solo in the Kentucky High School State Musical Festival, and a note.

The note read: "It isn't true. It isn't fair."

His mother's bible lay nearby. Apparently he had managed to hold on to it the whole way down.

After the police gained some control of the crowd—twelve hundred people worked in that building and the confusion and chaos were considerable—after the remains had been collected, and the ambulance departed, and the traffic snarls downtown sorted out, after they began searching for eye witnesses, it developed that no one had seen Artie jump. But many had heard him. He was shouting as he fell the eleven stories.

Artie's office, a cubicle, was on the first floor near a window on the Holmes Street side of the building looking out at the parking lot. His boss sat nine stories higher, on the tenth floor, just one floor beneath where the God-like creatures who ran the State Highway Department dwelled. Artie's boss wasn't in that day, so he missed the excitement.

Later that night on the porch at Jim Colby's, we sat in the dark. There was a sliver of a moon in the sky above the river. A faint scent of honeysuckle hung in the air.

Tracy was exhausted. She'd spent the afternoon and early evening with the police, then later answering questions from the media, and then finally with Artie's mother at the funeral home where Artie's body had been taken.

Jim looked physically beaten. He sat slumped in one of the big wicker chairs, his head down, his arms clasped in front of him, staring at nothing and muttering, "damn them, damn them, damn them."

The Saturday session had not gone well, they said. When Artie understood that his competence would publically be questioned, that some of their witnesses would say he's not too bright, that he didn't understand the rules and regulations and got in the way of getting things done, that his hand was out for kickbacks, his composure evaporated. Artie had been confidant that the facts were on his side and that the facts would win for him. That's what he'd been told and was what he believed. The facts would still win for him, they said. But these other things might be said, aloud, in public, for everyone to hear.

Artie began to withdraw then. He began to lose his concentration. He began to stutter. Seeing his distress, knowing it would be disastrous in the hearing, they asked him if he wanted to drop the case. He took a long time to answer. When he did, he told them no, don't drop the case. Then he thanked them and said he was going home and left.

That was Saturday. The sun was still shining, and it looked to be a nice, soft night coming on.

On Sunday, at church, Artie seemed subdued but not despondent. Tracy drove him and his mother home. Tracy knew he was upset, but there was absolutely nothing that suggested to her that he might do what he did. Nothing. He'd smiled when she left him and kissed her and thanked her again for all she was doing and told her to tell Jim Colby the same thing. Not sadly. Not goodbye-for-everly. Just Artie being grateful. That's what she made of it. Though she was uneasy.

Afterwards, Tracy had no doubt why he did it. Lord, the things our pride forces us to do. I understood that. I understood completely.

Whether Artie planned the result he got, we'll never know. I think he did. I think he decided to make an event out of himself.

Jumping from the spot he chose and at the time he chose didn't seem a random choice to me. Hundreds of people work in that building and quitting time for all of them is four-thirty. Almost all of them would be pouring out the doors and into the parking lots when he jumped. It would be hard to assemble a bigger audience or to create more havoc with downtown traffic than at that spot and at that time. It would be hard to stage something that would generate more attention. The media would play it high—statewide, possibly even nationwide. If the Administration truly had plans to dismantle the state civil service, the last thing they'd want was the attention Artie Skinner's dive would bring. I admired the brilliance of it.

I started to say this to Jim when I heard Julie Colby's voice from inside. "Are you all out there," she called. "Get some lights on. Pretend we're among the living."

Jim stirred in his chair. Tracy stood up from the porch step where she was sitting.

Julie appeared with a lighted candle. She began to light the candles that sat on the side tables by the swing and the chairs.

In the muted glow, Tracy's face was tear-stained, her hair mussed, her skirt wrinkled. Jim was rising, rubbing his hands across his eyes like someone coming awake. I had been stretched out on the swing, gently swaying back and forth as we each went through our private little requiems.

Julie went to Tracy. She took her hands and pulled Tracy close to kiss her on her forehead. "I know, dear," Julie said. "I know." She stroked Jim's cheek and said, "Don't despair, Robin," then hugged him full and hard. Then she sat down beside me on the swing. "You okay?"

I didn't know. I thought I was. I wasn't part of this fight. I'd been on the edge of it but hadn't stepped in. I was sorry now that I hadn't. I didn't like the feeling that was rising in my gut. I'd felt it before—anger and outrage and the aching sense that I am somehow responsible for making things right. When it peaks, if it peaks, I sometimes do irresponsible things.

Julie put her finger under my chin and lifted my head to look in my eyes. When Julie held your gaze like that, she seemed to see through your mind to your heart. After a moment she nodded and took her finger away. "Careful,' she whispered.

Jim mixed us a round of drinks. We sat in the flickering light, not talking, until the candles burned down.

Tracy was too spent to drive. She left her car at Julie's, and I drove her out to her uncle's farm where she was staying. She was asleep on my shoulder before we topped East Main hill. The little crescent moon had disappeared below the tree line by the time we got to the creek. I drove back alone with my window down, listening to the night rush by.

CHAPTER TWENTY SEVEN

The next day I moved into Rhae Dannan's office.

I knew I had to be careful. I had to give strokes, not throw my weight around, get people on my side, go slow. And I would, but for now I hungered to get at the monsters, to skewer the villains. I was going to go slow at a dead run.

Daylight was just breaking when I called Dulin.

"You getting ready to pick a fight?" he asked.

"Maybe."

"When you were breaking in . . . remember the rules Will Owens and I kept pounding into your head?"

"As well as my own name," I said.

"Rule Number One? The Dulin Monroe First Rule of the Game?"

"Don't do dumb things."

Will's rule about fights?"

"Never pick a fight you can't win."

A pause, "Okay then."

I asked him to call Lew Arbogast for me, tell him not to get excited and that I'd catch up with him later in the afternoon. I didn't want Lew to think I was moving in on him.

Paul Isham was next. I'd probably be getting him out of bed, but I didn't care. I wanted him to have the office ready for me by the afternoon. He was up. Making coffee. Listening to the morning news on the radio.

"Why the rush?"

"I've got people to see, places to go, things to do," I said.

"This is going to make people nervous."

"I'll handle it."

"Is this about the Skinner thing yesterday?"

"Maybe."

"Think, Theo. You're going to be chairman of Elkhorn Enterprises, Publisher of the *Journal*. You can't go running around tilting at windmills."

"Humor me," I told Paul.

The sun was up. From down the block came the clink of a city garbage truck upending a curb-side canister. I'd forgotten to put mine out. I got up from the kitchen table and walked to the window to check the day. Bright and clear. Sun warming the sidewalks on Wapping Street. Washington still in shade until the sun climbed higher. A little after seven-thirty. One more call to make.

Julie Colby answered on the third ring.

"You still serve breakfast to poor country boys trying to make their way in the Capitol City?"

Julie laughed. "Only if they ask politely and do the dishes."

"Is Jim up?"

"Shaving."

"Mind if I join you?"

"Eggs and bacon and blueberry pancakes. Ten minutes."

I was out the door and down the block to their place, showered, shaved, tie neatly knotted, khakis creased, and blue blazer over my shoulder, in fifteen.

Jim looked better than when I left him last night, but only marginally. He sat at the kitchen table with his head down and his shoulders sagging. He had his hands cupped around a coffee mug and seemed lost in deep and troubling thought. He hardly noticed I'd entered the room.

Julie was at the stove.

"Welcome to Sun Shine Inn," she said, nodding toward Jim. Then, "Jim, snap out of it. Theo's here."

Jim looked up, got me in focus and managed a half-smile.

Julie Colby would not indulge self-pity. Ever. She knew that everything has a consequence. She accepted that. Like Rhae Dannan, her ethic was play the hand you're dealt. No one I'd known could be more loving or tender or caring or comforting than Julie, but she had no truck with sackcloth, rue, or lamentations.

Jim's feeling of failure was not to be allowed, and from the tone of her voice, I was to take note that it was a new day, and we'd better get working on what comes next.

"Now that the Brain Trust is together, what's it going to be, gentlemen? Eggs and bacon? Blueberry pancakes? All of the above?"

She was standing with her hands on her hips, a scolding scowl on her face, daring us to go grim on her.

I had to laugh. Jim wasn't certain, then smiled, then laughed, too. Julie dropped her pose and joined in. The morning got brighter then.

Tracy arrived just as we were finishing.

I am always awed at the resiliency of women. Ten hours ago, Tracy was emotionally depleted and physically wrung-out. She was carrying a load of guilt and remorse I could hardly imagine. She was in pain, the worst kind of pain, the pain felt in the heart.

The Tracy Jordan who walked into Julie Colby's kitchen that morning had risen Phoenix-like from the ashes of that tragedy.

She was composed. She was focused. She was eager.

Where they find the inner resources to rise above the present, how they manage to set aside the pain and the disappointment and the despair thrown at them and still be loving and nurturing, is beyond explanation. Thank god no one expects that of men.

Tracy's energy and Julie's get-on-with-it attitude set the mood of the morning.

I cleared the table; Julie made more coffee, and we adjourned outside to the porch to review the bidding and decide what game we wanted to play and how we were going to play it.

I say "we" because I'd become a committed player. I'd made the decision. I was in. And in getting in, I'd pushed Niccan Dye's threat aside again. The manuscript he had, the one I'd left in Marne Young's care, the story of the Dannans and Jesse Bristow, could, I knew, if made public and believed, beat me up badly, maybe ruin me. It had to be dealt with. But not today. Today was for Artie.

The next day, Wednesday, was the day for Artie Skinner's hearing—two p.m. in the Main Conference Room of the Kentucky State Highway Department, tenth floor, the State Office Building, the same building from which Artie jumped, Commissioner Milton Tilton, State Personnel Board, presiding.

Would the hearing go forward?

With Artie dead, would there be a hearing?

"If Artie doesn't show," Jim said, "the Hearing Officer can dismiss the case. Or we can make a formal filing, asking that the case be dismissed. The case doesn't automatically go away. There has to be a formal action of some sort, and the attorney representing Artie will have to be present."

"Can't you still go forward with the case—present witnesses and evidence to clear his name of the charges?"

"I don't believe it's ever happened," Jim said. He looked questioningly to Tracy.

"Try a dead person? Not a chance, I'd think."

"Why not find out?"

CHAPTER TWENTY EIGHT

The story of Artie Skinner's death dominated local print and broadcast coverage that morning.

And again I had to admire Artie. If he really planned this as I thought he had, he couldn't have chosen a time that would generate greater media attention—just in time for the evening newscasts, but with plenty of time for the local dailies here and in Lexington and Louisville to work the story in detail.

Nothing more deadly dramatic had happened in recent memory.

The *Journal's* coverage was particularly powerful. Lew Arbogast already had a reporter looking into the Artie Skinner case for a story he planned to run the day of the hearing, so he had details and sources the others did not.

Lew threw all the resources he had available into the coverage. His reporters fanned out to find people who were on the esplanade when he jumped. No one actually saw Artie jump, but almost all of them heard his shouts as he plummeted.

They got comments from co-workers about the kind of person Artie was, talked with his Pastor at Buck Run Church and the music teacher who had been his mentor the year he won the State singing competition—wove into the story the humanizing quotes that helped make Artie something more than just a name to people who didn't know him.

Personnel actions like firings don't attract much public attention unless the person fired refuses to go quietly, contests the action, and demands a hearing. Even then, most appeals are never noticed. Hearings are routinely held. Decisions routinely made. No waves rock the State's boat.

Which should have been the case with Artie Skinner, except the Administration had leaked the details of the charges being made against him. They wanted to draw attention to the hearing.

The charges against Artie were damning: obstructionism, dishonesty, a fundamental inability to meet the requirements of the job—the kind of charges which, if made public and proven, would make it unlikely that Artie would ever find a job of any consequence anywhere again. The charges were contained in the formal letter of dismissal which would be presented at the hearing, a copy of which the *Journal* had obtained.

This information was used in the story, emphasizing that these were unproven charges and that the point of the hearing was to give Artie the opportunity to challenge the assertions, and if possible, disprove them.

Had the firing driven Artie Skinner to his death? Was the note "It isn't right. It isn't fair" found in his pocket trying to say that the charges against him were lies, that the case against him was fabricated and unfair? Was his dramatic jump from the top of the State Office building an attempt to draw attention to the injustice of it?

Lew Arbogast played the story as the banner head on page one. It was so powerful, it was picked up almost verbatim by the Associated Press and run out to its newspaper and broadcast clients across the state and in a slightly abbreviated version on the national wire.

By the time I arrived at the *Journal* that afternoon, Artie Skinner's jump had become the hottest story in the state

The Publisher's office at the *Journal* was no strange place to me.

I'd been in it often when Rhae sat in the chair, but long before that, too, when I was a boy, and Benjamin Dannan, Michael's father, was alive. Michael and I would sometimes go in with Mr. Dannan on Saturday mornings and roam through the backshop and the newsroom while he worked.

I liked Mr. Dannan. He took time with us. He was interested in what we thought. He explained things we wanted to know and never talked down to us as most adults did.

Benjamin Dannan was just a beginning reporter when Rhae's father noticed him. He was working at the *Bowling Green Daily News* in west Kentucky in his first job after graduating from the University of Kentucky. A bylined story about kickbacks to a local State Highway Department supervisor that got picked up by the Associated Press attracted the *Journal's* attention and was good enough to get Benjamin Dannan an invitation to come to Frankfort and talk about the possibility of a job

Benjamin was a natural—bright, skeptically curious, aggressive, and tenacious. He made friends easily and was a gifted writer. And for an Irishman, he was handsome. Shortly after his arrival, he and Rhae met—in the newsroom. Ten months later, they were married.

Benjamin Dannan moved rapidly through the chairs at the *Journal,* became managing editor, and then, when Rhae's father died, he was named Publisher. Benjamin ran the paper; Rhae took over the farm and the stables.

No, this office, his office, Rhae's office, wasn't a strange place to me. But it was hallowed ground. Benjamin Dannan was one of the most powerful and respected journalists of his day, and as Publisher of the *Journal,* he had made it one of the Commonwealth's most influential newspapers. Rhae Dannan kept that legacy alive. I moved in feeling like a pretender to an unearned throne, like an intruder at the Round Table.

The *Journal* building sits practically in the center of downtown, on Main Street, about a block west of the intersection of Main and St. Clair.

It's a tall one-storey Greek Revival style building of white glazed brick that takes up most of the block and projects an air of dignity and authority.

The County Court House is just a quick walk away if you take the short cut through Workhouse Alley, and the Old Capitol is only a block or so down St. Clair.

The State Capitol building itself, where the governor sits and the work of the people is done, is across the river and up the tree-lined streets of South Frankfort to Capitol hill—a little too far to walk unless you're in a mood to enjoy the day and not pressed for time.

The building where Artie Skinner jumped, the State Office Building, is about the same distance from the *Journal* building, but in the opposite direction down St. Clair to the Old Capitol, right on Broadway, past the train station to High Street, then left for four or five blocks to the intersection of Holmes Street and High where the old prison used to stand.

When I worked at the *Journal* my usual way in was through paper-boy's door off Workhouse Alley.

To get to the Publisher's office, you had to enter through the big door on Main Street.

I always felt a little out of place going in that door. The air of calm and propriety inside was as thick as morning fog. Nobody worked in their shirt sleeves. People inside had their jackets on and their ties knotted. The place was library-quiet. There was none of the excitement and noise of the newsroom, none of the energy. It made me uncomfortable.

But not that day.

The young girl at the reception desk expected me. Paul Isham came right out. "We need to talk as soon as you get settled," he said, then began to show me around the office. He introduced me to everyone in sight. I shook hands and smiled and said how delighted I was to be there and how I looked forward to getting to know each of them. When we'd made the rounds, he led me to my new office, which was side by side with his but larger, and said, as we stood at the door, with a sincerity I didn't expect, "Welcome back."

Mildred was already ensconced. She was sitting at her desk just outside my office door looking pleased and preening. In the world of associates, she'd taken on a new status.

I'm not embarrassed to admit I felt a chill as I stepped into that office for the first time as Publisher.

I stood still for a moment—just feeling.

Then I began looking around.

They'd done their best to get the office ready for a new occupant. The hardwood floors were polished, the large Afghan rug in front of the desk freshly vacuumed, and the books and trophies on the cherry wood shelves that formed the wall behind the desk, dusted and neatly arranged.

Rhae Dannan's personal papers and mementos had been removed and stored. The framed photograph I remembered of Michael as a six year old standing with his father by the barn at the farm was gone. The desk drawers were empty, the file cabinets cleared and waiting.

Except for the large portrait of Captain Hopkins in his Confederate Grey dress uniform and a large Sawyier watercolor of a rainy day on Wapping Street that was Mr. Dannan's favorite, the walls were clear.

There had once been a large window in the sidewall that looked out on the backshop. Through it, you could watch the bustle of a newspaper being made, but that wall was closed in and now served as a backdrop for a small conference table. There were two sturdy, red leather wing chairs sitting in front of the desk and a black leather couch on the back wall—a place to grab a few hours sleep when needed.

I brought with me no pictures for the walls, no trophies for the shelves. Move in and make yourself at home, Theo Clark.

I walked to the front of the big, old walnut desk that had been Captain Hopkins', and then Rhae's, now mine, and stood there assessing.

Rhae, I thought ruefully, you've chosen a reluctant and undeserving successor. And then, as clearly as I heard her that night in the storm, I could hear Rhae Dannan's voice. "Deal with it."

Paul Isham first, I thought.

I walked next door and stuck my head in.

"Got a minute?"

Paul was at his desk, the afternoon *Lexington Herald* spread out in front of him in his shirtsleeves.

My surprise was obvious. He shrugged, "I can't work in a jacket. In my office, when it's just me—shirtsleeves. Okay, Mr. Publisher?" The last with just a touch of sarcasm.

Holding up the newspaper on his desk, he said, "The Skinner story has taken over every front page. The *Herald's* playing it above the fold with a three column head this afternoon. You saw this morning's *Courier*. The *Times* will have it just as big. TV this morning, you saw the TV coverage? All channels. The Administration is hopping mad."

He motioned me to the chair beside his desk.

"I've been on the phone this afternoon with the Highway Department Commissioner, the Head of the State Personnel Board and (a pause for emphasis), the Governor's Chief of Staff. They are not happy people."

"Do we care?"

"The State printing contract is up for renewal in September, for chrissake, Theo. It's fifteen percent of the printing company's income."

Okay, Theo, is this where you have to start thinking like a businessman rather than a poet and a scholar? Don't do dumb things?

"The *Journal's* coverage this morning was literally dynamite."

I nodded agreement, not sure whether he meant it as a compliment or a criticism.

"Lew had more. A source in the State Highway Department, unwilling to be named but credible, who says the evidence that Artie was taking kickbacks is manufactured. Lew has another source who says the charge that Artie was mentally not up to the demands of the job was all built on verbal testimony from department employees looking to get his job or trying to curry favor with the new boss. To cap it, he has a source willing to be named who will say the Administration hoped to use Artie's case as the opening gambit in an attempt to get rid of the Merit System. If that information gets on the record, the story isn't about a suicide any longer; it's about a scandal."

"Why didn't he use it?" I asked in amazement.

"I wouldn't let him," Paul said.

"For god's sake, why not?"

"He didn't have independent confirmation for any of it. I wouldn't let him go with it until we were dead certain we could back up the accusations."

"Can he get it?"

Paul folded the paper on his desk and pushed it aside. He leaned forward in his chair, engaging me, wanting to make sure I grasped the seriousness of what he had to say.

"This is a fight we don't have to take on. We can watch this fight. We can write about it. But we do not have to get in it. We don't have to give the people who want the State printing contract for their cronies any more ammunition than they already have."

"And Artie Skinner," I said, "we forget about him? We let the outrage of that go?"

Paul replied, with conviction: "We do not have to get in this fight."

Keeping my temper, I nodded, said "Comments noted," and got up and left.

CHAPTER TWENTY NINE

My businessman's mind hadn't engaged yet. I wasn't sure I had one.

"See if you can find Lew Arbogast," I said to Mildred as I returned to my office.

"Ask him if he can join me for a few minutes."

Sitting waiting for Lew to make his way from the newsroom, I pondered Captain Hopkins' portrait on the far wall. He was, as they saying went in those days, a fine figure of a man. He was posed standing at the steps of a columned mansion in his Confederate gray dress uniform, sheathed saber at his side, looking confidently into the near distance. He was probably in his late twenties when the portrait was painted. He served with the Second Corps of the Army of the Potomac, Stonewall Jackson's boys, left in the final days of the war to fight a rear guard action against Phil Sheridan's advance down the Shenandoah Valley. They were outnumbered and outgunned, threadbare and hungry, their ammunition almost gone.

All they could do was die to buy time for General Lee.

They were wiped out at the Battle of Bell Grove, near Strasburg, in October with the crimson leaves falling.

Captain Hopkins managed to survive. He made it to Appomattox where Lee was preparing to meet Grant.

It wasn't much of a contest. Grant had such overwhelming force he couldn't be stopped.

They fought him anyway.

When they were commanded to lay down their arms, they cried standing in the smoke and the carnage, not willing to give up, they cried.

General Grant let them keep their sabers and their horses.

Lew Arbogast arrived while I was still at Appomattox.

He stood in my office doorway, waiting to be noticed and looking wary and annoyed. Lew had his jacket on and his tie knotted and was properly attired for officer country. He was probably as irritated by that little requirement as he was by the interruption to his day. He had a newspaper to get out and no time for games.

I motioned him in and to the wingchair by the desk.

He sat, and we both stayed silent for a moment, each wondering what was on the other's mind. I went first.

"Dulin called you; told you I was moving in. Told you not to get nervous. That the move had nothing to do with you?"

He nodded but didn't relax.

"I'll explain."

"The Artie Skinner story this morning. Beautifully handled. Great job," I said.

He acknowledged the praise with a dip of his head but still was not at ease.

"I want to come back to that, but first let's get clear on why I've moved in here. It's not to second guess you or get in your way or interfere with the way you're running the paper."

I was using my sincere voice and smiling and trying to project as much warmth as I could.

"I'm here because I need to be. I need to get in place, get settled, and start understanding what's involved with being Publisher. I can't do that as a visitor. I have to be here and be part of the operation. That's the only reason. Make sense?"

He frowned unconsciously as he turned it over in his mind, then nodded.

"Good. Now put it behind you and tell me about the Artie Skinner story. You have more information than you used, information that could blow this story into something big enough to give the Administration heart-burn?"

Lew relaxed then and sat back and laid out for me what he had. As he talked, I could feel his eagerness to get on with the story and take it wherever it would lead.

His sources, he felt, were golden. They had personal knowledge; they had no axes to grind, and one would speak for the record. The other two could be convinced to do so if it was absolutely necessary.

"And Paul wouldn't let you use the information because you don't have corroborating confirmation?"

"Yes, but we can get it. We just ran out of time last night."

I didn't hesitate.

"Get it."

Lew stood up as I did.

"Paul explained to me about the printing contract. You're going to risk that?"

I fantasized I could see Rhae Dannan smiling.

CHAPTER **THIRTY**

Wednesday.

Artie Skinner's day—the day he was to clear his name and be reinstated to the position he'd earned and honored as a loyal, hardworking, fully capable servant of the people, the job that defined Artie Skinner to himself as a man of accomplishment and respect.

Except he was lying in a casket at the Rogers Funeral Home on Second Street across from the school.

A cold rain puddled the sidewalks, and wisps of fog were floating up from the river as I dressed.

Jim Colby and Tracy Jordon were going to throw their little hand-grenade that afternoon.

The two of them were reluctant, but I kept pushing. What was there to lose? Keeping Artie Skinner's issue alive was important. I'm not sure why I thought that, but I knew that letting whoever was ultimately responsible for this outrage slip by unmarked would be equally outrageous. And I knew for a fact that keeping a public spotlight on the act would ultimately light them up.

So, when the Hearing Officer convened Artie's appeal hearing and moved to dismiss the case on the not unreasonable grounds that the appellant no longer existed, Jim Colby would rise and, in righteous indignation, demand the right to clear his client's name of the scurrilous charges against him, dead or not, in the interests of justice and posterity. If that didn't galvanize media attention, nothing would.

I finished my coffee, found my Burberry, and stepped out into the morning.

The upstairs apartment over the Woman's Club that Julie Colby had found for me was convenient to the *Journal*, only a block-and-a-half walk down Washington past the Methodist Church, then right on Main to the *Journal*. But I pushed on another block up Main to Jim Colby's office.

The early morning rain had given way to a mist-like drizzle that laid a soft haze over downtown. If I looked through half-shut eyes, I could imagine myself stepping back into Main Street of the early nineteen hundreds, all muted colors and graceful shapes and a feeling of anticipation and expectation in the air.

Jim and Tracy Jordon were in the small conference room in his second floor office, papers spread across the conference table. Jim was in his shirtsleeves with tie loosed. Tracy was in jeans and a Vanderbilt sweat-jersey, her titian hair in a pony tail.

"I'm going to change," she said hurriedly when she looked up and saw me enter, "I'm going home and shower and fix my hair and put on my uniform and look like a respectable lawyer. Don't worry."

Jim laughed. "We were in here before daylight. Get a cup of coffee. Pull up a chair. We're going over our plan for this afternoon."

He pushed back, put his hands behind his head and his feet up on the table. "It's crazy, you know. We can't find any precedent. No one has ever insisted on going through with a trial to vindicate a dead man."

"They have no idea what you plan?"

"No. I had a call from the Highway Department's attorney late yesterday afternoon telling me I'd have to be present at two p.m. in the Personnel Department Hearing, so the case can be formally dismissed."

"What will they do when you show up and demand the hearing go forward?"

"They'll mess their pants and go blind. It's never happened before. They won't know what to do. I'm not sure we know what to do."

"Our best guess," Tracy said, " is that the Hearing Officer will tell us our demand is ridiculous and that we're wasting the state's time and money. But all he can do is adjourn the session and put the attorneys to researching the situation and coming up with an opinion that will allow him to dismiss the case."

"So you'll carry today?"

"We'll carry today. But there's not a snowball's chance in hell for later."

"A day at a time, old buddy, a day at a time, " I said.

The Court House clock was striking seven by the time I got around to trying to run down The O'Donnell. Seven o'clock on a mid-week night in Manhattan. He could be anywhere.

The girl on the night desk at his office, when she recognized my name, told me that Mr. O'Donnell was with a client but could be reached in an emergency. I declared this that, and she put my call through to the phone behind the bar at The Bull & Bear in the Waldorf on Park Avenue.

"Theo?" I could hear the tinkle of ice against glass and the low hum of conversation in the background.

The bar was in the form of a large hollow square. Guests crowded around the perimeter while bartenders in starched white shirts and black bowties hustled drinks from inside. There would be the are's, the wannabe's, the once-were's, and the no-longer-are's-but-ain't-giving-up's, standing shoulder to shoulder, laughing, telling lies, whispering secrets, winding down and gearing up.

I could picture Jay leaning back against the polished walnut bar, a brunette beauty on the stool to his left and a pinstriped captain of industry on his right. With his Irish charm and his sophisticate's polish, he'd have them enthralled and in no way aware he was just a country boy from the Volunteer State.

"I need a man with a devious mind and a righteous streak," I said when he answered.

"Louder. I can't hear you."

"The barbarians are at the gate."

"What the hell are you talking about?"

"Can you spare me a day? Sunday? Can you run down here for the day? I need to confound and confuse some people, and I need your Machiavellian mind to help me refine the plan."

"Sunday? I sleep on Sundays."

"Eastern's got a nine o'clock out of LaGuardia that'll get you here by eleven. I'll pick you up at Lexington. We'll have a grand lunch at a little inn in the Bluegrass that'll suit you, spend a couple of hours scheming, then put you back on a plane and have you back to Manhattan in time for your Sunday night assignation."

"Barbarian, huh, as in bad guys? Am I gonna enjoy this?"

"Guaranteed," I said.

"You're serious? On a Sunday? It can't wait?"

"Can't wait."

"You will owe me really big."

"Just like always."

He laughed. " Meet me at the gate."

Artie Skinner's funeral was on Saturday morning. It was held at the little church that sits on the bank of the creek at the Forks of Elkhorn. Tracy Jordan sat with Artie's mother and his uncle. I sat with Julie and Jim Colby. The church was full, and people were standing around the edges.

A man I didn't know delivered the eulogy. He talked of how good a man Artie was. He was so sincere you had to believe him. The preacher asked if any others would like to say a word. Several did, a women who sang in the choir with Artie, a young man Artie had helped coach the church basketball team. Then finally Jim Colby. There were a number of us present who had been in school with Artie at Frankfort High. Jim spoke about that. Nothing saccharine or sentimental, only that we liked him and were honored to have known him; and, with an edge of anger in his voice that couldn't be concealed, that Artie Skinner would be missed and remembered.

The manner of Artie's death wasn't mentioned.

It was a fine June morning, bright and clear, a little breeze coming in through the open windows and the sound of the creek flowing by.

Sunday.

Lexington.

The O'Donnell was whistling as he came down the corridor at the airport. He had on a white Palm Beach blazer, a blue button-down, a yellow paisley tie, navy blue slacks, a killer smile and a jaunty walk. He looked like he owned the place, or soon would.

The boys from Kentucky and Tennessee—the ones from the valleys of Virginia and the tidewaters of the Carolinas—from the piney woods of Georgia and the rich earth of Mississippi and Alabama and Louisiana—they're the ones who weave the spells.

They have an air of gallantry about them that in the threatening canyons of Manhattan is reassuringly appealing. They are polite and well-mannered. They are seductively well spoken. They never check and raise. And they are relentless.

The city draws them like a magnet. It's the excitement and the danger of it—and the promise, oh yes, the promise—because under their cloak of civility and charm, these boys intend to take the prize—the fame and treasure that only the Capitol Of The World possesses.

There are the Ivy League types, of course. They own Wall Street, but their narcissism and arrogance are off-putting, and their grail is merely money.

The boys from the Midwest are tough enough, but they lack the polish.

The ones who come all the way from the West do well, but the town's a little too demanding for them, too contentious.

At the top are the boys from the Bluegrass. I say this with true humility. The O'Donnell doesn't agree, but I humor him. He comes from Sewanee—in the foothills of the Cumberland Plateau south of Nashville near the Alabama line, a place of gentle valleys and farms almost as well favored as the Bluegrass—almost.

As I'd said, we met and became friends in Manhattan. As country boys in the big city, we were natural allies, and our like for each other cemented it.

Jay was as good as they get at the game he played. "It's about getting people to do something, or not do something, or letting you do something," he'd tell me. "Something specific. Something important like buying your products or supporting your stock price or voting for your candidate or letting you build that pipeline you want to build. It's about moving people to take action on something that makes a difference. It's about getting results. That's where the fun is. That's the way you win."

Jay won a lot. He was now a partner in his firm. His counsel commanded kingly sums, and you had to stand in line to get it.

"Okay, where are these barbarians?" he called out as he got near. "I've a late dinner with Ellen Asterhart, you remember her, at the Four Seasons tonight. Can't be late. Show me the villains, and we'll do them in, and I can get back on time," laughing and pounding me on the shoulder when he reached me.

The O'Donnell is about six-two, the build of a pulling guard, black wavy hair, boisterous. The crowd streaming past us couldn't help noticing—two mature, well dressed men, hugging in the middle of the hallway.

"Later," I said, disengaging myself. "Lunch first, then work."

I'd booked us a private dining room in a the Fox Hill Inn at Midway, a picturesque old mansion just far enough out in the country to be rural, but still close enough in to be convenient. It sat under oaks that were as ancient as the Revolution, on a rise overlooking a small stream that meandered though green fields, bordered by white fences. From one of the rocking chairs on the porch, you could sit with your julep in hand and conjure up any dream that pleased you.

I remembered that.

Allie and I had been there once. An October night. The sky laced by branches and full of stars.

No dreams this day.

This day was a day for machination. I had a master conniver sitting beside me.

For The O'Donnell, the more difficult the challenge, the more intrigued he became. Most often this was purely an intellectual exercise for him. Be smarter than the other guys. Out think them, then out maneuver them. No passion involved. It was all a brain game with him, like chess, but infinitely more fun. I was sure that the scheming surrounding Artie Skinner's death would outrage him as much as it did me. Between us, I intended that we'd come up with a plan that would make the Administration wish they'd never laid a glove on Artie Skinner.

Jim Colby and Tracy Jordan were waiting for us.

I'd promised The O'Donnell a Bluegrass lunch that would please him. The Fox Hill Inn didn't disappoint. They'd set us up in a little room on the second floor with a window wall that looked over a meadow. Clusters of hedge parsley grew along the fence line. People dressed for church were strolling the shaded paths under big oaks or moving to and from the gravel parking at the side of the house. Sunday brunch at the Fox Hill Inn was a local tradition.

We started with country ham on beaten biscuits, moved on to a tart apple salad, then for the entrée, honest-to-god-old-fashion-home-made-fried-chicken with mashed potatoes and milk gravy and corn on the cob and green beans fresh from the fields and finished off with chocolate bread pudding in a bourbon sauce. No wine. Iced tea.

We sat around an oval table with white china and filigreed old silver on a wine-colored tablecloth—Jim and I at either end, and Tracy across from Jay. We talked easily, the three of them getting to know each other and sizing each other up. All Jim and Tracy had was my word that Jay was a wizard, and all The O'Donnell had was my word that the pair of them were bright and solid and could be counted on. They needed to make their own judgments.

When the table had been cleared, and the room was ours to be uninterrupted, Jay leaned back in his chair in a cat-like stretch. "Superior," and smiling at Tracy, "especially the pleasure of your company."

Then turning eagerly to me, "I've enjoyed all this immensely, old buddy. Now tell me why I'm here."

Forty-five minutes later, we were sitting on Dulin's patio, the town and the river below us. A water skier was cutting a foamy wake near the bend to Big Eddy, and a few power-boats loafed along on the stretch between the bridges. Sun glinted off the dome of the Capitol and etched shadows on the rock face of Fort Hill.

Tranquil. Serene.

Dulin brought us each a julep.

"I wanted you to see this," I said to Jay.

I walked him to the edge of the patio where Tracy and Jim were standing, so we could see all the way up and down the valley.

"The backbone of the economy here is State government," I began. "The Commonwealth provides most of the jobs. Its employees buy or rent most of the homes, keep the stores and the shops open, the gas stations busy, the movies running."

"Some of them come and go as administrations change," Jim added. "That's expected. But the majority of them, Merit System employees like Artie Skinner, they stay. They're the core. They're insulated by law from the political manipulations that decide who gets a job. They make up the cadre of experienced professionals who keep the day-to-day wheels of government rolling smoothly, regardless of who sits in the governor's chair or which businessman or big contributor has been appointed to run this or that agency. Without them, state government would be run by a bunch of amateurs or favor seekers. The economy here would be crippled and the state overall in serious danger of going over a cliff.

"Big job cuts are being ordered by the new governor. Everyone's spooked. But what has them really scared is the talk that he's going to make a run at dismantling the Merit System. Artie Skinner was to be the opening salvo in that campaign"

We told Jay all we knew and laid out all we had: how Artie died, the note found in his pocket, my feeling that he'd jumped deliberately. I told him about the material Lew Arbogast's reporters had dug up, most importantly that we had a source willing to say, for the record, that Artie had been set up and that his dismissal was to be the kick-off the administration's attack on the civil service system.

Jim Colby laid out the only gambit we had; how, as Artie's attorney, he had insisted the case be tried even though Artie was dead; how, when the hearing officer refused and dismissed the case, Jim had filed an appeal, and how we were now at an impasse waiting for the appeal to be ruled on.

The O'Donnell laughed when he heard that. "Force them to try a dead man. Ridiculous. But I love it. I wish I'd been there to see the confusion when you dropped that bomb." Still smiling, he looked around at all of us. "As much as I admire what you three are doing and the sheer gall of it, you're like Davy Crockett at the Alamo."

Not smiling now and deadly serious, "You're overmatched. You can't win this fight. Your appeal is going to be denied, and you know it."

Then focusing only on me, "So what do you really want?"

I looked around to Tracy and to Jim. They were watching me expectantly, unsure what I'd say. Dulin, too. He'd taken no part in the discussion, but I could see he was caught up with concern.

I swung back to The O'Donnell. He was watching me with that eager smile he sometimes had when he was waiting for the game to be named.

I recognized it. He was in. Smiling my own little smile now, I said, " I want a little magic. I want to expose the bastards. I want to blow their boat out of the water." And with more anger than I realized I felt, "And I want to get the record set straight on Artie Skinner."

CHAPTER THIRTY ONE

The afternoon had almost wound-down.

 The pleasure boats on the river were beginning to head in. We'd exhausted all the talk. There was nothing more to say, so we stopped talking and started looking up to see who could spot the first star— waiting for a pronouncement from The O'Donnell.

Tracy thought she saw a pinpoint of light at the top of the dome of the sky, but none of us did, so we didn't let her claim the honor. The O'Donnell, who had been standing at the edge of the patio looking down river, glanced up, agreed, then dropped into a rocker and angled it to face me.

"Here's what you do," he announced.

Dulin's head jerked up. I spun around.

"Light them up. Confront the Governor. Light up what was done to Artie Skinner. Show it for the dirty, despicable, underhanded act it was and hold them up to public scorn. Light up the plan to get the state's hiring practices back under political control. They won't be able to take it.

"You've got the weapons. Use them—the *Journal,* your position, Theo, at *The Atlantic.* You can draw so much negative media attention to this sorry situation that no politician could hold up under it. With the *Journal,* you can inflame statewide outrage. With the *Atlantic,* you can focus national contempt on what's being tried here. You don't need to actually use them. Just threaten to."

"Get with the Governor. Not an aide, not his Chief of Staff, go to the top, the guy whose reputation and political future is at risk. Show him what you've got. Lay before him the stuff that the *Journal* reporters have unearthed—people who'll expose the case against Artie Skinner to be bogus, people who will condemn the targeting of Artie as part of a plan to attack the Merit system, people who will lay Artie's death at the Administration's feet."

"You want me to take on the King in his castle? Armed with nothing more than a story?" I said, intrigued.

"It will work. With the weapons you've got, you can turn this into a crusade. If this guy has any political ambitions at all, and they all do, it will work."

Dulin fidgeted uncomfortably.

Jay said, "Give him the chance to save his career. All he has to do is have his Highway Commissioner announce, publically, that the case against Artie Skinner was flawed, that Artie's dismissal is being reversed and his record cleared. All he has to do is drop any plans to meddle with the Merit System."

He seemed to like the idea the more he heard his own words, smiling now and nodding his head in agreement with himself.

"And, oh yes, the renewal of the State printing contract—the most qualified low bidder, emphasis on most qualified, gets the contract. No finagling by the politicians. Guaranteed. He agrees, and the story goes away. If not, you run with it."

"Blackmail the Governor?" Dulin said, with a derisive snort.

"Not blackmail," Jay shot back, "negotiation. They threw away the rule-book when they went after Artie Skinner. Let them take the consequences. Don't angst about this. Do it."

He rocked forward and began to stand then, shrugging on his jacket.

"But leave the Governor some ego room. Suggest that he might not have known the particulars of the Artie Skinner plot. Maybe he didn't. If he's operating like a typical CEO, he told someone what he wanted to achieve and said get it done and didn't look over their shoulder while it was happening. Tell him you hope you'll be able to work together in the future for the best interests of the Commonwealth and the Capitol City. Honorable and reasonable men can disagree and still cooperate. Hang on to the material you have, though. It's your insurance. Now, old buddy," he said, looking at his watch and beaming, "you need to get me on an airplane, so I don't keep the fair Ellen waiting."

Paul Isham was apoplectically against it.

"The risk is too great. You can't push a governor around like this. More to the point, you can't embarrass his key advisors like that, his staff. The plan had to be theirs. Shove it back down their throats? These are powerful men, egotistical men. Humiliate them in their boss's eyes? They won't stand for it, Theo. They'll find a way to get you, to get back at the *Journal.* Do not do it. You don't even know that the plan will work. Do not do it!"

I had no argument with Paul's arguments. They were sound.

The thing is, I'd made my decision before The O'Donnell even had his jacket back on.

Rule #2 in the Will Owens Rule Book: "Don't pick fights you can't win. If you're in one, hit first, hit as hard as you can, throw away the rule book."

Rule #1 in both the Will Owens and Dulin Monroe rule books: "Don't do dumb things."

I didn't pick this fight.

I was going to hit as hard as I could and hit first.

The only rule I was going to pay attention to was win.

And though this may have been a dumb thing to do, I had my own Rule #1: "Go with your gut."

I thanked Paul for his advice. "Comments noted," I said.

CHAPTER THIRTY TWO

Paul Isham set the meeting with the Governor for Thursday. Time couldn't be cleared on the Governor's calendar before then. The delay worked in my favor. Lew Arbogast's reporters had two extra days to collect and confirm the additional information needed to buttress the story. And it gave me time to get back to the matter of the manuscript in Mr. Niccan Dye's hands, the one I'd left with Marne Young, the one that could— well, I wasn't sure what it could do. There is no statute of limitations on murder.

But that's beside the point. I couldn't remember in detail what I'd written. That time when Michael had come home and was running for governor against Jesse Bristow, when we'd begun to unravel the mystery of this father's death, when Michael and Allie were getting back together, and then when Michael had been killed and Allie had come to me; that had been one of the most difficult times in my life— more emotion, more anger, more hurt than I'd ever experienced. More than at Chosin. More than with the beaten body of Rose on the morgue slab before me.

Did I tell it all?

Did I tell how Allie held me by the hand with her eyes full of pain and told me to not let Jesse Bristow get away with it—and reached up and took my face in her hands and kissed me to put the final seal on an action I'd already planned to take?

Did I describe how Jesse Bristow died?

Did I write all that?

I'd have to go see Mr. Niccan Dye.

"Mildred," I called.

No response.

Louder. "Mildred."

A head poked around my office door. "Use the buzzer, Mr. Clark, the buzzer. These are the Executive Offices. Goodness," she said.

"Sorry," I said, properly chastised. "I'm just a country boy, not office broke yet. Cut me some slack."

She smiled at me, shook her head, "All right then. What?"

"Our friend, Mr. Niccan Dye. Remember him?"

She frowned, waiting.

"I need to attend to him. That friend of yours at the newspaper down there, the girl you met; think you could get her to get him to call you?"

"Call me? Not you?"

"I don't want to be in direct contact with him yet. Let him set the time and place. Not this week. My schedule's too full. But any time next week. Whatever works for him."

"You haven't told me what was in his letter," she said. "You said you would."

"Later. After I've found out what game Mr. Dye wants to play."

Tracy Jordon knocked on my door that night.

I'd worked late in the office, dropped into the newsroom to talk briefly with Lew Arbogast and, because old habits die hard, hung around until Page One was locked up, then walked home. There was the feel of rain in the air. Leaves shivered in the streetlights; thunder growled in the distance, and I felt that little tingle of excitement I always feel when a storm is moving in, waiting for the wind to go wild and the rain to slash and the sky to flare with lightning. I needed something rampageous, something raging.

Midnight. Maybe a little later.

I'd just gotten settled and had fixed a nice stiff bourbon and was standing at the window watching the wind in the trees when the knock came.

At that hour? I figured it must be an emergency of some kind, but why not call; why send a messenger? Something else? Oh, hell, Theo, go open the door.

Tracy Jordon stood there.

"It's going to rain rain," she said.

Surprised, I glanced over her shoulder and then back at her. Her eyes were sparkling, and she seemed to sway a bit.

"Is anything wrong?"

"No. No. I was down the street at Jim Colby's working late and saw your lights as I came past and on the spur of the moment, thought I'd stop in and ... it's okay isn't it?" She frowned, "I don't want to—"

"Tracy Jordon at midnight. That's better than okay," I said. "Come in."

She stepped inside just as the rain began.

"Would you buy a girl a drink at this hour and not think badly of her?"

"Anytime. What would you like?"

'Scotch, please. Single malt. Straight if you've got it."

I didn't. I hadn't planned on doing any entertaining and hadn't stocked a bar yet.

"Will bourbon do?"

"Oh," she said, embarrassed that she might have embarrassed me by asking for something I didn't have. "Bourbon is fine. Bourbon is best. I should have remembered. I'm in Kentucky. The world's finest bourbon. Yes, bourbon, please. Bourbon is perfect. No soda. No Coca Cola. Straight Kentucky style. On ice with just a little water. OK?"

I laughed. "It's okay, Tracy. I haven't had a chance to get prepared for guests. You're the first. Take your coat off and find a chair, and I'll hustle up the best bourbon and branch you've had today. The fixings are in the kitchen. Only be a minute."

When I returned, she was standing at the window watching the rain fall.

She turned when she heard me and reached her hand out to me. "Take me to bed, Theo."

Rain tapped against the windows all the night long.

I lay with Tracy nestled against me—her arm across my chest; her lips against my neck—breathing softly and trying not to wake her.

She was asleep beside me on the couch before she finished the drink I'd brought her. I lifted her carefully and carried her to my bed. She was in jeans and a man-style button-down shirt that wouldn't be much the worse for wear in the morning. I removed her boots, took off my loafers, lay down beside her. When she felt my body beside her, she turned and put an arm across me and kissed me on the neck and went back to sleep. I pulled the cover up over us.

She hardly moved the whole night through. I held her and stroked her hair and told her it would be all right.

By dawn the rain had stopped.

I woke her with a hot cup of coffee waved above her sleeping head.

"If you want to get out of here before the kids start down the street to school, or Julie comes driving by and sees your parked car, you better get up and get moving."

"Oh, my god," she said, sitting up, looking around confused.

"Theo? Oh my god, I didn't, we didn't—"

"You had a good night's sleep and reminded me I need to get some single malt scotch. Now get moving.

"I'm so embarrassed," she said.

"At needling me about the scotch or because you weren't able to seduce me?"

I think she started to throw the coffee cup at me, but decided not to.

"Next time," she squinted her eyes up and laughed. "Next time."

The door had barely closed behind her when my phone rang.

"I think you better come talk with Mommie."

"Julie?"

No mistaking the voice or the pique in it.

"It's barely daylight."

"Coffee's on, and I'm making pancakes. Real maple syrup. Don't make me send Jim to get you."

"Is he up?"

"No, but he will be by the time you get here."

He was. Siting at the kitchen table. Looking hung-over. But putting a brave face on.

"Robin Hood here had a little too much bourbon last night. Thank goodness he was only feeding wine to Tracy. Here, let me look at you."

Julie pulled my face close to hers.

"You don't look any the worse for wear ... considering."

"Considering"

"I saw Tracy's car parked in front of your apartment as I came back from early Mass this morning. What's going on?"

"Nothing."

"She's there all night, and nothing's going on?"

"She showed up a bit past midnight last night. She needed a little comforting."

"In bed?"

"She was emotionally strung out. I wouldn't have taken advantage of that."

She studied me for a long minute. "You wouldn't, would you? But that doesn't stop you from letting others take advantage of you. You know what the girls called you in high school? Straight Arrow. That's why the mothers loved you. Doesn't it get frustrating? Trying to do the honorable thing all the time?"

"You're mad at me for not taking her to bed!"

Julie scrunched her eyes up and shook her head." No. Yes. I don't know. It might have been good for her. Might have been good for you."

A long pause and then a long sigh. "Oh, Theo what am I going to do with you. You're worrying me. Something's weighing on you. I can see it in your eyes. I can hear it in your voice when no others are around. It's not Artie Skinner, and it's not this fight you're going to get into. Is it the responsibility Rhae Dannan put on you with the paper and all that? Or is it what you were running from when you left? You're home now. You're with people who love you. Don't you want to be home? Let us in. Talk to me, Theo. Talk to Allie."

CHAPTER THIRTY THREE

Allie.

Allison Boatwright Sinclair.

I don't know that she would have chosen me. I think she would have, but I didn't give her the chance.

Pride.

I couldn't take her the places Michael could, couldn't give her the things he could. That was important to me. I had no car, barely had the money for the movies and something after. I don't think it made any difference to her, but it made a difference to me. My ego.

The time Allie and I had together, the spring and summer of our junior year and the autumn of our senior; that time was grand. She was so honeyed to the taste and so sleek to the touch that I hungered to be near her. There were girls with better figures and girls who were prettier, but none who were Allie. We talked, and we laughed, and in a way I still don't understand, we fit. We fit like I've never fit with anyone again.

But I walked away.

Michael didn't.

He and Allie became an item. They made a handsome couple. When I left for Korea, I thought they'd marry. Matrimony wasn't in Michael's plan.

I saw her some when I got back, but stayed away from anything intimate. I was afraid of starting something I couldn't control.

Later, when Michael came home to run for governor, they gravitated to each other again. I stayed on the sidelines, not intruding, telling myself I was truly hopeful it would work for both of them and telling myself I meant it. But then Michael was killed. I carried the word of it to Allie, driving all that long way from Harlan through the rising dawn to reach her. She cried in my arms when I told her.

Through all of it, from the first time we kissed on the swing on the porch at her mother's house to now—the taste of Allie, her touch, the look of her in the moonlight—through all the time since, the thought of her has never left me.

Talk to her? It had been years since I'd seen her. I wasn't even sure she was real. She might be a fantasy I'd conjured. Talk to her? Tell why I left her again after Michael's death when she was fragile and hurt. Justify that. Make that all right. Tell her how much the thought of her fills my mind? Ten years gone and no contact, no word from me? Talk to her?

CHAPTER THIRTY FOUR

Mr. Niccan Dye of Cumberland College chose the next Sunday after church for our meeting. One-thirty in the afternoon. In the library on the campus. It would be quiet there on a Sunday afternoon, and we'd have no trouble finding a table in a corner where we would have privacy. He would have the manuscript. I could inspect it there.

"That okay, Mr. Clark? I said it would be. I said you'd be there," Mildred said as she followed me into my office. "He called while you were out. The girl at the paper got him to."

So I was to play on the enemy's field. Okay. It's what I asked for. I'd rather start on his home ground where he felt comfortable. But that was only part of the reason. I owed Marne. I'd leave early, get there mid-morning and find the little churchyard where she lay. Sweet Marne. A rattlesnake. Damn.

"Is it okay, Mr. Clark?"

"Yes, it's fine," I said. "How did he sound, Mr. Dye? Was he mad? Sound put-out? Threatening?"

She reached for my Burberry to hang it up outside. "He sounded fidgety, like he felt he ought to apologize for making you drive all that way, but wasn't going to because he's as good as you are, and you better know it."

"Did you get any feel for the kind of person he is?"

"He's nervous. Like he's in to something he's not sure of."

I tried to picture him but gave up because people almost never look the way you think they will.

"Are you going to tell me what this is all about?"

"It's a game. We're just beginning."

The flick of her head was a comment on her dissatisfaction with my answer.

"It's going to rain again," she said as she turned and left.

I returned to the file on my desk. I'd asked each of the business managers to prepare a précis on their operations for me—a synopsis, a summary explaining their business. I was going through them as thoroughly as I do when researching a major story. When I finished, I'd have at least a fix on what they did, and why and how. That week, I was concentrating on the commercial printing business, Elkhorn Press, preparing for my meeting with the Governor.

There was no preparation I could do for my meeting with Dye. There were no documents to go over, no records to check. Dye had whatever there was to be had.

I hadn't dealt with blackmail before. That's what I thought his game was. In all the crime stories I'd read, the only way to handle blackmail was to eliminate the blackmailer.

So I sat there and thought, Theo, old friend, you were doing really well—a job you loved, all the money you needed, companionship and comfort at your ports of call; phantoms in the night getting weaker and no boredom or disquiet as you made your daily rounds.

Now here you are, picking a fight with a governor, trying to get a dead man's name cleared, at risk of having a story you wrote years ago come back to hang you, being saddled with the responsibility of running a set of businesses you know nothing about, and facing a job you think you're going to detest. Don't forget the phantoms. Oh, no, don't forget them. You'd almost worn them out, but now that you're back here, they're gaining strength.

The roof fell in, old buddy. You're up to your ass in alligators.

Sometimes I talk to myself. I tell myself things and ask myself questions. Sometimes some of what I tell myself is interesting. Sometimes it's even useful. No little voice with magic solutions whispered in my ear that time—only the echo of Rhae Dannan's incantation.

CHAPTER THIRTY FIVE

Nothing so distresses the ambitious and the avaricious as their name in print with their schemes exposed. So sayeth The O'Donnell, and so attesteth I.

I planned not only to tell the Governor what we had, but also to show him. We worked through the night and the early morning on our cudgel.

I didn't want our reporters involved in this gambit, so using their notes, Lew and Dulin and I wrote the stories. What we produced was a dummy front page with a banner headline screaming across the top that read **Administration Linked To Suicide** and a deck proclaiming, **Skinner A Scapegoat For Planned Attack On Merit System,** to show him what we'd run if we had to.

We filled the page with stories backing up that charge. The most damning story quoted a memorandum from the Governor's Chief of Staff outlining a plan to eliminate the Merit System and to put all hiring and firing under the control of the Administration, consistent with the Governor's promise to "run the state like a business."

The first step would be to create a case, the memo said, that would show the system hires people not capable of doing the jobs assigned them. Artie Skinner was to be the scapegoat. He was targeted because he was a burr in their side. He kept insisting the rules and regulations be followed, slowing down the operations of his department and interfering with his superior's plans. Whatever was needed to get rid of him was to be developed and packaged as a case. The secretary who gave us the memo, Janet Wilson, worked in records. She filed the memo. When she saw Artie's name and read what was written, she copied it, and after he'd jumped, she brought the copy to the *Journal*. She couldn't stomach "the way poor Artie was used." Mrs. Wilson is Merit System, too. "If they come after me to fire me after reading this, they better watch out," she said.

We had a long sidebar on the suicide note found in Artie's pocket. What was he trying to say, the reporter asked people on the street the day of Arties's funeral? Artie had written, "It isn't true. It isn't fair."

"I don't believe for a minute the charges they trumped up against Artie Skinner," Jimmy Estes, who worked with him, said. "Artie wasn't no rocket scientist, but he was smart enough for that job. Kickbacks? No man alive was more honest than Artie. None of that stuff is true."

"I knew Artie," May Underwood said. " He was a sensitive man, very careful of what people thought of him, and they were humiliating him. It drove him to kill himself. That's awful. It's not fair, making up trash like that, hounding a man like that."

It was a beautifully written story. Not my work. Dulin's. It would bring tears to your eyes.

They were all damn good pieces. I'd hire us if I were looking for staff. And it was better than you can imagine to be sitting in a newsroom in the shank of the morning again with time running out and a big story in your hands.

We played a three-column photograph of the State Office Building with a black dotted line showing the path of Artie's fall and used shots of mourners coming out of the church by the creek after the funeral and Artie, big smile on his face, getting his Employee Of The Month Award.

When we had it finished and looked at it, the impact was more powerful than any of us thought it would be.

By then, daylight had come. We'd had the newsroom to ourselves after the paper went to bed and worked unnoticed and uninterrupted. Now, admiring our handiwork and feeling that steely affection men who accomplish difficult tasks together develop for each other, I knew that whatever came in the future, we'd be a team.

Paul wasn't part of it. He was adamantly against what I planned. You can't walk into his office and threaten the Governor, he kept telling me. You're going to make an enemy out of the most powerful man in the state. For what? You're out of control, Theo.

So I didn't tell him about the dummy front page. He wasn't going to see it until I spread it out for the Governor to see.

Dulin understood what Paul saw, but saw it differently. The risk was very high and what we'd win if we won might give us a warm feeling but not add to the bottom line. He was with Paul on that. Whether we could win remained to be seen, he felt. But as to whether a governor, this Governor, could be intimidated (I was glad he'd dropped the word blackmail), Dulin smiled and rubbed his hands with relish and said "Let's find out."

Perhaps it wasn't fair bringing Dulin into this. He had fought his battles and won his spurs. But that afternoon at his place conniving with The O'Donnell and laying out the plan for the game we were about to begin, Dulin got so caught up in the thinking that there was no way to keep him on the sidelines. Not that any of us wanted to. He had a range of experience that neither Lew nor I had, and a basketful of chits that might be very useful. His biggest help to us, though, would be his steadiness. I have a tendency to get carried away, to get wrapped up in enthusiasm or taken over by outrage, and it causes me, or has caused me, to do that thing they tell you angels fear to do. Dulin would be my buffer. He had no patience with wishful thinking. If he was on the team, I was half-way confident we had a chance of pulling it off, but only half-way.

We tucked the killer front page carefully away inside a copy of the morning's *Journal.* I folded it under my arm, protecting it as if it were the original of the Magna Charter, and we walked out together through the newsroom door—a day to go.

CHAPTER **THIRTY SIX**

Mornings in the early summer in the Bluegrass can be nearly perfect. There is nothing harsh or glaring as the day comes on. The light is soft and the morning welcoming. Usually there is just enough breeze to put a little flutter in the leaves and lift the scent of rose and honeysuckle into the air. The sky is clear and blue. A few puffy white clouds float lazily alone. It's just warm enough to be comforting, but there's a breath of cool in the breeze that lets you know you won't get too hot when the sun gets high.

This was one of those.

We assembled at Julie's for breakfast—Paul Isham, Lew Arbogast, Dulin, and me. Tracy Jordon was there, and Jim Colby, of course—Paul because he was the one who would accompany me to the meeting with the Governor—Lew because he was a part of this now. The rest of us, Dulin and Jim and Tracy and me, we were the ones that put together the plan with The O'Donnell. And Julie? What more propitious place to launch our attack than from Julie's kitchen?

Seven of us. Eight o'clock in the morning. Julie by herself in the kitchen. She must have been up for hours to pull it all together—bacon, country ham, scrambled eggs, biscuits, pancakes, real maple syrup and blackberry jam—all by herself, and all of it hot and waiting when we arrived, and looking as fresh and relaxed as if the whole bundle of it had magically appeared. I think there is nothing beyond Julie's capacity. I wonder at her and am glad that our friendship as kids hadn't developed into something more. We might have been good together as lovers, but we were superior together as friends.

There was a big wooden picnic table on the back lawn near the river under a sycamore that filtered the morning sun. We filled our plates and carried them out there. I thought Tracy might be a little shy or embarrassed. She wasn't. She sat her plate next to mine and slid in beside me, smiling a smile I didn't understand saying, "Good morning, Sir Galahad." Before I could react, she put her hand on mine. "You were very gallant the other night. Thank you." Then smiling teasingly, or at least I thought she was teasing, she said, "The next time I show up at your door at midnight, I won't be tipsy."

"The next time?"

"Life is full of surprises." She patted my hand and turned to Dulin, who was just taking his seat beside her.

We made our little pleasantries, the how-are-yous and sleep-wells and what-a- beautiful mornings, as is expected and well mannered, but turned almost immediately to smoothing out the plan for the meeting with the Governor in the afternoon.

Paul would accompany me. He was the man who had set up the meeting and who was seen by the Governor's staff as the man with clout and the authority at the *Journal,* He'd told the Governor's Chief of Staff he wanted to introduce me to the Governor and that we wished to discuss information uncovered regarding the Artie Skinner suicide and get his advice on its handling.

Once the meeting began, I'd tell the Governor there were issues I wished to discuss privately with him and ask that Paul and the Chief of Staff be excused. The Chief of Staff would undoubtedly object. He, or his people with his approval, had probably organized the Artie Skinner affair, and he'd want to be present to protect to his backside. I'd insist. The Governor would dance around but in the end, support his Chief of Staff. I'd acquiesce.

Through all this, I'd be respectful and mannered. No belligerence or combativeness. I would make it clear I knew I was in "The Presence" and would be appropriately impressed.

Ego.

Nothing hooks an ambitious man like ego. Play to his ego, The O'Donnell preaches.

Then, with the Governor relaxed, the Chief of Staff suspicious, and Paul Isham fearing doom and damnation, I'd present our story.

Verbally at first, recounting what we knew and confirming that we had verification of the facts—just to set the stage—then, for the coup de grace, unveil the front page we'd print if we had to.

"The drop-kick," Jim Espy said.

Dulin and Paul looked at each other with raised eyebrows.

"Yes," I said laughing, "the drop-kick."

On game days, we all had rituals. Chilton had to be the first in the locker room. He'd show up an hour or more ahead time, a *Bat Man* comic book in hand, and sit in front of his locker lost in it until the rest of us got there. Jim Espy had to be last. He'd never enter until we all were there. Big Jack, a tackle, got fully decked out in his game uniform—pants, pads, jersey, even his helmet—before he'd put on his shoes—left shoe first, then the right.

Every game, home or away, we followed our rituals. It isn't that we thought they brought us luck. It's that we knew we'd have bad luck if we didn't.

Mine was a walk around the field. Counter clockwise. Making sure I stayed on the sidelines and circled both goals. Rain or shine or anything in between. I'd drop my gear in the locker room and, still dressed in my street clothes, make the circuit of the field. Alone. Studying the contours. Looking for the spots where footing might be tricky.

Just before kick-off, we huddled for the little prayer that was the team ritual at the start of games. Michael always led it. He never asked that we win. Winning was up to us. All he asked was that we be helped to play our best.

This day felt like a game day. Excitement in the air. Tension. I could hardly wait.

Kick-off was three p.m. I would meet Paul Isham at the Governor's office in the Capitol at two-thirty—early, but I'm a believer in Lombardi time. In the meantime, with time to kill, I decided to go back to the office and run once again through my notes on that phenomenon Isaac Adair—Governor Isaac Adair.

I left Julie's and was in my office at the *Journal* by mid-morning. I asked Mildred to hold my calls, get me a sandwich and cup of coffee when lunch time came and otherwise see that I wasn't disturbed.

Governor Isaac Adair was a story I'd like to have written.

He came out of nowhere. He was Hollywood-handsome, had a cover-girl wife and a reputation as a buccaneer on the battlefields of corporate commerce. He'd won a fortune betting he could take a small Cincinnati pizzeria and make it a national money machine. He was a lawyer, not a businessman, but late one night in the kitchen of a college friend about to go out of business, Isaac Adair bet he could save it. A couple of bourbons chased by beer helped trigger the decisions, but he had absolute confidence in himself. As a student working part time, he'd sold life insurance to people who couldn't afford it so successfully that he drove a Cadillac convertible and lived in an off-campus condominium with a heated swimming pool and a putting green. Tony's pizza was great pizza, and he bet he could sell that, too. Tony put up a case of Ancient Age, hoping to lose, that Adair couldn't. In less than a month, Isaac Adair had recast Tony's Pizza as Antonio's Luscious Luccan Pizza and created so much demand that the little storefront on the edge of the Xavier campus was drawing people from all over town.

They expanded to Columbus where the Ohio State kids gobbled it up, then to Lexington and got the same response from the UK crowd. In a few years, concentrating on college towns, Antonio's Luscious

Luccan Pizza was the most profitable pizza chain in the nation. In the process of all this, Isaac Adair found out he had a genius for marketing. And found he liked it better than practicing law. Growing certain that he could beat any competition he came up against, he took down his lawyer's shingle and bought out Tony. The world was his oyster.

Isaac Adair's decision to run for governor surprised everyone—especially the politicians. He had no political experience and, so far as anyone knew, no interest in politics. Though he was a native son, born and raised in the Bluegrass and a graduate of Centre College where his father was a professor, he'd been out of state for most of his career. No one expected him to enter the primary. When he did, no one expected him to win. The Democratic Party had already picked the man it planned to place in the governor's chair next.

Isaac Adair's decision seemed an afterthought to many and to some only a publicity stunt for some project that would soon be revealed. He entered the race almost at the last minute—just two months before the primary. No one thought he was serious.

But he was. Using his personal fortune, Adair launched a radio and television advertising blitzkrieg that overwhelmed his opponents. While his messages were dominating the media, he delivered himself in person to the voters, shaking more hands and kissing more babies in more rural parts of Kentucky than any candidate ever had. The man was pure charisma. He had rock-star aura.

The Party's anointed was blown away in the primary. His Republican opponent in the general election didn't stand a chance. Governor-elect Isaac Adair strode into the governor's office pledging to run the state like a business and bring a little panache to the government.

On paper I liked him. He seemed energetic and interesting and open. He looked like the kind of man you could trust—the kind who would get things done.

Why, I wondered, with all he had, why would he want to be governor? He had money and prestige and seemed to be enjoying what he was doing. What was missing?

Mildred had just given me my one-thirty call. I finished my ham and cheese, took the last sip of coffee, wadded up all the papers and tossed them in the trash and stood up to start out for the big game.

I would have felt a little more comfortable had there been a playing field to walk around, but since there wasn't, I decided on the next best thing. I'd walk around the Capitol. Maybe that would serve. I'd made that walk many times in the past—in the early mornings in my first incarnation at the *Journal* after we'd put the paper to bed, and I was making my usual circuit of the sleeping city before heading home for bed. I'd made it with Allie in the moonlight. I couldn't remember having made it in daylight.

My usual route was out the carrier's door of the *Journal* onto Workhouse Alley to Main, turn right and follow Main all the up way up through the silent and deserted streets to the New Bridge, cross the river there, then up Capitol Avenue, broad and majestic in the morning dark with the Capitol Building basking in spotlights at its top, stay left on the walkway that circles the Capitol, pass the Mansion sitting off to the side through sculpted gardens and then the Floral Clock, then up the stone stairs to stand leaning on the marble balustrade and gaze down Capitol Avenue all the way to the river and the town beyond, thinking nothing in particular, just letting the feel of it please me.

"You better a get a move on, Mr. Clark. Want me to drive you? It'll be hard to find a place to park up there."

Mildred was at my office door holding my suit coat. No blazer today. No button down. Command presence was called for. Navy Blue suit. White Brooks Brothers straight point collar shirt with French cuffs. Red power tie. Gold cuff links with a subtle UK emblem. Black spit-polished Church Iconic Westbury's with the silver buckle. I considered pinning my Silver Star ribbon on my lapel, but backed off that as too showy. He probably wouldn't know what it was, anyway.

I thanked her for the jacket, shrugged it on and told her I thought I'd walk it. She seemed a little dubious about that but didn't argue.

"OK then. Are you going to walk back? Want me to pick you up?"

"May not be necessary. I may be brought back on my shield."

She frowned and looked puzzled.

"A joke. In ancient times, the mothers of Sparta told their sons when they left for battle to come back with their shields or on them. Win or die."

She frowned again. "I wish you wouldn't joke, Mr. Clark. I worry."

"I'm sorry, Mildred. It's just my way of shrugging off tension. I promise I'll come back with my shield."

The Capitol City has two capitols—the old and the new. The Old Capitol, vintage eighteen thirty, sits on a tree shaded, four-acre tract that was, at the time it was built, the town square in what was the middle of town. I suppose it's still in the middle of town though town had changed and spread. Most of the stores and businesses that were downtown have dispersed to the malls that have grown east and west of town along the roads leading to Lexington and Louisville. Fort Hill, with its quarried cliffs, is to the Old Capitol's rear—the river a short walk west down Broadway—and to the east, the rise of East Main Hill.

Louisville and Lexington fought bitterly to get the Capitol, but they didn't have the river. The Kentucky River transects the state, running south to north from the timber and coal-rich mountains of the Cumberland Plateau through the fertile bottomlands of the Bluegrass, to the northern border of the state where it joins the Ohio. The river was the road to riches in those days—the cheapest, safest way to get the state's rich mineral resources and agricultural crops to the young nation's markets, and for the products of the rest of the world to make their way to Kentucky buyers. Though the river meanders some two-hundred-sixty miles through the heart of the state, Frankfort is the only town on its banks.

I favor the Old Capitol. It has more drama and romance than its successor across the river. Henry Clay orated there. Confederate cavalry occupied it briefly during the Civil War. The only Kentucky governor ever to be assassinated was shot and bled on its sidewalk. On spring nights with moonlight filtering through the leaves, it looks like the Greek Temple its architect designed it to resemble.

The New Capitol, new being a relative term since it was built in 1930, seen looking up the broad avenue that leads from the river to its marble steps, is grand—in my view more stately and imposing then even the nation's Capitol, which it resembles. It rose when the old Capitol burned, the third to burn at that site downtown. Everything was moved south across the river to the new site on the hill, and the business of the people transacted there from that time forward.

In any event, two capitols, one Capitol City—me on my way on foot to the newest.

CHAPTER THIRTY SEVEN

Paul Isham was already in the Governor's anteroom when I arrived. He looked every bit the Bluegrass patrician—tall, silver haired, aristocratic face and bearing. If there was any incipient class awareness in our good Governor's psyche, Paul's bearing would spark it. I wondered if that would be an advantage.

The Governor's office was on the first floor of the Capitol building, just off the rotunda where statues of Kentucky native sons Abraham Lincoln and Jefferson Davis stand and Henry Clay and the pioneering surgeon Ephraim McDowell. The doors to the anteroom were open and tourists where strolling through the rotunda and moving up and down the marble stairways to view the Senate and House Chambers on the second level.

Three others were in the anteroom—two men in business suits at a table in the corner checking through a sheaf of papers and a young woman of uncommonly shapely build holding a legal size envelope. She was staring fixedly across the room at the Governor's secretary who was ignoring us all.

Paul and I took seats around a small bench beneath a photomural of colts in a Bluegrass pasture. Paul had a thin, black leather briefcase that looked as if could contain only the most important papers. I didn't own a briefcase. All I had was the morning's edition of the *Journal* with the Artie Skinner front page folded carefully inside.

Almost whispering, Paul leaned across to me. "You're determined to go through with this?"

I merely nodded. He shook his head in resignation and sat back.

"What's in the case," I asked, motioning to his brief case.

"A knife to slit my wrists with," he said scowling.

We had nothing more to say, so we sat silently waiting to be called into the presence.

At ten minutes before the hour, a small man in a black suit came hurrying in. He went immediately to the secretary's desk, said something to her, turned and nodded curtly to Paul, then opened the door to the Governor's office and went in.

"Richard Rosen" Paul said, "the Governor's Chief of Staff."

Rosen was a partner in an Ashland law firm specializing in coal and natural gas issues. He was one of the businessmen Governor Adair was surrounding himself with to run the machinery of government.

As Rosen went in, the young woman with the envelope and the noteworthy build stood up and walked rapidly to the secretary's desk. Fuming, she pointed to her watch and tossed her head angrily. The secretary looked at her for a moment, smiled sweetly, and turned back to her work.

Promptly at three o'clock, the Governor's office door swung open and out he himself came, all warmth and smiles and energy. He came directly to me, so rapidly I barely had time to get to my feet before he was reaching out for my hand and saying, "I've really been looking forward to meeting you, Mr. Clark. It's a pleasure, a real pleasure. I'm an admirer. I've been reading your stories in *The Atlantic* for years. Great stuff. Powerfully written. Yes, it's a pleasure to make your acquaintance." He turned to Paul, "And you, Mr. Isham, yes, a pleasure. Well, let's see what I can do for you," he said, wheeling and ushering us both before him into his office while the secretary stood at attention, and the lady with the body stared.

Isaac Adair, the fifty-fifth governor of the Grand and Glorious Commonwealth of Kentucky, was as good as advertised. The news stories that described him as charismatic and forceful got it exactly right. He came on like a tidal wave. Unless you had hold of something, you were going for a ride.

He steered us to a big leather couch in a small sitting area forward of his desk and eased down in a wingback facing us. Rosen, the Chief of Staff, appeared and took a chair by the Governor's desk, not in the circle of conversation, but appended to it.

"Can we get you something? Coffee? A sip of bourbon? I'm sure we could find some, couldn't we," he said turning to Rosen.

"Thank you, no, Governor," Paul Isham responded. "We don't want to take too much of your time. We appreciate you seeing us on such short notice."

The Governor waved his hand graciously, "Happy to do it, Mr. Isham. Happy to do it. Now what's on your mind?"

As opposed as he was to what I planned, Paul nevertheless played his role. He explained that I was the new head of Elkhorn Enterprises; that the businesses and the newspaper had played an important role in the life of the city and the state and that we hoped to continue to do so and that Mr. Clark wanted pay his respects and then discuss a matter of mutual interest.

I wondered what they expected, he and Rosen. An apology probably. For the Artie story. Supplicants before the throne doing damage control.

Ego.

Feed the man's ego.

I was duly respectful and complimentary. Adair's feat in dashing in and snatching the governor's chair to everyone's surprise, truly impressed me. So did his record as an entrepreneur. And so did he. He was friendly and engaging. A certain glint in his eye, though, made me think he might be the kind who checks and raises. When I'd finished my little song and dance of expected veneration, I stood.

We'd been sitting casually. Now I rose—a bit of gamesmanship handed me by the head of a retiring member of the British Parliament "My boy, if you wish to take command, stand when you speak. Speaking while seated is only conversation. Standing to speak is delivering the revealed word."

The Governor seemed surprised. Rosen started to rise as well, assuming, I think, that I was standing to leave. Paul stayed seated. He knew what was coming.

"Governor," I said, "there is a matter of some delicacy I need to discuss privately with you. I wonder if we might excuse Mr. Isham and Mr. Rosen so that we can talk in confidence."

The Governor frowned at me, looked to Rosen, perplexed, then back to me.

"Well, let me think. I don't believe anyone's chasing after me with a paternity suit. That good looking young lady outside is after something else. I haven't embezzled anybody. No outstanding speeding tickets. All my gambling debts are current." There was no anger in his voice, more a note of curiosity, even amusement.

"What in the world could you have, Mr. Clark, that is so confidential it can't be discussed in Mr. Rosen's presence? He's my Chief of Staff. I trust him completely. No," he said pleasantly and smiling. "He stays. Now sit down and unburden yourself."

The conversation didn't last long. Rosen pulled his chair over beside the Governor's. I continued to stand.

I told them what we had. As I talked, the Governor's look of curiosity eroded into concern. Rosen fumed and twisted in his chair.

I unfolded the Skinner front page and spread it out on the table before the Governor. He leaned in to read it. Rosen crowded in over his shoulder. The sense of shock in the Governor was palpable. Rosen looked up at me with so much anger I almost blanched.

"We're prepared to run this tomorrow, Governor," I said, "unless"

"You're threatening me!"

"No, Governor, I'm bargaining."

He swung around to Rosen. He pointed to the headline:

Administration Linked To Skinner Suicide

A Scapegoat For Planned Attack On Merit System

"Richie, how much of this is true?"

I didn't give Rosen a chance to answer.

"Governor, I believe that you knew about none of this. I think you told your staff what you wanted to achieve and left it up to them to get it done. You're a CEO. You operate like a CEO. You set goals and leave it up to your lieutenants to make it happen. You don't look over their shoulder. You rely on them. I think that's what happened here."

It was a reasonable enough explanation. I don't think he wanted to know how his people got done the things he wanted done. I think he could be cheerfully ruthless but would not knowingly be ruthlessly lethal.

Somewhere in Will Owens' or Dulin Monroe's playbooks is a rule about not backing people up against a wall unless you have to. Leave them room to make the decision you want them to make without losing face if you can. And that, as The O'Donnell advised, is what I was trying to do with Governor Isaac Adair.

"Governor," Rosen tried to break in.

The Governor waved him silent.

"You play poker," he said, looking up from the front page spread out before him.

"Sometimes."

He studied me very carefully, him sitting looking up at me standing, eyes locked on mine.

"You don't look like a man who bluffs," he said finally.

"He's blackmailing you, Governor," Rosen almost shouted in his outrage.

"Quiet," the Governor said. Then to me, "What do you want?"

Men who know when to fold deserve respect. It takes a steely discipline to accept reality. Even more discipline to control your ego while the winner rakes in the pot.

If you're the winner, you want to be very careful at this point. You don't want to be boastful, or overbearing, or condescending.

So, as civilly as I could manage, for my anger at the way Artie Skinner had been pushed to his death still seethed, I told the Governor what I wanted.

I wanted Artie Skinner's good name restored.

I wanted the Highway Commissioner to issue a statement saying that the dismissal of Artie Skinner was based on flawed information and was being reversed and that Artie would be re-instated, posthumously, to the position he'd held. I wanted the statement to say that Artie Skinner was an exemplary public servant, and the state apologies for the disservice done him."

Rosen exploded. "We're going to do no such thing. We're making no apologies. The Highway Commissioner is not going to eat crow in public!"

"Shut up, Richie," the Governor said, never taking his eyes off me. "Why are you making such an issue of this?"

"Artie Skinner was a friend of mine," I said. "What was done to him was outrageous."

"Do you go to these lengths for all your friends?"

"For the ones who get killed, I do."

He let that sit for moment while our eyes locked.

"Is that all of it?"

"No sir. I want the maneuvering to get rid of the Merit System to stop."

"Who the hell do you think you are?" Rosen snarled.

"And I want assurance that the lowest fully qualified bidder will, as the law requires, be awarded the State printing contract when the current contract expires. No games played. No cronies favored."

The Governor waited to be sure there was nothing more. We regarded each other in a tense silence for not as long as it seemed at the time, but it seemed very long indeed.

Had I overplayed my hand? Had I made an enemy of the most powerful man in the state, and was I going to wind up with nothing to show for it?

He sat back, took a deep breath and exhaled slowly, then turned to say over his shoulder to Rosen. "Go sit down, Richie." Then to me, "You, too, Mr. Clark. You bother me towering over me like that."

He waited while we rearranged ourselves, then he stood so that he did the towering, walked slowly across the room to his desk, leaned back on the edge of it, and folded his arms across his chest.

"Richie, I'm very disturbed about what Mr. Clark has told me. No," he said holding up his hand as Rosen started to respond, "you can explain later."

"I knew nothing of this, Mr. Clark," he said, turning his attention to me. "I intend to run this State like a business. I think this Merit System you're so interested in makes that very difficult. I told Richie, and others, that I want to see if we can't improve on it. I asked them to look into it. I regret this particular result. The statement you want will be issued tomorrow. Richie, see to it," he said.

"As for the State printing contract, you have my word that the bidding process will be exactly to the letter of the law. If your company is lowest qualified bidder, you'll get the contract. If you're not, you won't."

"Now, my "maneuvering" as you call it.

"You want my 'maneuvering' to stop? That was a request wasn't it, not a demand. Yes, I'm sure it was a request," he said with a sardonic smile. "I've been governor for almost six months now. I'm just starting, Mr. Clark. The system we use now to hire and fire is paralyzing. I need more flexibility, a better system, one that allows us to get the people we think we need, put them in jobs we think they fit, and if they fail to perform, fire them and replace them right away—without all this bureaucratic nonsense that slows things down and makes holding people accountable almost impossible. So, no. I'm not going to stop. I'm going to dismantle it if I can. If we have to fight about that, so be it.

"You're getting two out of three. Don't be greedy, Mr. Clark. Take your winnings and walk away."

It was a strange win.

When we gathered at Julie's that night for the post mortem, the mood was subdued. Of course we felt good. We'd won. Not a clean sweep, but we'd won. Artie Skinner would be vindicated, his name cleared, his reputation restored. Those who read between the lines would also recognize that the dirty little plot to get political control of the State's hiring and firing had been exposed and, for the moment, frustrated.

We all felt that strange mix of exhilaration and relief that comes with victory in a game with high stakes and an uncertain outcome. Tracy Jordan particularly. She was the one who had the most emotional investment in Artie, who had felt his hurt most directly. She glowed.

I called the news to The O'Donnell. He was still in his office. "Hot diggity-damn, Theo," he cheered, "You pulled it off."

"You had doubts," I laughed.

"Never. The good guys always win. Except when they don't. Way to go." Then, more soberly, "But watch your back now, buddy."

Paul was there. And Dulin. And Lew Arbogast. We were all proud of the job Lew and his people had done in building the case, and we were impressed, relieved is the better word, to have it confirmed that the *Journal* had the muscle to make a governor back down.

Still, we weren't sure of what we'd done. Without any question, a serious enemy had been made of Richard Rosen, the Governor's Chief of Staff, and of the State Highway Commissioner, who had to issue the crow-eating statement. Both were powerful men with big egos. And the Governor? Had I made an enemy there? I'd played in many hard games and come off the field bruised and bloody, but feeling no ill will to my opponent, in fact often feeling a sort of kinship, or at least an honest respect. Would that be the case with Isaac Adair? Or was he a win at all costs and damn the competition type? I wondered how much influence Rosen had on him. The Governor promised me a level playing field for the printing contract. Would Rosen try to tilt it?

Paul Isham still thought it was a mistake to confront the Governor and still saw nothing good coming from it. But he couldn't hide his pride that we'd done it.

Dulin shared some of Paul's concern, but he'd worry about that tomorrow. "Tonight," he said, "tonight we drink toasts and marvel at how good we are."

I was as exhausted as I'd ever been. The tension of preparing for my little song and dance, the stress of the probable consequences, the actual performance in the Governor's chambers with adrenalin pumping so furiously I could feel it coursing—all that drained me.

After I left the Governor's office, the well-stacked young lady glared at me as I walked out. I made my way back down the broad avenue to the New Bridge. I stopped for a moment to lean on the rail and look down. The river was running clear. A powerboat pulling a skier cut a wake upriver. The sky above the cliff under Daniel Boone's grave was cloudless and of that deep blue it gets on summer afternoons. Some of the tension began to drain away then. I managed to hold it at bay all the way to that last toast at Julie's. "To Artie," we drank, "May the good guys always win."

No phantoms came that night.

Tracy Jordan did.

I slept most of Friday. By late afternoon, I was up and dressed and in the office.

The killer front page, the Artie page, was spread out before me on my desk. I was sorry we hadn't run it. But I got what I wanted. Almost what I wanted? No. I got what I wanted. The printing contract was a secondary issue to me.

The Highway Commissioner's statement had been issued about five, the close of the business day at State. The timing of the release and the fact that no one was around to answer questions made it obvious that they hoped to slip it through with as a little attention as possible. But that wouldn't happen. There was still too much interest in Artie Skinner's death, too many questions about why he jumped.

Lew Arbogast would play his story on Page One in the coming morning's edition of the *Journal*. The headline would read something like:

State Apologizes: Skinner Reinstated Posthumously

A big photo of Artie would accompany it, along with a sensitive profile of Artie written by Lew's feature editor, and Dulin's piece about the meaning of the suicide note—the only piece we'd lift from the killer front page, but too good to let disappear. The overall impact would be dramatic and powerful, not as powerful as the material we weren't running, but powerful enough.

I smoothed out the killer front page on my desk and very carefully folded it and slipped it into a large manila envelope. The envelope would be the first addition to the safe deposit box I was going to open at Farmers Bank in the morning.

Rest in peace Artie Skinner.

CHAPTER THIRTY EIGHT

Williamsburg is a town of about five thousand lying in a meander of the Cumberland River in the mountains of southeast Kentucky, just north of the Tennessee border—the County Seat of Whitley County and the home of Cumberland College. In its day, Williamsburg was said to have more millionaires per mile than any other place in America. Coal mining and lumbering were the big things then. But the millionaires' mantle has passed to other places.

I left before daylight, sliding through the dawn down past Lexington and Berea and out of the Bluegrass and up into the Cumberland foothills.

I hoped to be at Marne's grave while the morning was still fresh.

She was buried in the cemetery of a small church a few miles outside town. The road to it was gravel and one-lane, and the fields all around were in corn.

Church was starting as I got there; the late arrivals hurrying to a door at the side of the building.

I parked on the grass and sat back for a moment, unwinding from the long drive and taking in the layout of the place. There was a gravel lot in front that was almost full—Fords and Chevys mostly, several Buicks, some well used pick-ups, one late model Jeep Wagoneer. Solid family transportation. The few people still trailing in were in their Sunday best—the men in suits and ties, the women in summer finery. The church sat in a grove of elms. It was quiet and peaceful there.

Off to the side was the cemetery. It was small, and from the look of the weathered gravestones, very old. The markers were in irregular rows, most standing, some leaning; a few with writing on them that wasn't readable any longer, were beginning to sink. The graves were well tended, the grass mowed. There were flowers at many of the headstones.

I wandered up and down the rows. A bobwhite's call floated up from the distance. The scent of plowed earth and wild roses was in the air.

Marne's grave was on a small rise near the back where you could see the sycamores by the creek.

I wasn't sure how to say an Ave.

The words that came to me were from the Rubyiat:

"For some we loved,

The loveliest and the best..."

So I said them, kneeling in the morning sun. I'd brought a long-stemmed white rose with me. Marne favored white roses. I laid it on her grave, and as I'd done at Rhea's grave, put my fingers to my lips and touched the kiss to her tombstone.

Across the way the closing hymn was being sung. The singing filled the morning like the sunlight.

I don't go to church anymore. Once I did. Every Sunday—with my mother. Then she died. And I stopped.

Sometimes now on Sundays, alone in strange cities with a certain mood on me, I go. I find a church where there is singing. The singing draws me. Something in the singing makes me feel at home and safe.

The church door was open, and the windows, too, letting the breeze flow in and the music flow out. No one noticed as I slipped in. I took a seat at the back by an open window. The benediction would be next. I could use a benediction.

One-thirty was my appointed time.

Mr. Niccan Dye, he of the manuscript and the undeclared agenda—Niccan Dye would be waiting. Or I assumed he would. It was his turf; he'd picked the spot and the time.

He'd want to be on site first, in position and watching the mark approach. Be careful, Theo. Be relaxed. Be courteous. Show no sign of apprehension or concern. Play to his ego, but make it clear you can cut him off at the knees if you choose.

I'm good at giving good advice to myself. Not so good at following it.

I assumed I'd know him when I saw him. We'd not met. I'd seen no picture of him. But you can always tell who's looking for you. The one glancing around expectantly, uncertainly—that'll be the one. Though I didn't think I'd have to scout up Niccan Dye. I was sure he'd seen a photo of me in the coverage on my ascension to the Dannan throne. He'd recognize me.

The singing ended, and I scolded myself for letting my thoughts wander. The preacher had finished and was asking us to rise and stand for the blessing. I did as the others did, not expecting anything to come of it, but hopeful.

A large man with friendly smile and work-hardened hands was at the door as I left. He extended his hand to take mine, recognizing me as a stranger, and telling me how glad they all were that I had come to worship with them.

"Visiting?" he asked.

"No, just passing through," I said.

"You come back," he said. "You're welcome here."

I was surprised to feel that he meant it. His friendliness took a bit of the edge off the combativeness that had been building in me. Maybe a good thing. I'd have a more "Christian" attitude for the afternoon.

I thanked him, walked back through the cemetery past Marne's grave to the creek and passed the time until I had to leave for town, sitting on the trunk of a big sycamore, skipping stones off the water and stringing together memories of the times with Marne and Michael, and the acts that led to the writing of the manuscript.

Nicholas Dye was waiting outside the library, glancing up and down the long, straight city street on which the library building sat, one of the several that ran through the campus. A building I took to be a dorm was on the corner.

The campus was on a hill above town, spacious and welcoming. There was nothing pretentious about it, but it was neat and bright and felt comfortable, comfortably functional. Exactly what the Baptists of the eastern mountains intended when they joined together in the late eighteen hundreds to build a place to educate their children— a place they could afford and sustain. This was it. Two governors, five generals, preachers, teachers, captains of industry, solid citizens of note and achievement, and Jean Ritchie, the folk singer, had so far issued forth.

And Niccan Dye.

I'm sure he recognized me from the distance. And I marked him immediately. So we had each other in our mutual sights as I made the long walk down toward him.

Having in my mind, as I did, the image of a man looking to bleed me of money and reputation, a blackmailer of evil intent, I expected someone slithery.

I should have known he wouldn't be. Marne Young would never have taken such a protégé. And no Melungeon I'd ever met was slithery.

Niccan Dye would be Melungeon. Of course he would be. Or have Melungeon blood. Given Marne's field of specialization and interest and her position as Director of Appalachian Studies at the College, her graduate assistant would be, if she could manage it, a Melungeon. And given Niccan Dye's position as founder and head of the student group Melungeon Proud, he'd have Melungeon blood.

The Melungeons I met through Marne with Michael as we were trying to unravel the mystery of Michael's father's death, were tall and well formed and carried themselves with simple dignity. They were strong, even the older men, fast, and disconcertingly watchful—like a cougar on a stand. The women were very handsome.

They were already there in the remote regions of the Appalachians when the first white settlers arrived. Small groups of them. People where people weren't supposed to be.

They dressed like the English. They spoke English with a rich Elizabethan accent. Yet they weren't English. They weren't even European. Their color of skin was like that of someone deeply tanned by the sun, or tending to dark copper like a Cherokee, or burnished olive like a Turk or Egyptian. But they were none of these either. They, themselves, didn't know their origin.

They kept to themselves. They were clannish and didn't intermingle. Because they were strange and mysterious, stories grew up around them—about healing by the laying on of hands, about the ability to see in the dark and find game when no one else could—about the casting of spells and foreseeing the future. About magic. Which in time led to fear, then to bigotry and discrimination.

Niccan Dye watched me through hooded eyes as I approached. He was small in build, perhaps an inch or so shorter than me, but not fragile. He looked like what we called a "pony back" in the days when I played football—light, muscularly compact boys who could move like lightening and prance around tacklers like they weren't there. He had on a blazer and rep tie and khakis. Whether he was dressed for church, or to impress me, or because he had a campus image to maintain, I had no idea. He had curly hair, black, and dark brown eyes.

He neither smiled nor offered me his hand. He was tense and on guard—like a man eyeing a snake, not taking any chances.

"Mr. Clark," he said.

I nodded.

"In olden days, men shook hands to make sure one or the other wasn't carrying a club," I told him, extending my hand. Reflexively, he took it. I smiled. He let go rapidly, embarrassed. "Come inside," he said and turned and led me through the door into the library, past the librarian's desk to the far side of the room to a table that sat beneath a window. Tall book shelves on either side formed a little cul de sac of privacy there. He motioned me to a chair in the heart of it and, without saying a word, placed a large manila envelope on the surface before me. He laid it down in front of me almost tentatively, as if he was at once both uneasy and uncertain of what he was doing.

I glanced at it, moved it aside as if it were of no immediate interest, folded my hands in front of me on the table and looked back up at him. He was still standing, watching me warily.

"Sit down, Mr. Dye." I tried to make it sound not unfriendly.

"The manuscript is in that envelope," he said pointing.

I nodded. "Right now I want to know about Professor Marne Young. Sit down. Tell me about the snake."

There were only the two of us in all that big room—cocooned in the quiet of a summer Sunday afternoon with books all around and dust motes floating in the sunlight from the window.

I could see his surprise and confusion in the way he stepped back and the way his chin rose. He hesitated, then finally pulled out the chair across from me and sat down.

CHAPTER **THIRTY NINE**

They were dancing.

They stomped and sang and shuffled in circles. They swayed and moaned and fell to the floor.

The beat of the music was like the pulse of the blood. They twirled and clapped to it. The whole room was in motion. It was a strange dance, primitive and pounding.

The snakes were in wooden boxes on a long table in front of the alter, twisting and hissing, agitated by the sound and the movement, rattles buzzing, forked tongues testing the wire mess tops that held them in.

Niccan and Marne stood back against a wall, transfixed.

There was talk that the sects were dying out, that the fundamentalists were dwindling as education made stronger inroads into the back-country and that the snake-handling churches would disappear.

Professor Marne Young knew better. The word of God thundered through these mountains. It was to be taken literally. It was to be obeyed. And the word was *"And these signs shall follow them that believe. In my name they shall cast out devils; they shall speak with new tongues. They shall take up serpents; and if they drink any deadly thing it shall not hurt them; they shall lay hands on the sick and they shall recover."* It was right there in the Gospel of Mark

No, the churches wouldn't disappear because the people who believe wouldn't disappear. Throw all the logic and rationalization that can be mustered at them and it will make no difference. The Holy Spirit will lift them up. The Son will lead them home. Believe and obey and you will be saved. They know this in their hearts. No, they wouldn't disappear.

Marne and Niccan had been late. They'd taken the wrong fork on the gravel road that climbed through a stand of fire-blackened pines and by time the found the church on the ridge the afternoon was half gone. There had been the singing and the preaching and the testifying and the laying on of hands and now the service was moving to its climax.

There were perhaps fifty people, almost as many women as men. The women, young and old like, were all plainly and modestly dressed. The men wore long sleeved shirts but no ties.

Marne and Niccan tried to be inconspicuous. Outsiders weren't welcome. The faithful were clannish and private and proud. They had no wish to put on a show for the curious or for thrill seekers. They were deadly serious about their religion; so deadly serious that they risked death each time they walked in to a service. And what they were doing was illegal. The handling of deadly poisonous snakes was illegal.

That Marne and Niccan were permitted in was due to Niccan's aunt and in partial deference to Niccan's standing as a son of the mountains. He was no outsider. His father was known, a full-blooded Melungeon born and raised in sight of Black Mountain.

Niccan's aunt, his mother's sister, was a Pentecostal. She was a friend to the people of The Church Of God With Signs Following. She had been a friend to George Hensley.

Hensley started it all.

He was a repentant sinner, a bootlegger, trying to get right with God. One day, on a mountainside in east Tennessee, he was sitting in the shade reading his bible and praying. He'd just finished the passage in the Mark, the "they shall take up serpents," passage. When he looked up from the page a large timber rattler was coiled in front of him ready to strike. Hensley knew it was a sign. Knew he was being tested. Without hesitation he reached out, grasped the serpent as the Bible commanded and then and there, so he testified, the Holy Spirit infused him and sent him out to spread the word to the good people of the Cumberlands.

Over the ridges and up the hollows of the mountains that make the Kentucky-Tennessee border he went, preaching salvation and rapture to those who proved their faith by obeying the word as Mark had proclaimed it. Take up the serpents. Drink the poisons. The ecstasy of the Holy Spirit will come upon you. You will speak in tongues and heal the sick by the laying on of hands. You will be saved and pass rejoicing through the gates of Heaven.

The promise blew like wildfire through the mountains in those early years of the nineteen hundreds.

Of course they had to be circumspect. There were so many disbelievers, so many who were envious of the power the Holy Spirit gave them.

And of course the practice was seen by many as delusional or even, among the conventional churches, heretical.

And of course a few people died – people whose faith wasn't strong enough or people whose faith was strong enough but whose time had simply come. Even George Hensley himself. He died of a rattler bite later down in Florida where he was conducting a service.

And of course the authorities tried to ban it.

So it is understandable they wouldn't let outsiders in unless someone trusted vouched for them.

Aunt Jose did.

Niccan was a favorite of hers.

The church was an old one-room schoolhouse that had had been fitted out with benches arranged in rows, though no one was sitting.

Along the flanking walls the windows were open to let in the breeze and the afternoon light.

As the music built and that strange shuffling dance intensified a wave of excitement ran through the whole room, infusing everyone, even them.

Suddenly a man emerged out of the crowd. Three women danced behind him, encouraging. A younger woman, face flushed, joined in. A few people feel to their knees, lifting their arms and shouting.

The snakes, timber rattlers and cottonmouths, were in a frenzy on the table in front of the altar, pounding against the wire mesh tops that held them in.

The man danced closer, then quickly reached into the nearest box and grabbed a serpent. Just as rapidly, he reached with his other hand and withdrew another. He thrust them aloft.

The crowd clapped. "Praise the Lord" and "Alleluia Amen," rang out.

The beat of the music grew faster. The man began fondling the snakes, wrapping them around his arms and neck, weaving through the crowd and shouting, "Witness what faith can do!"

He raised a fist with a hissing rattler into the air in punctuation and as he waved it about it twisted free. Marne was alongside. It landed on her shoulder, slithered down and raced for the open door. People scattered frantically.

Niccan, like everyone else, tried to get out of the way. When he recovered, Marne was on the floor at the base of the window. There were fang marks on her neck. Her eyes were wide, her breathing shallow.

She died in less than twenty minutes.

Rattlers don't usually kill that fast. Usually there's time to try first-aid or get to a doctor, not much, but some. Marne didn't have the chance. This was a big rattler, a Timber rattler with full poison sacks and mad as hell. Marne got it all. Compounding the attack was her own body chemistry. A chemical in the rattler's venom triggered anaphylactic shock. Anaphylactic shock kills almost instantly.

Niccan had tears in his eyes when he finished the story. He coughed, rubbed his eyes to clear them, then took a deep breath and turned to the window, looking away from me as he spoke. "She was my mentor. She shepherded me through my studies. She backed me when I wanted to form the Melungeon students group on campus. There aren't many of us. The administration was against it. They didn't want attention drawn to our differences. Professor Young understood. She understood how important it is that we take pride in who we are. She's the one who was helping me get accepted at Georgia for my doctorate."

He paused, then turned back to me." You went to her grave today?"

"This morning. It's a beautiful setting."

"I picked it," Niccan said. "You were friends, close friends?"

"You read the manuscript," I said, pointing to the still unopened envelope in front of me.

He nodded.

"Then you know."

"What was she like as a young woman?"

"Smart and sweet," I said, unhesitatingly.

"I imagined," he nodded. "And Jesse Bristow?"

"I suspect that's in the manuscript, too."

"You said you half-way liked the man."

"Did I? What else did I say?"

"You said you killed him. Shot him in the forehead with a twenty-two."

"Did I?

"He's a hero to us, to Melungeons, and to most of the people here in the mountains."

"I know. I understand there is even a statue of him in the Courthouse square in Harlan."

"You killed him. You say so in the manuscript."

"That manuscript is over ten years old. I don't remember what's in it. How do you know it's not intended to be a piece of fiction?"

"It doesn't read like fiction."

"I'm a good writer."

'It isn't fiction. It's story. A true story. You say so at the end."

"A fiction technique."

"You didn't write fiction then. You don't write fiction now. I've read your biography. I've read your stuff."

"Maybe I was seeing if I could."

"It's not fiction. It's a true story. You didn't intend it to be published until after your death. But you intended it to be found and published. You even say so in the story."

"Another fiction technique to give the piece believability. Why, for god's sake Mr. Dye, if I had actually committed a murder, if I had actually killed one of the best known and most powerful men in the state, why, if I'd done that, would I want it known at any time? Why would I put it all down on paper? That makes no sense." I said all this smiling, as if I was amused that he'd drawn such a wrong conclusion to so obvious a situation.

"I can't explain that. Mr. Clark. But you did."

"This manuscript," I said pointing to the still unopened envelope "is my property. I was no longer trying to sound amused or companionable. I wanted anger in my voice. "You have no right to it. You've read it, and you think you know something, but you have no verification or proof of any kind."

Leaning toward him, frowning, making sure I had his eyes, I whispered, "What are you up to?"

In a way Niccan reminded me of Jesse. Not that the two were alike, or at least I didn't think Niccan Dye had the same ego or arrogance that Jesse Bristow had. It was that he had an honesty and an openness about him that reminded me of Jesse. I had been sincere when I said there was much to like about Jesse Bristow. He could be kind and surprisingly generous. He looked out for his own. His word was good. I suspected Niccan Dye had many of these qualities. He didn't match at all the picture in my mind of an extortionist. And increasingly less so as I watched his reaction to my challenge. It had rocked and confused him. He expected, I think, that I would be immediately defensive. My claim that he was holding property that belonged to me, and he had no right to it, surprised him. His body language and tone of voice from the start had been almost apologetic. I had the impression he was reluctant to do this and was forcing himself to confront me. Or someone or something was prompting him.

He glanced nervously away. A lone student, a girl, was at the librarian's desk. The two of them were talking quietly. The afternoon was still spilling light through the open window and dust motes were still in the air as Niccan Dye gathered himself.

"Read it, Mr. Clark," he said, pointing to the envelope. He pushed back from the table. "Take it with you. Refresh your memory. Then we'll talk. I made a copy. So if you think of destroying the evidence, don't." He stood, looking down at me. "You killed Jesse Bristow, and you thought you'd gotten away with it." He turned and walked away and said over his shoulder as he did, "You've got a week."

"A week to do what?"

"Make an offer."

He nodded to the librarian as he left, not looking back at me. She glanced toward me. Curious. A stranger. What was he doing in her library on a sleepy Sunday afternoon in June? With Niccan Dye?

I gathered up the envelope and stood to leave as well. The envelope was heavy. How many pages, I wondered: how many words did it take me to tell that story? It felt like a full manuscript, like a book. I was in no hurry to re-read it. It would take me back to a time I didn't want to live through again.

An offer.

I said my thanks to the librarian and made my way to my car.

CHAPTER **FORTY**

Almost midnight.

In the armchair by the window that looks out on Wapping Street.

A cup of black coffee on the reading table beside me and a snifter of Hennessy in my hand.

I'd put it off as long as I could.

I opened the clasp on the envelope and pulled out the manuscript.

There was no title page.

The slug in the upper left hand corner of the first page, blackface, eight point type, read: *Dannans/Bristow. Page 1*

The line below it: *TOC*, my initials.

The line below that the date: *June 25, 1970.*

The head, in twelve point Times New Roman, all caps, centered atop the copy, read:

The True Story of the Dannans and Jesse Bristow

I was reluctant to open it. Michael would be in there. And Allie. And Rhae. All the people involved with that time would be there. Jesse Bristow and the Melungeons. All of them.

I sat the manuscript back down and walked to the window. A light rain was falling. It had put a glisten on Wapping Street and was blurring the streetlight on the corner. I was tempted to grab my Burberry and head out into the night, to make that long walk through the empty streets up to the Capitol with the rain falling and nobody out.

I had started the writing on a night like this. At the *Journal*. At my desk in the newsroom at the *Journal*. Everyone had gone except me. In my mood that night, I couldn't face the prospect of a lonely apartment and the challenge of trying to find sleep while all the images I was trying to escape raced through my mind.

I began the story that night. I worked on it in spurts through the rest of that summer and almost until the day I left, intending never to return. When I finished it, I assembled all the pages, put them in an envelope and gave it to Marne for safekeeping.

Now it was back to me.

I got comfortable in the chair again, took a sip of the cognac, and hefted the manuscript. Exactly two hundred sixteen double-spaced, typewritten pages. I thumbed through them, looking for the condemning passage, the one that described the execution of Jesse Bristow.

Yes—the execution. That's what I meant it to be. An execution. Fully justified and efficiently delivered.

"Doing it was amazingly easy ..." the passage began.

I settled back, almost as interested in seeing if I had written it well as in what I had confessed to.

"I left the Journal that night by the alley door just after deadline but before the page forms were locked up and put on the press. No one noticed in the rush of getting that morning's edition ready. Even if anyone had, no one would have thought anything of it. My habit of rambling the streets was so established that notice would have been taken only if I hadn't ducked out into the night.

"I crossed the bridge and walked casually up Shelby Street, all but invisible in the heavy shadows. One car passed. When I reached the office where I knew Jesse Bristow to be, the office he kept above the party headquarters in sight of the Capitol, I climbed the outside stairs to the landing in front of the door. I was uncommonly calm.

"Jesse answered my knock and, when he saw who it was, opened it and let me in. He turned and led the way back into the office and took his seat behind the desk. He looked up at me, smiling.

"By then I had the pistol out. The shot took him in the center of the forehead. A small hole appeared. He frowned. A trickle of blood started down toward his right eye. He lifted his head as if to say something, the frown still on his face, then slumped forward.

"I stood there only a second, letting a feeling of relief wash over me. And for an instant, just a touch of regret. There was something about the man that I liked. But he had started the game and set the rules."

So that's how I'd told it.

It was accurate but it needed polishing. I didn't intend it to be published at the time. I intended it to be found with my things when they laid me down and to be the source for some later writer's telling. It was a draft, a first draft. If I had intended it as finished copy, I would have been more elegant in the phrasing, more careful with the descriptions, so I told myself to console my writerly ego.

Everything was there.

Jesse was working alone that night in the office he maintained above the Democratic Party headquarters, a block down Capitol Avenue from the Capitol Building. The primary election that would decide the Democratic gubernatorial candidate was just a week away. He expected to win easily now that Michael was out of the way, and with it, the governor's chair. The Democrats had a lock on the state, and whomever the Republican candidate turned out to be, the odds of their winning were almost zero.

The outside stairs were well shielded by trees, so there was little chance anyone would see me even if anyone was on the street at that hour in that neighborhood, which was unlikely. The night was chilly. Though we were in early May, spring hadn't come entirely. I had on my Burberry to ward it off and had the collar turned up high—for warmth and to make it more difficult to identify me if I was accidentally seen.

Jesse looked tired when he opened the door. He frowned at first. "What the hell are you doing here at this hour?" he asked, but being Jesse, opened it without thought and let me in. I followed him; he took his seat at his desk, and turned to me, curious.

One shot. Center forehead. The force of it rocked him back in his chair.

I was very careful to be sure I left no sign of my presence. I checked that there were no footprints and carefully wiped the doorknob clean as I left, and the door locked automatically behind me. All the downstairs doors and windows were already locked. The staff did that when they closed each evening.

When the police came, they found no sign of a struggle. No entry had been forced. A dead man in a locked house. No murder weapon. No witnesses. No apparent motive. No suspects. Perfect.

Leaving was as uneventful as getting there. All of South Frankfort seemed asleep. The only light came from the streetlights on the corners of each block. I stayed in the shadows the trees threw and not even a car passed to make me nervous. The little twenty-two went into the river as I re-crossed the bridge. My grandfather taught me to shoot with that little gun. I got good enough with it to hunt squirrels in the autumn in the big oaks along the creek at his place. It was the only handgun I ever owned. It meant a lot to me.

The presses were running when I slipped back into the *Journal* through the alley door that morning. No one had missed me. I had taken care of what had to be taken care of. I had done what I had to do.

CHAPTER FORTY ONE

At that time and through these intervening years, I'd never felt guilt about the killing of Jesse Bristow.

He was as responsible for Michael Dannan's death as if he had pulled the trigger himself. He had manipulated a young man who worshiped him into doing it for him. Was it murder if Jesse didn't actually pull the trigger? I thought so. I think so still.

And there was Benjamin Dannan.

Jesse Bristow let Michael's father bleed to death while he sat and watched.

Was that murder? To sit and do nothing while Benjamin Dannan bled to death in the snow? I thought so. I think so still.

Both Dannans, father and son, dead. And Jesse Bristow the agent.

I've never been sorry. I've felt no remorse. There would have been no justice had I not acted. Was there an edge of vengeance to the act? Yes. But my motive was never retribution. It was justice. I felt righteous.

Still at odd times all along—in dreams—in the sleepless hours before dawn when old regrets come crawling in—I'd hear whispers.

"You killed a man in cold blood. With malice aforethought. A man who was no threat to you, who had done you no harm. What gave you the right?"

Harsh. Accusing. The ghosts of my Baptist upbringing—the old thou-shalt-nots pecking at my psyche. I realized this. But it brought no comfort in the dark.

That night, that night after I returned from Williamsburg, that night after I'd put the manuscript down, the voices no longer whispered, they thundered so loud I thought I might not make it sanely to the dawn.

When daylight came, seeking solace, I did what I had not done before.

I took myself to a man of religion, a friend, a pastor, a man of my own generation whose ministry I admired and whose opinion I valued.

"Can a man who killed in cold blood be rid of his ghosts? Can he get absolution?" I asked.

"Is he sorry? Does he repent?"

"The man he killed, killed two others and went unpunished."

"Vengeance is mine, sayeth the Lord," said my friend.

"An eye for an eye, sayeth the Lord," said I.

"Judge not lest ye be judged," he countered,

"Let not the wicked go unpunished," I offered.

He shook his head sadly. "This friend of yours, he knew the rules. I have no pass to give him."

"There is a story," I said. "The night before the battle of Orleans, Joan of Arc assembled her commanders and asked them to kneel and pray. Her favorite, the knight Etienne La Hire, declined. 'Prayer's do not win battles, my lady,' he said. Joan insisted. La Hire knelt, and raising the hilt of his sword cross-like to the stars, this is the prayer he made:

"Fair Sir God,
Pray do by La Hire
as La Hire would do by you,
if you were La Hire,
and he were God."

My friend frowned. "He would challenge God?"

"He would ask for justice."

"Chancy."

I nodded. "It seems the only option."

He slowly began to smile. "Work on your story. The Lord moves in mysterious ways."

The week passed. I immersed myself in the businesses of Dannan Enterprises, trying to fill my head with enough details to crowd out worries about what Niccan Dye might be planning and to distract the phantoms.

The full moon of June came that Saturday night—the Strawberry Moon.

We were on the porch at Julie's, the moonlight so bright the trees cast shadows, and the river sparkled.

Tracy Jordan was beside me in the swing. Julie and Jim Colby were inside, opening the wine.

Tracy said, leaning close to me, "Did you get that Glennlivet?"

Remembering, I laughed and turned to her. "The lady who likes single malt scotch and lace on her panties. No Glennlivet. Glennfiddich," I said, teasing.

"Well, I suppose I could make do."

She ran a finger down my check, turning my head to hers.

"I'll be leaving soon." Not playfully now, "You'll miss me?"

I was surprised. Tracy Jordan not around. She'd grown on me.

"I thought you might stay. I thought Jim was offering you a position with his firm. I thought you liked it here."

"That means you'll miss me?"

We were both silent, searching for something in each other's eyes.

Julie broke the momentary spell, stepping out onto the porch with her tray and stopping when she saw our faces. "What's going on here?" she asked.

Tracy moved a bit less close to me. I sat up straighter.

"Tracy just told me she's leaving."

"Oh," Julie said. She looked around for Jim who was coming out with the wine.

"You've decided for certain, Tracy?" Julie said. "Jim's blandishments haven't swayed you?"

Tracy sighed, stood up then and walked over to lift a glass of wine off the tray Jim held.

She looked around at each of us in turn. "I loved being here. I loved the time I had with each of you. It's time now for me to get back to work"

Julie walked over and kissed her on the cheek. Jim did as well. I hesitated, then stood and added mine.

Later that night—almost midnight—there was a knock. I had the Glennfiddich open.

After, as we lay with moonlight on the pillow, she said, "Julie told me about Allie."

"What did she say?"

"That Allie was your first love."

Silence.

"That she put a spell on you."

Silence.

"Is she right?"

She rose up on her arm to look me in the face. She waited, watching.

"Not talking, huh? "She kissed me, "You could be worth staying for, Theo Clark. But not for sharing," then put her head on my chest. "Wake me before daylight."

CHAPTER FORTY TWO

I woke thinking about Niccan Dye.

Tracy Jordan was gone. The bed was still warm where she had lain, and her scent sweetened the air. It wasn't quite light yet. The room was in heavy shadows and chill. We'd left the window open for the breeze, but an early fog was rising from the river, and damp was on the pillow.

I struggled awake, trying to recover what I'd been dreaming. It wasn't about Tracy. It was about Niccan Dye. About waiting for a sound. About waiting for the sound of Niccan Dye dropping the other shoe. That's what was punching me. Waiting. Waiting while the other guy got ready to dismember me. That's what pulled me awake.

After Chosin, after the debriefings at the hospital in Tokyo, one of the Navy doctors told me I had a constitutional aversion to threat, that when faced with threat, I had to act, I had to eliminate the threat. It wasn't something voluntary. It was hardwired into my psyche—a primitive reaction, a predator's instinct, he said. "That will make you a fine battlefield commander, but unless you plan a career in the Marine Corps, get a grip on it."

So I lay there in the morning chill getting a grip on the adrenalin surge that woke me.

The week Niccan Dye had given me in which to make him an "offer" was up.

"Make an offer," he said. "You have a week."

Nothing good could come from that.

If I made an "offer," at the very least I tell him I'm willing to be manipulated. What would it get me? An opportunity to make a higher "offer," and another and another ad nauseaum with the threat never going away? Not a good option.

What if I made no offer? What if I ignored him?

He blows his whistle and takes what he has to some media outlet for a big exposé? But what does he gain from that? A fee for the exclusive rights to the story? How much? A couple of thousand? Could be big money for a graduate assistant at a mountain college, but I had the feeling Niccan Dye would have something a little more grand that that in mind.

What else?

The extortionist could be eliminated. Could I? Would I? I didn't want to think about that. Was there another option?

I could brazen it out, I supposed, hold on to my claim that the manuscript is the draft of a story—a piece of fiction—not the "confession" Niccan Dye imagined it to be. Not sure what the fall-out of that would be, but a possibility.

Or I could eliminate the extortionist.

Say I cloak myself in righteous indignation. Say I refuse to play his game. I refuse to be blackmailed. Make it public and let the devil take the hindmost. Would he have the guts for that—to be publically branded a blackmailer, a low-life villain, kiss his academic career goodbye? The notoriety could be hurtful to me and to the *Journal*; it might even put me at personal risk. One of the hot-bloods out of the hollows, with the killer of Jesse Bristow identified, might feel compelled to get revenge and become a hero in his own right.

A risk—but acceptable.

What about the legal risk? Was there a real one? A charge of murder? A conviction?

There is no evidence to support Niccan Dye's claim. No weapon. No witnesses. Nothing that in any way could tie Theo Clark, the highly respected journalist who doesn't even have a parking ticket to his name and is soon to be Publisher of one of the state's most prestigious newspapers; nothing to tie him to such a heinous act. Is there any District Attorney in the state who would bring a case based on nothing more than a passage in a manuscript the author swears is a work of fiction?

The publicity could be a career-maker for an ambitious D.A. Or a career ender. How could the charge be made to stick with no evidence and the accused insisting on his innocence?

Big gamble for a D.A. to take. Odds were against it, I thought, but it's never smart to try to predict what chances a really ambitious man will take.

Better yet, say I don't wait for Niccan Dye to go public.

Say I take the initiative. Say I take all this stuff and shove it down his throat.

Bingo!

I liked this. I liked the way it felt.

I call a press conference. I accuse Niccan Dye of stealing a manuscript I'd left in the care of a friend—a draft of a story, a piece of fiction I'd written based on the deaths of Michael Dannan and Jesse Bristow that has a character named Theo Clark avenging the murder of his best friend. Niccan Dye thinks the story is a confession of murder. He threatens to make it public unless I pay him.

Blackmail.

I accuse Niccan Dye of the crime of blackmail.

I announce that I am bringing suit against him for slander and that after I've had the chance to review the manuscript and shape it into the finished piece of fiction it was intended to be, I'll publish it myself.

Damn, I liked this. I liked the surprise of it and the aggressiveness of it. Take control. Hit first, and fast, and very, very hard.

Could I make it work?

Worth a try, buddy boy— worth a try.

"Grab hold a something, Niccan Dye, you goin' for ride," I said smiling into the mirror as I finished shaving and started down the stairs.

The feeling of euphoria lasted just past the Methodist Church.

Drop this bomb myself? Call the attention of the whole state to Jesse Bristow's still unsolved murder, put myself in the center of it and count on fancy footwork and my boyish charm to extricate me? What the hell am I thinking?

I turned around there. Walked back to my apartment. Got my car out of the garage in the alley behind, and hoping Dulin Monroe was up, started for the hill to Balk Knob, thinking how cold a summer fog can be.

CHAPTER **FORTY THREE**

Dulin knew nothing about my "interaction" with Jesse Bristow.

I had told no one about it.

Except Marne—that night—that one night when the weight of Michael's death and Jesse's killing so bore me down I could hardly breathe—that night when she cradled me and told me "it's all right"—through that night, through that long, long night.

Now Dulin.

I needed Dulin to tell me whether what I planned was as ridiculous as it now seemed, whether the outlandish scheme I'd manufactured out of wishful thinking had a chance of working, whether the risk to me, the risk to Rhae Dannan's legacy, was even worth considering. He'd have to know the story.

So Dulin Monroe on a Sunday morning with the sun shining bright on his hilltop while a cold grey fog filled the valley, got the actual story of the Dannans & Jesse Bristow—with Theo Clark for a chaser.

Dulin made breakfast while I talked. Moving from the stove to the table, pouring coffee, cracking eggs in the skillet, glancing at me from time to time, intent on what he was doing but studying me, eyes crinkled questioningly, sometimes staring off into space, considering.

We moved out onto the deck—out into the sunshine. Dulin paced, as if he needed to be moving. I told it all as completely as I could. As accurately as I could. Trying to make no excuses for myself. Sometimes he'd frown. Sometimes he'd stand and walk to the railing and look out over the valley. Sometimes he'd fix on my face and try to read my thoughts.

That I'd killed Jesse Bristow in cold blood seemed to neither surprise or disturb him.

What affected him was Benjamin Dannan's story, was the revelation of Benjamin Dannan's affair with Jesse Bristow's young sister and her death trying to abort the baby they had conceived.

The particulars of Benjamin Dannan's death were still a mystery, his reputation still unsullied.

"So that's why Benjamin died," Dulin said when I'd finished, "trying to fix something he'd broken. And he bled to death while Jesse Bristow sat and watched."

He turned away from me to look off up the valley. "I think I would have just as soon not have known, Theo."

We sat for a long while; neither of us speaking. There was no one for whom Dulin had more admiration than Benjamin Dannan, no one for whom he had more respect. It is a hard thing for a man to learn more than he wants to know about his heroes.

The sun gradually cut through the fog in the valley. The town began to appear and come to life. Cars were making their way across the bridges; church bells called the faithful.

Finally Dulin roused himself. He stood, stretched. "Coffee's cold," he said. "I'll make some new."

When he returned, he'd shaved and changed. There was a sadness about his eyes, but he'd put the past away.

He stared at me for a moment, deciding something. When he had, he stepped down off the deck and motioned me to follow. "Pretty morning," he said. "Let's walk." There was a footpath I hadn't noticed, a small trail that angled up the ridge and disappeared into shale and cedars. "Leads to a little water hole. See if there are any quail around."

When the trail leveled off, and we could walk side-by-side, he paused to wait while I caught up.

"So," he said, "you and Jesse Bristow."

He shook his head, wonderingly. "The Bristow murder is still the biggest unsolved mystery in the state. And you're thinking about blowing it wide open? Damn."

He started back up the path again then, talking to me over his shoulder.

"Rhae thought all along it was you. No. She knew it was you. You told her?"

"I wanted to, but she wouldn't let me.'

He nodded. "Of course. She wouldn't have wanted you to have told her anything that at some point could come back to hurt you. She mentioned it to me only once. When you left—trying to understand why you'd left—she told me what she thought then."

The path ended at a fallen gate. An overgrown pasture was just beyond it. Wild blackberry bushes loaded with berries crowded what had been the fence line. The ripe berries, as big as marbles, were so deep a purple they looked almost black in the sunlight. Those still ripening were a bright red against the green of the thorn bushes.

"Best quail cover in the universe," Dulin said, pulling one of the branches forward. "The thorns keep the predators out. The berries make excellent food. Damn shame the State's tearing them out along all the county roads. Too hard to mow around." He carefully slid his hand up a branch and broke off a thorn, a half-inch half razor sharp triangle that could tear through flesh as easily as clothing. "In the early days, the Cherokees wove blackberry fences around their camps. They were shoulder high. Practically impenetrable. Kept the bears and the wolves out, and enemies wouldn't even try."

He pulled a berry off and popped it into his mouth, a smile as he bit down on it. "I'll come back this afternoon and pick a pail. July and August. Blackberry picking months. Fresh blackberry cobbler tonight. You can stay? No. I imagine you have things do."

There was an outcropping of small boulders off to the left of the gate. Dulin led me there and sat down in the shade of a maple that looked as if it might have been there as long as the rock.

"Is there a way out of this thing with this Niccan Dye short of the nuclear attack you're planning? I'm not saying I'm against the plan you outlined. It's bold and it might even work. I'd just hate to see you do it. I'd hate to have it all made public. Even if you can get away with this "fiction" fiction. If you do this and you're successful, you'll ruin the boy, you know that. He is a boy, right? Who is he? What's he after?"

When Dulin asked it, I realized I didn't know. From the first moment, I'd assumed Niccan Dye was after money—a bank of his own he could draw from whenever he felt the urge and not worry about being overdrawn. What other reason could there be? My head? Revenge for the murder of a hero? Expose the dastardly villain? Maybe. But why go to the trouble of contacting me? Why not go public with what he had and to hell with me? No. It had to be money.

Watching me struggle for an answer, Dulin said, "You don't know, do you? Hadn't you better find out?"

CHAPTER **FORTY FOUR**

July

Niccan Dye wanted me to open the bidding. Gave me the manuscript. Told me to "make an offer." Gave me a week in which to do it. Let the mark set the starting price. Keep boosting it up from there. Good tactic, Niccan ole boy, but ain't gonna play that game. In fact, ain't gonna play at all. Ain't gonna make no offer. Gonna wait and see what you do and then with due regard to Dulin Monroe's concerns, I'm gonna knee-cap you. Gonna demolish you, damn you for putting me through this.

I didn't respond to Niccan Dye.

The deadline passed.

I called the O'Donnell. Told him what I was up against. Told him the whole Jesse Bristow story. Told him what I planned. If I was going to have to go to war, I'd need him to be my strike-force. Would he?

"Bad guy?"

"Bad guy."

"Justice?

"Justice."

"You didn't really quote La Hire's prayer to the preacher."

"As he would do by you if you were La Hire and he was God."

A laugh.

"Count on it."

"I'll owe you."

"You always do."

Three days later, Wednesday, July second, the Fourth of July week-end coming, Dulin Monroe turned up at my office a little after lunch. He had a small pail of blackberries in one hand and an envelope in the other. He set the pail down on my desk. "Fresh picked. Dribble a few spoons-full over a bowl of vanilla ice-cream with a shot of bourbon to flavor before you go to bed tonight. Pure indulgence. Then in the morning, a bowl-full with a little milk. Cream if you've got it, but milk will do. No need for sugar. They're succulent sweet. You'll think of a way to thank me. Now ask me to sit down." Which he did without my asking and held the envelope up in front of me.

"Just for you," he said, opening it and beginning to read.

"Niccan Dye is twenty-two. Son of Henry Dye and Margaret Seekings Dye. She died in a flash flood when Niccan was in his early teens. His father is a foreman at the Priest Hollow coal mine in Harlan County and lives in Twila, south of Harlan near the Tennessee line. Niccan (don't call him Nick) is squeaky clean. No police record. Honor student in high school. Academic scholarship at Cumberland College. Just completed work on his masters and hopes to be admitted to the University of Georgia in the fall to begin work on a Doctorate in Cultural Anthropology (his mentor, Professor Young's, specialty). No money to speak of. His father has helped underwrite some of his expenses at Cumberland College and will help with expenses at the University of Georgia if Niccan is admitted to the program, but Niccan will have to continue to work at outside jobs to support himself through school. At present he's earning money as a tutor and works Saturdays at a local garage. He's a good mechanic. He lives off-campus in a small apartment above that garage. The college faculty, but for the little flare-up when he agitated for the creation of a Melungeon student organization on campus, are generally complimentary. He is seen as disciplined, focused, ambitious, and self assured ... and given a break or two, a credit to the college and a winner."

Dulin laid down the letter and looked at me with a stern expression.

"This sound like an extortionist to you?"

"What is that?" I asked, pointing to the letter.

"The background on Niccan Dye. Maybe I'm more curious than you are about him. I called on an old friend at the newspaper at Harlan. Asked him to do a run down on the quiet for me. So this is him. Niccan Dye."

"Why?"

"Because I think Niccan Dye has stumbled into something that can hurt him and hurt you and drag a much respected man's name through the dirt and open old wounds that ought not be opened. I don't think he knows what he's risking, and I don't want you wading into this with guns blazing until you know what the young man wants and are certain there is no other way. Go find out."

He left then, leaving the letter open on my desk.

While I sat there churning Dulin's remarks, Julie Colby called. "We'll go to the Club for the Fourth. Hot dogs and hamburgers, blankets on the grass, fireworks.

You'll enjoy it," she announced brightly. "No arguments. You are part of the Establishment now. You need to be out and among them."

I started to protest but realized it would be futile.

"I've asked Allie to join us."

"You didn't."

"I told her you'd pick her up. About six-thirty. Jim and I will meet you there."

"Julie—"

"Don't be late. They'll start the fireworks as soon as it's dark."

No fair. No fair!

In less than an hour, Dulin had saddled me with a responsibility I didn't want, and Julie was shoving me through a door I was reluctant to open. And all I had to show for it was a small bucket of blackberries

"Mildred."

Poking her head around the office door, "The buzzer, Mr. Clark. The buzzer. This is the executive floor. Don't yell for me."

Propriety. Thank god for propriety. It keeps us sane and civilized. I smiled. "Sorry. Our friend Niccan Dye? You arranged a meeting with him for me. I want you to arrange another one please. Next week. Wednesday. Two p.m. Here. In my office.

Can you do that, please?"

"You haven't told me what happened in the first one," she scolded.

"When I know, I'll let you know."

There was nothing special about Wednesday or two p.m. What I wanted was Niccan on my ground. I wanted him in an unfamiliar setting where he'd feel uneasy. I wanted him off balance and apprehensive.

I had a plan for Niccan Dye.

I had no plan for Allison Boatwright Sinclair.

I had left without saying goodbye. I came back without saying hello. I'd let years pass without a word. I felt like a coward and a heel and a nervous schoolboy being pushed to ask the prettiest girl in the class for a date.

If I'd had a plan, it would have made no difference.

Allie greeted me with a slap.

Right hand.

Then the left.

Then she fell against me, hammering with her fists on my chest. "I'm mad at you. Mad. Mad." Then she was crying, and I put my arms around her, partly to comfort her and partly to cushion the blows, and she relaxed. Then she stopped and looked at me and ran her hand gently down my cheek. "Did I hurt you?" Then she pushed away and wiped her eyes.

"All that time, and I didn't know if you were hurt or where you were or if you were all right. And then you come home and you don't call. What are you thinking?" She moved as if she was getting ready to pound me again. But stopped. Stared at me with her hands on her hips, "I need to fix my face. Make yourself a drink. Everything's where it always was."

All this took place in the open doorway.

I'd arrived just a bit early at the little ranch-style cottage in the subdivision outside of town where she lived when I left. It was farmland then. Now it was mostly streets and well-manicured lawns. Allie's house, though, still backed up against fields. A broad pasture was just beyond her fence line, and it sloped down to a pond that the sun's lowering rays flicked sparkles from. I could hear cattle, but not see them– the pitch of the land hid them. It was that time of afternoon when things get very quiet waiting for twilight to come. I stood for a moment, admiring, then turned up the walkway to Allie's front door.

I knocked.

The door opened almost instantly.

I didn't even have time to duck.

Cheeks still smarting from that greeting and with not a single idea in my mind of how to react, I made my way to the kitchen where a bottle of Ancient Age sat on the counter with a silver ice bucket and a silver julep cup beside it.

I'd never seen Allie that mad before. I'd seen her angry. But smacking-people-in-the-face mad? Never.

I started to make a drink then stopped. How much had we changed?

My wondering was brought up short by a soft voice saying, "Let's start all over."

I turned. Allie stood there, more appealing in reality than in the imagining of my dreams.

I can't decide how to describe Allie. I can lay out the adjectives and mix them and meld them, but the result never comes close. Eyes the blue of the purest sapphires, hair the gold of sun on summer hay, a body sleek and sensuous. Sweet to the hand. Even sweeter to the taste. Will that do? She is just exactly the right size and shape and feel and nature for me. Perhaps I am bewitched.

"I'm sorry, hero. I had to get it out. It's done. I'm sane now. Are you okay?"

I knew it was all right when she called me "hero." When I got back from Korea, I had a scar on my cheek and a Silver Star. Partly to keep my ego in check and partly because she was proud of me, Allie started calling me "hero." She did it at times when she thought I was getting too full of myself. She did it at times when she thought I needed the stroking. I knew she used it with affection.

We didn't make it to the club that night.

That night Allie and I talked—sitting on the little brick patio at the back of the house watching the sun go down. I sipped bourbon. She toyed with chardonnay. When we got hungry, she made eggs and bacon, and we ate by the light of a single candle.

We talked of what we'd done and what had happened in the missing years— told most of it. I left out some. She did as well, I imagine.

When full dark came, we spread a blanket on the grass and lay side-by-side, watching the distant fireworks light the sky. There was a half-moon that night that stayed politely in the background while the fancy colors flared. When the show was over, and night came back, it was almost dawn.

"I'm seeing someone," she whispered. "No one you know."

The thought chilled me, but of course she was. My god, had I expected time to stand still?

She took my hand. "Don't go away again, hero."

CHAPTER FORTY FIVE

At least Julie waited until daylight.

"You stood me up!"

I struggled awake. Seven-thirty, my bedside clock announced. Still dark in the room; a bit of gray seeping through the window. I knew before I picked up the phone who the caller would be.

"Well."

I had no response to "well."

"Don't you hold back on me. We waited until the whole show was over, and everyone had left. People were expecting you. I was embarrassed. What happened?"

"What did you expect to happen when you put together your devious little plan to throw me and Allie together?"

"You stayed all night"

"You've a salacious mind, Julie Colby."

"Come tell me all about it."

"Julie, it's Saturday morning. People sleep on Saturday mornings. We've established that you're not my mother, right?"

"Oh, Theo, dear, you couldn't do without me," she said. "Now hurry. The coffee's on."

They were down in the backyard at a wooden table under a sycamore by the river, the morning cool but soon to warm as the sun got higher. Julie had on a red sweater; Jim, a faded Vandy sweat-jersey. Little jewels of dew hung on the wild roses. Jim gave me a knowing smile as I walked down. "You get distracted last night, buddy? We waited."

"Hush," Julie said, swatting at Jim, "Ignore him. It's such a pleasant morning we decided to have a little coffee down by the water before starting on breakfast."

Turning to Jim and smiling sweetly, she said, "Jim dear, could you go find something to do while I give Theo the third degree?"

And then to me and with an even sweeter smile, "Now come sit down here next to Mama Jules and pour yourself a cup of coffee and bare your soul."

I had to laugh. And she did, too. Jim, still giving me that knowing smile, started back up the path to the house saying, "I hate to leave you alone with this conniving woman."

A moment or two passed, letting Jim get out of earshot and the morning settle around us.

"Was she who you thought she'd be?"

"I don't understand."

"Allie. Was she as you thought she would be? She couldn't be. The Allie you've been carrying around in your mind is a fantasy ... someone you've conjured up ... a girl you thought you were in love with at eighteen and walked away from and have regretted ever since and have let take over your imagination. The Allie you were with last night is real. Did she measure up to that perfect lover who lives in your dreams?"

"Julie! Damn! That's going too far."

She stopped, realizing that she had. She took my hand, "Oh, Theo I want you to be happy. But you have to come to grips with what to do about Allie."

"Allie said she's seeing someone."

" Beau Sims, James Beauregard Sims, of the Fayette County Sims. Blue bloods. It's serious. At least it's serious as far as he's concerned. He has a farm outside Versailles on the way to Lexington. Horses and tobacco. He is a handsome man and attentive, and he runs in all the right circles and knows all the right people. Beau would be very good for Allie."

"And Allie, how serious is she?"

She shrugged. "Some, I think. More if you hadn't come back." She looked at me and seemed to be almost pleading. "What do you want, Theo? You're home now. You're going to be an important man in this town and this state. Maybe Allie is to be part of that. Maybe she isn't. Beau Sims knows what he wants, and he'll get it if he can. What do you want? If it's Allie, you better do something about it. For god's sake, Theo, quit dancing around."

I once told Allie I didn't know what to do about her. She said, "no, hero, what you don't know is what to do about you."

I still didn't know, yet Julie wanted me to decide whether Allison Boatwright was a chimera or real. She wanted me to decide now. It was important to the future she had in mind for me. And if I wanted Allie to be a part of it, I'd better move because there was a rich, handsome, appealing man who would probably be better for her than me.

I hadn't yet reconciled myself to what Rhea Dannan had done to me—or for me. Brought me home. Circumscribed my world. Loaded me with the weight of her legacy. And I had Niccan Dye in the wings ready to ring down hell and damnation on me. And now Allie? I had to decide what to do about Allie? Now!

I had no ambition to be an "important" man. I wanted to keep doing what I'd been doing—poking into things that interested me; roaming where I wanted, when I wanted. Writing what I felt like writing. Unfettered.

Julie didn't take her eyes off me. Sometimes I thought she could read my mind.

"What if I don't want to be an important man?"

"That wouldn't change anything where Allie is concerned. You don't have a choice anyway. You're not going to fail Rhae Dannan and once you take over everything, you'll become a real force in this city and the state. You'll be a power. You could be governor. Michael wanted it but didn't get there. You could if you want it."

"Lord, Julie. No."

She crinkled her eyes, half smiling, "For now. Wait and see."

She let that sink in then said, "Allie first."

CHAPTER FORTY SIX

Niccan Dye was punctual.

Mildred in her excitement practically blew through my office door. "He's here. Downstairs at the receptionist's desk."

I checked my watch. Two minutes to two. Three hours from Williamsburg to here. Find the *Journal.* Find parking. Allow some extra time for that. Would he have allowed for the unexpected on the highway? A flat. An accident. And a little lunch. He wouldn't want to come into this with hunger gnawing at him. Grab a sandwich once he got here. A little more time for that. Four hours minimum. Five if he was nervous about being on time. So Niccan Dye had probably been on the road since nine this morning. Maybe left right after breakfast. A long day already. All that way alone with only the radio or road noise for company. All that time alone to think, to anticipate, to worry. Perfect.

"Well, go get him," I said to Mildred. "Bring our favorite stranger up."

I was ready. The office was immaculate. My desk was clear of everything but the manuscript. It lay there centered on the polished surface, all alone. A small wooden owl carved from ebony sat atop it. It drew the eye.

If Dulin was right—if hard working little Nick (don't call him Nick, but I toyed with the idea of doing that just to piss him off), if hard working Niccan was just a nice young man who'd stumbled on to something he didn't understand and who, if I wasn't careful, could blow us both up, I had a plan.

If Dulin was wrong; if hard-working Niccan-the-Nick was a larcenous little miscreant with blackmail on his mind, I also had a plan. Never mind the luck.

"Mr. Dye to see you." Mildred was at the door. He was standing just behind her. Mildred fluttered, stepped aside and shooed him in.

He took a few steps into the office then stopped, as if unsure whether to come all the way in. I stood and walked around the desk to greet him, hand extended, smiling as big a smile as I could manage. He took it. Maybe my weak attempt at humor at our first meeting had an effect.

"Come in. Sit down. Some coffee? Mildred, could you get us some coffee, please."

I took his arm and steered him to a seat at the small conference table by the wall, trying to be the picture of affability—warm, welcoming, friendly. That would change. I'd start nice, but when I got to the meat of the matter, I'd come on like an outraged bull. I don't know what he expected. Anger. Suspicion. Aggression. He'd get them all. But not at first. At first, a bit of softening.

Niccan was dressed exactly as he had been at our first meeting. Blue blazer, rep tie, khakis a little wrinkled from the long drive but creased and neat. His take-me-seriously outfit, I guessed. I'd done similarly— in a navy blue suit with a starched white shirt setting off a blood red tie. Take-me-fearfully was my aim.

Mildred brought the coffee, hovered over Niccan like he was a visiting celebrity, her curiosity hardly contained. I made small talk— how was the drive, any trouble finding parking, first time in a newspaper office—to ease into what was to come.

I learned that the drive was okay, he'd found a parking spot down the block, had never been in a newspaper office, but had been to the

Capitol once—with his senior class on a school trip, saw the Governor's office, met the Governor.

It was a one-way information exchange, Niccan answering my questions but asking none of his own. He was tense and monosyllabic.

"Newspapers are fascinating places. If you've never seen how one is put together, you'll be surprised. When we have time, I'll show you around. Right now we have a matter to decide." I said this matter-of-factly, no threat in my voice, no anger on my face.

Crossing to my desk, I lifted the little ebony owl off the manuscript carefully and held it up for us both to see. "I was in Ghana covering a coup that failed. Covering the losing side. One of the losers, an old tribesman, an Ashanti, gave me this. For luck. His grandfather had carved it. The Ashanti believe the owl is a protector. Beautiful workmanship, isn't it?"

I handed it to Niccan to see more closely, to feel the smooth of the wood, how cool it was to the touch.

"This, though," I said, hefting the manuscript, "deciding what to do about this will require more than luck."

I sat it down on the table between us and took my seat. Time to turn up the heat.

"This is what I know about you," I began, and recounted all the information Dulin had found for me. "You've impressed a lot of people. You impressed Marne Young. Which impresses me. But you're a puzzle. Nothing that I know about you, or have heard about you, in any way suggests that you're an extortionist."

He jerked forward at that, starting to speak.

I stopped him. "Let me finish."

I pressed on. "You know what an extortionist is. Scum. Weak and unprincipled and despicable. A criminal. Extortion is a crime. The way you've come on makes it seem you have blackmail in mind. 'Make me an offer,' you said. Money. What else could you mean but money?"

I shook my head. "None of this sounds like the Niccan Dye I've been told about. Someone's pushing. Someone's prodding. Who? Who's putting pressure on you to do this dirty thing?"

He stood up, anger in his eyes.

"No. Don 't tell me. I don't care. It makes no difference." I motioned him back down.

He glared at me. I glared back. "We're going to need some privacy." I walked to the open door, leaned through it to tell Mildred, "I don't want to be disturbed. No phone calls. No visitors. Nothing until I open the door again and give you an all clear."

The surprise left her speechless.

I closed the door and returned to the table. "Now," I told Niccan Dye, "I'm going to tell you what your options are."

We broke a little after five. Niccan looked dazed and conflicted and anxious and tired.

I'd done most of the talking.

I told him that if his intent was blackmail, I'd destroy him. I laid out the plan I'd worked with The O'Donnell. The charge of extortion I'd bring against him. The press conference I'd stage, charging him with stealing a story I'd written based on the Jesse Bristow killing. A story with a character bearing my name which he threatened to release publically and claim that I, the real Theo O'Hara Clark, had been the shooter. Unless I paid him to keep it secret. A story I'd imagined, a piece of fiction. Ridiculous. I promised him that if he persisted with his threat, I'd draw so much public attention to his attempt, heap so much ridicule on his character that any career he might hope to have would be forever blown away. I had the resources to do it. I had the know-how to do it. I could and would do it.

But that didn't need to happen.

I had an idea that might appeal to him, I told him, one that appealed to me.

We both owed Marne Young. Me for the help and comfort she'd given me during the time with Michael Dannan. He for the support and opportunity she'd given him as he started on his career. We both loved her in our own way.

I proposed we honor her. With scholarships in her name and memory. Scholarships which I would fund. For young men and women of Melungeon blood. Full ride scholarships. Two each year. One for a male student of merit; one for a female student of merit. Established in her name, the Marne Young Scholarships. Established at Cumberland College. He, Niccan Dye, would be named a perpetual member of the scholarship committee.

As for the manuscript, he'd treat it as any other document among Marne Young's papers. Catalogue it and see it placed in the college's archives where it would remain until some researcher stumbled across it. Perhaps he, years in the future, when he was a distinguished professor of Appalachian Studies at whatever university was fortunate enough to secure his services, would "find" it—after I'm dead, of course—and finally write whatever he'd choose to write about Jesse Bristow and the Dannans—and Theodore O'Hara Clark.

Did that idea appeal? Did it seem an honorable finesse to a perplexing problem?

Niccan listened, angry sometimes, defensive some, but mostly like a man in a situation he hated and could find no way out.

His biggest problem, I learned later, was ego.

The idea of blackmail had not been Niccan's. It had been his girl's—the girl he'd like to be living with but wasn't. Cumberland College was Baptist. Serious Baptist. Good Baptist girls didn't do that sort of thing. And if they did, and the College knew of it, they'd be gone. This girl, a graduate student, too, had, I supposed, all the physical attractions a twenty-two year old male would find irresistible as well as the kind of mind that appealed to a budding academic. She was an economics major. She understood money. She was ambitious. When Niccan told her he'd found a document in Professor Young's file that could put an important man in jail, her immediate thought was money. Niccan needed money to get his doctorate. She needed money to finish work on her master's. Trying to eke out what they needed in after-class jobs was hard and slow.

Niccan didn't tell her who the man was or what he'd done. She thought it had to do with sex or embezzlement. "Sell it to him," she told him, "what do you care what he did? Didn't hurt us or anyone we know. What good is sending him to jail? Make him pay by really paying. Paying you. Sell it to him."

Niccan was repelled by the idea. But she kept at him. He resisted her arguments until one night, over beers by the river, exasperated, she told him, "I think you're afraid. I think the fact that's he's an important man intimidates you. I don't think you've got the balls to confront him."

That did it. He could hold out against mockery of his morality, but not against derision of his masculinity. So Niccan braced me. Now he was faced with gambling that what I said about making a pre-emptive strike myself was an empty threat Or going along with my idea of honoring Marne Young, burying the manuscript in the archives, and confirming his girl's suspicions that he was a wimp.

"Think it through carefully," I told him. "But don't take too much time. A week. If I haven't heard from you in a week, I'll call that press conference."

He'd be driving through dusk into dark on his way back to Williamsburg. I hoped he'd pay attention. I was beginning to both like and feel a little sorry for Niccan-the-Nick Dye.

CHAPTER FORTY SEVEN

Waiting is its own kind of hell.

A week I'd given Niccan Dye. A week. Ah, hell.

I wasn't truly confident that the card I threatened to play would win the game. I thought it would. The O'Donnell thought it would. Dulin thought it might.

Still, there was always the chance that some ladder-climbing D.A. would bring charges if Niccan made the manuscript public.

Even if that happened, could a conviction be had solely on the basis of a few lines in a manuscript with no evidence at all to back up the charge? No witness, no weapon, no motive? Might depend on where the trial was held. In Bristow country? Finally nail the killer of Jesse Bristow, hero and paragon? Leave it up to a jury of good men, tried and true, from Harlan county? If Niccan-the-Nick didn't go for my gambit, and some salivating servant of the people saw a golden opportunity, Lord deliver me, there'd be hell to pay.

While I waited, there was no want of matters to distract me—the farm, the stables, the printing operation—all still areas of relative mystery to me. I focused on the printing operations and on the work being done to prepare our bid for the new State printing contract. There was nothing useful I could add to the formulation of our bid. But I wanted to be knowledgeable about it. I intended to hold the Governor to his level-playing-field, no-special-favors pledge. So I spent my days that week with the printers.

Nights, well, the nights were long. Sleep came hard, and when it did, Jesse and Allie rattled it—Jesse with that hole in his head, looking for the twenty-two; Allie, just on the edge of my consciousness, with a man I didn't know, laughing, looking over her shoulder at me with an expression I couldn't read, walking away.

I fell back into my routine of roaming the early morning streets, showing up in the newsroom near midnight, waiting until the page proofs were ready and then, when the press began running, letting myself out the carrier's door to walk the sleeping city.

I think I knew every street in town, had ridden my bike down each one of them, or played through autumn leaves along their sidewalks, or walked my dates back home on moonlit nights, seeking the shadows of the big old trees that lined the way to hide in.

Roaming in the darkness, I could imagine the town as it was when I was a boy, see it the way it was then. I could let the memories wash over me, bring back the feeling of belonging. My Camelot.

I felt at peace when I'd finished these little pilgrimages and as dawn crept in over the trees, sleep would come

The week passed with no word from Niccan Dye.

When it came, Dulin Monroe brought it.

Niccan was in the hospital in Williamsburg. The police had found him in the gutter of a back street near the river, unconscious and bloody. His right arm had been twisted out of the shoulder socket. He had a ruptured spleen, three broken ribs, a dislocated jaw and his upper body and thighs were so badly bruised he couldn't move. Not a hit and run. Niccan had been savagely beaten. Dulin's friend at the newspaper in Corbin had relayed the news.

"Not your doing, I know," Dulin said. "You would never punish anyone like that. But who would ... and why? There are blood feuds in the mountains that last generations, and we know little or nothing about Niccan Dye's personal baggage, but the timing ... he gets damned near killed a week after he comes to talk with you. The manuscript? Could this be about the manuscript?"

I didn't know, but I left immediately to find out.

Niccan had difficulty speaking— the wired jaw, the stiches in the cut over his eye—they made conversation painful. He didn't want to talk anyway. He'd told the police all he knew, he said, which was almost nothing. He'd been working late at the college, walked out into the parking lot to find his car, and that's all he remembers. No names, no faces. Didn't remember what happened. A total blank. Nothing.

I didn't believe him.

The hospital room was pleasant enough. A window looking out to the hills. Lots of light. Roomy. He had to take his food through a straw and even with all the pain medication, moving his beaten body hurt badly. The shoulder joint had been reset, but he had to keep his right arm immobile. He could handle the TV remote with his left hand because he was left handed. The real piece of luck was that the rupture to the spleen wasn't so severe that an operation was necessary.

We talked. Or I talked.

I told him I didn't believe him. I told him that if he was trying to protect someone, or if he was trying to adhere to some code that said you don't settle your grievances by going to the police, you settle them personally, I said that if he was that delusional, I'd have him transferred to a mental hospital.

I told him that someone almost killed him—and might the next time. Whoever that was had to be found and dissuaded (yes, I used the word dissuaded, it sounded more genteel.) I told him he could trust me with the names. I told him he could trust me to take care of it. No police. No fanfare. I told him I needed him alive and well so we could settle this matter of the manuscript. I didn't want it floating loose. I didn't want it in someone else's hands. I told him this was for me as much as for him.

I don't think Niccan would have believed that I was motivated by Christian charity. That I was motivated by self-interest, though, was something he could accept.

This is what he told me:

He had returned from his meeting with me, conflicted and exhausted. The drive was long and tiring, and the last half of the return trip was in fog so thick he could hardly make out the lights of the car ahead.

He'd come with his courage in hand and ready to prove he had the backbone to make a powerful man pay—real money. Not an act that could be called blackmail. An act of penance for sins committed. But my threat of building a bonfire around him took him by surprise and scared him. More startling was my proposal for the scholarships honoring Marne Young. That appealed to him very much. Struggling with the tension of the drive and weight of the decision he had to make, wrung him out.

She was waiting.

He hadn't expected her to be. She had the door open at the top of the stairs and was standing, smiling, hardly able to wait to get the good news.

She grabbed his hands and pulled him in and kissed him. His apartment over the garage was anything but romantic, but it seemed so then—lit by candles, Segovia's dulcet guitar playing softly in the background. She wore a one-piece dress (it has a name, but he knew nothing about fashion, a shift perhaps), black, sleeveless, cut low, clinging so that each curve beckoned; her auburn hair pulled back; her graceful neck exposed; her brown eyes sparkling as she made him sit and brought him wine.

He was overwhelmed. She had never been so aggressively seductive, and he had never been in so much need of comforting and understanding. Miraculously, a bad day was turning into something he thought he might remember forever.

He would. But not in the way he was hoping.

"Tell me," she said, gripping his hands and leaning forward eagerly.

That's when the evening began to come apart.

Niccan had no talent for artifice. He told her exactly what happened— that he had not demanded the money they'd discussed in return for staying silent. He said he wasn't sure he would. He told her about the scholarships, about honoring Professor Marne Young. He told her how appealing that was to him, how much better that felt to him than lining his own pockets, how much more good it would do.

Her eager smiled turned to disbelief, then to a glare, then to fury. She jumped up, eyes sparking, threw what remained of the wine in her glass full in his face, spun around as if to leave, then spun around again. "You wimp. You sorry excuse. Don't you dare back down on this. If you won't put it to him, I will. Tell me who he is. Tell me what he did. I'll get the money." She was in his face, shouting, spitting mad. "Tell me!"

He didn't. He wouldn't.

Two nights later, as he was walking to his car after working late, they grabbed him— her cousins— drove him to a deserted cabin south of town, and beat him with ax-handles to get him to talk.

She watched.

Ax handles were the preferred punisher and convincer in that part of the country. They are not as big as baseball bats, but they are hard and flexible and can be swung full force and inflict maximum pain yet not be as lethal as a similar blow from a baseball bat—if care is taken. Try not to break any bones. Stay away from the face and the head. Go for the legs, the buttocks, the torso, work on them—more cushioning there; the bruises are deeper there and last longer. And the pain. There are few pains as bad as the pain from one of those beatings.

The Ku Klux Klan introduced the practice in the days following the Civil War. An ax-handle beating was as good as a whipping and less final than a shooting. In the time of the fight in the coal fields to get unions established, the thugs working for the mine owners refined the technique. Others saw its advantages, so the practice survived.

Ax-handle beatings were rare now, but when the other little tortures evil people fashion failed to produce the agreement being sought or the information wanted, some people, desperate or self-righteous or reptilian, remembered the old ways and used them.

Her cousins were Ajax and Jimbo Haines—sons of her father's brother. They were twins—big, dull-witted bullies. They worked at odd jobs and lived together by themselves in a cabin off Lost Creek Road.

She?

She was Melody Haines and had been the song in his life.

"Tell me," she kept chanting in rhythm with the blows.

He told them nothing.

Nothing about the manuscript. Nothing about the killing of Jesse Bristow. Or my name. Nothing. They finally stopped beating on him. He doesn't remember when. He was unconscious.

Niccan gave me all this reluctantly, laboring it out through his wired-up jaw; the pain medication wearing off and the look of betrayal in his eyes.

"I'll take care of it," I told him. "Rest now. We'll finish our business when you're well."

CHAPTER **FORTY EIGHT**

Strange things happen in the mountains.

Shortly after midnight on a Friday in July, roughly a week to the day after Niccan Dye had been admitted, Ajax and Jimbo Haines, twenty-one year old twin sons of Hiram Haines of the county, stumbled into the emergency room at the Baptist Regional Medical Center in Corbin, the same hospital where Niccan Dye lay.

They weren't beat up, but the strangest thing—each had the thumb on his right hand chopped off. They were in a state of shock and incoherent.

A bit later that morning, just about daylight, a local police cruiser on a routine round, found Melodie Haines, a cousin of the Haines boys and a graduate student at Cumberland College, standing on the steps of the Court House in downtown Williamsburg, dazed and crying. She was dressed in nothing but a short red night-gown that stopped mid-thigh and was held up by the thinnest of straps. More shocking—she was bald.

By mid-day, the talk of it was all over town.

The loss of a thumb might not seem so big a matter, but the Haines boys would think it so. They wouldn't be able to hold a knife or button a shirt, swing an ax or open a door with that hand. And they'd be left-handed beer drinkers. That was a serious thing.

The girl, though not physically hurt, was the victim of humiliation. Her hair would grow back, but the gossip and speculation about why it was done to her would be hard to live through.

The Haines boys said they'd been set on by a gang of hooded men as they were leaving their cabin to come to town. They were taken to the woodpile at the back of the cabin; their hands held down on the chopping block, and their thumbs sliced off with a bowie knife.

A big man with a gravelly voice stopped the bleeding, picked up the severed thumbs, placed them carefully into separate plastics bags and shoved the bags into their jeans pocket. "Something to remember us by," they said he said. Then they'd been put in a car and pushed out at the door to the emergency room.

The girl's story also had men in black whose faces were hidden by hoods. She woke to find them standing over her bed. They gagged her, tied her, took her to the kitchen, hacked off her long auburn hair with a big knife then shaved her head smooth. They'd brought along a set of electric clippers for the purpose. She wasn't hurt. There was no sexual threat. They just shaved her head.

After that, she was blindfolded, loaded in a car, and dumped on the Court House steps— in nothing but her nightgown—and with her head shaved bald. God, it was awful.

The Haines boys and Melodie said they didn't know who the men were or what they wanted. They just came and did these awful things without saying anything at all.

But of course, they said something. They said, "Don't touch Niccan Dye again. Ever. If Niccan Dye is bothered again, in anyway, we'll be back. You'll like the result even less. Don't forget what I've said. Run if you see Niccan Dye."

I know this is what they said because it is the message I asked them to deliver.

For the record, it was not a gang. It was two men.

If you travel far enough, rattle around in quarrelsome places often enough, you find yourself becoming friends with men of a certain kind. Over time, for one reason or another, for one act or another, you wind up beholden to each other.

These two men and I were of that association.

In the last month of the war in Viet Nam, I was with a Special Forces A Team near the Cambodian border. There was an ambush. Though I was there as a journalist and a non-combatant, when the VC triangulated us, nobody cared. The team leader tossed me a weapon, and I took up a position and started returning fire like the others. We held out until nightfall and then, helped by the dark, made a break. No one had been killed, but several of the team were badly wounded. We carried them with us. My guy had part of the muscle in his upper thigh blown away. I carried him piggyback down the mountain. And the next day through the jungle. And the third day through the high grass and the rice paddies until we made it out of Indian country. He was a master sergeant now with the Special Forces training command at Ft. Bragg in North Carolina. All he asked when I called was, "who and where?" The manner of how the message should be delivered was left up to him.

When he called to report, he apologized. Organizing the logistics took more time than he anticipated. There were no problems. They flew out of Fayetteville into Knoxville, picked up a car there, slipped in and out of Williamsburg unnoticed and were back at base in less than twenty-four hours. The message was delivered. He believed it had registered. "Thanks again for the ride," he said.

I refused to feel guilty about the Haines. I started to, but I decided against it. I had enough to feel guilty about, and anyway, damn it, they deserved it. Niccan Dye was safe and the compulsion in the Haines' avaricious souls to learn Niccan's secret had been erased. Chalk up one for the good guys.

Jesse Bristow? I still heard that accusing voice in the early morning dark, but it was getting weaker, and I was growing more comfortable that at the end of days, the game might wind up being played the way La Hire asked it to be played.

Allie, though, was an ache in my mind. What was I to do about her? If I kept dancing around, I might wind up not being able to do anything at all because she'd have walked away with someone else.

Ah, Scarlet, don't desert me now.

CHAPTER FORTY NINE

August

Three weeks from the day the Williamsburg police delivered his battered body to the Baptists Regional Medical Center in Corbin, Niccan Dye was released from the hospital—a Friday, the first day of August.

He was upright and ambulatory, the desk nurse told me when I called that morning, and glad to be out of there. We were old friends by then, she and I. I'd been calling regularly to check on his progress.

Niccan's father collected him. Friends from the college were waiting at his apartment above the garage to celebrate his recovery.

Niccan's beating and the thumbless and hairless Haines were still a prime subject of conversation in Williamsburg. No one could imagine why Niccan Dye would attract such violence. The beating made no sense, so of course this fed the rumors and the talk.

What made less sense and was more disturbing was what had happened to Melodie Haines and her cousins. The boys' thumbs chopped off. The girl's head shaved. Why? The twins were pigs and bullies, but they hadn't done serious harm. And the girl, she was a student at the college, a good student. Some said she was too full of herself and ambitious to a fault, but to be left near naked in the center of town with her head shaved bald? And this gang in black running around and dispensing mayhem at night, are they a danger to anybody else? Not good. Not good at all.

The police didn't have any answers. They could find no reason why the Haines twins and the girl were targeted. They had no idea who the gang was or where they came from. Or whether they would come again.

Things were a bit tense in Williamsburg. Doors were double-checked at night and windows closed. The uneasiness would pass. People lose interest and newer outrages demand attention. Except every time Jimbo Haines forgot and reached for a beer with his thumbless right hand and dropped it and every time Ajax Haines came weaving down the road trying to manage his truck with his left hand alone, they'd remember.

The girl, Melodie, left town the day after the shearing. That's what people called it— the shearing. She hadn't returned. Whether she would was a matter of considerable speculation.

I'd bet that she wouldn't be back. How could she explain what happened to her? She had been shamed—left half-naked in the middle of town with her hair cut off. There was a message in that. The women would gossip. People would look at her and wonder. No, I didn't think she'd be back.

Dulin didn't ask me about any of this. He came into my office when he learned Niccan was going home.

"Are you going to go see him?" he asked.

"I guess I'll have to. We haven't finished our business," I said.

"I heard about that affair down there, that girl getting her head shaved and her cousins having their thumbs wacked off. Bizarre."

I nodded and waited.

"Well," he said, giving me a look that was neither approving nor disapproving, "they have their own ways down there." He started to leave, then stopped and turned back to me. "That unfinished business you have with Niccan Dye; I'm trusting you're going to work that out without setting the whole countryside on fire."

"It's up to him," I said.

Though I had been calling daily, I'd not spoken directly with Niccan and had asked the nurses not to tell him that I'd been calling. Set aside the pain, he had enough to struggle with.

He had to face the fact that his girl almost had him killed, trying to learn a secret he wouldn't reveal. He had to decide what to do about me and my manuscript. And he had the torture of waiting to learn the University of Georgia's decision on his admission to its doctorial program, a happening almost as important to him as getting a pass at the Pearly Gates—and an answer he should already have had. Pain medication might help while his body healed but would do nothing to ease the anxiety his load of worries laid on him.

I wouldn't want to have to deal with it.

Two weeks, I figured. I'd give him two weeks, and if I hadn't heard from him, I'd go find him.

There was no need. I got my answers the next day.

It was morning. The town was just beginning to wake. I was standing at the kitchen window above the sink, watching the paperboy on his bike working his way up the street when the phone rang.

I didn't recognize the voice at first.

"Niccan?"

"Mr. Clark. It's not too early, I hope."

"No, not at all. How are you?"

"I'm okay. I'm doing better. I'll be fine."

"That's good. That's great."

"I heard about Melodie and the Haines boys."

"I did too. What a strange story."

He paused, then, "Thank you."

I started to say you're welcome because he was, but I didn't. I let silence say whatever it would say to him.

"That's not why I called. Well, yes, it is why I called. And to tell you I've been accepted into the University of Georgia program. The letter was here when they brought me home yesterday."

That was good news. Big news. "Congratulations," I said, really feeling good for him.

"And to tell you that the Dannan-Bristow manuscript is going into the college archives with no annotations to attract attention to it and that I'd be pleased to be part of the plan you have to honor Professor Marne Young."

A sense of relief washed over me so strong that it surprised me. The prospect of actually having to do what I told Niccan Dye I'd do must have been weighing more heavily on my psyche than I realized.

I'm not sure Niccan's decision surprised me. I had the feeling from the beginning that he was a reluctant player. He seemed to have an incipient integrity that was offended by the idea of extortion. I didn't think the lure of money would overcome that. I wasn't sure about the power of whatever or whoever was working on him.

I believe Niccan had already made his decision before he got back to his apartment that night. I think he made it on that long drive down to Williamsburg alone with nothing but his conscience. Melodies' blandishments, however tempting, didn't make any difference. Neither, as it turned out, did the ax-handles.

I liked the boy. I was going to help him if I could. I had the money, or soon would have it, and the connections. I could help ease his way through school, help get him started in his field. And together we'd honor Marne Young.

"Niccan Dye," I said, "I can't tell you how pleased I am that you've made this decision. It's the right one. For you. And for me. We'll make a good team. We'll start working on Marne's project whenever you're ready. Heal fast and well."

With the threat of my exposure gone, the day was remarkably brighter, and my morale substantially improved. I'd been under pressure so long, I'd forgotten how good being able to relax felt.

October.

Probate should close, and the keys and the checkbook to Rhae Dannan's empire should officially be mine no later than mid October—and all those responsibilities and all that pressure.

Early August now. The rest of this month and September to go, to get ready for it.

San Francisco.

Escape back to San Francisco. Watch the fog steal in over the bay at night. Draw the morning sun around my shoulders sitting on the dock at Sausalito. Take Kit to dinner at the top of Telegraph Hill and watch the lights blink on. Rest and relax.

Kit Bedrosian.

I hadn't seen her since I left her with my keys and my car and my other life.

Yes. I'd take a break. San Francisco. A week. Maybe two. Put Allie and Jesse Bristow's ghost and the load Rhae laid on me on hold—put a ribbon around them and leave them behind.

What's the song? What's the line? "Open up that Golden Gate." Yeah, California, here I come.

CHAPTER FIFTY

Kit and I had a window table in the Carnelian Room atop the Bank of America building high up on Nob Hill. We could see the ships lying at anchor in the roads on the other side of the Bay Bridge and the big fog bank waiting just outside the Golden Gate. The heart of the city was beneath us—the Financial District, North Beach, the Marina, the Presidio—sparkling with lights which would soon disappear in the fog rolling in.

"The coldest winter I ever spent was a summer in San Francisco," Mark Twain said when he was a young reporter here. Fog is the culprit. It forms over the frigid waters of the California Current that sweeps down from Alaska. Some nights it's so thick the tops of the buildings on Nob Hill can't be seen. Across the bay on the other side of the Oakland hills, sunshine bathes the countryside, and temperatures climb into the hundreds in the summer. But not in the city. In the city, summer visitors need jeans and sweat jerseys, not shorts and tee shirts—and a warm coat.

August days can be hot and humid in the valley of the Kentucky. I was happy to escape to the embrace of the fog—and to be sitting across a candlelit table from Kit Bedrosian.

It was good to be back with Kit.

Some women are so sour that nothing pleases them, and they lay guilt out lavishly; some are so self-centered they have no feeling for anyone but themselves, and some so insecure they constantly attack or constantly make excuses to protect their limping egos. Most women are strong. They have to be. But not many are tough—tough in the sense they don't fool themselves or let others fool them; tough in the sense they'll make hard decisions that hurt. Not many of us are tough in this sense—neither women nor men.

Some women, a few, a very few, are of a sweet nature and selflessly comforting.

Kit Bedrosian was in this last little cohort—strong and brave and tough and, if you didn't cross her, sweet.

This was my last night. Tomorrow morning, I'd be on a plane back to the Bluegrass.

My escape had been grand. Three days in the High Sierra. A small cabin on the shore of Lake Tahoe. Nights so quiet I could hear the stars as they moved through the night, and the sky so full of them it seemed they might spill out. Bright days on the Truckee wading in fast water and laying casts at the foot of the riffles for the rainbow that should be there. Taking my time. Savoring the solitude. A couple of days in the wine country, biking the small country roads past the vineyards and enjoying the fine little restaurants Kit touted me on. Then back into the city, to catch up on the matters I needed to catch up on and to sink myself in its riches— like a fortune found beside the sea.

It was grand—and I was leaving.

Kit didn't think I should go. She thought I should stay. She thought I should stay here and live the life that suited me, the one that made me happy.

She had never given me bad advice.

She had guided and pushed and promoted my career. She managed my business affairs and took care of the things I should take care of but couldn't when I was off on assignment. We were a very good team. No, we more than that. Neither of us put words to it, either to our ourselves or each other because words make things real; they give shape to things that have to be dealt with. We left that thing alone.

Kit slowly stirred her Manhattan and then carefully took the maraschino by its stem and, looking up, leaned across the table and placed it in my mouth. We both laughed. A joke from one of our first encounters.

She lifted her glass to me in a toast.

"Don't ask me to be faithful. Be content with what I give. Love me only when I'm with you. When I'm gone, forget I live."

"What?" I asked, surprised.

"A line from an old cowboy song. It just came to me. It might have been written for you."

I started to protest, but she put finger on my lips. "Or for me." She smiled a wicked little smile and drank down her toast.

"You're really going back."

"That's my plan."

"You don't have to. I know you think you do. I know you feel that you can't let Rhae Dannan down. That you have to go home and keep her kingdom safe and become a rich man and live the life of the landed gentry with races horses and mint juleps and beautiful belles at midnight balls in columned mansions. But it will kill your soul, Theo Clark." She leaned forward, conviction in her eyes and repeated, "Kill your soul."

She took my hand in both of hers. "You're not a businessman. Your mind doesn't work that way. Numbers bore you. You won't be happy in that world. And the money, all that money— it won't make the difference. Not to you. Money's not enough for you."

She squeezed my hand and let go, sitting back and looking as if the reasonableness of what she was saying must be obvious to me.

"You've never seen the Bluegrass, have you?" I said.

"Don't you try to change the subject on me," she said.

"I want you to see it. By moonlight. The full moon of September. The Harvest Moon. Will you come see it?"

She half laughed. "Be serious."

"I am being serious."

"Pay attention to what I'm saying."

"I have to go back, Kit. I'm obliged."

The city had disappeared. Only the tops of the towers of the Golden Gate Bridge poked through. The whole world outside was a cloud and we just above it.

She sat in silence, studying me. Finally she said,

"Why are you called Theo? Ted is the diminutive of Theodore. Theo sounds Greek. You're Irish. Sometimes you Irish act as if you have no sense at all."

CHAPTER FIFTY ONE

The eight-thirty to Cincinnati was wheels-up on time. The mimosas had been served and breakfast was coming. We had climbed out of the fog that blanketed the bay and cleared the Oakland hills and were in bright sunlight moving across the gold country toward the Sierra. We'd float over the high desert on the other side, scale the Rockies, cross the high plains, ford the Mississippi without getting our feet wet and be on the ground in Kentucky by mid-afternoon.

Every time I made the trip, I marveled at the people who did it by wagon train—four months if they were lucky, six months more likely—or not at all if the weather or the water or the terrain killed them, or the food ran out, or a sickness took them—or if they were just too weak, or the hostiles rode them down.

My people arrived too late to be tempted. Just before the Civil War. I don't know how they would have fared. Well, I think. They were tough. The way across from Ireland all the way to Kentucky was test enough.

Kit's people, the Bedrosians, could have done it. They're Armenian, the people of the highlands of the South Caucasus, the land where Noah found harbor for the Ark on the tip of Mt. Ararat after the Great Flood. Her parents clawed their way out of Turkey in the First World War, escaping the genocide that killed over a million of their people. They would have made it.

Kit.

She was still in my mind.

We had eased through the fog down California Street to the wharf, leaning into each other for warmth and comfort, her arm through mine. The street was almost deserted, and only an occasional car came by. We had coffee at a little café Kit knew near the Ferry Building, fog outside, only two other couples inside; soft music playing in the background; a muffled fog-horn sounding now and then. We took a cable car back up Nob Hill to the Mark and had brandy there. Kit wanted to. In World War Two, the Top of the Mark was where the boys heading off into the Pacific took their girls on their last night.

Kit was right. I liked the life I was living. It suited me. Free and easy and exciting and uncomplicated. Responsible to no one but myself. Responsible for no one but myself. Trade that for—what? An obligation?

"Pardon me, Mr. Clark. The seat-belt sign is on. We'll be landing soon." The stewardess stood over me, smiling.

By the time I picked up my car and was on the road to the Capitol City, the sun was low, and the sky was beginning to take on the colors of twilight. I ran south for about an hour through scrub-cedar and gulley country into the Bluegrass. At Georgetown, I left the interstate and turned west onto the little two-lane that winds along Elkhorn Creek and over rolling pastures all the way to East Main hill and down into the center of town.

Though I didn't expect her to be, Mildred was still at her desk. I think she really missed me. There was a little package of M&Ms on my chair with a ribbon tied around it and a card saying, "Welcome Back." She fussed a bit—took my briefcase, wanted to know did I have a good time, looked eager and excited, knew I must be tired after such a long trip, did I want coffee?

When she finally stopped fluttering, I looked at my watch. "It's almost seven-thirty," I said. "It's nice you're here, but there's really no need to have stayed so late."

She shook her heard firmly.

"Mr. Isham needs to see you and Mr. Monroe wants you to call him first thing. Allison Sinclair called, too. And you better call Mrs. Julie Colby. She's been checking to see if you were back. They all sounded like it was important they talk with you as soon as they could. I didn't think a note would get that across. I thought I should be here to tell you."

"Mildred, you keep this up, and you're going to get on steady."

CHAPTER FIFTY TWO

I decided to begin with Paul Isham. It wasn't late, but even if it had been, that would have made no difference. He'd be up past midnight. Dulin, too. Working on morning newspapers gets you in that habit.

Paul lived in a new condominium on the avenue leading to the Capitol that was spacious enough to entertain in and with an address toney enough to be impressive. He staged small, intimate dinner parties there for important advertisers and the movers and shakers in business and politics—expertly catered affairs and, for Kentucky, superbly wined—the sort of chore I'd have to pick up after October when probate closed, and Rhae Dannan's empire fell on me.

I let his phone ring until the answering machine cut in. I left a message that I'd called. If it was an emergency, call or come knock on my door.

Julie next, then Dulin.

Allie?

Not tonight. It would be too late by the time I finished with Dulin. Tomorrow. I'd get Allie tomorrow. It seemed safer to be making that contact in the daylight.

Julie answered on the first ring.

"You're looking for me?"

"Where are you?"

"At the *Journal*. I just got back"

"We're watching boring TV. Come down. You can tell us all about California. I bet you haven't eaten. I'll make you something. And I have something I want to ask you."

I was hungry. Might as well.

I put my car away in the garage in the alley, dropped my luggage off in my apartment, and walked the two blocks down to Julie's. There was no fog off the bay but there was a pleasant enough little breeze and a trace of magnolia in the air.

It turned out that what Julie wanted to ask me was about a "homecoming"—a party to welcome me home and re-introduce me to everyone.

"We'll do it in October after you're are official," she said. "We'll do it on a night when the moon is full. I know how you like full moons. Friday, October twenty-fourth. I checked. It will be fun. It will be great for you."

"Julie, I don't know. I'm not comfortable being the center of attention, you know that. Aren't you making too much of all this?"

"Listen to Mama Jules, Theo Clark, this is something you need to do. People want to see you in the flesh. They want to size you up. Those who knew you want to re-connect. Those who didn't, want to now. Not a really big party. Fifty or so. Very relaxed and informal. I'm thinking hot-dogs on the river bank. We'll make little bonfires and let everybody sit around and roast their own while the moon comes up. Chips. Pickles. Fresh from the bakery buns. Marshmallows and Hershey bars. Beer and bourbon. Scotch and gin for the outlanders. We'll have a ball, and if you're that bashful I'll hold your hand all night. Humor Mama Jules, Theo. She knows what's good for you."

She was smiling and eager and so certain this would be a good thing that I couldn't refuse.

Turning to Jim who was standing nearby. "I need some help." "

"Not me, buddy. I have to live here."

Laughing, I gave in. "Okay, Mama Jules, you got me."

As I was leaving, she asked, "Have you talked with Allie?"

I hadn't. I'd called one day last week, but she wasn't in. I didn't leave a message. Allie kept turning up in my dreams—beckoning, walking away, tempting, repelling. Words from a play or a poem, I don't remember which, kept coming to me as I lay sleepless in the dark.

Waking at night I go to my window, scanning the stars in the portion of sky,
fixing on one that hangs yonder over the street of the house where you lie.
If you sleep, do you dream.
If you dream, is it of me?
The clock strikes.
I hear your voice in the chimes, repeating your words when I ask if you love me.
Always.
Never.
Sometimes.

"Don't tarry, Theo," Julie said. "She's always been drawn to you and you, poor Theo, to her. The strange thing is that you keep trying to ignore it … and she lets you."

"Julie, please."

"Decide, Theo."

After Chosin, after we'd thawed out and healed and were waiting to go into back into the line, and I was being moved up to squad leader, my sergeant told me, " Don't rush a decision. Wait until you know as much as you can. But don't wait too long. The chance to make it may be gone."

Midnight was near by the time I got to Dulin's.

He had hot coffee ready and a bottle of Hennessy XO on the table on the deck. The night was cooler up on the ridge, but still warm. Moonless, though. Wispy clouds obscured the stars.

"In it or in a snifter?" Dulin placed a cup of coffee in front of me and was holding up the bottle of Hennessy.

"I just got in from San Francisco, and I'm still feeling classy. Snifter."

Grunting dismissively, he laced about a finger and half of the amber liquid in a crystal snifter and poured his in a cup in which I think there was coffee but was not sure.

I lifted my glass to him. "In the words of the immortal Bob Regan, 'death to your enemies.'"

"That may be more appropriate than you know," he said. "Who's Bob Regan?"

"An old friend. New York. One of the great ones. The Sage of the Oracles of Ore."

"The what?"

"Never mind. Why have you got me up here at this hour?"

He took a slow sip from his cup.

"You had a good time, and you didn't miss us, right? And you're happy to be home, and you can't wait to get at all the exciting opportunities that are waiting, right?"

Oh damn, I thought.

"Henry J. Kaiser—you know who he was? A great industrialist. Hoover Dam, Liberty Ships, aluminum and steel, delighted in doing things people said couldn't be done."

Dulin sat his cup down and leaned back with his hands behind his head and looked at me like he was truly curious about how I'd react to what he was about to say.

"Henry J. used to say that problems are just opportunities in work clothes."

"I don't think I want to hear this."

"You're not going to get the printing contract."

"I knew I didn't want to hear this."

"The bidding rules read that the contract goes to the lowest and best bid. Your bid won't be 'best.' It may be lowest, but it won't be best. 'Best' is decided by the bid officer, and he's going to decide that 'best' is the bid of Morris & Company, a Lexington printer, because they have a new six-color press. Yours is four years old. You may have the lowest bid, but Morris & Company gets the contract."

"There's that much difference in the presses?"

"Of course not. The difference is that the Morris people were big contributors to the Governor's campaign—and none of them pissed-off the Governor's Chief of Staff.

"Is there anything we can do?"

"About the bid, no. About the impact, maybe— if you can figure out a way to make up the lost revenue. Fifteen percent of your print company's revenue comes from that contract. A fifteen percent hit is a very big hit to that group."

"The bids aren't due to be opened until the end of the month. You're sure about this?"

"A friend—one of the old-timers they're keeping around in the Governor's office while they learn the routine, eavesdropped on a conversation between the Chief of Staff and the bid officer. He wanted me to know, so we could start planning for the hit."

"The Governor promised me no favorites would be played and that the contract would go to the lowest qualified bidder."

"They made a very slick finesse from 'qualified' to 'best.' The contract goes to the lowest and 'best' bid—which isn't yours. The message in this is that you've made a real enemy. I'm not sure the Governor is it, but the Chief of Staff definitely is. You blew the whistle on him. You have a real 'opportunity' here, my friend."

I left Dulin's too charged up to begin to think about trying to sleep. I drove for a while with the windows down, and the air of the early morning flowing around me. There were no cars moving on the streets, not even a big-rig on the interstate. The only action was the stoplights flashing their semaphore at the empty intersections.

I drove past Allie's, the words from the poem in my mind, but gauze-like clouds hid the sky, and there was no way to tell if a star hung there over the house where she lay.

The lights were on at the *Journal* where the presses were running, but I didn't go in. I drove on up to the Capitol and parked and walked out on the broad plaza in front and took a seat on the steps and stared off down the avenue at the town asleep and thought how right Kit was. I didn't like this game.

That afternoon, Paul Isham had a different opportunity for me.

The consortium people were back.

Paul was in my office almost before I got through the door. Not in shirt-sleeves. In jacket and tie. Serious business. He stayed standing while I took my seat at my desk.

With Rhae Dannan's death and a new owner about to step in, the consortium wanted the opportunity to present their proposal again—revised, expanded, one which they believed the new owner would find very attractive. How soon could we talk?

"Rhae turned them down. Let's not waste their time and ours," I said, looking up at him. Not liking looking up, but thinking that if he's standing, he won't stay long.

He leaned forward onto the desk, "These are important men. This is an important undertaking. At least do them the courtesy of listening to what they have to say."

" Ah, a matter of manners. I see. Sorry, Paul, I'm not up to speed yet on the etiquette of the corporate world." I wasn't sure the sarcasm would register, and I probably should have resisted the urge, but Paul carrying water for these people irritated me. "All right, I'll play the game for now. Set a time and let me know."

CHAPTER FIFTY THREE

The day was winding down.

State workers were already on their way home.

Downtown offices would close shortly.

Those few shops and stores still trying to hang on as the impact of Governor Adair's job cutbacks ate away at the economy would shut their doors later, hoping to eke out a little more business.

August days in the Bluegrass are long. The sun wouldn't set until around nine, so we'd have one of those lingering twilights. The downtown streets would be empty well before dark, and the town would be silent and lifeless. That saddened me. The loss of the vibrancy that I remembered saddened me.

I closed the last file on my desk and realized I still hadn't returned Allie's call of the day before.

Allie would save me from the melancholy mood I seemed to be sliding into. I needn't be obvious. I could casually suggest dinner. Give us a chance to discuss whatever she had in mind and to talk— about the weather, about UK football, about whether the actor Ronald Reagan had a shot at beating Carter for the presidency—or if either of us was brave enough, about us.

In the years I was away, Allie had made a career. She was now the Administrative Manager for the second largest accounting firm in the city. You wouldn't look at Allie and think numbers, but she was very good with them. Her mind worked that way.

She would still be there, at work, at least until six, so she told Mildred. If she wasn't in her office, I should try her at her home.

It was a little after six. She wouldn't be watching the clock. I called, made my apologies and excuses, and asked if I could salvage some of my sullied reputation with drinks and dinner, short notice though it was, if she wasn't otherwise engaged. We could cover what she'd called about then. I thought we would go to the Country Club, have a nice dinner out on the deck, watch the stars come out.

She hesitated, "I'm not dressed for the club."

I thought for a moment, "The Fox Hill Inn, then. We were there once. This side of Midway. You liked it."

After a moment she replied, "I remember." Another pause, longer. "Pick me up at my place in about an hour. It won't be too much out of the way."

The moon was waxing gibbous, almost full, but setting early. Just the rim of it was visible above the tree line as we drove and gone by the time we took our table.

We were out back on the edge of the patio at a table open to the sky. The night was warm; the light was soft. Twilight was barely hanging on.

Driving up, we'd talked easily. We always had. Allie was unusual in that way. There was no need to make conversation just to be making conversation, no feeling that you had to entertain or amuse. Long silences were okay. There was music to listen to and the land to admire.

I was in that latter space, wandering down in the valley with Willie Nelson when she asked, "Do you have someone, hero?"

She asked it so softly I almost didn't hear.

She'd shifted in her seat, so that she was facing me.

"You must have found someone. Somewhere."

Willie Nelson was at the part where the poor boy sitting in Birmingham Jail is listening to the wind blow and the evening train go by.

She turned her eyes away and faced forward, saying to the windshield, "I have."

I looked quickly at her. She had the look of a person who has found something that will do.

Which was James Beauregard Sims.

He didn't sparkle more in Allie's telling than he had in Julie Colby's when she told me about him. Handsome and fun to be with. From an old and prominent Fayette County family. They'd met two years ago at, of all places, Rhae Dannan's Derby Day Party. He was attracted to her and relentlessly attentive. In a very short time, they became an "unofficial" couple. She was his date at the round of dances and parties that made up the Lexington social year, and they were with each other, regularly, for dinners and concerts, the races, and UK games. Beau was always up to something. He couldn't stand to be bored. He had taken her on a Caribbean cruise last spring. It was the first time she'd been to New Orleans, the first time she'd been aboard a ship. She loved Jamaica. She loved New Orleans. Oh that Beau, he's something. (That's me, not Allie. James Beauregard Sims was already beginning to irritate me, and I hadn't even met him.)

"And you? Have you? Found someone?"

She turned back to me then. We were just about at the little turn-off on to the side road that would take us into Midway and to Fox Hill.

Had I? Kit came closest. None of the others. But no, no "someone." I hadn't been looking. To Allie I only shook my head and smiled.

She crinkled her eyes at me. "All that time. All those places. And no one."

I let the thread of the conversation drop as we were led to our table and didn't pick it back up when we were seated. I knew all I wanted to know about James Beauregard Sims, and I didn't want to dig into my own little mound of emotions at all. Allie didn't push it. She seemed satisfied.

Juliet Harrod Colby didn't entirely approve of Allison Boatwright Sinclair.

They were friendly in that strange way women have of being supportive and compassionate and protective of each other, even though they may disapprove or even dislike them.

Julie and Allie had many of the same friends, moved in the same circles, but they weren't close. When they were together, they seemed to be comfortable enough with each other, but they made no effort to seek the other's company or be involved in the other's projects.

I know Julie was there for Allie during the dark times—when I went off to war and Michael off to university, and we left her there alone, and she married the wrong boy, and then the divorce, and then Michael's death, and then my disappearance. Julie had been there to lean on and draw strength from. And Julie had been there to encourage and support her as Allie put her life together. All of that. Without question.

And yet Julie didn't entirely approve of Allie. Or didn't approve of Allie for me. She thought Allie should never have let me walk away that summer before Korea, should never have been so spiteful (her term) as to marry the boy she married while Michael and I were away, should never have taken up again with Michael when he came home to run for governor.

These were evidence in Julie's mind of flaws, flaws of character and conduct. Julie made no pretense with me about this. The day Tracy Jordan left to go back to St. Louis, she told me that if I were a little boy, she'd spank me. "If you had made any effort, Tracy would have stayed. She'd be a perfect partner for the kind of life you can make for yourself here. But you're under the spell of a phantom. The Allie in your mind doesn't exist. The one that does exist won't be good for you. Allie is strong, and she's disciplined, and she's smart, but she is not the one for you."

I thought of this as I watched Allie in the candlelight. We'd finished dinner while the twilight faded and were taking our time with a good Sonoma chardonnay. Allie seemed more relaxed. She'd been tense about getting the matter of Beau Sims out in the open with me. I wondered if that had been the reason for her call.

Julie could be right. The Allie in my mind might not exist. I may have created her out of a remembered kiss on a moonlit night, out of a boy's fantasies and a young man's need. That could be. But still, but still a man needs dreams.

"A penny for your thoughts," Allie brushed my hand.

"Was I lost somewhere? It's either the wine or you."

"Where were you?"

"Here. With you. On another night. The moon was full that night."

"We watched it go down," she said.

"While I was away in California, you called."

"To talk.

"About James Beauregard Sims?"

"Partly."

"And?"

"You, hero.

"What about me?"

"You still haven't decided what to do about you."

The evening didn't progress as I thought it might, had halfway hoped it might, though I had nothing more in mind when I called Allie than to find an antidote for the melancholy creeping up on me. James Beauregard Sims lurked in the back of both of our minds. In mine, he was frowning and shaking a finger.

The prospect of Allison Boatwright Sinclair and Beau Sims holding hands in the moonlight was something I didn't care to consider. I didn't ask her if it was going anywhere. I didn't ask if it was serious. I heard what she said and filed it away in one of those little rooms in my mind where I stuff things to be dealt with later. I don't know whether she was surprised or disappointed or puzzled by that.

And I couldn't tell how my answer about "a someone" affected her. I don't know whether it pleased her (I didn't give that answer to please her; it was the honest reaction to her question) or whether it saddened her. Her comment that I still hadn't decided what to do about me seemed to be said in resigned disappointment.

The drive back to her place was quiet and pensive. We listened to music and spoke very little.

At her door, she turned and took my face in her hands as she sometimes did and, though we were in the shadows, pulled me close to look in my eyes in search of something. After a moment she pulled my face down to hers, kissed me a long, lingering kiss. "One of these days," she said.

I stood there in the dark as she walked away—wondering.

CHAPTER FIFTY FOUR

I broke the bad news to the manager of Elkhorn Printing on Monday morning, letting him have his weekend unclouded by the rain that was going to start falling on his operation soon. I took Paul Isham with me and asked Dulin to come along. Dulin no longer had any official standing in any of the companies, but they all knew him and respected him, and I thought his presence would add a layer of reassurance to the proceedings. More and more, I was coming to rely on his gravitas. I knew he'd give me an honest critique of how well or how badly I handled the situation. There were jobs at risk—mortgages and car payments and doctor's bills and groceries for families who were living well. I knew the anxiety would be considerable. I wanted to cushion it as much as possible, but I had no experience at this sort of thing. I'd dealt with the anxiety of men in battle, but I was leading the squad and running the same risks they were, and they trusted me and had confidence in me. I was running no risk here. There were no shared experiences to draw trust from.

My weekend wasn't as relaxed as I hoped the printing plant manager's had been. Except for Sunday. I spent Sunday afternoon with Julie and Jim Colby. We ran upriver in Jim's inboard past the beach at Big Eddy, almost to the locks and dam at Alton Station, staying cool in the breeze made by our passing.

Jim put out the skis, and Julie and I took turns crossing the wake of the boat and making big arcs in the middle of the river. When we tired, we tied up at the little dock at Julie's family camp downriver from Big Eddy.

A hopeful breeze had tried to assert itself and the sun had been low enough that the big oaks gave shade there. Jim had brought along a portable radio, and we set up deck chairs on the dock in the shade, dug out the beer and listened to the Reds go down two to five to the Pirates.

Sunday night's gibbous moon would be full Monday night. It was low in the sky and on its way to setting as Julie spread our dinner on a picnic table under the trees. When dark came, we headed back down river, sipping sauvignon and watching the stars come out, drifting slowly under the two bridges and around the bend to Jim's little dock at the foot of Wapping Street.

As I started up the bank to the house, Julie asked me, "Have you talked with Allie?"

"Last night."

"Did she tell you about Beau?"

"James Beauregard Sims. Yes."

"What did you say?"

"Julie, it's been a great afternoon. I've enjoyed it and appreciated it. I have a really hard day tomorrow. I don't' want to think about that or Beau Sims. All I want is to enjoy the little buzz I have on and go home and turn on some music, and lie in the dark, and go to sleep, and sleep without dreaming, and wake up in the morning ready for whatever I have to do."

She didn't say anything. We stood there silently thinking our separate thoughts. Mine why she cares so much about what does or doesn't happen between Allie and me. She, probably, why I'm so stubborn about making a decision she sees as obvious and right.

"Pleasant dreamless sleep," she said softly, kissing me on my cheek and shooing me up the path.

I slept well enough—for a time. Then Jesse Bristow came.

He had a judge with him carrying a large leather-bound Bible in one hand and a scale of justice in his other. Jesse points at me, whispering something to the judge that I can't hear. Two soldiers, in Russian paratrooper camo, appear. They take me by the arms. The judge points to the wall. A door opens. Heat pours out and beyond it flames leap from the frame. They push me toward it.

Then, in the way dreams move you about, I'm sitting in a cavernous movie theater, empty except for me.

On the screen, a man in a white shirt and white pants and barefoot, sits in a spotlight in a chair in the middle of a darkened room. He hears whispers and keeps turning his head to try to see who is making the sounds but the glare of the spotlight blinds him.

Over the sibilants of the whispers, a voice like the boom of a cannon blasts out, "What gave him the right!"

The bodiless voices whisper, "Nothing."

The cannon voice booms louder, "Who gave him the right!"

The whispers rise "No one!"

The room goes silent. The roof gives way to a roiling, cloud filled sky. Lightning flashes and thunder cracks. An immense bearded face suddenly fills the sky. The voice is angry and devoid of mercy, then muting to a whisper cold as ice, says, "Vengeance is mine. Mine alone. Off with his head!"

I feel a tap on my shoulder. Sitting beside me is a little bald man in a cleric's collar. Jesse Bristow is with him. "That's right, you know." He turns to Jesse, bobbing his head up and down. "Vengeance is his, yes-indeedy-dog, vengeance is his." Jesse wipes at a stream of blood from the hole in his forehead and gives me a leering smile.

I recoil and start to run. A door opens. I dart through it and find I'm in a confessional. I've never been in a confessional, but this is a dream and I know it's a confessional. It's cramped and there is a little window on one side with a screen I can't see through. A voice, a woman's voice, low like a contralto's, says "Yes, my son."

I'm confused. Even though this is a dream, I know there are no women priests. Maybe I'm not in a Catholic church. But what other type of church has confessionals?

The voice speaks again, a bit impatient. "Well? I haven't got all day."

I blurt out, "What I did was righteous. He was getting away with it. I did the right thing."

"I should care about this?" the voice said.

"What about hell fire and damnation," I shot back.

"You're in the wrong pew. I don't do murderers. I do thieves and adulterers."

I jump up, angry, and hit my head against the top of the confessional—and wake up.

Ah, damn.

I thought I had outrun Jesse Bristow. He didn't come haunting while I was in San Francisco. Maybe the distance was too great. Maybe he was afraid of flying. Or maybe it was Kit and her Armenian spells. I'd had no visits since I got back, but that was only three days ago.

Enough. No more.

I did the right thing. Go to hell, Jesse, if you're not already there.

As of that very moment, on Wapping Street in the Capitol City of the Commonwealth of Kentucky in the witching hours of a late August morning, I declared myself done with the insidious sense of guilt that was planted deep in my childish mind by preachers and teachers scaring me with visions of hellfire. I declared my act righteous, rejected remorse, and announced myself willing to gamble that, all evidence to the contrary notwithstanding, God is fair and just and will honor La Hire's prayer and let it serve for us all.

I told the little voices to get the hell out of my head and take the ghost of Jesse Bristow with them.

Ed Johnson was waiting nervously for us at the entrance to Elkhorn Printing in the row of industrial buildings that spread along Holmes Street east of town on the edge of Thorn Hill. I'd called him at home that morning to set up the session, the consequence of not spoiling his weekend.

He looked worried. He had no idea what to expect but clearly something unsettling, else why would the new boss be dropping in on him on such short notice? Dulin and Paul Isham were with me.

Coffee and doughnuts were waiting in the little second floor conference room overlooking the parking lot, and the air conditioning was on maximum. The morning was already hot, and the humidity was rising. I often found myself going through two shirts and three handkerchiefs a day. Getting back in harmony with the summer climate of the Kentucky River valley was a struggle.

Ed Johnson had his jacket on as he ushered us inside, but I shed mine as soon as we were seated, and all but Paul Isham followed.

Ed Johnson had been running the printing operation for Rhae Dannan for almost twenty years. He was in his early fifties. He had been a linotype operator earlier.

I remembered him. He was one of the best.

As a boy with Michael rambling around in the back shop while we waited for his dad, watching the men at the linotype keyboards creating words out of molten lead that slid out on silver slugs of type was watching magic happen. The linotypes are gone, but lord, they were marvelous to watch.

Ed now had fifty people working for him. Their printing contracts covered everything from business cards and advertising flyers to slick color magazines and legal forms. Most of his people were long-term employees, ten years or more. I'd done my homework.

I told Ed what we'd learned. That the State printing contract wouldn't be renewed. That it would go to a competitor who had a newer color press. When I told him this, he stared in disbelief. "That's ridiculous." He glanced around, incredulous. "Our price is right. Our quality can't be beat. We never miss a deadline." He turned to Dulin, "What happened?"

Dulin looked first to Paul Isham, then to me. "The new administration likes them better than it likes us."

Ed Johnson nodded then. "Damn the politicians!" He swung to me, almost pleading, "That's the biggest chunk of our business."

All three of them had me locked in their sights. Paul with an I-told-you-so expression, Dulin curious, expectant. And Ed, with pure apprehension.

We were seated around a small conference table. Ed had put me at the head of it. Dulin and Paul were on my right, their backs to the window. Ed was to my left, facing out into the morning glare.

I stood, fixing on Ed, "This hit is bad, but it's not fatal. The bids won't be opened and the winner officially announced until next Monday morning. Until that time, we keep what we know to ourselves. When we break the news to your people, I want at the same time to tell them how we're going to work our way out of this problem. You've got a week to pull the plan together. This is what I want you to build it on: look at everything you're doing and decide that if you weren't already doing it, would you start doing it now. If the answer is no, cut it. If you've got deadwood on staff that you've been too lazy or too tender-hearted to drop, drop them. Other than that, I don't want anybody to lose their jobs. And I don't want you pulling back. I want you aggressively going after business to replace the business we're losing."

Paul broke in. "You can't make up this kind of loss without a severe cut in jobs. And you can't generate enough new business to offset the lost revenue."

"I didn't say anything about making up the loss. If we have to take a hit to the printing company's profits, we'll take the hit ... and recover. Okay with you, Ed?"

Ed Johnson seemed stunned for a moment, then straightened up smiling.

Paul Isham shook his head in unconcealed disgust at my ignorance. Dulin sat back, watching noncommittally.

I never pretended to be a businessman.

But I was, or shortly would be, chairman of Elkhorn Enterprises. I had consulted with my one-and-only shareholder during the dark hours between shutting up Jesse Bristow's voices and daylight coming—my one-and-only shareholder—me—and decided that I didn't have to drive every last dollar of profit to the bottom-line as rapidly as possible. I could do what I wanted.

"Do it then," I said to Ed and shook his hand, and we left.

Back in my office at the *Journal,* Dulin sprawled comfortably on the leather couch getting ready for the argument he knew was coming between Paul and me. I walked to my desk. Paul Isham came in last. He hesitated a moment, then closed the door behind him. The expression on his face was that of a man who had had his suspicions confirmed and was pleased at that but appalled at what being right meant. He remained standing while I took my seat.

I looked up at him questioningly and waited.

"You cannot run this company this way." he said, pounding his fist into his hand to emphasize his words, "If what we saw in Ed Johnson's office is an indication of your approach to managing these businesses, Elkhorn will go broke."

Actually, I felt good about what happened in Ed Johnson's office.

I glanced at Dulin who said nothing.

"Sit down, Paul," I said, pointing to the chair by the side of my desk. "Actually, we'll come out of this stronger. Ed will clean up his operation. He'll get rid of all those things that are started because they were needed at one time but are not dropped when the need isn't there any longer. He'll finally move on people who aren't pulling their weight or whose jobs have run out, but he's holding on to because he's too nice a guy to let them go. And his people will be reassured and more productive."

Paul remained standing, fuming and frowning.

"We'll be leaner," I said, "more efficient, more aggressive. Yes, we'll take a hit, but we'll make more money and be more competitive when we finish. This is an opportunity, Paul, an opportunity in work clothes."

I heard Dulin chuckle.

Paul hadn't conceded anything. He swung around to Dulin for support.

Dulin sat up straighter on the couch. "As long as the one-and-only shareholder is willing to take the hit, I'm happy."

I realized I was happy, too. For the first time since coming back, I was happy with my situation.

I'd been fighting against the change Rhae Dannan's bequest demanded I make in my life from the moment I learned of it. I'd been searching for some honorable way to justify to myself that I could be true to Rhae's charge and yet not have to pick up the burden that came with it. I didn't want the responsibility. I didn't want the money. I didn't want to come back and face my phantoms. And yet, as much as I denied and resisted the feeling, I wanted to come home.

I can't explain. Maybe it's an Irish thing. We're drawn to home. Maybe our spirits are bound to the land we spring from. Maybe we're anchored to home ground. Maybe blood and bone and mind and heart are so infused with the look and the feel and the smell of the place that it is always in our memories. Maybe it's a spell conjured from river mist and bluegrass meadows.

I slapped my hand down on my desk, stood up, opened the office door and asked Mildred, who was hovering nervously outside, if she would arrange some coffee for us. Then I turned back to Paul and Dulin.

"All right then, gentlemen," I said, feeling liberated and eager, "let's be clear. I didn't ask for this. I didn't want it. But I have it, and by damn, I'm going to make it sing."

CHAPTER FIFTY FIVE

The work week passed hurriedly.

I established a routine to get me through the day as efficiently as possible. An early morning run. Breakfast—a full breakfast that I'd either make myself or take at the White Tower across the bridge. Be in the office by nine and deal with the calls and the letters and the meetings that wash up there until noon. Break free then and spend the afternoon focusing on the businesses—hie myself out to the farm, the stables, and the printing operations to learn and understand the play of their games as rapidly as I could.

In the evenings, if I could manage it, I'd have dinner alone. I'm not naturally gregarious. But there were invitations that had to be honored, so those opportunities would be rare.

Whatever the evening held, I'd try to close it out in the newsroom, ostensibly getting an early look at the next day's news, but the real reason was to draw comfort from the chatter of the tickers and the rhythm of the talk. Then after a while, as I had done since I was a young man, I'd walk out into the night through the sleeping streets, remembering things past and making plans until I was ready for sleep.

I intended to stay with this schedule until I was confident I understood what I had and what we could do with it.

Tuesday, the Tuesday after the long Labor Day weekend—the day already hot, and the humidity rising, but the sky cloudless and a forecast of a few cooling showers by nightfall—I'd just gotten into my office when Mildred told me the Governor's Chief of Staff was on the line.

There was no preamble.

Richard Rosen said, coldly, "I am calling as a matter of courtesy to inform you that the State printing contract is being awarded to Morris & Company of Lexington. The Governor asked me to call. He promised you a level playing field. Your company's bid didn't meet the test of 'lowest and best.' The official notice will be posted shortly. I understand this piece of business is a major part of your printing company's income. Isn't that a shame. Well, I imagine a man of your character can rise above a little set back like this. "

And hung up.

I don't know what I resented more. The hypocrisy. The dishonesty. Or the smugly satisfied tone of Richard Rosen's voice.

I called Ed Johnson at the printing plant.

"The balloon just went up. Let's assemble your people and lay out our plan."

It was a good plan. Ed had gone over it with me the day before— made him late for his church's Labor Day Picnic, but he went away a much relieved man. I made no changes to his plan except to tell him to hire the two best print salesmen he could find. I wanted a full court press on new business, and he'd need extra muscle to bring it in.

There would be some early retirements; a few jobs would be eliminated but with a generous separation package to ease the pain, and a slew of antiquated work practices would disappear. Elkhorn Printing would be at break-even by midyear next year, and in the black before that year was over.

Take that, Richard Rosen.

When I returned from Ed Johnson's meeting, I called in Paul Isham.

No preamble here either.

"Call your friend at the consortium. Cancel the meeting. Tell him the *Journal* is not for sale. Thank him for their interest and wish them well."

"You don't even want to hear what they have say?"

"Whatever they have to say will make no difference. I have plans. You can tell him that."

"You?" Paul said, astonished. "Plans? For god's sake, Theo, don't begin tampering."

I should have been insulted by Paul's disrespect, but I felt too good to be put out. The meeting with Ed Johnson's people had gone very well. The result we'd get would be very positive. The plan I had was exciting and challenging and, if we could pull it off, golden. Paul deserved to be a part of that if he wanted. I started to say to him, stick with the Kid, Black Hawk, but knew he wouldn't have the slightest idea of what I was referring to.

Even so, the thought made me smile and smiling, the slight surge of anger that I had begun to feel disappeared.

The smile alarmed him further, though. "Are you all right?"

"Cancel that meeting. If you don't like the game I plan to play, you can cash out with my best wishes and go play any game that pleases you."

Perhaps I shouldn't have been so blunt. This thing I wanted to make happen, this prize I wanted to win, would take believers. I had no place for doubters.

The idea had been voiced to no one yet. It wasn't even fully formed yet.

I called out to Mildred. "Mr. Clark," she came back sharply. "The buzzer, use the buzzer!"

Worth a smile that. Put me in my place.

"Call Mr. Dulin Monroe. Tell him he needs to invite me to lunch."

Her frown told me she didn't approve of my manners, but she placed the call anyway. "He said to tell you that he regrets he didn't do a better job of teaching you respect. Meet him at Jim's Place on the river by the dam at one-thirty."

Paul walked out without a word.

The idea I was playing with was simple—and maybe impossible.

We'd build our own media empire. We'd use the *Journal* as the flagship, but instead of daily newspapers as the consortium planned, we'd build ours on weeklies—the small town newspapers that are the souls of the communities they cover.

The weeklies are as integral a part of the life of their towns as the local schools. Their advertisers are loyal, and their readers are passionate. Every town of any size had one. Georgetown, Versailles, Shelbyville—they were almost in arms' reach of us. We'd start with them and move out until we had as many of the weeklies in the Bluegrass as we wanted. The Bluegrass is the richest market in the state. We'd link them all with the *Journal* and have the strongest news and advertising medium in the most lucrative market in the Commonwealth.

It could be golden.

If it could be done.

The author of the Don't-Do-Dumb-Things rule would know.

Dulin Monroe rocked back in his chair when I finished. "Aren't you the guy bucking at being saddled with thinking like a businessman and burdened with a fortune?"

"Come on, Dulin, I'm serious."

"It would take a ton of money. Where would you get it?"

"Partly from our own resources. Partly from financing. I've a good friend in New York. An investment banker. One of the best. He can arrange these things."

"What makes you think the owners of these papers will want to sell?"

"Maybe no one's asked them. Maybe they retain a share of the ownership. Maybe they see the possibilities. I don't know. My guy in

New York can work that out." I tried a Don Corleone smile, "We'll make them a deal they can't refuse."

Dulin didn't laugh. Instead he shook his head slowly, not as if he was rejecting what I said but as if he was having difficulty believing I said it.

A waitress moved in to clear our plates. Dulin kept looking at me as if he couldn't quite comprehend what had happened. When she left, he said, "Do you grasp the implications of what you're suggesting?"

"Probably not," I admitted, "but it's an exciting idea, isn't it."

"Pulling it off would keep you from getting bored. No doubt about that."

"Is it a dumb idea?"

He didn't hesitate, "It's a fantasy."

"Okay, but other than that, how do you like it?"

The waitress showed up again. "We have homemade Key Lime pie. Coffee?"

I smiled and said no. Dulin was still squinting at me.

"You realize that the odds of pulling this off range from damn little to worse than none." He shook his head. "You're going to try it anyway, aren't you?"

CHAPTER **FIFTY SIX**

One thing I know for certain. I'm not as smart as I think I am. So I've never been hesitant to get smarter people to help me.

Often I get help from people who don't know they're giving it—by listening to what they say, by watching what they do and how they do it.

For this thing I had in mind, Benjay would be key—Benjamin Bolanger IV, of the Boston Bolangers, investment banker par excellence. Only someone with Benjay's talents and contacts could assemble the financing that might be needed and design a strategy for the acquisitions.

And I would need someone with the management skills to put the organization together and to see to its day-to-day running. I'd be good for the plans—for the energy, for the enthusiasm and the problem solving, but once the organization was up and functioning, seeing to the day-to-day management of it would bore me mightily.

And a consigliore—someone of wide experience whose judgment I trusted completely, my chief advisor, my second.

There was only one candidate for that job. Dulin Monroe.

Paul Isham was very much in my mind as I ran through these possibilities. When I took over officially as publisher, I'd want the *Journal* editorial operation reporting directly to me. The Managing Editor Emeritus title would disappear. Would there be a place for Paul then? Should there be?

None of these questions were raised at lunch, but I would need answers soon. I had it in mind to start on this exercise as soon as I felt I had a firm enough grasp of the overall operations to be comfortable in turning attention to this new challenge.

Begin putting the team together in January. Was that possible? Was I pushing too fast? The Donner Party, rushing to make it to California before the winter snows closed the Sierra passes had been seduced into taking a short-cut that turned out to be a disaster. They reached the mountains later than they should have and were snow-bound near Lake Tahoe. Some froze. Some starved. Some turned to cannibalism. Less than half of the eighty-five who started the journey survived that horror. One of the survivors, a young girl, writing to a friend in Illinois who was to follow later, closed her letter with a single line of advice, "Hurry as fast as you can, but don't take no short cuts."

I would.

Go fast.

And take no short cuts.

Dulin was standing outside on the deck at Jim's Place watching the river when I left. He seemed pensive and subdued. He hadn't encouraged me to go forward. But he hadn't encouraged me to desist either. I think he was of two minds on the matter. He realized the considerable problems my idea held, but recognized the considerable opportunities the idea could generate and was intrigued by them.

I think the thing that fed his hesitancy was whether Theo Clark had the skill to pull it off. More importantly, whether Theo Clark had the determination and the commitment.

I've never been guilty of a lack of confidence. I've done dumb things and made wrong decisions and many mistakes, but I've never been too timid to try a thing because it was thought to be impossible. I don't say this in any self-congratulatory way. It's more of a fault than a strength.

This idea I'd discussed with Dulin was just the first step toward a far more significant, far more difficult goal I'd set for myself. Did I have the discipline for that, the heart?

Yes, I wondered, too.

CHAPTER FIFTY SEVEN

September, tantalizingly, began its slow segue into autumn.

My days were filled with the routine of the businesses. With a real purpose now in mind, I concentrated even harder on learning—long days at the farm and the stables and with Ed Johnson as he began executing his recovery plan.

Days were getting shorter. The evenings cooler. School would be starting soon and football season.

I love fall, can hardly wait each year for it to come—even in San Francisco where it is barely noticeable. There is a crispness in the air, a feeling of excitement and possibilities that none of the other seasons possess.

One step at a time, I cautioned myself. This first. The other thing later. And in between the matters that must be taken care of. Winding down my writerly life neatly and with no strings dangling. Taking my leave from *The Atlantic* with good feelings all around. Handing the Afghanistan story off to whomever the editors chose to carry it on.

And Kit. I hadn't considered a future without Kit Bedrosian in it somewhere, and when I did, I found the prospect disturbing.

And Allie.

I still cannot explain the strange hold she has on me. It was there at the first day and has never lessened. Allie is like a song that keeps running unbidden in my mind. I know the tune of her as well I know the beat of my heart. But I can't find the words. For some things there are no words. And even if words can be found, sometimes they are not said. To put words to a thing is to make it real.

Julie Colby would say I am cowardly. Julie is a romantic. She thinks every man needs a special woman—someone to love and be loved by, someone to care for and be cared for by and that I'm afraid to make the commitment that would produce that result for me. She thinks I'm too cowardly to accept the responsibility for another's happiness. She could be right. I try not to get too close to anyone, or let anyone get too close to me.

I may not have managed that with Allie.

Have I with Kit?

Neither of us expects of the other more than the other is eager to give. When we're together, we're together. When we're apart, neither lives in the other's mind. We have a satisfying relationship.

Kit had never seen Kentucky. She knew a big horse race was run there every year, and she knew there was all that gold at Fort Knox. They made bourbon in Kentucky. She liked bourbon—a dab of sweet vermouth, a touch of bitters, and a maraschino cherry—no other way. There was a brand of country music that she favored, in limited doses, and it carried the name of the region I kept talking about. It was a pleasant enough place, she was sure, but you wouldn't want to live there.

I wanted her to see it. When I suggested she come, she was reluctant, but her curiosity won out; the net result of which was that in less than thirty minutes, her flight from SFO into Louisville would be on the ground, and I'd be greeting her with a julep in hand.

When Daniel Boone first saw the country that would be called The Bluegrass, he thought he had stumbled into Eden. This was just before the start of the Revolutionary War. He'd found a pass in the southeastern mountains, crested the Cumberland Plateau, and was standing on the peak of a high ridge. A vista of gently rolling hills and succulent meadows stretched as far as his eye could see—rich and tranquil and welcoming—like nothing he'd seen before. Eden beyond the mountains.

The settlers who followed him up the Wilderness Trail agreed.

They wrote back to their friends in Virginia and the Carolinas, in Tennessee and Georgia—to those all along the Eastern Seaboard who were looking for opportunity but were barred from this paradise by the rugged wall of the Appalachian Range that ran like a barricade from central Alabama all the way north to Newfoundland.

Come, they said. The soil is richer than you can imagine. Game abounds. The streams are clear and sweet. The weather temperate. Come.

And come they did— aristocrats and rednecks, craftsmen and backwoodsmen, merchants and farmers—they came.

And they found that what they'd been told was true. The Bluegrass was as close to Eden as they were likely to come on in this life.

Whether a San Franciscan bred and born would find it so was uncertain, but there is an enchantment to the Bluegrass that seduces almost everyone. Possibly even Kit Bedrosian.

I think she was as glad to see me as I was to see her. It had only been a month, but we both accepted now that a major change was occurring in our lives. I wouldn't be living in San Francisco any more. We wouldn't be working together any longer. I wouldn't need an agent when I settled into my new role at the head of Rhae Dannan's empire. There would be no reason to be in each other's life then.

We both knew that something was ending. Or beginning.

The lyric to the cowboy song Kit whispered teasingly to me that last night in San Francisco ran through my mind. "Don't ask me to be faithful/ Be content with what I give/ Love me only when I'm with you/ When I'm gone, forget I live."

I held out the julep as she came through the gate into the terminal. "What's that?" she asked, a suspicious frown forming.

"A mint-julep. You're in Kentucky."

"I like Manhattans. "

"This one's for me. To toast your arrival."
She laughed and threw her arms around me.

By the time we'd gotten her luggage and I'd retrieved the car, we were in the middle of the evening commute. To the locals, the Watterson Express Way that would take us around Louisville was a parking lot. To Kit, used to the pile-ups on the Golden Gate and the Bay Bridge, it was a walk in the park.

At the eastern edge of town, I cleared the Watterson and made for old Highway Sixty rather than the four-lane interstate. The sun was going down, and the long shadows of evening were beginning to reach across the land. The drive would take us out through Shelbyville and Bridgeport on a meandering two-lane road with well-tended farms and rolling pastures spread out on either side all the way. There would be very few cars, and Kit could watch night softly begin to wrap its arms around a section of the Bluegrass.

I'd decided to house her at the farm. There were good hotels around, but nothing the equal of the Mark or the Plaza, and I didn't want to start off with unfavorable impressions.

The main house at the farm, the old Hopkins homeplace, Rhae's home, on the rise above the meadow, looking out to the creek, would be perfect. It was mine now, part of the inheritance.

The house was a gracious old two-story of sprawling dimensions built by Captain Hopkins, Rhae's great-great grandfather, in the Federal style. There was nothing pretentious about it, none of the Grecian columns or soaring porticos that fronted so many of the old mansions in the Bluegrass. It was a place, simply, of elegant simplicity and enormous comfort.

The house was painted white and had a roof of Welsh slate that was blue-grey in the sunshine and black in the rain. The slate had been cut from the mines at Blaenaue Ffestiniog and brought all the way across the ocean from Wales to satisfy Captain Hopkins' fancy. The Captain never explained why he wanted the slate roof. There were no others around. I remember as a boy, the sound of rain on it at night, soothing me to sleep.

Kit would find it charming.

Rhae's cook and housekeeper (now mine if I chose to live there) were there to take care of her. Kit would wake to colts in the meadow and the flash of gold and red along the creek as the sycamores and the oaks took on their fall colors. She'd have breakfast on the porch as the sun dried the dew from the grass, and birdsong and the sound of water over stones from the creek.

Of course she'd be charmed. I'd be there to make sure of it.

Not that I would stay at the farm with her. The housekeeper would be scandalized and my reputation at risk with the cook. If I favored breakfast at the farm with Kit, I'd have to get up early and drive out.

I wanted Kit to see the whole of the state—east to west, north to south. It is a magical place. Jesse Stuart, the poet of W Hollow, believed, "Kentucky is neither East nor West nor North nor South. If America can be said to be a body, Kentucky can be said to be its heart." See it all, and you can believe that. But there wasn't time. Kit could spare four days. So we'd concentrate on the heart of Kentucky— The Bluegrass—the Eden beyond the mountains.

"Yes," I told her as we drove, "The grass really is blue—in the spring, when it's budding. It grows two to three feet high, and when you look out across the fields and the pastures, with the sun on the grass and a light breeze moving through, you think you're seeing waves rippling on a peaceful sea. Sometimes you pull your car off to the side of the road and just sit and watch."

I explained that the broad geographic region called the Bluegrass takes up a large part of north central Kentucky, but the heart of the Bluegrass, is the Inner Bluegrass. It is smaller and more beautiful. The Inner Bluegrass is a gently rolling plain of rich black soil laid over limestone rock that spreads in an irregular circle from just above Cynthiana in the North to outside Paris in the East, past Berea in the South and a little beyond Shelbyville in the West. The soil is so fertile because of the high phosphate content caused by the underlying limestone. It is the richest agricultural area in the state, and hands down, the most handsome landscape in the country. We were just on the edge of it. Frankfort and Lexington are almost in its center.

"We'll concentrate on the Inner Bluegrass," I told her. "You're going to see horse barns grander than the mansions on Knob Hill and little country cemeteries more beautiful than parks. If it appeals to you, we'll canoe down Elkhorn through the autumn leaves. I'll show you where the best bourbon in the world is made, and we'll sit in the garden at Liberty Hall with the full moon shining and watch for the ghost of the Grey Lady. Abraham Lincoln and Jefferson Davis were both born in Kentucky, did you know that—the President of the United State of America and the President of the Confederate States of America—born in the same state and in the same year. Strange, isn't it that their paths took them to such different ends? Their statues stand in sight of each other in the rotunda of the Capitol building. There is an almost cathedral-like feeling there. We'll go there and let the silence take us back and wonder.

"And later we can dine like the landed gentry in antebellum mansions or check out the funky restaurants. Or we can drive down to My Old Kentucky Home in Bardstown, so you can see where Stephen Collins Foster wrote the song, and I'll teach you the words."

She laughed, "Don't you dare try singing to me."

We were nearing Frankfort then. The sun was below the horizon. I wanted to stop at the Louisville Hill overlook, so she could see the lights coming on and the town bedding down in the folds of the river.

We got out and stood by the stone wall at the edge of the overlook. In the twilight, the Capitol seemed almost close enough to touch. Across the river, the Arsenal looked like a storybook castle perched above the town. The Post Office spire and the Catholic Church steeple were silhouetted against the sky. Streetlights were beginning to click on in the neighborhoods, and the flash of brake lights marked the way up East Main Hill. In another half-hour, it would be full dark.

Kit edged up against me and took my arm.

"So this is what home looks like."

"Some of it."

"It gets better?"

'You'll see."

CHAPTER FIFTY EIGHT

So she saw.

All that.

And more.

I'm still not sure what I expected, or even what I wanted, by showing Kit all I wanted her to see.

The moon did its part—the Harvest Moon—the full moon of September—bathing the countryside in its fairy light. Drive the back lanes of the Bluegrass on the night of the Harvest Moon, and you'll become slowly spellbound. There is a feeling all around that something exciting, something immensely satisfying, is about to happen. The pale blue light that bathes the countryside is the light by which magic is made.

I think Kit felt that.

We'd stopped on the side of a lane to Georgetown and were sitting side-by-side on one of the old stone fences. There was a small creek just beyond. We were watching the moonlight on the water rippling by.

"Sometimes I forget you're Irish," she said, turning to me. She reached for my hand. "All you Irish are poets, aren't you?" she said, "poets and lovers." She turned to me then. "How did you ever manage to make it into the Marine Corps? How could such a strange thing happen? All that blood and brutality. You are a gentle soul,

Theo Clark. How did you ever manage to fool them? How did you ever manage to get through it?"

She was very serious. What kind of man are you really? That's what she was asking. Did I know? I knew there are too many people inside me to say for certain which one I am. I know some of them well. Some are only passing acquaintances. A few I don't want to know. The question was too hard to answer. She would have to provide the answer herself. I danced around it.

"Fool them? The Corps could hardly wait to get me," I said, bantering. "Yes we're silver-tongued and muse-inspired, no doubt about that, but you left out the warrior part. The Irish are the fiercest and finest fighters the world has ever seen. The Corps knows that. And a Kentucky boy with the blood of Irish warriors running in his veins? They greeted me with open arms. An Irisher from Kentucky led the route of the Barbary Pirates and inspired the line about 'to the shores of Tripoli.' He's buried here. First Lieutenant Presley O'Bannon. And the Minstrel Boy, he was Irish. Jeb Stuart and Jubal Early. The Irish Brigade that turned the tide at Gettysburg. Sargent York, the most decorated soldier of World War I, and Audie Murphy, the most decorated soldier in World War II. Irish. Warriors. The record will show it. None better. That part about lovers, well—all the world knows we're a modest race. I couldn't speak to that."

I was smiling what I hoped was a winning smile, but Kit wasn't in the mood for banter. In the morning she would be on a plane back to San Francisco.

Despite the magic and the moonlight, it wasn't a night for playing. It was a night for things to be said that should be said if they were going to be said at all. Or left unsaid and regretted.

She slid down off the wall and stood facing me while I still sat. Our eyes were on the same plane. A sad little smile played on her lips.

"You're staying," she said.

"You're leaving," I answered.

She leaned up to kiss me softly.

"What happens now?"

I slid down from the wall, and we stood face to face in the moonlight, our shadows merging. I took her hands. They were warm and firm. I tried to see in her eyes what answer she wanted, but saw only the question.

"I don't know what happens now. Do you?"

She looked away from me and up to the sky. "The moon is so bright it hides the stars," she said.

"They're there."

"We're both afraid of it, aren't we?"

"It?"

"Us."

We lapsed into silence after that. Kit leaned back against me. I put my arms around her. We watched for a star to appear and listened to the creek while the moon went down.

I spent the rest of the night at the farm—with Kit—and figured I could sweet talk my way through the cook's suspicions when morning came.

Later at the airport, as she was ready to board, "There must be reasons for you to come to San Francisco," she said.

"I'll find some," I said. "You'll come back? You haven't seen the Derby."

"No. You come to me. People would talk if I came back here."

She didn't hug me or kiss me, just touched her lips demurely to my cheek. "Come when you can. And," she said as she walked away, "don't listen to cowboy songs."

CHAPTER **FIFTY NINE**

October

Rhae Dannan's empire formally cleared probate and passed into my hands the first Monday of October.

There was no fanfare. No rockets went off; no marching bands played. No crowds assembled to hail my coronation. A simple call from the attorney. That was all.

After all the angst and anticipation, it was a disappointment.

But fanfare or not, Theodore O'Hara Clark was now officially the monarch of Elkhorn Enterprises—suzerain of a farming complex that was the largest and most lucrative in one of the richest counties in the state, pasha of a thoroughbred racing and breeding stable of renown and promise, czar of a commercial printing operation rejuvenating itself and growing, and, to him, most notably of all, Editor and Publisher of the *Journal*, the Capitol City's best, and only, daily newspaper.

Not to be overlooked, of course, was a portfolio of investments as rich in the aggregate as all these assets combined.

Who could tell what he might do with all this? Who could tell what all this might do to him?

Others may ask it out of curiosity. I asked it of myself out of concern.

My first call was to Dulin.

"It's done," I said. "Game time now. Will you come play? Keep me from doing dumb things? Help me get this right. I need you."

There was a long silence. I thought he had put the phone down and walked away. I could hear birdsong in the background. He must have been outside on the patio on his third cup of coffee, watching the morning. When he came back on, he said, "Remember the afternoon I sent you out to the Hockensmith farm? I had a tip on a murder, and no one else was around. I couldn't wait for any of the other reporters to show up. Someone might beat us to the story. You were all I had. You were still in school, finishing up at UK and working nights at the *Journal* to help pay your way through. A rookie. No experience. Turned out to be the biggest story of the year. Turned out you handled it so well the *Herald Tribune* came and took you to the big city. Is that boy still in you—that drive, that determination?"

He went silent again, and I knew he wasn't asking me. He was asking himself if he believed it.

After a while he said, "My coffee's cold. Don't go away."

I heard the door on the deck slide open. A long silence. Then it slid closed.

"You still there?"

"I'm still here."

"I don't know that I can help you. But if I can, I will."

I didn't need to call Paul Isham.

He came into my office shortly after my call to Dulin. I've said that Paul is as distinguished looking a man as I ever seen. He had all his dignity wrapped tightly around him that morning.

Paul of course knew. As Executor of the Estate, he was the first to know. The attorney called Paul, then called me. There was no call to me from Paul. No word of encouragement or congratulation.

He laid an envelope on my desk. "My resignation," he said.

I let the envelope lie, looked up at him standing rigidly in front of my desk, "You've decided you don't want to play?"

"Play! That says it all,' he almost hissed. "This isn't a game! It's deadly serious. You're in so far over your head, you'll never see the light. You'll run Rhae's legacy into the ground. I refuse to be a part of that."

Paul didn't understand. He didn't see the simple truth of things. It's all a game. Business. Politics. A game. With winners and losers. It's about proving who's smartest, who's toughest, who's got more talent. It's about finding out who can get knocked down and get back up and win. All the time. Every day. A contest. A competition to find who's best. There's no point to it otherwise. I picked up the envelope and turned it slowly in my hands, as if weighing it, then placed it back upon my desk.

'Well then, I wish you luck with whatever comes next for you."

I meant that. Paul Isham had earned it. His skill and dedication had helped make the *Journal* the force it was. He'd been a rock for Rhae Dannan after Benjamin Dannan's death. I would shed no tears at his departure, but I did wish him well. Which meant nothing. Paul's anger was palpable. He shook his head dismissively.

"I won't pretend we've been friends. Once, though, I was grateful to you. For killing Jesse Bristow. There was nothing linking you to it—but we knew. I knew. Rhae knew. Even Dulin knew. If you hadn't done it, I would have. To avenge Benjamin."

Recalling all that, he softened a bit and his voice took on a note almost resembling regret.

"You were smart to leave when you did. Rhae made an awful mistake in bringing you back. You'll fail, Theo. When that happens, the *Journal* can be what it ought to be—the flagship of a chain of powerful newspapers that blanket the state—and you can go back to playing the *games* you know how to play. The consortium is naming a new executive—an Executive Director of Newspaper Operations. The announcement will be made tomorrow. I'm that man. We'll use my name and my reputation to help acquire the few remaining papers we want. The *Journal* is still at the top of that list."

I stood up then. It didn't seem proper to remain seated. "I wish this was ending differently." I extended my hand. He didn't take it.

CHAPTER SIXTY

With Rhae's empire now my responsibility, with the game clock now running, Dulin and I huddled.

Someone to look after the day-to-day running of the various businesses; I needed one of those. In the corporations I'd covered, they call that the Chief Operating Officer.

And someone to manage the numbers and the finances of all the businesses—a Chief Financial Officer—one of those, too.

Dulin would be my second— my chief advisor. I wasn't sure what title that responsibility should carry, and Dulin didn't care. We opted for simplicity—Chief Advisor to the Chairman. It seemed prestigious enough to carry weight with strangers. His reputation alone would be sufficient everywhere else.

Satis Arnow, the banker from East Kentucky who had played an important role in Michael Dannan's run for governor and with whom I'd become close friends, would find us the CFO. He knew the best financial minds in the state.

I decided to ask Jim Colby to take the Chief Operating Officer spot. Jim had a mind for management and an MBA from UK to round out his resume after he'd passed the bar. I knew him to be organized and disciplined and as good with people as anyone I'd met. I had reason to believe he was tired of practicing law and ready for something with more challenge—challenge like what he'd get if we moved forward with my plan.

Dulin and I discussed and agreed to all this over dinner at the farm— my farm—that night.

Betsy, Rhae Dannan's housekeeper and cook, who had been with her since her childhood, passed while I was away. The new cook, Mrs. Anderson, hired by Rhae, was new to me. She set us an excellent table and a fine meal of quail and kale.

I still hadn't moved to the farm. I wasn't sure I would. The old house was dear to me. I'd spent much of my boyhood and young manhood there, playing and working with Michael and later, helping with his campaign when he came back to run for governor. I even had my own room there. But there were too many memories in those rooms, intense and bittersweet after all that had happened. I was hesitant to go live among them. Still, I had to move somewhere. The little apartment over the library wasn't an appropriate setting for the Chairman of Elkhorn Industries and Editor and Publisher of the *Journal.*

Julie would have some ideas.

Dulin and I took our coffee and brandy outside when dinner was done. We sat in rocking chairs on the porch and watched the night come down. It was cool and too late in the year for fireflies over the meadow, but pleasant and quiet and no breeze to speak of. The creek made its soft sounds, and the stars started poking through. It was the time of month of the dark of the moon. The night would be raven black and the sky so full of stars, the Milky Way would seem a solid path.

The moment felt right to tell Dulin what I really intended.

Build the little media empire I'd already told him about, yes. But, even if we could manage it, that wouldn't be enough. I needed more than that. I needed something that would take hold of my soul and dominate my thinking and spur me to goals I had no reason to expect I could reach but had to try for.

I let the moment pass. I'd asked Dulin to come out of retirement to help me achieve a goal he thought was probably impossible. I'd wait a while to tell him about the other thing.

My ascension to the throne of the Elkhorn Enterprises did not escape the notice of the press. The *Journal*, of course, played the story prominently. I asked Lew Arbogast to keep it small and make it modest, but the formal change in the ownership of the *Journal* and Elkhorn Enterprises was too big a local story to play down. It made Page One. The *Lexington Herald* played it page one, too.

DANNAN PROBATE CLOSES

Clark Takes Over

Frankfort, October 7 -- Theodore O'Hara Clark, a Frankfort native and Editor At Large of *The Atlantic Magazine*, today took charge of one of the Commonwealth's leading newspapers and largest personal fortunes.

As heir to the late Rhae Hopkins Dannan, who died in an automobile accident this spring, Clark becomes Chairman of Elkhorn Industries and its farming, thoroughbred stables, and commercial printing operations as well as Editor and Publisher of the *Journal,* the Capitol City's daily newspaper.

While not related to Mrs. Dannan, Clark was "like a second son," friends said. He and Michael Dannan, Mrs. Dannan's only child, were best friends from their boyhood days, and Clark was principal advisor to Dannan during his run for governor.

Dannan, a last minute dark-horse entry, was ahead in the polls when he was shot dead by a crazed gunman at a campaign rally in the closing weeks of the campaign.

Jesse Bristow, his opponent, was considered the certain winner then, but Bristow himself was assassinated several weeks later. Bristow's killer remains unknown.

Through most of his career, Clark was a reporter and columnist for the *Journal*. His weekly column was widely syndicated and considered one of the most influential political columns in the Commonwealth. He unexpectedly resigned from the *Journal* in 1970 to travel and write. In 1975, he was named Editor At Large of *The Atlantic.*

Clark is a United States Marine Corps veteran. He was a rifleman during the Marine's celebrated breakout from the Chosin Reservoir encirclement the first winter of the Korean War and was awarded the Silver Star for gallantry in action and a Purple Heart for wounds suffered during the fighting.

He is a Frankfort High School graduate and holds a Journalism degree from the University of Kentucky.

In addition to his work at *The Atlantic*, Clark was earlier a reporter for the *New York Herald Tribune* where his coverage was nominated for a Pulitzer Prize.

He is forty-eight and unmarried. Clark has been living in San Francisco, but will now make his home in Frankfort.

This is the story that was picked up by the wires and run out on the state and national circuits. I could have done without the mention of the medals. And I wished the Bristow killing hadn't been mentioned at all. But the story was accurate and fair, and no one gave me a chance to edit the copy.

I told myself to start getting used to being written about.

Dulin and I met with the business heads that afternoon. Being the pro-tem boss was one thing. Being the boss in fact was different.

Now that I was official, I thought they should know what I had in mind. I announced Paul Isham's retirement and Dulin's agreement to come back to help me get this right. They liked that. They knew and trusted Dulin. No one seemed particularly upset that Paul was leaving. They respected him. They wouldn't miss him.

I told them to tell their people to stay relaxed and focused. No big changes are coming. We're doing well and will continue to do well.

After the meeting ended, I asked Lew Arbogast to hang back a moment.

"Paul's out of the picture now. So it will be you and me and Dulin. You're comfortable with that?"

"Perfectly," he said smiling.

"Then can you find room for a new column?"

"Whose?"

"Mine. I want to resume writing a weekly column. For the Sunday paper. In time it might get good enough again that we can syndicate it again. Can you indulge your publisher? I promise I won't bore your readers."

"Resurrect your old column," Dulin broke in. "Helluva idea. It'll make some people very uneasy ... delight most everyone else. Can you do it? Will you have the time?"

"I'll make the time. What do you say, Lew."

"Can I afford you?" Then he laughed. "When do we start?"

"Soon."

The cards and calls came pouring in.

Mildred spent most of the day taking messages and opening notes of congratulations and good wishes. Shortly after noon, a local florist struggled in with an enormous funeral wreath on a green metal stand. It read "In tender memory of the old Theo Clark. RIP. Long live the new one." It was signed "The Callucci Boys: Jay, Brian, and Benjamin Bolanger IV."

Mildred was shocked. I fell back laughing. My New York trio. The story must have been run out on the AP national wire, and Brian saw it at the *World-Telegram.*

Later there was a phone message from Kit, "Theo. So much. Don't let it change you."

And a call from the Governor's secretary. "The Governor would like Mr. Clark to lunch with him privately. On Thursday in the Sun Room at the Mansion at one-thirty. Is that possible?"

Mildred asked.

"Yes, of course," I said. A private audience with the Governor. For what reason? What had he in mind? I couldn't possibly pass that up.

There was nothing from Allie.

The next few days were a blur of document signings and accountant reports as Rhae Dannan's empire became mine. I went in early and stayed late but made it through the nights with no visits from Jesse Bristow or little accusing voices in my head.

I was dealing with issues I'd never dealt with before. The money brought with it a demand for attention to matters I wasn't interested in but now had to be. The chairmanship brought with it responsibilities I found heavy—responsibilities for the businesses that Rhae Dannan's family had built over the years, but more sobering to me, responsibilities to the people who worked for us to keep those businesses running smoothly and successfully.

I thought of Kit's admonition. "Don't let it change you." How could it not?

Dulin moved into the office vacated by Paul Isham.

Mildred became Executive Assistant to the Chief Executive. She loved the title. Her work load was to be considerably expanded, so since the *Journal* didn't have "secretaries," we hired an "assistant" to assist her with the calls and the mail and the scheduling and all those things secretaries did—a bright young girl, Sara Dixon, right out of Mrs. Lovelace's Secretarial School in Midway—young enough not to resent reporting to Mildred and eager enough to be delighted with the job.

We began to settle into a routine.

CHAPTER SIXTY ONE

The Executive Mansion is the home provided by the people of Kentucky for their governor's comfort and convenience while he looks out for their welfare and makes their lives better.

It sits on the east lawn of the State Capitol grounds surrounded by lush gardens and stately trees and faces west to the Capitol Building, where the work of the people is done.

The Mansion is modeled on the Petit Trianon, Marie Antoinette's opulent hide-away near the Palace of Versailles and is almost as impressive as the Capitol itself, with twenty-two strikingly furnished rooms, a staff sufficient to the needs of the occupant, and an air of nobility which pleases the landed gentry of the Bluegrass. Kentucky takes good care of its governors.

As is my practice, I was early so as not to be late.

The Governor had not yet made his way across from the Capitol. I was ushered to the Sun Room where we were to lunch.

The room was at the rear of the mansion, overlooking a lawn that sloped down to the ridge above the river. A large picture window took up the far wall, the east wall. In front of it was a small round table with place settings for two. The floor was hardwood, highly polished and gleaming in the sunlight, and the walls a soothing light pastel green, Colonial Green, I believe it's called. One flanking wall held a large pastoral landscape and the other an arrangement of portraits of ladies of an earlier age, none of whom I recognized but probably should have. Outside, the afternoon was bright and sprinkled with the orange and scarlet leaves of autumn.

A white-jacketed waiter appeared and asked if I cared for anything. Wine? A cocktail? I declined and stood enjoying the view while waiting for the Governor to make his entrance.

Dulin and I had gone over all the scenarios we could conjure for what this meeting might be about. And could imagine no reason for it. So I waited with my curiosity fully engaged and prepared for nothing.

For my part, I had no agenda other than to try to determine whether the Honorable Isaac Adair and I were going to be enemies. Friends was unlikely. There is, always has been, and probably always should be, a healthy wariness between the media and politicians. One rarely trusts the other.

A slight commotion at the back of the room caused me to turn. A State Patrolman was opening the door for the Governor, who stepped in with Richard Rosen, his Chief of Staff, at his shoulder. The two were in animated conversation. The Governor saw me and nodded and smiled, still in conversation with Rosen. They stopped just inside; Rosen made some final comment to the Governor, glared at me, then turned and left.

The Governor advanced, grinning. "I'm afraid you're not Richie's favorite."

Motioning to one of the chairs and expanding the grin into a full-faced smile, he said, " Glad you could arrange time for this in the midst of your coronation. You seem to have caught the brass ring."

As he had at our first meeting, Governor Isaac Adair radiated charm.

"So it's official now. We're going to be very happy to have you as a full-time Kentucky resident again—and taxpayer. Excellent." He laughed and reached for a little silver bell that sat on the table.

Almost immediately the waiter reappeared. The Governor nodded. Lunch arrived. A Salad Nicoise, accompanied by a small baguette on a butter plate and a glass of just-cold-enough Chablis to compliment.

"I have a weakness for Salad Nicoise," the Governor explained. "The brasserie Perraudin, on the rue St. Jacques on the Left Bank, is responsible. Do you know it?"

I did. It surprised me that he did.

"The flavor of the anchovies mingled with the rest of it is what hooked me," he went on. "Fresh anchovies are impossible to find here. I have them flown in. You probably recognize the Chablis. A Girard from the Napa Valley. If this doesn't suit, the kitchen can whip up almost anything you want."

I was perfectly satisfied.

The Governor kept the conversation moving along this line— Parisian restaurants we liked, California wines we favored, the sort of inconsequential talk that's mildly interesting and lets the actors preen a bit.

We didn't get to what he had in mind until the coffee came.

"So tell me" he said, shifting back in his chair and swinging his gaze to the scene outside then back to me, "so tell me," he said with a brotherly smile and an inviting note in his voice, "can we be friendly? Note I didn't say friends. I said 'friendly.' I'm sure we'll disagree on some things, but reasonable men can disagree and still be friendly. There are important changes I want to see made in this state ... important changes that *need* to be made in this state. Your newspaper and your influence can be important to that effort. I'd like you on my side."

He gave me that brotherly smile again and leaned toward me. "Can we be friendly?"

Isaac Adair was the sort of man you would want to be friendly with. He was successful and sincere and handsome and disarmingly charismatic. And he was Governor. I was perfectly willing to be personally friendly with the man. I liked him. But I don't think that's what he had in mind. I think he meant would I support his actions, or at least give him a pass when I disagreed.

I smiled back as brotherly as I could.

"Governor, I'll be the friendliest guy I know when I agree with what you're doing. When I disagree with it, I'm afraid I might get a little contentious ... to help you see the right path, you understand. Nothing unfriendly. Just a reasonable man disagreeing in a friendly way."

He grimaced and nodded and sat back in his chair.

"You haven't had money or power before, have you?"

The question seemed odd.

"Money? No. It's never been important to me. Power? That's never been important to me either."

I thought about that for a moment, "But I have had a taste of a certain kind of power— the power of the press. You've heard of it? It topples kings and exposes villains. Why do you ask?"

"It's a friendly question. You've just been given a big dose of both money and power all at once. I hope it doesn't spoil you."

A little knowing smile, a sip of coffee, then eyes back on me.

"Well, let's at least agree to be friendly about our disagreements."

"Done," I said, extending my hand. "You're still going to make a run at dismantling the civil service system?"

"It institutionalizes mediocrity."

"No it doesn't, Governor. It insures that the work of the people is done by qualified professionals who are free of politics."

"You give it a generous interpretation. What else do we disagree about?"

"I don't know yet. Maybe I'll be in favor of much of what you hope to do. You haven't told me your plans."

He only smiled.

We both stood up to take our leave.

As he walked me to the door with his hand fraternally on my shoulder, the Governor said, "Richie doesn't like you. He has considerable influence over agencies of state government—agencies that might be important to your businesses. I hope that whatever transpires between the two of you doesn't get in the way of our relationship."

On that happy note, Governor Isaac Adair and I parted— friendly.

CHAPTER SIXTY TWO

Richard, Richie, No-Middle-Initial Rosen—I was tempted to make a doggerel rhyme out of that, it had a nice little rhythm to it.

Richie Rosen. A powerful man. Has you on his list. Pay attention, Theo. Not someone to make light of.

I let that thought marinade in my mind as I walked back to the *Journal*. I'd walked up. Mildred thought that in my new exalted position I shouldn't be walking the streets of town like I was just anybody. She'd wanted me to drive, or would drive me, or would have someone drive me.

"You don't see the Farmers Bank's president walking to the Capitol. You don't see the Mayor walking up to the Capitol. For goodness sake, Mr. Clark, give a little thought to appearances." Bless her heart. Mildred Polsgrove, like Julie Colby, was determined to make a man of consequence of me despite my many failings.

I favored walking.

Walking didn't get me anywhere faster than I wanted to get there. Walking let me see my surroundings complete, not just a snapshot as I whizzed by.

Walking let my mind work.

I could take a problem like Richard, Richie, No-Middle-Initial, Rosen and slip it into the back of my mind and let it rattle around in there while I walked. By the time I got where I was going, often I had an idea of what to do. Sometimes I didn't. But most of the time, letting my mind dissect the problem without my conscious interference worked well.

So I gave it Richie Rosen and enjoyed the afternoon and the walk.

Kentucky's Capitol rests serenely majestic near the top of the gentle rise that climbs up from the river to the top of the valley. Homes and lawns and quiet streets and schools and churches surround it.

The broad lawn in front of the Capitol that I was passing, we'd played touch-football there on autumn afternoons when I was a boy; we'd kicked, laughing and wrestling, through big mounds of crinkly leaves piled on the sides of the streets on our way home after school back then.

I thought about that as I walked. I thought about the fun we had. I thought about standing on the New Bridge at night with the Capitol gleaming up on the hill and thinking that someday I'd like to be the man who sat in that big chair up there and did great things—or a foreign correspondent filing vivid copy from bloody battlefields, or a fishing guide making long graceful casts on the Madison in Montana, or a Clarence Darrow-like lawyer protecting the good guys from the bad. There was so much out there waiting in those days, in the tomorrows upcoming.

I played might-have-been games with all that until I reached the *Journal.*

Dulin was in my office.

"Well?"

I shucked my coat. I'd gone up on the hill properly suited as I had for my first meeting with His Excellency. Conservative blue suit. Conservative white shirt. Conservative tie. Dignity incarnate, although not the equal of Paul Isham's person. I hung my jacket on the back of my chair and loosened my tie. Sara, the new secretary, dashed in almost immediately. Looking apprehensive but undeterred, she snatched my jacket from the chair before I could sit down and hung it up properly where it belonged. I caught her glancing expectantly through the door. Mildred was nodding approval.

Dulin almost laughed.

"Well," he repeated.

"I had a nice walk," I said. "It's a beautiful afternoon."

"Isn't it? What happened?"

In all honesty and after due reflection I said, "I'm not sure."

The Governor had been gracious and hospitable. The Salad Nicoise was first rate. We knew many of the same restaurants in Paris. I gave him the name of a few California wines I thought especially fine. He invited me to his box at the UK football games. It was an odd session. Like a little sparring before a main event.

"It was pleasant. He was pleasant. There was nothing hostile. He wanted us to be "friendly." Not friends, but "friendly.""

"What does that mean?"

"I think it means he wants us to go easy on him when we disagree. Remember, he's spent his entire career in business. He's been relatively insulated there. He hasn't had the media throwing darts at him, and he hasn't had to stare at morning headlines that call him a crook or an idiot. He's thin-skinned. I think criticism upsets him mightily. I think fighting upsets him; certainly upsets his sense of himself and might even upset him physically. I think when he fights, he has someone else do it for him."

I swung into my chair, now devoid of the jacket, and Dulin took a seat beside the desk.

"Are we in a fight?" he asked.

"We will be. He still intends to try to dismantle the civil service system. We'll 'disagree' about that, but I told him we might favor much of the program he has in mind once we learn what it is, and if we do, we'll get behind it."

"Did he take kindly to that?"

"He put his hand on my shoulder and walked me hospitably to the door, telling me he hoped Richie Rosen's dislike for me didn't get in the way of our relationship."

Dulin frowned. Rubbed his hand across his cheek. Looked away and then back.

"My source in the Governor's office," he said, "tells me that Rosen was behind the loss of the State printing contract. He had the bid language changed to favor Morris & Company. The consortium owns Morris & Company. Rosen has an ownership interest in the consortium. The consortium still wants the *Journal.* Paul has joined the consortium. I don't like this one damn bit."

CHAPTER **SIXTY THREE**

Sun Tzu, in *The Art of War,* advises "know your enemy."

This is what we found out about Richard Rosen.

He had influence. He wanted more.

He had money. He wanted more.

He played to win, and he wasn't fastidious about rules or consequences.

Rosen's law firm was devoted to advancing the interests of its coal and natural gas clients. Rosen made his money finding ways to engineer waivers that allowed his clients to slide around strip mining regulations. He got them permits to blast the tops off mountains to get at coal seams, then dump the overburden down in the valleys—savaging the environment and threatening the little communities with floods that could drown them in coal waste and mining debris.

He was a big man in the biggest business in the eastern part of the state. He was ambitious to be a big man in the biggest business in the entire state—the government.

Ego.

Mildred had assembled some of this information. I sent her to Ashland to do on-the-ground research the day after my meeting with the Governor. She got much more, of course. Rosen was born in Newport, right across the Ohio River from Cincinnati—which may have had something to do with the consortium connection. He was an only child. Father a bartender in one of the Newport sub-rosa gambling clubs. Mother a grade school teacher. Undergraduate degree from Oberlin, a small liberal arts college on the banks of the Ohio with one of the most beautiful campuses in the country. An LLB from University of Cincinnati. Unmarried. A masters level bridge player. Vacationed every year, alone, usually in the winter, in Jamaica.

Would some of that help us to know our enemy? Maybe.

Satis Arnow gave me the rest.

Satis was the most important banker in that end of the Commonwealth. As I've mentioned, he was a principal member of the team that almost put Michael Dannan in the governor's chair. Satis was with us when Michael was shot. He was wounded by one of the bullets that passed through Michael's body. He and I became close friends.

Satis' evaluation was unflattering.

"Rosen is devious. He's cunning and without principles. Which may be his greatest strength because nothing gets in his way. I can see why Adair wanted him. I can't see why Adair put him in as Chief of Staff. From what I understand, they couldn't be more different. Rosen has about as much warmth as a stone, and I don't think he has ever experienced anything resembling empathy. They must make quite a contrast when you see them together—tall, handsome Governor full of charm, short, sour-faced aide radiating menace at his side."

Satis gave a half-laugh then. "Maybe I'm being too harsh. The man has that effect on me. My best advice—don't turn your back on him."

We digested all this, Dulin and I. The question was: what sort of enemy was Rosen—a panther in the night, stalking and aggressive, or an alligator, submerged, waiting for the prey to get in reach.

My unfettered mind, to which I'd given the Richard Rosen problem on my walk back from the Governor's office, had come up with no solution. My conscious mind had no answer either.

Dulin thought the gator more likely and that, like Teddy Roosevelt, we ought to walk softly and carry a big stick—and make sure our backs weren't exposed.

This seemed the only available option, and I agreed, but it wasn't comforting. All my experience told me to attack. Don't wait to be hit. Hit first.

CHAPTER SIXTY FOUR

The more I was around her, the more I was convinced that Julie Colby had an in with higher powers. The night she'd set for my "homecoming" was the kind of late October night you could get only with that kind of influence.

We'd had cold winds and dreary rain most of the week, but that day, the Friday before Halloween; that day dawned dry and clear and sparkling, and the moon, the full moon of October, the Hunter's Moon, rose that night just as the sun was setting, and it was so big it filled the sky.

At the camp, small campfires dotted the grassy bank above the river. Around them congregated little groups of people, laughing and talking, roasting hot dogs on skewers and downing bourbon and beer out of paper cups.

I knew most of them, or should have known them—people I'd gone to school with, people I'd worked with, people who knew of me and people who Julie thought should know me better.

That was the point of this whole thing—to "re-introduce" me to them, to "welcome" me home. We were maybe fifty or sixty in all—bankers and merchants and teachers and preachers, state office heads and a few of the county's big land owners—the human infrastructure of the place, the people who made it and ran it.

Allie was there.

Unaccompanied.

I had halfway expected that if she came, James Beauregard Sims would be with her. Even so, we had very little chance to talk. Julie kept moving me from group to group to make sure I'd meet and talk with everyone. For a moment, a brief moment on the porch, we were alone.

"You okay," she asked.

"Holding up," I said.

"This isn't your kind of thing, hero."

"Noblesse oblige," I replied.

"Poor hero," she said. "Have you decided what to do about you yet?"

"What should I do about me?" I asked.

"Poor hero," she said again, "so conflicted. You should make up your mind."

She left as Julie came up the steps to collect me.

People were beginning to leave. I stood at the top of the hill, shaking hands until everyone had made their way to their car.

By ten it was only Julie and Jim and the cleanup crew and me. We sat on the dock for a while and watched the moon. The moon of this month, the first full moon after the Harvest Moon of September, is called the Hunters Moon. By the time it rises, the crops are harvested, and the trees have shed their leaves. The deer are fat, and the land is open to a light almost as bright as day. Game has nowhere to hide. Tracking is easy. Hunting is easy. This is the moon that Indians and settlers waited for to fill their larders for the long cold winters.

Though I didn't think of it in that way until later, I began my hunt that night.

I had reconnected with good friends. I had made friends with people who, until then, were only casual acquaintances. And people who were strangers got an idea of who I was and what I was like.

A start on a nucleus began that night; a start on assembling the core I would need when I made my run for governor. I hadn't intended it to be that. I hadn't expected it to be that. But it was, and no one had any idea of it except me.

We went back to Julie's for a nightcap and a postmortem. Bundled in sweaters and sitting out back on the porch and perhaps too euphoric from what was so warm a reception and so sincere a welcome, I decided to lay out my plan, my near term plan not the other one, to Julie and Jim.

I told Jim I wanted him to leave his law firm and join me, become Chief Operating Officer of Elkhorn Industries, help Dulin and me build a media conglomerate in the Bluegrass and live rich and happy ever after. I explained the plan to him, detailed why I thought it could be successful.

Julie reacted first, smiling ruefully and shaking her head. "Say no, Jim."

"It's a sound plan, Julie," I said.

"Say no, Jim."

"Why?"

She rose from her chair and walked over to Jim, took his face in her hands.

"You're Robin Hood. The people of Sherwood Forest need you. You wouldn't be happy in the castle."

Turning to me she said, "I know you have great confidence in him. I know how well you get along. I know how comfortable you'd be with him in charge of the things you think you're not good at. And I know how uncomfortable he'd be trying to make sure he didn't let you down. He's a lawyer. You're a dreamer. Both of you get headaches from numbers. You need someone who really understands how to make businesses work, not Jim."

Then back to Jim, "You know I'm right."

In the moonlight, I could see his face quite clearly. He was smiling.

"It's tempting, old friend, and I'm flattered that you want me, but the lady knows us both too well." He leaned up and kissed Julie on the forehead. "I'll pass."

I must have flinched. I was so sure that Jim would be immediately taken with the idea and that Julie would support it—the three of us working together (it would be the three; there would be no way that Julie would stand by as a spectator while Jim and I had all the excitement). I was so sure that I was right, the possibility I was wrong never entered my thinking.

Julie saw the surprise on my face. "Ah, Theo, love, you know I'm right. Listen to Mama Jules. Don't surround yourself with friends who you hope can do what you want them to do. Go find the professionals who've proven they can. Leave your friends alone to be friends."

CHAPTER SIXTY FIVE

I met James Beauregard Sims the next day, Saturday, the twenty-fifth day of October, the last day of the fall race meet at Keeneland. He was there with Allie, or rather I suppose I should say, Allie was there with him.

They had passed up the trappings of the dining room in the clubhouse for a tailgate party on a grassy lawn near the paddock.

At Keeneland, you feel as if you're a guest at a small private estate—a place of tradition and privilege where gentlemen and their ladies gather to watch the sport of Kings.

Lawns like carpets flow over the grounds, and stately oaks and maples are all around. The mood is genteel and dignified. There is no infield at Keeneland as there is at Churchill Downs were the Derby is run, no raucous crowds, no tasteless garb. Keeneland is aristocrat country. Beau Sims fit perfectly.

I was there with Julie and Jim Colby. Our path took us past the space where Beau Sims' party was in progress. Allie saw Julie and waved to her. Julie smiled a mischievous little smile at me, waved back, and said, " Let's go meet your competition."

Very high on the list of things I had no interest in was making the acquaintance of James Beauregard Sims. But there seemed no graceful way to avoid it. We'd been seen. We'd been invited. It would be impolite to forge ahead without stopping to say hello. Julie was never impolite. Well-raised Kentucky girls mind their manners.

There were four people in folding chairs, sitting around the tailgate of a Ford Country Squire wagon that was pulled up on the grass beneath a large maple. The open tailgate held several large wicker picnic baskets and two bottles of—I could make out from where I stood—Very Old Old Crow, one hundred proof, bottled in bond. There seemed to be a wine cooler behind.

Allie was standing next to a man who frowned as we advanced. He came forward eagerly, though, as if we were long lost friends.

Beau Sims.

"Come join us. Have a drink. First post isn't for an hour yet."

Cordial. Friendly.

We were introduced all around. Beau Sims already knew Julie but had not met Jim. The others, his guests, knew none of us. Allie handled that.

Beau took my hand in a manly grip and shook it enthusiastically. "I knew Rhae Dannan only casually—through the horses. She was a grand lady. I know you'll do her legacy proud." He reached out and put his arm affectionately around Allie. "You and Allie go back a ways, I understand, and Julie and Jim. Well, welcome back. Take a seat. What can I get you?"

"I'll get it," Allie interjected, slipping out of Beau Sims' embrace. "Bourbon, two ice cubes. Right?" She kissed me on the cheek as she turned to the makeshift bar, whether to counter Beau's show of possessiveness or just because she felt like it, I didn't know. I usually didn't know why Allie did things. Julie narrowed her eyes in amusement.

I had tried not to do much thinking about Beau Sims. But he was almost what I thought he would be— if I had thought about him.

A little taller than me—maybe six-one. Solid build. No gut. Looked strong through the shoulders. I remembered he'd been on the UK swim team. Dark blond hair worn a little long for my tastes but stylishly cut. Handsome in a patrician way like the Blueblood he was. Brown eyes, heavy black eyebrows that ran on a slight upward slant.

Manicured nails. I always noticed nails. I once spent time in the company of a man I admired, a closet intellectual masquerading as a salt-water fishing guide. He considered manicures to be unmanly.

James Beauregard Sims held the stage while we were there, like a peacock preening his colors to attract the female and warn the intruder. I got his message. So did Julie, and she coughed to hide her laugh.

Allie said very little. There wasn't much chance for any of us to say much. Beau had command of the conversation. She caught my eye from time to time. I could read only curiosity in her glance.

I waited long enough to satisfy Julie's sense of propriety, then I reminded her that we had to get along.

We said our "nice-to-meet-yous" and "hope-to-see-you-agains" and hurried off. James Beauregard Sims and I would not be friends. I wondered if Allie cared.

A glorious afternoon.

Clear skies, a sylvan setting, trees sporting their finest fall colors, attractive people ringed around the paddock, a table in the clubhouse overlooking the track—and across the room, Richard Richie No-Middle-Initial Rosen.

Rosen had arrived with tasteless pomp—an escort of two State Troopers on motorcycles to clear the way through traffic, a black Lincoln Continental to the door of the Clubhouse.

He and his party were escorted, with show, to a large circular table in the center of the room.

They made a stir. Rosen was recognized. Heads turned. A few who caught his eye smiled and nodded. One man, in the far corner of the room, waved.

Rosen seemed to be enjoying the attention.

With him, to my surprise, was Paul Isham. There were two other men I didn't recognize. One was a tall, heavy-set older man with a haughty glare and a slight limp; the other a younger man dressed as if he had stepped out of a *Gentleman's Quarterly* spread on what the well dressed gentlemen wore for a day at the races.

Paul saw me but made no acknowledgement. Rosen did as well. Our eyes locked for a moment. He gave a grunting little sneer of dismissal and turned back to his guests.

Ostentation is always a bad idea for a politician. It's off-putting for the voters. Rosen, though, was not a politician. No one elected him. Isaac Adair appointed him, chose him to be his Chief of Staff, put him in one of the most powerful jobs in the Commonwealth, the Governor's eminence grise, the man with the behind-the-scenes power to pull the strings of government to advance whatever cause he favored and answerable to no one but his sponsor.

Rosen should have preferred to be invisible. The most effective ones are. His ego appeared to be trumping his judgment.

I thought that might well be the case with many of the appointees Governor Adair had put in the top spots of the state's agencies. Highways, Finance, Health & Welfare, Public Safety, Personnel—all the key jobs necessary to the running of government had been put in the hands of corporate executives or private businessmen, men who had been successful at the business of business, on Adair's contention that government can and should be run like a business, and the way to insure results is to have successful businessmen manage the process.

Except government isn't a business. It's a compact we've forged among ourselves in hopes of securing our mutual welfare, safety, peace, and harmony. It has its own rules, its own hierarchies, its own procedures and expectations—unique to it because it is, in itself, unique. It can't be run like a business. I wondered how long it would take Adair to find that out—and what damage would result in the interim.

Ah, well—the presence of Richie Rosen wasn't going to spoil the day for me. We finished lunch and were ready to head to our box, when on a whim I can't explain, I decided to rise above Paul's snub and go say hello to the man.

Paul stood when he saw me coming. He was the most dignified looking man in the room, and probably the most apprehensive.

He made the best of the situation. He extended his hand and managed a smile and began to introduce me to his seated companions, then them to me.

"You know Richard Rosen."

Rosen glowered.

"And this," he said, gesturing to the big man with the limp, "is Hector Tapp, Chairman of the consortium, and Marvin Volker, his assistant. They've been wanting to talk with you. What a lucky coincidence." Paul, regaining his composure, tried to smile again.

Only Volker stood. He told me what a pleasure it was to meet me and how much he'd appreciate the opportunity to talk with me at some time when it was convenient, but hopefully soon because things were moving fast with the consortium and that the *Journal* remained very important to its success. "Paul and I think we've come up with a way that the *Journal* could come into the consortium and still honor your commitment to independence."

So these were Paul's new playmates.

"Shall I call in the morning? Perhaps we could get together one day next week—any day, any time; whatever fits your schedule. Paul would join us."

I glanced around. Rosen was still glowering. Chairman Tapp was frowning. Paul was watching me anxiously.

Volker probably sold used cars to finance his way through college. He had that sort of encouragingly forceful personality.

"Marvin. It is Marvin, isn't it? I don't want to seem impolite, and I certainly don't mean to be rude. The consortium may be a very good idea, and I wish you luck with it, but it holds no interest for me. So there's no need to waste your time or mine. It's been good to meet you, gentlemen. Good luck with your picks today."

As I turned to leave, Rosen growled from where he sat, "You arrogant son of a bitch, you'll wish you'd played ball."

The sound of it caught me like a slap. I turned and started toward him. Paul saw my anger and immediately stepped between us. Volker glanced quickly around to see if others had noticed, then stepped in beside Paul. "Smile, dammit," he said to Paul. Across the room, I could see that Julie and Jim were standing at our table, waiting expectantly for me to join them.

"Tell the man hiding behind you," I said into Paul's forced smile, "he just did a dumb thing," and spun and walked off.

"What was going on over there?" Julie asked when I reached them. "It seemed tense."

"Not to worry," I told her. "Richard Richie No-Middle-Initial Rosen just decided something for me."

Julie wasn't satisfied with my answer. "Something made you mad. Don't get mad. You're not a nice person when you do."

Jim grabbed both our arms. "We need to get our bets down." As he hurried us out he said, "Who were those men with Rosen?" When I explained, he said, "Strange. The big man with the sour look, he owns South Fork Coal, one of the biggest in the business. He's the man pushing mountaintop mining. I thought he was just a client of Rosen's law firm. He's the consortium, too? You pick big-time playmates, buddy." When we got our bets down and returned to the box, Jim said, "The Governor's Chief of Staff and a powerful coal baron? Watch your step, buddy, watch your step."

CHAPTER SIXTY SIX

Too much emphasis is placed on waiting to turn the other cheek. We seem to believe we have to let the other guy hit first.

The saner course, it has always seemed to me, is, if someone is getting ready to pound you, deck him before he can. If there is a credible threat from a capable enemy that will do you real damage, eliminate it—with finality—scorch the earth; take no prisoners; demolish it with such intensity, it will never be a threat again.

Rosen fit both categories.

I had no idea what his next move might be. I had no intention of waiting to find out.

Rosen had fear, intimidation, influence, and avarice on his side.

I had a newspaper.

It wasn't a fair fight.

The morning after Keeneland, I called Lew Arbogast and Dulin Monroe into my office. My editor. My consigliore.

I explained there seemed to be a new urgency in the consortium's ambition to make the *Journal* a part of its empire and that I thought any and all weapons available would be used. I told them I believed Rosen to be the key. I had no inkling of what pressure he could bring to bear from the position he held in the Governor's office or what strings he could pull, but I wasn't going to wait to find out.

"Take out Rosen, and we take out the threat."

Dulin was an uneasy listener. The threat to the *Journal* he understood. There was another threat that bothered him. "You're not letting this get personal."

"Hell yes, it's personal," I shot back. "But that's beside the point. Rosen's out to get us. I know what you're getting at. You're concerned I'm about to use our newspaper as a weapon in a personal vendetta. I won't. You wouldn't let me. Lew wouldn't let me. We'll do this by the book. We'll play it fair."

"I had to raise the caution," Dulin said. "Lew, you're comfortable with this?"

Lew, a little bleary-eyed because we'd called him earlier than he'd normally make it to the newsroom, but alert and eager, said only, "What's the plan?"

We decided to find out what the people of the Commonwealth should know about the man who sat at the right hand of the Governor, the one who whispered in his ear and pulled the strings.

Lew assigned two reporters to the story—our best investigative reporter, P. T. Thomas, a taciturn, gangly, middle-aged man who stuttered slightly when he became excited, and a disarmingly friendly young woman, Annie Parson, in her third year at the *Journal* after graduating from the University of Louisville with dual degrees in English and Criminal Justice, and whose energy was equaled only by her determination to get the story.

Experience and ambition.

Experience went to Ashland, Rosen's base of business operations, Ambition to Jamaica, where Rosen spent his winter vacations—alone.

Ashland is the largest town in East Kentucky—an industrial town— steel, chemicals, railroads. Population under thirty-thousand. Not a metropolis. Sits in the northeastern edge of the state on the banks of the Ohio River. West Virginia is just across the river.

Rosen ran his practice right up against the limits of the law but not beyond. No bribed judges or pistol-whipped witnesses, no illicit campaign contributions or vanished files needed for litigation. Nothing visible. Nothing incriminating. But there were rumors, gossip, talk that the man was not constrained by convention or propriety. His ambition was palpable. The town was not big enough, the setting not grand enough, the clients not rich enough. He deserved bigger. He deserved better.

Cross-fade to the Capitol City of the Grand and Glorious Commonwealth of Kentucky. Not the biggest nor the richest city in the state. Just the seat of power. That's where the big and the rich came as supplicants. That's where the cornucopia of state treasures overflowed.

Enter Isaac Adair, Governor-to-be, delivered to him by Hector Tapp, CEO of South Fork Coal, satisfied client and significant contributor to Governor Adair's campaign coffers. Chief of Staff? Power and prestige on a statewide scale? The bigger and the better he lusted for.

You know the saying about power—that power corrupts and absolute power corrupts absolutely? Rosen didn't have absolute power, but he had sufficient. His word could get you a prestigious job or could make sure a lucrative state contract come your way. He could get you a road built or a plot of land condemned for the motel you wanted to open along the new state highway that had not yet been announced, but which would soon be under construction.

Or the reverse. He could make bad things happen to you as well. That's power enough.

P.T. Thomas dug, but didn't find anything damning in Rosen's time before he came to the Capitol. A few things odoriferous, but nothing that a story could be hung on. All that changed dramatically when P.T. came back down out of the mountains and began nosing around the Capital city.

Rosen was feared. And in many circles, reviled. In the year he'd been in the job, he'd wielded his power with such arrogance and insensitivity that he'd created a cadre of enemies. P. T. tapped into that. He found the few inside and outside the Administration who, if they could be convinced their identity would not be revealed, were more than willing to let us in on enough of Richard Rosen's sins to bring him down.

They are always there somewhere. People who have been injured, or taken advantage of, or humiliated. People who haven't been appreciated, or sufficiently rewarded, or jettisoned for spite or revenge. And sometimes people who are just plain outraged at the way the powerful work the system or take advantage of the weak.

You must be careful when you find these people. Sometimes their facts are fabricated to do damage to the man they hate. Sometimes their memories are wrong. Sometimes they just want attention. Every fact has to be checked, and cross-checked and corroborated.

We did all that.

When we'd finished, Richard No-Middle-Initial Rosen was the tiger to whose tail we were about to light a fire.

Item: Kickbacks. Rosen was receiving a percentage of the premiums paid to the successful bidder for a recently awarded multi-million-dollar State Unemployment Insurance contract— premiums worth millions—a contract Rosen's influence had secured.

Item: Misappropriation of state funds. A paved road through a Bluegrass meadow and up a little hill leading to the new home Rosen was building on a small farm he'd acquired on the way to Keeneland. Built by the State Highway Department with State personnel and paid for out of the department's budget.

Item: Misuse of State workers. State grounds keepers were detailed to cut his lawn, State Troopers to walk his dogs (two poodles, a beagle, and a German Shepard) and secretaries to pick up his laundry.

The man's sense of entitlement was astonishing.

And Jamaica—Rosen's winter forays to the Island In The Sun. We thought there might be something there. He went every winter. Every January. Alone. Took a villa at Golden Eye on Oracabessa Bay on the North Shore east of Ocho Rios near Ian Fleming's place. Two weeks. Never came back with a tan. You'd think a man like Rosen would want to flaunt his time in the sun, would come back bronzed, strut around showing off while the rest of his Kentucky peers limped pale and listless in the grey of winter. Strange, that.

Annie Parsons, our indefatigable young reporter, turned over every stone she could find, became friends with the beach boys and the hotel help, with the local cabbies and the bay front bartenders, the charter boat captains and the back country guides.

No dirt. Lots of gossip and speculation about the man who came every year to Villa 17, but no dirt.

He kept to himself, drank moderately, didn't party. On occasion, he'd hire a jeep and go off up in the mountains. By himself. Leave before daylight, back before dark. Mysterious. There was nothing up there except a few Rastafarians and a lot of ganja plots. Jamaican marijuana smuggled in through New Orleans was booming business back home. But Annie could find no connections between the trade and Rosen, and we wouldn't let her pursue it further. It was a long shot at best;, too much danger was involved, and we had all we needed.

So Annie came home. With a lovely tan and an empty notebook.

We had put four weeks into the reportage.

CHAPTER SIXTY SEVEN

December

The demolition of Richard No-Middle-Initial Rosen began with the column I wrote, my first, noting the Publisher's privilege and announcing my intention to resurrect the column I'd written in my first incarnation at the *Journal*—a weekly commentary I hoped people would remember and would welcome back. It would be a Sunday feature and play on the editorial page; it's proper placement since the opinions expressed therein were not to be confused with news.

In that column, I announced our intention to take a close look at the men who were in charge of state government. We would do a series on these men— profiles on their backgrounds, their experience, their achievements, so we could all understand their credentials and be reassured about their qualifications to manage the business of the people. Governor Adair believed government can and should be run like a business. He had put businessmen in charge. We thought we ought to know them better than just by what could be gleaned from the press releases announcing their appointments. We would begin the series tomorrow (Monday) with a profile of Richard Rosen, the Governor's Chief of Staff.

There is an axiom in politics and business: Never pick fights with people who buy ink by the barrel.

We strung the Rosen saga out through most of November. I wanted to provide time for other news outlets to pick up on our stories; time for a buzz to ignite and for outrage to build.

We started mild— the use of state employees as servants. The photo of the State Patrolman walking Rosen's poodle on a leash (a miniature poodle, for God's sake! What real man owns a poodle!) was embarrassing, even to people who didn't care for the State Police.

Then we escalated to the misuse of state funds (the private road to his new home put in by the State Highway Department and paid for out of its budget.)

The coup de grace was the kickback story. Outright fraud. Illegal. Go to jail if convicted.

We had it all. Cross-checked and verified by credible sources. Enough to force an investigation by the State Attorney General.

Richard No-Middle-Initial Rosen resigned the afternoon that story played, the fifteenth day of December. He had been in the job just a week shy of a year. The Governor made the announcement, not Rosen.

Covering his derriere and hoping to show how strong and responsible a governor he was, Isaac Adair said in his official press release, "In light of recent public revelations regarding the conduct of Richard Rosen, I have today asked for and accepted his resignation. Nothing but the highest standards of conduct will be tolerated in this Administration." There was more, but it was only posturing.

The Rosen resignation dominated the news cycles for the next two days. The Associated Press tried to reach Rosen for comment.

He had left for Jamaica.

CHAPTER SIXTY EIGHT

We approached Christmas week feeling very, very good, Dulin, Lew Arobogast, our stellar reportorial team and me. We'd won.

Rosen was gone and with him, the threat to the *Journal*.

The consortium was gone, too.

It had been intending to use Rosen's muscle with the state agencies that could hurt our businesses to force the *Journal* into its folds.

Paul Isham confessed this—not to me, to Dulin—that the consortium was a paper mirage. All the hype about building a media empire that would dominate the state was only hype. The *Journal*, with its prestige and position as the Capitol City daily, was to be the lure to attract other key city dailies— the *Ashland Independent* in east Kentucky, *The Paducah Sun-Times* in the west, *the Bowling Green Daily News* in the center of the state, and the *Middlesboro Register* on the southern border with Tennessee—these the core with the *Journal* as the driver. Without the *Journal*, the consortium couldn't fly. Paul was resigning. He apologized.

Yes, this would be a good holiday, a big holiday, the first Christmas I'd spent in Kentucky in almost ten years—the ghost of Jesse Bristow purged from my mind, the threat to Rhae's empire blunted: Allie close by, maybe in reach if I reached: memories of Aunt Maggie's fruit cake and egg-nog on Christmas eve and waking on Christmas mornings when there was still a Santa Claus, and the toys you wished for were under the tree.

Snow.

There might even be snow. We had big snowfalls at Christmas time when I was a boy, and we'd take our new sleds, and there'd be a big bonfire up at the top of Shelby, and we'd fly all the way down from the Capitol to the river. What was the line? "Backward, oh backward, turn time in your flight. And make me a boy again, just for tonight."

Julie, as was her nature, was taking charge of Christmas. I was to come to her house for Christmas Eve. A few friends, people I knew, would be there. We'd have egg nog and sing carols around an open fire. Then I was to join her family for dinner on Christmas Day. Mama Jules. Looking out for the orphan boy.

I had a different plan. Christmas dinner at the farm. With Dulin and Paul. A pleasant, relaxed evening with an old friend and a repentant one and good memories we shared of Rhae and Michael and other holiday nights at the farm. Capping its appeal, I'd get to set the menu—filet of beef tenderloin with hollandaise, twice baked potatoes, scalloped oysters, creamed spinach and green bean casserole and candied carrots and warm yeast rolls with melted butter. We'd start with a garden salad and end with a Charlotte Ruse. A Trefethan Cabernet for the dinner. A nice Tawny Port with coffee for the desert. And Ancient Age and branch to begin it all with.

I still hadn't decided whether to move there.

My little apartment over the library suited me, but Julie insisted, and I agreed, that in my new role I needed something a little more grand, a little more spacious, a place in which I could entertain as would be expected of me—large enough for dinner parties, fashionable enough for cocktail gatherings. The farm was all of that and with a charm more appealing than any place I could find in town, but it was a long drive out a twisting country road. And it had those memories that I wasn't sure I wanted to live among.

Ron Rhody

Julie brought the compromise. Christmas Eve at her place. Christmas Day at the farm.

Did I want her to invite Allie for Christmas Eve? It was probably too late. Beau Sims surely would have already asked her. But she would if I wanted.

I hadn't seen or talked with Allie since that day at Keeneland. I should have. I seemed to be in the grip of a strange form of paralysis. I wanted. But I wasn't exactly certain of what I wanted. That's not right. The honest fact is I was resisting accepting the certainty of what I wanted.

"No?" Julie frowned at me. "What was that story you kept telling me about your Marine sergeant, about making decisions—never wait too long because the chance to do it may be gone. You paid attention?"

Christmas came and passed, and it was a good Christmas, but there was no snow, and I could find no one who could make me a boy again, but it was good to be who I was and where I was.

I did talk with Allie. On Christmas morning. To wish her merry Christmas and to see if she might be free for New Year's Eve. "Beau has something planned," she said, "and for New Year's day. Next time?"

I spoke with Kit later, allowing for the three-hour time break to the west coast, and waiting until I was sure she'd be up.

"It was a beautiful night here," she said. "No fog. Stars everywhere. The lights on the bridges like necklaces across the Bay. You missed it. I missed you."

I said, "Are you coming to see me?"

"No. You come here. You need an antidote for all the Bluegrass and moonlight."

"We'll flip a coin."

"No. We'll pick a number. I'll tell you if you get it right." We both laughed.

"Happy New Year, lady."
"Happy New Year, country boy."

CHAPTER **SIXTY NINE**

January

The Governor was back and wanted to see me.

Richard Rosen had resigned on the Monday before Christmas. The Governor left that afternoon for his Christmas holiday, two weeks in the Bahamas—a private villa above a private beach on Eleuthera—a little golf, a little fishing, some snorkeling, and some lying in the sun sipping Mojitos while recovering from the rigors of attending to the business of the people of the Commonwealth.

Needed. Deserved.

He was back now.

Same routine as before. Late lunch. The Sun Room.

As is my practice, I was slightly early. As is his style, he was moderately late.

The small table set for two was, as before, centered in the picture window looking out on the back lawn of the Mansion. The day was cold and rainy, the lawn winter brown, the trees leafless and their trunks black in the grey light. Gloomy. It was a gloomy day.

The Governor was beautifully tanned, the picture of health, and he emanated energy, but he was not smiling broadly as he had been at our earlier meeting.

"Let's speak candidly," he said as we took our seats, and the service began.

No Salad Nicoise, today. No wine. A small cup of potato-leek soup, cheeseburgers and fries, black coffee on the side. Hot and hearty. Fit the cold, gloomy day.

"Are you out to cause me problems?" he began without preamble.

"The Rosen story?" I said. "The man was a pirate, Governor. He got what he deserved. You should be more careful with your appointments."

"You've made a number of people very uneasy."

"Your other appointees?

"This series of stories you're planning to run, these "profiles" on my cabinet secretaries, are you just looking for dirt to build circulation, or are you trying to dig up material to embarrass me?"

"Neither, Governor. These men wield real power. They manage budgets of substantial amounts. They're like barons ruling their own special fiefdoms. They answer to no one but the King, in this case, you. It seems to me the people have a right to know what qualifies these men to handle the responsibilities you've given them and to have a sense of what kind of men they are. That's all we're doing, Governor. Providing information. No axes to grind. No agenda. Just information."

"Why is it that I have trouble believing you?"

"Because you're wary of the media. Most politicians are. Most businessmen are. They don't trust the press to say things the way they want them said. They're afraid we'll find out things they don't want found out and tell things they don't want told. The press has the power to hold them up for everyone to see. They don't like that. They don't like that they can't control us. I understand that. You're right to be wary. Just as the public has every right to be wary of any force that can exercise power over it. If people were a little more skeptical about what they're told—by politicians, by advertisers, by preachers—we'd all be better off."

"You didn't like Richie, did you? Do you like me?"

"Sir?"

"Candid. I said let's be candid."

I don't believe I've ever had a man ask me, "do you like me?" It doesn't seem the sort of thing one man would ask another, at least in that way. A woman, yes. But a man? I was at a loss for a moment.

"I like you well enough," I said, recovering. "You're a likeable fellow. I don't like what's happened to the town as a result of these across-the-board cuts you've ordered in state personnel. It's ham-handed and counter-productive. And I'm against getting rid of the State Merit System as you seem determined to try.

"And I object to the arrogance of people with no experience thinking the way they run a business is the way to run government. That's nonsense. The only people business managers are responsible to are their investors and their shareholders. All they have to be concerned about is their bottom line. Government has to be responsible to everybody. Its demands are monumentally more complex than simply making a profit. The differences are huge. Government can be more efficient. There is a much waste that should be eliminated. But thinking that government can, or even should, be run like a business is just wrong. And the experiment is going to weaken the system."

It was a long speech. I couldn't tell from his expression what he thought of it. He didn't frown or glower. Isaac Adair had the sort of face that seemed to always be on the verge of a smile regardless of the circumstance. There was no rebuttal or argument with what I'd said, rather he asked, "How much damage did Richie do me?"

That fast switch surprised me, too.

I considered for a moment. "You can't run for re-election, so in that sense, none. If you're planning on running for the Senate when your term as Governor is over, probably very little. People forget. The immediate damage? Some. It calls into question your judgment. If Rosen is typical of the men you've put in high positions in the state, you have a problem—actual and perceived. Actual in the sense that if they are crooks or incompetents, it'll be found out and add to your discredit. Perceived in the sense that most of them are now probably suspect, and consequently, their effectiveness can be limited. The series we're running can help dispel some of that suspicion ... if they're clean and competent. My advice to you is to review very carefully the appointments you've made. If there is anyone you have the least question about, get rid of them. Quietly if you can. Noisily if you have to. But do it. And advise the others to cooperate with us. We'll be fair."

We sat for a long moment just staring at each other. The day had gotten darker, and the rain had intensified.

"You have a ride back downtown?" the Governor asked, motioning to the situation outside.

"I drove."

He pushed back and began to stand. "I'll have a Trooper with an umbrella walk you to your car."

The rain faded into a fine mist as the day wound down. Streetlights were coming on well before quitting time. I did a little after-action report for Dulin on my meeting with the Governor then headed out.

Christmas lights were still up all over town. With the soft mist blurring the outlines of the buildings and the sidewalks glistening, I felt I was in a Sawyier painting and could almost step back in time. I would have made it Christmas Eve of the year before Chosin. There was a snowfall that night and I was with Allie. We walked arm in arm through stillness and the beauty of it and we were happy and there were no tigers lurking in the dark.

CHAPTER SEVENTY

We gave the Governor's appointees series to Annie Parsons. She was young, eager, attractive, and appeared totally unthreatening. We thought the subjects would feel more at ease with her. Never mind that she was as tenacious as a pit-bull. Or that she left no question unasked and no lead unpursued.

Dulin would be her mentor. Lew, her final editor. She couldn't have better coaches or be under more responsible supervision.

Her first piece was on Llewellyn Jones, a middle-aged banker from a large bank in Louisville. He had a wife and two boys in middle school, had moved to a leased home in a gated community just outside town on the road to Lexington to be nearer his work after being named by Governor Isaac Adair to head the Finance Cabinet. By all accounts, a solid citizen. Except he had no experience in Government or in governmental finance.

Annie spent two weeks on the reportage. She spent a day bird-dogging Mr. Jones at work, a day with Mrs. Jones and the boys, and the rest of it digging. Mr. Jones was nervous. He had no direct experience with the press. Almost all of the Governor's appointees were in that boat. They were small businessmen, entrepreneurs, and a few professionals, men insulated for the most part from public attention, and in whom the press had only occasional interest.

Mr. Jones had noted the Rosen stories—Annie shared a by-line with P.T. Thomas on all of those—and was apprehensive. But he did what all smart people do when confronted with the press. He answered her questions honestly; said he didn't know when he didn't know; he didn't volunteer information that might open up lines of questioning in areas he had no business visiting, and he made no attempt at dancing around or fancy footwork.

The story came out fine. For us. For Mr. Jones. For our readers.

Llewellyn Jones was as advertised. Competent, honest, hard working, and apparently dedicated to seeing that the business of the people was conducted honestly and effectively.

We hoped they'd all be that way. We wouldn't know until Annie had finished her reportage and written her stories.

Dulin and Lew and I were going over the reactions to the story in Dulin's office when Allie called. I excused myself to take the call in my office. Allie seldom called me. She almost never called at work.

"This is a surprise," I said when I picked up. "You okay?"

"I'm fine. I just wanted to catch you before you left for the day. Did I pull you out of a meeting?"

"No, no, it's fine."

"Have dinner with me. On Friday. The eve of New Year's Eve. I'm otherwise engaged on New Year's Eve, but I want to see you. We can get an early start on welcoming the New Year. At my place. I'll make something simple. You bring the Champagne."

She sounded odd. Something in her voice. No matter. Of course I'd make it.

"I'll have to cancel my flight to London and rearrange a meeting with the Queen, but for you … what time?"

"Be serious, hero. Seven. Give me time to get home and get organized. Seven?"

"At your door. No later than."

I had a curious feeling about this. Not something I could give a name to. Not something I'd find on my mind when the four o'clock willies knocked. But strange.

When Friday night came, it was raining again, that cold, bleak rain of January. Allie had a fire going in the fireplace and candles on the mantle when I arrived. She was dressed in a white cowl-neck sweater and faded jeans that looked as though they'd been cut by a tailor and molded to her form. She was barefoot. She often was when she was at home.

Her hair, as I believe I've said, is the color of summer hay in sunlight and her eyes are blue like the deepest blue of the finest sapphire. As a girl, her smile, the way she carried herself, her form, had us all captivated. As a woman, after the revealingly-dressed and the couturier-clothed, the trophy wives and the blue-blood beauties have been scanned and considered, Allie stands out. She's not the most alluring or the most sensuous or the smartest or the most interesting woman in the room, but she seems to be. And that's enough to earn attention.

She had mine completely.

She greeted me with a quick kiss; led me to the couch by the fire. I had bourbon. She had Chardonnay. We talked of Christmases past and holiday dances and songs we liked and where-were-they-nows. She made scrambled eggs and bacon (again), and we had strawberry jam on the toast. Black coffee. Then brandy for me and Kahlua for her, back on the couch in front of the fire as the embers burned down.

The conversation then was rambling and of no consequence, and the only thing I truly remember was what she finally got around to saying.

"Beau asked me to marry him."

There was just the light from the fireplace and the candles, and the room was lullingly quiet except for our breathing and the crackle of the fire and music playing somewhere in the background.

'Beau has asked me to marry him. What do you think I should tell him?"

I won't try to describe what I felt when she said it.

There was a long silence; I remember that—a long, long silence. And I remember a part of the lyric of the song that was playing, "*and I sing you a song in the moonlight, a love song ... .*" Strange that I remember that.

"Do you love him?" I finally asked.

"We get along well."

" But do you love him?"

"He's kind and considerate and generous. He's pays attention to me and wants to take care of me."

"But do you love him?"

"Must I?"

She reached her hand and turned my face to hers, "What has love ever gotten me?" Shaking her head slowly, she said softly, "Poor hero. Poor me."

I left shortly after that—the Champagne unopened and the things I could have said, the things I should have said—all left unsaid.

The engagement of Ms. Allison Boatwright Sinclair to Mr. James Beauregard Sims, was announced on New Year's Day. There was to be a May wedding. It was expected to be the big event of the spring season.

That act would end the show, wouldn't it, would write finis to the long running saga of Theo and Allie, would remove her from my mind and bar her from my dreams? It would free me from the spell of her, wouldn't it? It would do that, wouldn't it?

Julie thought the outcome perfect. For Allie there was security, certainty, comfort, and prestige. For me, an end of the foolishness over a woman who didn't exist, and who in any event, would have been wrong for me. Wouldn't she?

" You decided, no."

"I didn't make a decision," I protested. "Allie did."

"Yes you did. You decided not to decide."

"I did no such thing."

"Oh, but you did. You dithered and delayed and avoided and refused to face up to yourself. You might not have been aware that you were making a decision, but you were. She saw that. She did what was the only sane thing for her to do. Be happy for her. Buy her a nice present, wish them both well, and get on with being whatever it is you've decided to be."

CHAPTER SEVENTY ONE

October

The full moon of October rises tonight—the Hunter's Moon.

A year.

It has been a year since I ascended to the throne of the Dannan Empire—a year and a half since Rhae Dannan's death brought me back.

I think I have things fairly well in hand now.

The businesses are running smoothly. My demons are dispersed. LaHire and I are ready for the test on Judgment Day.

The manuscript that tells the story of how Jesse Bristow died and at whose hand is safely stored away in the research stacks at Cumberland College and unlikely to be stumbled upon.

The thumbless Haines boys are dangers to no one but themselves. Melodie is probably a danger to someone, but not to Niccan Dye. She's in Chicago. Her hair has grown back. She's a blond now.

The scholarship in Professor Marne Young's memory, as promised, has been established, and Niccan is completing his first year of Doctoral studies at the University of Georgia. I've arranged a stipend for him, so that he can concentrate on his studies and not be worried about food and shelter.

I'm relieved all that's behind me.

Is Allie?

Ignore that. That's not a question for tonight. That's a question for another night.

For now it is enough to know that the burden Rhae Dannan laid on me has been shouldered well, it seems.

I've put my little organization together. Satis Arnow found me a gem of a CFO running the finances of a growing manufacturing company in Grayson. She's in her early thirties and scarily thorough.

Benjy took the Chief Operating Officer job himself. He came down to assess the problems and the opportunities in the small media empire of weekly newspapers I am in the process of assembling, and fell victim to the charm and grace of the lifestyle in the horse country around Lexington. Benjamin Bolanger IV, he of the old-line Boston Bolangers, cashed in his stock in the investment banking firm of which he was partner, sold his Park Avenue apartment, deserted the big city and bought a small estate near Versailles. He is the driving force in the growing fortunes of Elkhorn Industries. And Lew Arbogast has the *Journal* purring.

Dulin and I spend more time than probably we should on the *Journal,* but it's the bedrock of the empire and where our hearts are anyway. Circulation has increased nicely, due in part to our series on Governor's Adair's appointees, and my reincarnated weekly column has been well enough received that we're starting the syndication process.

I'm still not a businessman. I don't think I ever will be. But I have people around me who are, and I'm encouraged that Rhae Dannan's legacy is in good hands.

Though it is a grand assembly she handed me, I'll lose interest soon. I'm not big on running things. I'm better at fighting dragons.

So when we have the Dannan empire fully in hand and growing, I intend to go for Governor.

Yes, I know. Dumb idea. But I believe I can make a difference. I've been given too much not to try

I have three years. Isaac Adair's term will be over then. Three years to scout the territory, plan a campaign, build an organization and gain enough name recognition that people will know I'm on their side.

I haven't told Dulin or even Julie about this yet. I will tonight at the party Julie's hosting to mark the anniversary. Dulin will think I've lost my mind. I once asked him what advice he'd give a man planning to run for governor. "Don't do it," was his reply. Julie will be delighted.

Kit?

I'm not sure how Kit will feel about this. I'm hoping she'll be enthusiastic and will want to be a part of it. But Kit marches to the beat of her own drummer. I'm on the morning plane to San Francisco to find out if we're in step.

So tonight marks the end of the beginning and tomorrow the beginning of whatever comes next.

I'll stop by Rhae Dannan's grave on my way out of town in the morning—to leave a rose and a kiss on her headstone.

"Come home," she had said in her last letter to me, the one that changed my life. "You belong here, Theo. Come home."

Ah, Rhae, I'll whisper so she'll hear.

I'm here.

I'm home.

Rest easy.

THE END

ABOUT THE AUTHOR

 Ron Rhody was born and grew up in Frankfort, a small town nestled in a bend of a river in the heart of Kentucky's lush Bluegrass country and the state's Capitol city. He attended Georgetown College then transferred to the University of Kentucky intending to enter law school but became attracted to journalism instead.

Rhody has been a reporter, a sportswriter, a broadcast newsman, and covered the Kentucky Legislature before moving on to a career as a corporate public relations executive in New York and San Francisco, and later as a consultant to Fortune 500 companies on communications and public relations issues.

He was Executive Vice President, Corporate Communications & External Affairs at Bank of America during one of its most demanding decades as the bank skirted bankruptcy, fended off a hostile take-over attempt, and rose again to the top ranks of international finance.

Earlier he had been Corporate Vice President, Public Relations & Advertising, for Kaiser Aluminum & Chemical Corporation, directing the communications strategies for the intense marketing battles and international expansions and downsizings that were endemic to the world aluminum industry.

Rhody is the author of *Theo's Story (2010)*, *Theo & The Mouthful of Ashes (2011)*, and most recently, *When THEO Came Home (2013)*, which completed the Theo trilogy.

His non-fiction works include *The CEO's Playbook: Managing The Outside Forces That Shape Success*, *The Art & Craft Of Writing For Public Relations* with Dr. Carol Ann Hackley of the University of the Pacific, and *The Soccer Book: A Spectator's Guide*.

He and his wife Patsy now make their home in Pinehurst, North Carolina.

ALSO BY RON RHODY

A prominent widow is found dead at the foot of the cellar stairs in the family home on a farm in the lush Bluegrass section of Kentucky. Her head has been bashed in by an old flatiron and her mouth stuffed full of ashes. The county is shocked – horrified at the brutality of the murder and mystified at the use of the ashes. The victim's married daughter, her only child, is  a suspect. Theodore O'Hara Clark, a young Marine recently returned from the Korean war and finishing up his university studies while working part-time as a rookie reporter at the local newspaper, is assigned the story because he's the only one around when the tip comes in. If he can unravel the mystery, he'll be on his way to the big time in Manhattan.

Theo & The Mouthful of Ashes is the prequel to *Theo's Story*.

THEO & The Mouthful of Ashes is available at Amazon.com, the Kindle and bookstores everywhere.

In October of 1941, the coatless body of a prominent journalist is found lying in the snow beside a lonely road in the mountains of east Kentucky, over one hundred miles from his home. No one knows why he is there, or how he got there. Though the story is the biggest in the state that year, the mystery is never solved. *THEO's STORY* is the first book in the THEO trilogy.

THEO'S STORY is available at , the Kindle and bookstores everywhere.

Your son or daughter has just joined the school soccer team and there you are on a pleasant afternoon, standing around a grassy field, watching a lot of kids running back and forth kicking a ball and you are clueless to what they are doing.

Soccer, a Spectator's Guide is for all those who find themselves at soccer games and are not entirely sure of what's going on.

A must read for all parents with soccer players in their family. Available on Amazon and in bookstores everywhere.

At last, a book that explains the how and why of writing for public relations from the perspective of a world class professional and a noted academic. It offers the ideal combination of practice and pedagogy, serving as an advanced text for graduate students and a comprehensive reference for young professionals. A badly need volume written in a conversational style and user-friendly.

Available on Amazon and in bookstores everywhere.

www.ingramcontent.com/pod-product-compliance
Lightning Source LLC
Chambersburg PA
CBHW021440240626
47153CB00001B/221